I0659659

THE RAVEN

Book #2 – The Nina Chronicles

Stan Morse

The Raven is a work of fiction. Names, characters, places and incidents either are the product of the author's imagination or are used fictitiously, and any resemblance to actual persons, living or dead, businesses, companies, events, or locals is entirely coincidental.

All rights reserved. No part of this book may be reproduced, scanned, or distributed in any printed or electronic form without permission. Please do not participate in or encourage piracy of copyrighted materials in violation of the author's rights. Please purchase only authorized editions.

Published by Stan Morse

All Prose and Artwork: © 2020 Stan Morse

ISBN: 978-0-9898513-7-4

Ivan Cakic designed the Raven and background, arranged through 99designs
Ashley Goff designed the Crest of Clarissa, also called the "Swirl Star"
Special thanks to Hailee Lehman for setup of the interior and the cover
Special thanks to early draft readers for their invaluable feedback. JoAnne and Olivia Strandberg, Nick and Theresa Moran, Earl Papac, Amy and Kya Holmes, and Joy and Emma Crowe. Special thanks to Madeline Barkley for review of the final draft.

OTHER BOOKS BY STAN MORSE
Circling the Earth in a Wheelchair
Brothers of Summer
Goering's Gold
The Order

For Brielle and Dylan

CHAPTER 1

Raven perched near the top of a birch tree, studying two young females who sat talking at a round wooden table on the back deck of a large house.

Every human he'd ever spied on had glowed with a reddish aura, like the one surrounding the smaller girl. But the tall girl was enveloped in a shimmer of pure Robin's egg blue.

It was practically heart-stopping.

When they finally went inside, Raven launched from his perch, swooping past the rope swing dangling from the huge maple in the center of the backyard, landing on the table.

He hopped down onto the nearest slatted chair and sniffed where the smaller girl had sat. Finding her scent pattern unremarkable, he quickly hopped over to the taller girl's chair.

Raven had whiffed hundreds of human smells during his twelve seasons, but none were remotely close to the essence of this girl. Hers was a scent pattern that was in perfect harmony, perfect balance.

Raven immediately took flight, returning shortly with a worn gold band clutched in his curved beak, a wedding ring he'd found three summers ago and then hidden away in the knot hole of an ancient pine.

He landed in the middle of the table, dropped his gift, and quickly lifted off with great happy beats of his glossy black wings, knowing that his great purpose in life had finally arrived.

CHAPTER 2

During the two weeks following her rescue Nina had become more and more frustrated. Wasn't her new foster dad, Frank Miller, who was a lawyer, supposed to report kidnappings to the police? And why hadn't her former foster dad, Dan Torgerson called the cops? After all, her kidnapper had slugged him so hard that one of his eyes had swollen shut!

And then there was Dan's wife, Evelyn who had so desperately wanted to adopt Nina. She had last seen Evelyn with her hands and feet bound with rope, duct tape across her mouth, sprawled on the sofa in the downstairs den. Nina hadn't gotten so much as a phone call from Evelyn to ask how she was doing. How could she have given up so easily?

And what about the mysterious Charlie Dozen? Or Clarissa? And what had happened to her kidnapper?

As Frank drove the family to Waterfront Park to watch the 4th of July fireworks, Nina's questions began to pop like a string of firecrackers.

"Do you think Charlie will come tonight?"

Frank sighed, hands suddenly moist on the wheel. With a brief glance in the rearview mirror, he said, "I don't know."

"Have you talked to him?"

Frank shifted uncomfortably. "No." He sounded tired, and more than just a little frustrated.

To his right, Anna's left eyebrow raised a little. She continued to stare straight ahead, but her lips were now pressed tight.

"Have you heard from Clarissa?"

"No." And this time his denial came with a firmness that said the questions were trying his patience.

He was lying. Nina *felt* it. She pushed back in her seat, and looked in frustration to the Millers' adopted daughter Chantha, who just shrugged.

When the Volvo finally pulled to a stop at the city park's front gate, Nina saw Selena standing with her parents and her kid brother just inside the fence. She hadn't spent much time with Selena since the rescue, and she didn't want to spoil the moment. She bit her lip, letting go of asking questions, at least for the evening.

"Nina! Chantha!" Selena shouted, as the Volvo's doors opened.

The two girls scrambled out.

Frank said, "I'll go find a parking spot," sounding relieved.

Anna nodded, and pushed open the passenger side door.

The three girls hugged, and for a moment everything seemed fine. And then Nina saw Selena's little brother staring angrily in their direction. She whispered to Selena, "What's up with Benny?"

Selena's reply came loud enough for Benny to hear.

"He went into my room yesterday and started using the computer Trisha gave us. Mom caught him playing some stupid online game, and now he's on suspension. They wouldn't even let him buy sparklers for tonight."

Chantha frowned at Benny, who stuck out his tongue in reply. She turned to Selena. "Why does he think he has any right to use our computer?"

"He says that since Trisha's gone, there's no reason why only I should get to use it."

"That doesn't make any sense."

"Yeah, well, you try and get a ten-year-old boy to make sense!"

Ernesto heard this, and saw Benny's reaction. He threw hard looks at his daughter and son. "That's enough," he said. "You two are not going to wreck this evening with another one of your fights. If you don't behave, I'll take both of you straight home and you can sit in your rooms instead of enjoying the fireworks." Immediately followed by a *sorry about this awful mess* smile directed at Nina and Chantha.

3

Benny turned away, staring out across the vast lawn to where kids were playing, his eyes pure daggers.

Anna, who stood in the middle, took a stab at breaking the tension.

"When Frank gets back, we'll go down to the beach. You girls can pick out a spot and we'll lay out a separate blanket for you."

Maria nodded approval, glancing at Benny, who was now pretending to ignore everyone. In a firm voice she said, "Benny can keep the grownups company tonight."

Benny spun around. "I want to go and find my friends!" He stomped a foot on the ground, hands clenched into fists.

"You're on suspension," Maria said firmly, followed by an offer of what she hoped might calm him down. "After you've eaten, and *if* you mind your manners, you can go and look for your friends, but *only* if you promise to stay inside the park fence."

Benny's response was to collapse dramatically onto the grass.

Ernesto took a step toward his son, but Maria waived him back. "Let's wait for Frank," she said, trying to sound calmer than she felt.

Ernesto threw a hopeless look at Benny before turning away in frustration.

Everyone now did their best to ignore the boy writhing and groaning on the ground.

When Benny finally realized his fit was getting him nowhere, he sat up, and then stood up; once again staring with envy at other kids who were running around and having a perfectly grand time.

When Frank came trudging back from the parking lot, they all walked down to the beach. Maria and Anna unfolded a king-sized blanket, and then spread out a queen-sized blanket far enough away to allow the girls some privacy, but still within safe watching distance.

Out of the big blue ice chest came bowls of fried chicken and potato salad, cans of soda, chips and salsa.

The girls soon retreated to their blanket.

After Benny had eaten two chicken legs and guzzled a can of root beer, he was released to go in search of boys his own age.

Everyone finally began to relax.

As the girls settled in to await the fireworks, Selena couldn't resist bringing up what was still a sore topic.

4

"I still can't believe what Trisha did."

"Yeah," Chantha agreed. "She was a total witch." She looked to Nina for confirmation.

Nina was sitting cross-legged on a corner of the blanket, staring out across the lake as if she hadn't heard. The look on her face reminded Chantha of a similar reaction from a day in early June.

They had just completed the first summer business class, where Trisha Peterson had shown up—as if by magic—and taken control of the classroom. It had seemed as if the retired businessman, Irv Goodwin, who had taken on the teaching project as a volunteer, hadn't even been in the room.

When Chantha and Nina later sat on the back deck of the Millers' home, talking about Trisha's unexpected appearance, Nina had said with nervous concern, "That Peterson woman is weird." She went on to describe what felt like a "connection" between herself and Trisha, revealing that she'd had similar feelings about two other people who'd recently arrived in the valley: Clarissa, and Charlie Dozen.

"It's like we're all connected by some invisible force." And then her face had taken on a light-years-distant gaze. As if she was sensing something *Out There*.

Chantha wanted Nina to be *here* on this wonderful 4th of July evening, not obsessing about some imaginary connection. She turned to Selena, and said a little more loudly than was necessary, "We definitely want to move ahead on the manufacture of bunnies. Are you still on board?"

"Absolutely!" Selena said, looking to Nina for confirmation.

It seemed for a moment as if Nina hadn't heard. But then her eyes shifted from the distance and refocused on Chantha; she smiled and nodded.

Selena's excitement now seemed to fade a little.

"But . . . how are we going to figure out everything we need to do without—" she barely avoided saying "Trisha" (she had adored the willowy blonde) "—someone to help us understand the business stuff?"

"There's always Irv," Chantha volunteered.

"I guess," Selena conceded. "But he's such a dork. And he's like, ancient!"

"We'll figure it all out," Nina said confidently. "After all, there's no hurry. Right?"

Selena sighed and rolled her eyes.

The girls realized there was nothing more to say on the subject. They nibbled on potato salad and chicken and chips, and made small talk as the sun set behind the mountains.

As stars began to twinkle, there came a bright flash overhead, followed by a huge *BOOM!* They lay back on their blanket, cozily shoulder to shoulder, watching colorful explosions light up the night sky.

♦

Two hundred yards from where the girls lay on their blanket, a rough-shaven man with the build of a professional fighter, appearing to be in his early thirties, leaned against a tree.

On this hot summer evening Gunther wore jeans and a white tee shirt, pretending to enjoy the fireworks, while glancing as often as he dared in the direction of Nina, hoping he was far enough away to keep her from feeling the *resonance* all members of the Order felt when they came close enough to another member.

He'd made no attempt to contact her, even though he very much wanted to. But Clarissa had warned him to steer clear if he wanted to remain in the U.S. This was a threat with very real teeth. If he were deported back to Germany, the Watchers would certainly find him. His decision to switch sides in the battle between Clarissa and the Order must surely have infuriated the warrior who chaired the Council. Leading to an easy conclusion.

Pieter Silberhof must want me dead.

♦

6

Raven hated the booming and the bright flashes, but he refused to abandon his vigil over the male who leaned against the tree trunk below.

Not long after he had discovered the young female with the brilliant blue aura, he had spotted this second human, who possessed a dull blue aura. Now the newcomer was shadowing the princess. Could he be a friend? Or, was he an enemy? All Raven knew for certain was that the man he thought of as *Dark Soul* required watching.

CHAPTER 3

Charlie Dozen decided to skip the fireworks. Being a full-blooded Shoshone Indian, it seemed somehow wrong to celebrate the birth of a nation that had treated his people so poorly.

But there was a more serious reason for Charlie needing some time alone. He and Clarissa had been falling into ever greater disagreement about how to handle Nina, and something unfortunate had happened. During a walk they'd taken that morning, their disagreement had erupted into a full-blown argument.

As they paced side by side along the lakeshore trail, he had turned to her and said, "We must tell Nina what she is."

Clarissa's response had been unequivocal.

"No!" As if he must be hallucinating to think this was wise.

Charlie's frustration boiled over.

"The Council is eventually going find a way to get to her. They'll tell her about herself, and then she'll question why we weren't honest with her."

"I thought you understood, Charlie. She's too young. Let her settle in with the Miller family, get back to school in September, reestablish a regular life. She's had enough strangeness over the past few weeks."

"When *do* we tell her?"

"Charlie . . . you need to let me make that decision. And I'm telling you she's not anywhere near ready to know the truth."

"When *will* she be ready?"

"I don't know!"

"In a month? Six months? A year?"

Clarissa had raised a hand in protest, and spoken as if she were lecturing a slow student.

"Revealing the truth will force her to make decisions she's completely unprepared to make. She needs to know us better before we put her in that position. We need to reach a point where she can fully trust us to help her make the right choices."

Charlie's terse reply sounded more like an accusation.

"You're afraid, aren't you? You think she might want to go and check out the Order. You're worried you might lose her."

Twenty-one centuries of life had swum up in Clarissa's blue eyes.

"Yes, I fear what a fourteen-year-old girl's emotionally driven choices might be. You would be asking someone who is hardly more than a child to make decisions that will affect the entire human race. I want some insurance before that happens. I want a well-established friendship with us before we put her to that test. And this is not a subject I wish to debate!"

Charlie had stopped in the middle of the trail.

"I disagree. We can't help her if she doesn't know how special she is. If we wait, she's only going to resent us for keeping her in the dark."

Clarissa faced off, feet in a wide stance, arms crossed.

"Don't you dare tell her, Charlie. I'm asking . . . no, I'm warning you."

"Or what?"

She stared at him, dumbfounded. And her reply couldn't have been more hurtful.

"Please give me whatever time you think I deserve, after all that I've done for you over the years."

Having first met Clarissa in 1891, their friendship now stretched well into a second century. They had begun as lovers. For Clarissa, the infatuation had soon been replaced by a platonic friendship. But love's first blush had never fully faded for Charlie. Somewhere deep inside, the embers still burned.

And now she had reduced that love to a cipher in some imaginary ledger.

9

They had stood, face to face, neither knowing what to say next. The hurtful moment ended when Clarissa had simply turned away and walked back toward the Bosecker Inn.

Charlie turned in the opposite direction, and in pure frustration began walking. After several minutes at a determined pace, he sat down on the ground and stared out across the water, struggling with his emotions.

Two hours passed before he returned to the Bosecker, reluctantly reconciled to tell Clarissa that he would give her whatever time she thought she needed.

Something felt wrong as he pushed through the front door and entered the reception area, said "Good morning" to Iris, the young blonde receptionist at the front desk, and turned for the stairs that led to Clarissa's third floor room.

Iris had called out, "Mr. Dozen! Ms. Cumberland checked out over an hour ago."

Charlie stumbled, realizing what seemed wrong. The sense of Clarissa's presence in the building, her *resonance*, was missing. He turned and retraced his steps.

"Gone?"

His usually pleasant attitude was replaced by the frightening wolf-like presence Iris had witnessed once before, just a few weeks ago. Her nervous reply came in a jumble of words that sounded like an apology.

"Yes, sir. I'm sorry. She came downstairs with her suitcase just a few minutes after she got back." Iris grabbed under the counter for the sealed envelope, and said "She left you a note," laying it on the counter.

Charlie grabbed the envelope, ran one finger under the seal, and pulled out a roughly torn half-sheet of paper.

I need to make a trip to Europe and expect to be gone for a week. Please consider my request. Clarissa

He had glanced up, numbly said "Thank you," and walked quickly into the dayroom so that Iris wouldn't see that tears had begun to well up in the corners of his eyes.

CHAPTER 4

Frank and Anna were busy in the kitchen on a Saturday morning, taking advantage of the early hours to catch up on chores following what had been a busy week, especially with the previous night's 4th of July festivities in the park. As Anna stacked plates in the dishwasher, they both heard the distant *whoosh* and *thump* of the French doors leading to the back deck. Frank looked out the window above the sink and saw Nina and Chantha, still in pajamas, walking out onto the deck. The early sun was warmly lighting the cedar railing.

Anna stepped up beside Frank and slid her left hand into his open palm. His fingers gently closed around hers.

"I'm proud of what we've done," she said softly.

"Me too," Frank agreed, watching the girls walk to the deck's edge, pause at the railing, speaking words he and Anna couldn't hear. "They're perfect for each other, aren't they?"

"Yes."

They watched the girls for a long moment, before she said, "I know there's more you haven't told me about Nina. Now that she's a part of our family, can you please share what you were doing with Clarissa and that woman from San Jose?"

Frank had known this was coming. Theirs wasn't a marriage of secrets. And as co-guardian, Anna was now legally entitled to know everything about Nina. The problem wasn't Frank's unwillingness to share. The problem stemmed from Clarissa.

Before Nina's kidnapping, Clarissa had made an appointment with Frank at his law office. At first, she seemed like any other new client.

Then she'd surprised him, revealing that she wanted to help Nina, and asking if Frank was personally interested in her welfare.

Frank confirmed that he'd met Nina, heard her story about a disintegrating foster relationship with Dan and Evelyn Torgerson, and discussed the manufacture and sale of a stuffed bunny—a toy she'd been given by a woman whose name she couldn't reveal because she'd promised not to. He then assured Clarissa that he had Nina's best interests very much at heart.

Clarissa confessed that she was Nina's "mystery woman," and proceeded to tell him about the Order, and why its membership was so interested in the girl.

Stunned by the revelations, Frank assured her he would keep them secret.

Clarissa had countered with, "I'm not at all worried. You won't be able to tell anyone what I have told you because I'm going to place a mental block that prevents it."

After Clarissa left, Frank tried making notes about their meeting, but his pen simply wouldn't move across the paper. He tried making a recording, but again with no luck.

More recently, following the kidnapping, Clarissa had partially released the block so that he could talk freely to Valerie or Charlie. But for the rest of humanity, including Anna and Nina, the block was still firmly in place.

Frank now looked at Anna, and with pain in his eyes said, "I just can't."

Anna wasn't one to give up so easily. There had been too much strangeness. She suspected that extraordinary secrets were being kept. Somehow, Frank was being prevented from answering. The next logical source of information would be . . .

"Are you in contact with Clarissa?"

"No."

"Will you be in touch with her during the next few days?"

"I don't know," Frank said, clearly frustrated.

"Do you have a way to get in touch with Valerie?"

Frank's eyes brightened. "I've got a phone number."

"May I have it?"

Frank reached for his wallet, thumbed through the paper and plastic, and pulled out Valerie's business card and handed it to Anna.

"Would you mind if I gave her a call on Monday?"

"Not at all. That's a great idea." There was hope in his voice. Anna was about to ask why he thought this was such a great idea, when the girls rushed into the kitchen.

Chantha extended her right hand and said in an excited voice, "Look what Nina found!" Her fingers uncurled to reveal a gold wedding band.

Anna took it and searched for an engraving, but found just smoothly worn gold.

"Is it yours?" Chantha ask eagerly.

"No, sweetheart." Anna handed the band to Frank.

He made a brief inspection, and then asked Nina, "Where exactly did you find this?"

"On the deck table."

"Can you please show me?"

They all walked through the family room and out onto the deck and Nina pointed to a spot in the middle of the table.

"Odd," Frank said. "Someone must have put it there. But who leaves gold rings?"

Anna frowned. "Do you think it's a sign of something dangerous?"

"I'm not sure," Frank said. "But let's all keep a lookout for strangers in the neighborhood. And maybe we should think about installing a security camera."

As they stood puzzling over the mysterious ring, Chantha's face turned hopeful.

"So . . . what do we do with it?"

Frank realized what she was hoping for, but fairness now came into play.

"You said it was Nina who found it?"

"Yes," Chantha said.

"Then until we figure out how it got there, I suppose it's 'finders keepers." He handed the ring to Nina. "Unless someone comes around to ask for its return, you may keep it."

13

Nina took the gold band and slid it onto her right index finger, where it fit snuggly.

Chantha's mouth formed a reluctant smile, and then she gave Nina a hug.

♦

Hidden amongst a cluster of birch leaves near the top of the tree, Raven was upset when he saw the man holding the ring. Then the princess took it from him and slipped it onto her finger.

In a voice that sounded much like Frank's, but very soft, very quiet, very secret, Raven said, "*Nina.*" Followed by a guttural cackle of pure joy.

After the humans went back inside, Raven's mighty wings powered him off the branch and up into the morning sky. When he cleared the treetops he performed a loop-de-loop, partly for the simple thrill of flying upside down, but mostly to celebrate the delivery of his first gift.

CHAPTER 5

Clarissa's flight from Seattle to Amsterdam held some risk. Airport security was much tighter following the terrorist attacks on 9/11. Her U.S. passport was the best forgery available, but it was still a forgery. If anyone chose to dig deep enough, they would discover that "Alice Isabelle Smith" presently occupied a grave in a cemetery on the outskirts of a small town in rural Georgia. Clarissa was close enough to Alice's 5' 9", deep blue eyes, and medium brown hair to pass visual scrutiny. Even the nose—narrow, petite—was nearly a perfect match.

The assumed identity wouldn't have worked if the U.S. required biometric data on passports as did many of the European countries. But with no embedded chip containing data on fingerprints, retinal patterns, or facial recognition, the passport was a fairly safe bet.

A year ago, Clarissa would have hired a private jet for the flight. But her confidence in private jets had been shaken when Valerie used her laptop to track the Order's Gulfstream on its flight from Zurich to the East Wenatchee airport. It was a rude awakening, and a reminder that there were details about life in the twenty-first century that she needed to pay greater attention to.

There was a second reason not to order a private jet. She was certain the Order was now monitoring the movement of funds from her dark bank accounts. They couldn't block the transfers, but they had sophisticated tools for tracking where money went. Renting a costly Gulfstream would require a direct bank transfer. Once they identified which jet she had reserved, they could easily be waiting when she landed.

Conversely, a business class ticket on KLM, costing around five grand, could easily be paid for in cash. And with commercial air travel under an assumed name, she would remain invisible to the Order.

Still, the travel agent had looked a little stunned when Clarissa laid a stack of hundred-dollar bills on his desk.

After landing at Schiphol Airport on the outskirts of Amsterdam, Clarissa waited in line for customs, feeling exhausted. The flight had been long and without much chance for sleep, in part because the man next to her was the chatty type. She'd chosen not to reach into his mind and shut him up. Over the course of nine hours, a passenger suddenly turned zombie might raise concerns with the flight attendants.

But it wasn't just her talkative seatmate that kept her awake. Two other matters weighed heavily on her mind.

The first was the possibility of betrayal by an old friend.

Twelve years ago, Clarissa had hinted to Liesel Hartkorn that the baby girl she had discovered was special. When Liesel had shown up on the Gulfstream to spirit Nina away, it seemed their friendship might have been set aside for the expediency of attending to the Order's business.

And then there was Charlie. Clarissa was certain she had made a mistake. Much of her time on the jet had been spent trying to figure out how to make things right. But she arrived at no simple solution, no easy cure. Even worse, she knew that leaving had been the act of a coward. Worst of all, as she replayed their conversation over and over in her mind, she began to wonder if Charlie might be right.

When she reached the front of the line, the immigration agent gave her a close look.

"Passport?" he asked.

Clarissa placed it in the metal tray. The agent scooped it up, scanned the data page, and compared the photo to the woman standing on the other side of the glass.

"The purpose of your trip, Ms. Smith?"

"I'm on vacation," Clarissa said in a polite southern drawl and with a sense of wonder, as if a miracle had somehow allowed her this once in a lifetime adventure.

The agent smiled.

"For how long?"

"Seven glorious days."

There was a pause as he again studied her passport, leafing through pages which held no visa stamps.

"I see you haven't been to Europe since your passport was issued. Is this your first time to the Netherlands?"

Clarissa had no idea whether or not the deceased Alice had ever been to the Netherlands. Or even to Europe. There might still be a record for an entry if the dead woman had traveled abroad. *I'll have to make a guess that someone who lived in rural Georgia and died at the age of 41 wasn't a world traveler.*

"Yes," Clarissa said. "There's a first time for everything. I'm excited to see Amsterdam and maybe even some of Germany." She nudged the man with her mind. *Let me through.*

The agent smiled more broadly, reaching for the inked stamp, pressing it firmly on the first page in the passport, and handing it back to Clarissa with a brisk nod. "Enjoy your stay," he said, as his eyes shifted to the next person in line.

Clarissa carried her one bag to the x-ray machine for customs clearance—the final step for entry into the European Union's Schengen Zone. Once inside Schengen, she could travel freely across country borders.

The man standing beside the scanner asked if she was carrying any plants or animal products, to which she replied, "No." She was waived through and entered the terminal.

The Intercity Direct train to Amsterdam delivered her to an immense red brick station house. She found a travel office and approached the counter, where a young woman with light auburn hair pulled back into a tight bun asked, "Kan ik je helpen?"

Clarissa was capable of answering in flawless Dutch. But this woman who would sell her the ticket would also ask for her passport, and she might become suspicious of a woman from Georgia, who had no prior visa stamps, who spoke fluent Dutch.

"Do you speak English?" Clarissa asked, again in that lovely southern drawl.

17

"Yes, I speak English," the woman replied. "Can I be of help?"

"I'd like to purchase rail tickets."

"Of course," the woman said. "What is your destination?"

"Spain."

"May I see your passport?"

Clarissa reached into her jacket pocket and pulled out her passport and handed it to the woman.

The woman smiled, and asked, "To which city are you traveling?"

"San Sebastian."

"The coastal Basque country. It is a lovely place, especially in the summertime." She began tapping on a keyboard, intent upon what came up on her screen.

San Sebastian wasn't Clarissa's final destination. She was headed for Zizurkil, twelve miles to the south, in mountainous sheep country. A place she had visited once before, in the year 204 A.D.

At the beginning of the third century, she had gone in search of a woman rumored to have lived at the Western edge of the Roman Empire for over a hundred and fifty years. Someone who had completely avoided the Order. Clarissa now hoped this woman might know how to help her make Nina invisible to both the Order and to the "normal" world.

If . . . Livia was still alive.

CHAPTER 6

When Nina found Raven's next gift, early on Monday morning, she wasn't nearly as excited as she had been about the gold ring. In the middle of the deck table lay two keys on a chromed split ring. Nina carried them back into the house and found Anna in the kitchen, starting a first pot of coffee.

"There was something else on the deck this morning," she said, holding out the keys.

Anna briefly examined the key with an embossed Toyota Motors symbol, and then the second key, solid brass with *U.S.P.S. DO NOT DUPLICATE* stamped into the rounded head.

"Someone's going to have a hard time getting into their post office box," Anna puzzled, staring at the keys in her hand. "And their car . . ." She fingered the keys gingerly. "Why would anyone leave keys on our deck? It makes no sense." She looked up. "Did you see anything that looked strange or out of place when you went outside?"

"No," Nina said. And she'd scanned every tree and bush, including the big birch in the neighbor's yard. And then cautiously peered around both corners of the house, relieved to see nothing on the thin strips of lawn edged by tall cedar fences.

"Well . . ." Anna said, bewildered. "A gold ring, and now *this*."

At that moment Frank walked barefoot into the kitchen, wearing baggy blue shorts and a raggedy gray sweatshirt with *U.W. LAW* stenciled in faded purple. "I smell coffee," he said in a cheery voice. Then he saw Anna's concerned look.

"What's wrong?"

"Nina just found this on the deck table." Anna held out the keys.

He took them and jangled them in his open palm.

As Anna awaited his verdict, she poured a cup of coffee in his favorite mug, also bearing "U.W." in purple lettering. After he took the mug, Frank turned to Nina and asked, "By any chance did you or Chantha have a look at the table last night?"

They had played on the rope swing just before dinner time, and she was certain the table had been bare. She nodded, and said, "We were outside before dinner, and after that we watched TV in the family room. The blinds were open until it got dark. I'm sure we would have seen if someone came before we went to bed."

"Well," Frank said, "I'm definitely going to have the electronics store send someone out to install security cameras. And I'll call the sheriff so they'll know we've had a prowler. They may have had other reports in the neighborhood. We can't have someone coming onto our deck and leaving things." He stared hard at the keys in his hand. "But it's a strange thing to leave your keys on someone's deck in the middle of the night."

"I agree," Anna said. She turned to Nina. "Just to be safe, I want you and Chantha to stay indoors today, and keep the doors locked. Please keep a cell phone handy."

"I will," Nina promised. "Can I go tell Chantha about the keys?"

Anna heard excitement in Nina's voice and wanted to say this wasn't something to be excited about. But not wanting to encourage fear, she simply said, "Of course. But let her know to stay indoors, at least until we know who's leaving stuff on our deck."

When Nina was gone, Anna turned to Frank.

"Maybe I should stay home from work for a day or two? If the people who tried to kidnap Nina have come back, I don't want the girls to be home alone."

Frank wished he could tell her about the steps they had taken to warn off the Order. But Clarissa's mind block was there. He thought for a moment about Gunther. Could he be the one leaving things? Were they intended as some kind of penitence for the kidnapping? But that made no sense either.

There seemed to be only one sure way to find out. A security camera would tell the tale if the intruder returned.

Anna was waiting for an answer.

"I think the girls will be okay on their own," he said, trying to sound certain.

"Alright," Anna said, giving him a second look just to be sure. When he nodded to reassure her, she said, "I'm planning to call Valerie later this morning to ask if she can help the girls with the bunny project. Do you still think that's a good idea?"

"Yes," Frank said. "I think it's a great idea. Please let me know what she says. Right now, I'm running a little late and I need to get dressed for the office."

"I'll scramble some eggs and cut up some cantaloupe. Do you want a toasted bagel?"

"Yes, please."

She gave him a kiss on the cheek.

Frank grabbed the coffee pot from the warming plate, topped off his mug, and left the kitchen, whistling what Anna thought might be the Beatles tune *When I'm 64*. Frank was a lousy whistler, struggling to carry even a simple tune. But it didn't deter him one bit from trying.

CHAPTER 7

The doorbell rang mid-morning. Both girls walked to the front door, and when Chantha peeked through the security eye she saw a balding man in gray coveralls with *Ken's Computerland* stitched in red above his breast pocket, and below it, *Mark Potts.*

"It's the camera guy," Chantha said, turning the latch.

"Good morning," Mark Potts said, as the door opened. He glanced nervously from Chantha to Nina, seeming a bit confused. His eyes shifted down to the black tool case he carried, and then to the large cardboard box tucked under his right arm with the words: *DELRIDGE CAMERA SECURITY SYSTEM* printed across the top. Then back to the girls.

"Your father asked me to tell you that I'm from the computer store, and that you should give him a call to let him know I've arrived." Once more he looked from Nina to Chantha, and then back to Nina. "He said you could point out the problem area."

Both girls instantly knew what was bothering Potts.

On the very first day Nina had come to live with the Millers, Anna had announced, "We're going to tell everyone you are sisters. As far as we're concerned you are both our daughters from now on." This declaration had hugely pleased the girls.

But it was hard to imagine two "sisters" who looked more different. Chantha, a native Cambodian, adopted by the Millers shortly after birth, now four-foot-nine and not likely to ever be much taller than five feet. With a round face, pug nose, straight jet-black hair, oval eyes, dark skin.

Conversely, Nina was easily headed for six feet by the end of high school. With an athletic body, medium brown hair with just a hint of curl, eyes light brown.

Sisters!

Chantha shrugged off the moment.

"It's the deck table where things have been showing up," she said, turning for the family room.

Nina fell in step behind Chantha, with Potts trudging obediently behind, having decided it was a good idea to stop wondering. Remembering that his second cousin in Wyoming had adopted a seven-year-old black girl two years ago—a move that shocked everyone in the family. But they'd all readily adjusted when it turned out Gracie possessed an attitude that was a pure joy to be around.

So here was the twenty-first century in all its multi-racial glory. Cascade County wasn't flush with forgiving souls when it came to non-whites. But whose business was it to judge people for loving a kid?

Mark suddenly felt better about himself. If either girl had turned around, they would have seen a silly grin brighten his face for a long moment.

They passed through the French doors and out onto the back deck, where Chantha pointed to the round teak table.

"Someone's been leaving things in the middle of it."

"Okay," Potts said. He looked around and saw a place up under the eaves that was perfect for a camera. He made a note on a small pad, and then stepped off the deck and walked to one corner of the house. A strip of grass ran out to a gate that opened onto the sidewalk. He pointed to an eve at the corner of the house. "I'll put one up there just in case whoever it is comes in from the street."

He walked to the other side of the house and scanned along the fence. "Here's another spot," he said. And finally, he pointed at the bushes and trees at the back of the yard. "I'll also stick one somewhere out there."

He returned to the girls on deck. "I'll need to set up the base unit where there's plug-in power. Is there a good place inside?"

Nina volunteered, "Dad's got a home office, and I think that's where he wants it." It was the first time she had called Frank Miller "Dad" without thinking about it, and it gave her a thrill. It had come so naturally!

Chantha's instant smile was a mile wide.

"Okay," Mark said, realizing something special had happened, but clueless as to what it was. "I'll get started. And don't forget to call your father and let him know I'm here." He was now smiling along with the girls. There was joy in the air on this warm summer morning.

♦

Valerie was working at her stand-up desk on a statistical analysis for Wang Do, LTD, a Shanghai manufacturer of electronic components, when the intercom buzzed.

"Yes, Tina?"

"Miss Li, you told me to interrupt you if there was a call from *those people* up in Washington. Anna Miller is on line three."

"Thank you, Tina. I'll take it." Valerie thumbed off the intercom, and then pushed the button on the speaker phone.

"Hello, Anna. To what do I owe the pleasure?"

"Good morning, Valerie. Thanks so much for taking a moment. Do you remember when we talked about the girls wanting to manufacture the rabbit doll?"

"Yes." Valerie recalled a short discussion about an old-fashioned animal doll during a break at Frank's office. Anna had brought them a lunch of tomato soup and ham sandwiches, and then hung around until they had to shoo her out.

"They need help figuring out where to manufacture the dolls. I thought with your connections in China you might be able to offer them some ideas? Maybe even put them in touch with a company, or however that's done?"

"Sure," Valerie said. "I can make an inquiry or two. Is there any rush?"

"If they're going to move forward on the project, they should get started before school begins. That's just four weeks from now."

"I think that's doable."

"Great." Anna sounded relieved. "Can I tell the girls you'll be in touch?"

"Of course."

"And by the way," Anna continued, trying to sound casual, and sounding anything but. "Is there anything special I should know about what you all were working on? I asked Frank, but he doesn't seem comfortable sharing any of the details."

Valerie knew about Clarissa's block on Frank, and imagined what kind of emotional turmoil he must be going through. She improvised, hoping it sounded convincing.

"We did something to scare off the kidnappers so they wouldn't try again. But I think it should be Clarissa who gives you the specifics."

"Okay," Anna said, disappointed. "I'd really appreciate knowing if there may be something we should be doing to protect Nina."

"I'll try to get in touch with Clarissa right away so that she can get back to you," Valerie said, feeling a little gutless for the lie.

"Thank you."

A dial tone signaled the end of the call.

Valerie paused for a moment, considered the bunny part of Anna's request, and had an inspiration. She keyed the intercom.

"Yes, Miss Li?"

"Tina, I've got a special project for you. It's something that I think you'll like. And you'll even get to do a bit of traveling."

CHAPTER 8

Charlie decided it was time to pay Gunther a visit. Clarissa had been clear in her concern about his history of violence. "It's going to come up sooner or later that he gets into trouble, so you've got to keep an eye on him. And don't hesitate to remind him that we will have him deported if he gets out of line."

Iris was at the reception desk, reading a magazine. Her head came up when Charlie entered the lobby from the dayroom.

"Mr. Dozen?"

"I'm going out for a while, Iris. Please call my cell number if you hear from Clarissa."

She grabbed a pen.

Charlie gave her his number, and added, "Don't hesitate to let me know if she calls."

"Yes, sir."

Charlie rewarded her with a fleeting smile.

Iris returned a polite and respectful nod.

As Charlie drove southward along the lakeshore toward Langston, he began to obsess about what might have gone wrong. Eleven days had passed since Clarissa's departure. Had the Order taken her prisoner? Had the immigration authorities discovered she held an invalid passport and put in jail? Was it possible that she'd been in an accident?

When he finally parked in front of the apartments where they had stashed Gunther, it was a relief to have something else to think about.

The Belvedere was a squat three-story concrete building. At some point in the not-so-distant past the owner had tried to cheer up the exterior with a coat of red paint. The relentless summer sun had gradually faded the cheap latex to a dying shade of pink, with enough cracks and scabby patches to betray that previously the building had been painted indigo blue.

Charlie climbed the five worn concrete steps and pushed against a solid wood door that gave the building a distinctly prison feel. It banged shut behind him with a heavy *thud*.

A Formica-topped counter stood to the right in the cramped lobby. Opposite the counter, two steel-gray chairs bookended what might have once passed for an antique end table. A staircase framed the back wall.

From behind the closed door came the pounding beat of a polka, with plenty of horns and an accordion. Charlie tapped twice on the chromed call bell and waited. When no one appeared, he banged it hard three times.

The music softened and the door creaked open. A middle-aged Hispanic woman bustled up to the counter. "I'm coming, I'm coming," she huffed. After one quick look at the twenty-something Indian she said, "You want to rent a room?"

"No," Charlie said. "I'm looking for someone who is staying here. His name is 'Gunther'."

"The German? He is your friend?" Not so positive.

"Yes," he replied cautiously, wondering if there had already been trouble. "Is he still here?"

"He is still here," the manager said grudgingly. "Up on the third floor, in three-oh-five."

"Is it okay if I go up?"

"No problem," she said. And with this bothersome duty completed, she turned abruptly and walked back through the open door. It swung shut, and within seconds the Mexican polka was again blaring at full strength.

Charlie took the stairs two at a time. When he reached the third floor, a vague odor—something between *stale beer* and *dead mouse*—permeated the dimly lit hallway.

27

The door to room 305 was scarred and stained mahogany, with a crudely-glued patch where it had once been kicked. A tarnished brass cylinder lock was inset above the metal door knob. Charlie rapped with his knuckles. He heard the thump of shoes hitting the floor inside, and after a few seconds the sound of the lock being turned.

When the door swung open, Gunther stood in jeans and a black tee shirt, his well-oiled leather boots planted in a wide stance as though he might be expecting trouble. His hair was longer now, greased and combed to the right. The German stared at him for a few seconds, looking surprised and curious, before pulling the door wide and motioning Charlie in with a tilt of his head.

The furniture inside was pure yard sale. A metal-edged table, two chromed chairs with green vinyl seats, a short sofa covered in frayed brown cloth. A white plastic box fan in the far corner was vibrating with a rhythmic *whump whump whump*, the up-tempo *whoosh* of its blades nearly drowning out the sound of traffic drifting in through a window that had been wedged open with a can of pork and beans.

"You have finally come to check up on me," Gunther said, easing onto one of the chairs.

"I'm here to make sure you are doing okay," Charlie insisted, trying to sound sincere, as he sat down opposite Gunther at the table. He glanced around at the bare walls. In the kitchenette, an empty cardboard pizza box lay upside down on the metal drain board by the sink.

Gunther watched, and then offered, "It is not much."

"No," Charlie agreed. "It lacks a certain charm, for sure."

Gunther laughed. "Charm," he said, with dark amusement, "was never here."

Charlie nodded slowly.

Gunther tried to sound polite, feeling anything but. "How is the girl?" He had sacrificed everything for her rescue, and felt entitled to know if she was okay.

"She's doing well," Charlie said. "She's living with the Miller family and quite happy to be out of that place where you first saw her."

"The Torgersons." Gunther snorted in disgust. "They were not worthy of her."

It was at this point that Charlie began to feel sorry for the German. And now he wanted to find some way to make Gunther's life just a little more palatable.

"Do you get out much?"

Gunther's frown said no, he hardly got out at all. "I might get into trouble," he grumbled. "And that would lead to consequences . . ." There was no need to elaborate. Clarissa had made it very clear what would happen if he stepped out of line.

"Maybe you should do a little sightseeing?"

Gunther returned a resentful look, and in a voice laced with sarcasm said, "Any suggestions?"

"Well," Charlie offered, "there's the Stampede up in Omak. It starts this weekend."

"A stampede?" The only stampedes Gunther knew of involved cattle running wild.

"Sorry. What I meant was the 'Omak Stampede.' It's a big rodeo that happens every summer at the beginning of August. Plenty of cowboys and Indians." Charlie gave a rueful smile at the painful cliché. "I only recently heard about it myself. They've got a Baptist revival show, food trucks, plenty of whiskey. And every night there's an event they call the 'suicide race' where horse riders come down a steep hill and splash across the river. Someone told me that later in the evening things can get a little crazy." Charlie paused, to see if Gunther was interested.

A sly grin began to spread across the German's face. "I think I might like that," he said cautiously. What he was thinking was that here was a chance for some action far enough away from Langston and Cascade County to be safe. And if it was being recommended by Clarissa's lackey, how could she possibly complain if he got into a fight?

Cowboys, Indians and whiskey. It sounded promising.

29

CHAPTER 9

Clarissa rediscovered Zizurkil in the green hills of Spain's Basque country, a few miles inland from San Sebastian. Since her last visit the population had grown from a few hundred to around three thousand.

She'd come here eighteen centuries ago, traveling from the Order's compound in the Helvetia province—an area that would eventually become the canton of Zurich, Switzerland—riding a spirited mare on good Roman roads, only recently made safe again by the Emperor Septimius Severus, following the chaotic reign of the emperor Commodus. The journey had taken two weeks, but the excitement of seeking out a potential new member made it seem more of an adventure than a task.

When she finally sensed Livia's powerful resonance, it confirmed the rumors: this reclusive woman possessed of all the powers; a rarity matched at that time only by Clarissa, and Eustachus of Athens.

They came face to face on a grassy field near a small cluster of adobe buildings with red tiled roofs and modest gardens, a few chickens, an occasional pig, and a lingering flock of several dozen sheep.

Livia stood with her feet defiantly planted, as if braced for a fight. She was slim and whipcord strong, with a Spaniard's dark skin. Her chestnut hair fell in a single braid to the middle of her back. Deep brown eyes flashed a gravity of resentment for the unwanted visitor.

"What is your business?" she demanded.

"I come from the Order with an invitation for you to join."

"I want no invitation."

"We still wish to make the offer."

"Then you must tell them it is rejected. Now go away. Leave immediately, or I will set the shepherds upon you."

"Violence is prohibited against a member—"

"I am not a member!" Livia had screamed. And then, in a caustic dismissal, "And I feel no compulsion to obey your silly rules." She put two fingers to her lips and blew a shrill whistle. Three young men, brandishing sturdy wooden staffs, appeared from behind a small rise and ran toward the two women.

"Peace!" Clarissa had cried. "I will leave you to your tribesmen." She had jumped onto her horse and galloped away.

Now, standing in that same field, which hadn't changed much during in the intervening centuries, Clarissa stared in frustration across the lush green grass where a handful of sheep grazed.

She had already asked around the village, framing her questions as if seeking a legend and not an actual person. Her inquiry had been met with blank stares, except for one old man, bent and crippled by a curvature of the spine. Standing in the doorway of his house he had looked her up and down with scorn. "You do not have the right to ask," came his raspy accusation. "You should not even dare to voice such questions."

Clarissa was puzzled by his anger. Did it imply that Livia was still around? Or, had the man lost his ability to reason? Perhaps he was just being a good Basque, telling outsiders to mind their own business?

He stood protectively hunched in his doorway for a fractured moment, quite as foreboding as any stone gargoyle, before turning and slamming the door in her face.

That was three days ago, and since then, nothing. Clarissa turned and began to walk back toward the buildings of Zizurkil. As she paced along the hardened dirt track, a blue van sped into view and then braked to a stop just beyond the low stone wall edging the field. The word *POLICIA* was emblazoned in white on its side; an unlit rack of blue lights was bolted to the roof. As she approached, the driver's door opened and a man dressed in a blue uniform stepped out. The red beret angled on his head marked him as one of the Ertzaintza—the local Basque police.

31

She was nearly to the wall when the officer called out, "*Señora,* may I have a word with you?"

"Of course," she said, stepping through a cut in the waist-high stonework and facing the officer. "What is it that you want?"

At which point he pulled a pair of handcuffs from his belt, and in a stern voice said, "You are under arrest."

Clarissa was ready to use her power of control when a police cruiser rounded the corner, tires squealing, blue lights flashing. It skidded to a stop and three more officers piled out, hands on the butts of their holstered pistols.

For Clarissa, control of one person was easy; two was certainly possible; but four armed men would be a challenge. And they looked *ready.* If Livia was behind this arrest, she would have certainly taken the precaution of mentally hardening the officers to resist Clarissa's mind control.

The crisp *click* of holster guards being unsnapped decided the moment. Clarissa held out her hands, watching in stunned silence as the cuffs were slapped onto her wrists. The officer then grabbed her firmly by one arm and led her to the van.

CHAPTER 10

The girls' birthdays all fell during the month of August. Last year they had made a pact to celebrate together on the second Saturday of the month, with successive yearly parties rotating between their houses. The first party was held at Chantha's. This year a piñata party was planned for Selena's backyard.

As they sat around the table on the Miller's back deck, Selena now sounded utterly defeated.

"Let's hold the birthday party at your house again, Chantha."

"No way," Nina said. "It's your turn."

"But it'll be a disaster," Selena moaned, hands waiving in frustration.

"No, it won't!" Chantha insisted, looking to Nina, who nodded in agreement.

"Yes, it will! Benny's being horrible! He threatened that if we have it at our house, he'll make sure we regret it."

Nina remained determined.

"Isn't Benny still on suspension? Couldn't we just ask your parents to make him stay in his room?"

Selena's frustration exploded. "He's got them totally fooled. He pretends to be nice when Mom or Dad are around. But when they're gone, he's not nice at all. No way are they going to make him miss my birthday if it's at our house!"

Chantha didn't like what she was hearing, and asked, "What do you mean 'not nice'?"

"He says mean things to me. He threatens to mess up our computer. I have to lock my bedroom door whenever I leave. He's a total pain."

"Well," Nina said firmly, "I think three fourteen-year-old girls should be able to figure out some way to handle a ten-year-old boy."

Chantha's furrowed brow eased a little. "Absolutely," she agreed.

Selena's look of relief confirmed that she truly did want to have the party at her house.

"It's a done deal," Nina proclaimed.

"Yeah," Chantha said, raising a hand to give Nina a high five, and then high fiving Selena, who hesitantly asked, "Do you think we should invite anyone else?"

Last year they had decided it would just be the three of them, plus their parents. But Selena was now picturing a boy it would be fun to invite. A few weeks ago, she had asked her mom and dad about the possibility of dating, and they had both immediately said, "No!" Inviting him to a birthday party seemed like a good back door approach.

Nina felt the opposite. Even a "safe" date, like to a movie, meant asking permission from Frank and Anna. It was too soon to be raising the subject. And beyond that, Nina wasn't sure she was anywhere near ready for boys. "I think it should just be us and our parents this year," she said firmly.

"Yeah," Chantha agreed. "Just us."

"Okay," Selena relented, trying not to sound disappointed. She quickly shifted to another subject. "Are we going to do gifts the same as last year?"

Nina and Chantha nodded yes.

The previous summer they had decided not to spend more than ten dollars on each other. Even that modest sum had been a challenge for Nina. She had settled upon bouquets of wildflowers, arranged in fancy glass vases bought for fifty cents each at the local thrift store. She felt embarrassed at having only spent a dollar, but it had worked out better than she could have hoped. Chantha and Selena were practically moved to tears upon seeing their uniquely beautiful presents.

Even as she agreed to the same rules as last year, there was one gift Nina wanted more than anything else. She knew it couldn't come from her girlfriends, even though it wouldn't have cost a penny. But she would have prized it above anything store bought.

Nina wanted answers.

CHAPTER 11

With a growing sense of frustration, Frank finally appealed to Charlie for help.

"Nina is asking me questions, and when I tell her I don't know the answers, I'm certain she knows I'm lying."

Since his June meeting with Clarissa, Frank had known about Nina's innate ability to sense a lie. *Truthing* was what members of the Order called it. It would be active even though she was unaware she possessed the skill.

More importantly, Frank believed Nina deserved the truth. Teens were confused enough without piling lies onto their fragile sense of self-worth. Nina might have the greatest potential on earth, but like all kids her age she was constantly trying to piece together what life was all about.

"How am I supposed to be a good dad when I'm forced to lie?"

Charlie had been counting on Clarissa to handle situations like this. But three weeks had passed since her abrupt departure, and he was now certain that something bad had happened. She would have been careful not to carry anything on her person that would lead foreign authorities back to Cascade County. And since he didn't know the identity on the passport she was using, there was no way to launch a search. This left no option but to wait . . . and hope.

He now recalled what Clarissa had told him three months ago when she'd recruited him in New Orleans to move out west to protect Nina. If something bad happened in her absence, he was to trust his warrior's instincts and find a solution. Clarissa's disappearance certainly qualified as something bad.

Charlie reached a decision.

"I'm willing to have a talk with Nina about the Order."

A look of relief flooded Frank's face. "You'd do that?"

"Yes. But I'd like to hold off for just a few more days. If Clarissa doesn't return soon, yes, I'll begin the process. Can you wait just a bit longer?"

"Do I have a choice?"

"I'd like to give Clarissa a chance to come back to us."

Frank sighed, knowing he'd already gotten more than he might have hoped for. "Okay. I'll tough it out." He quickly shifted to another issue that had been weighing heavy on his mind. "What's happening with Gunther?"

"I talked to him earlier this week at that rundown tenement where he's living."

Frank had seen the Belvedere, and thought 'rundown tenement' was being generous, telling Charlie, "I've had a couple of tough luck clients who lived there. It's a pit. Do you think we should maybe move him somewhere nicer? Sort of a bribe to keep him interested in cooperating?"

"That might work for a while," Charlie agreed. "But it'll take more than a move to nicer digs to keep him out of trouble. He's eventually going to find some way to let off steam. Earlier this week, I offered him something to get him out of town for the weekend. I suggested that he go up to the Omak Stampede."

Frank pictured what he knew about the Stampede, and wondered if this might just be pouring gasoline onto a smoldering fire. "Isn't that risking him getting into a fight?"

Charlie shrugged, and offered, "He'll be outside the valley. And if he gets into a dust-up with a cowboy or two, I don't see any harm in it. Besides, it'll let him burn off that nervous energy he's been storing up. Worst case scenario, we may have to bail him out of jail."

Frank was imagining the disaster possibilities for something over which he had no input, no control. "I just hope he doesn't get into real trouble."

Charlie laughed. "Trust me," he said confidently. "Gunther knows enough not to seriously injure some drunk who takes a swing at him. He's had more than two centuries of practice at it. He'll be just fine."

CHAPTER 12

Maria and Ernesto Hernandez transformed their back yard into a party paradise for the girls' Saturday afternoon birthday celebration.

Long wires were stretched along the house eves, hung with pink, blue, yellow, and orange streamers that fluttered in a warm breeze.

Four round tables were evenly spaced on the lawn, each draped with pink-patterned table cloths, centered by pottery vases holding bouquets of chrysanthemums and dahlias. One table was loaded with bowls of pulled pork and chicken *carnitas*, a vegetable tray, guacamole, refried beans, rice, and a brown crock filled with spicy potato salad. A wooden bowl brimmed with fresh warm tortillas.

A second table held a three-layer cake with white frosting, with a red sugar rose beside each girl's name and a huge number "14" in blue in the center.

A washtub near the back door was filled with ice, stocked with soda for the kids, beer for the adults.

A beach-ball-sized piñata hung from a high wire strung between the house and a tree. Several long sticks lay on the grass, for when the girls would be blindfolded to take turns trying to smash it and release a shower of candy and presents.

The girls had chosen to wear Mexican-styled summer party Dama dresses, with layered skirts of silky tulle fabric cut just above the knees. These had been specially ordered through Langston's Hispanic general store *Tienda Maria's*. Nina's was light blue, Selena's a vibrant red, and Chantha's was an elegant creamy white the sales girl had called "champagne."

Raven was also present, perched near the top of a pine in the neighbor's yard, hoping that by day's end there might be bits of food fallen in the grass. As he spied down across the fence, he saw a young boy come out from the house, pick up a stick beneath the piñata, and grip it firmly with both hands, as if it were a club.

Another dark soul. But not dark like the warrior's soul. Dark because he is a lonely creature, wanting his own way and never feeling satisfied.

Nina also saw Benny grab the stick, and it captured her attention. He'd been mostly keeping out of sight, seemingly unprepared to carry out his earlier threat. She had though this perfect behavior strange, even if it was welcome. But when he purposefully walked out from the house and picked up the stick and waived it around in a threatening way, she became concerned.

Benny soon laid the stick down, walked to the serving table, and started loading up a paper plate with food.

Let go of it, Nina thought, shifting back to something that had earlier caught her attention.

Chantha now walked up with a plate of fruit salad, set it on the table, and pulled out a chair. After she sat down, she lifted a fork and stabbed at a slice of cantaloupe. "Whatcha thinking about?" she asked, nibbling on the cantaloupe.

"I dunnow," Nina said, staring up at the pine tree in the neighboring yard.

Chantha followed her gaze. "Sure you do. When you get that look you've always got something on your mind." She nodded toward the pine tree. "What's so interesting up there?"

"A raven. He's been sitting on the same branch for the past half hour."

"So?"

"Don't you think that's strange?"

"Not really. Do you?"

"Have you ever watched ravens before?"

Chantha thought for a moment. She'd certainly *seen* ravens before, but she'd never actually *watched* one. "I guess so," she finally said. "What's so different about this one?"

"They never sit in one place for very long. I've never seen one sit still anywhere near as long as this one has, especially in the middle of the afternoon. They're usually out flying around looking for food. And other birds are usually chasing them off if they sit somewhere very long because ravens like to eat other birds' eggs and chicks."

"That's gross," Chantha said, losing interest in the cantaloupe. She stared up at the pine tree. The raven appeared to be looking straight back at her. "Maybe it's hoping we drop some food?"

"Yeah," Nina said. But she thought it was something different. She remembered when she'd first met Clarissa, in the old forest up beyond the ski hill. A raven had landed on a nearby branch at the very moment she'd realized she was lost. It had let out a loud cry before flying off. *Could this be the same one?*

As Nina watched the raven, Frank came strolling across the yard to check up on his girls. "Chantha, how are you and Nina doing?"

"Fine, Dad," Chantha said, standing up to give him a hug. "Thanks for coming to the party."

"Yeah," Nina agreed, throwing one last glance at the raven before standing up to give Frank a hug.

"I'm so happy you're here, Nina," Frank said. "I'm going to grab a can of soda. Do you girls want anything?"

Both said "No."

Frank walked back across the yard to the iced tub and grabbed an orange soda, popped the tab, took a couple gulps, and gave a satisfied belch.

Selena and her mother now came out from the house, and Selena called out, "We're going to do the cake!"

Nina finally gave up watching the raven. She and Chantha stood up and walked over to the table where Ernesto was lighting fourteen gold- and silver-colored candles.

Benny now showed interest in what the others were doing. He laid his plate down on the grass and walked over to join them. He even gamely sang along with the "Happy Birthday" song, which everyone first sang in English, then in Spanish, with Nina and Chantha doing fairly well in Spanish (they had practiced), and Frank and Anna awkwardly humming the unfamiliar words.

41

The girls then held hands and together blew out all the candles. Little wisps of smoke swirled from the dying orange tips.

"Who wants ice cream with their cake?" Maria asked.

"I do!" the girls—and even Benny—shouted. Maria went inside and returned with a half-gallon carton of vanilla, dishing out generous scoops before setting the carton in the ice bucket with the sodas and beer.

Benny took his plate and once more retreated to the back of the yard, practically as far away from the tables as he could get. He sat down on the grass and began to gobble down cake and ice cream, once again ignoring everyone. This drew concerned looks from his parents, and even Frank and Anna exchanged brief worried glances.

Still . . . Benny seemed content to be by himself, and as long as he behaved, the adults—and the girls—were willing to let it go.

Selena nearly said something mean, reconsidered, and instead sat in silence, enjoying not just cake and ice cream, but what seemed like a total victory.

CHAPTER 13

Charlie sat on a park bench near the Portage waterfront, wishing he were able to attend Nina's birthday party, when the cell phone in his pocket buzzed. When he saw the caller ID read *Okanogan Sheriff,* he thought it must be a misdial. For a moment he considered ignoring the call. But if it actually was the sheriff, and if it was actually meant for him . . . Charlie touched the green icon and held the phone to his ear.

"Hello?"

"Am I speaking to Charlie Dozen?" The man sounded totally serious.

"Yes."

"Mr. Dozen, this is Sergeant Ben Hughes with the Okanogan County Sheriff's office. Do you know a man named Wolfgang Arthur Spindler?"

For a moment Charlie didn't have a clue. And then he remembered Gunther having a passport with a name that had Wolfgang in it. He cautiously said, "I recently met a German with a name something like that."

"Do you know if he has any family in the area?"

"He didn't mention anyone," Charlie said. "Why?"

There was a pause, as if a decision were being made. And finally, "Mr. Spindler was involved in a fight three hours ago, up near the Omak Stampede grounds. We're not sure how it happened, but some of our local boys got into it with him. Apparently, Mr. Spindler punched two men out. The third guy, well, he pulled a pistol and shot Mr. Spindler several times. It's pretty bad. The medics stabilized him and put him on a helicopter to the Confluence Hospital in Wenatchee. As I understand it, he's being prepped for surgery as we speak." Again, a pause, as if to emphasize just how serious things were. "The hospital called to ask if there was anyone they could get permission from for a decision."

"Jeez," Charlie said, two thoughts rushing to mind. The first one being regret for having sent Gunther to the Stampede. Followed closely by what might happen if the police began to investigate what Gunther had been up to during the past few weeks.

The sergeant's words now came quickly. "We found your name and number on a slip of paper in his pocket, along with his German passport. I figured to call you first, just in case you knew if there was someone already here in the U.S. that we could contact. Otherwise, our next step will be to contact the German embassy. Is there anything you know that might help us?"

"No," Charlie said, wishing he'd never mentioned the Omak Stampede. He had no idea how airtight Gunther's passport might be. *But it can't be perfect. Nothing ever is for us.*

"Do you know where Mr. Spindler was staying?"

Charlie almost said "No" but then he remembered the Hispanic woman who'd come to the counter at the Belvedere. She would certainly remember him, and would no doubt report his visit to the police if they showed up asking questions.

"Yes," Charlie said. "I visited him once in Langston at an apartment building."

"Do you have a name or an address?"

"The Belvedere," Charlie said. "I don't remember the street it's on, but you can't miss it. It's a big pinkish concrete building, three stories high, and just about as ugly as they come."

"Alright," the sergeant said stiffly, not sounding amused about the apartment building's appearance. "Thanks for your help."

"No problem," Charlie said.

As soon as the connection went dead, Charlie tapped in Frank's cell number.

CHAPTER 14

"It's time for the piñata!" Maria hollered.

Still isolated at the back of the lawn, Benny began to grin.

The girls dutifully carried their empty plates and plastic forks to the garbage can, and then walked over to where the sticks lay beneath the piñata.

Ernesto set his beer on a table, and strolled across the yard to where his son sat cross-legged on the grass. Benny was concentrating upon the commotion of the girls blindfolding Selena for a first turn at the piñata.

As Ernesto reached Benny, he said, "Son, why don't you come over and join the rest of us? I'm sure the girls will let you have a swing at the piñata if you want."

Benny's grin vanished. He shook his head violently.

From near the top of the pine tree, Raven was looking down on the father and son, sensing the love energy coming from the man, and a surprising surge of darkness surging from the child. It made Raven want to fly over and bomb Little Dark Soul's head with a load of poop. But he sensed something important was about to happen, and it was better that he remain an observer and not become a participant. So instead of launching for a bombing run, Raven settled down on the branch.

"You don't care about me," Benny said angrily, eyes squinting up at his father.

"Now Son, you know that's not true. Your mother and I love you every bit as much as we do your sister. But sulking out here accomplishes nothing."

Benny turned his head down to stare at the grass.

Ernesto waited.

When Benny refused to look up, Ernesto glanced back and saw that Selena was now taking wild swings at the piñata, as Nina and Chantha jerked cords to swing the colorful globe beyond the range of her stick. Ernesto sighed, took one last look at Benny, whose head was still down, and fought off the urge to grab his son's arm and hustle him off to his room for a time out. He reluctantly turned and started walking back across the lawn.

As Ernesto rejoined his wife and the Millers, Maria called out, "Your time is up, Selena!"

Chantha looked at Nina and said, "You go." But Nina said, "It's your turn. I'll go last."

On the far side of the yard, Benny said in a low voice that only Raven heard, "Aww . . . why couldn't my *sister* have busted it open."

At that moment Frank's cell phone began to buzz. He pulled it from his pocket, saw it was from Charlie, turned to Anna and said, "Hon, I've got to take this. I'll be in the house."

"Don't be too long," she replied, immediately shifting her attention back to the girls. Frank disappeared through the door, lifting the phone to his ear as he walked.

Selena took off the blindfold and began to stretch it across Chantha's eyes, tying a bow at the back. Nina handed Chantha the longest stick, and then gently spun her around, pointing her in the direction of the dangling piñata, and said, "Go for it."

Chantha took three steps forward, made a wild swing, and missed the piñata by two feet.

Selena was now pulling the cord to move the piñata, while Nina shouted directions to help Chantha aim her swings. "No . . . higher and to the right. Not so high. On your left!"

On her sixth swing the tip of the stick nicked the piñata; bits of orange and blue crepe paper fluttered in the warm summer air.

"Higher!" Nina urged. She looked at Selena, nodding to where she should move the piñata.

As Chantha drew back her stick for a round house swing, Selena pulled the piñata until it was directly over Chantha's head.

"It's right above you!" Nina yelled.

Instead of the major league home run swipe Chantha had intended, she instead swung the stick straight up. It connected dead center with the piñata, which burst open, showering hard candy, small toys, and something quite unexpected, straight down upon her head.

Benny had expected the zip-locked bag of dog turds to remain sealed. But since the time he'd snuck into the kitchen and put the loaded baggie into the piñata, the heat of the day had gradually liquefied its contents. By the time of the party, they were the consistency of watery oatmeal.

When the baggie struck Chantha's shoulder it popped open, splattering soft turd across her arm and down the full length of her champagne dress.

"¡Ay, Dios!" Maria cried. She grabbed a bar towel and raced for Chantha, who by now had felt—and smelled—the feces. She ripped off her blindfold and stared in horror at the brown ooze dribbling down the right side of her body.

Benny's grin transformed into a look of panic.

Chantha began to cry, as Maria wiped globs of poop from her shoulder and dress, all the while promising she would get her cleaned up, saying there were fresh clothes in the house and she could take a shower and she would be perfectly alright. All of which had practically no effect upon Chantha, who was by now sobbing.

Ernesto realized who was responsible and began to march across the yard toward Benny.

Benny would have run away, but the back yard was bordered by a six-foot high wood fence. He sank down onto the grass and drew his knees up to his chest, wrapped his arms around his legs, and buried his head against the tight blue cloth of his jeans.

Raven was fascinated by the energies that now emerged. The man, marching in the boy's direction, blazed with an aura of red ferocity.

The boy's energy darkened to a burnt crimson and coiled around him like oily storm-water surging from a street drain.

When Ernesto reached Benny, he grabbed him by one arm and yanked him to his feet, and then began to drag him toward the house. Benny struggled, but it barely slowed his father down.

As Ernesto and Benny approached the princess, Raven saw little sparks of blue energy begin to form around her. It started as an aura around her head, and then fully enveloped her body, twisting into a virtual tornado. The electric blue vortex became so intense that Raven could barely make out her face.

A warmth had blossomed in Nina's cheeks. It quickly spread to her chest. She focused on Benny as he came close. They were practically face-to-face when her angry words tumbled out.

"You stupid little fool!" Nina shouted. "How could you do this?"

As the princess spoke, Raven watched the blue energy blast outward, crashing into Benny's body like a battering ram.

To Ernesto it felt as if Benny had been pushed backwards as Nina delivered what sounded—and felt—like a command.

"If you can't act like a decent person, you should go find a shovel and climb up into the hills and dig yourself a hole and crawl in and never come out again!"

Benny panicked, and somehow managed to pull free from his father's grip. "I'm sorry," he blubbered. "I didn't mean for it to break open." He struggled for better words, failed to find them, and collapsed onto his hands and knees. He then puked up every little bit of partially digested hamburger, cake, ice cream, and orange soda, soaking the freshly mown grass in a frothy mess.

Up in the pine tree, Raven watched the blue energy tornado swirl and punch and then spin down within seconds, totally in awe of the power of his princess.

And in that instant, he knew exactly what his next present had to be.

CHAPTER 15

With her hands cuffed and feet chained, Clarissa sat wedged between two Ertzaintza in the back of the van, expecting to be driven to the coastal city of San Sebastian. The officers in the van weren't giving off emotions which signaled deadly intent, so the worst-case scenarios she imagined were either being rebuked by Livia, or deported after a hearing before a local magistrate.

When the van made a sharp left turn on the outskirts of Zizurkil and headed inland, Clarissa became concerned. She turned to the officer on her left, who was clearly the commander of the group. He cut her off before she could question where they were going.

"You must say nothing. If you speak, you will be sedated." He reached inside his jacket and withdrew a small case, opening it to reveal a syringe filled with a clear liquid.

This at least confirmed something important. They knew she was dangerous if she were allowed to talk. And that meant someone who *knew about the Order* must be controlling the agenda.

Clarissa settled back in her seat, and tried not to look too scared.

The van sped up into the green coastal mountains until it reached a point that was little more than a dimple between two hills. Here the driver turned onto a rutted dirt road. After several minutes of bumpy road they entered a narrow valley, leaving a trail of dust which settled in the scattered clumps of brush and wild grass lining the road.

The final destination turned out to be a solitary stone-and-mortar farmhouse. A microwave antenna was bolted to the red-tiled roof. The front door stood half open.

Clarissa felt no resonance coming from inside, which meant Livia wasn't awaiting her arrival. Her sense of fear surged.

After they unshackled her feet, she was led from the van, with one officer on each arm, and escorted inside while two officers remained posted up in the shade out front.

The main room was centered by a mahogany dining table and six chairs. There were no decorations on the plastered walls. A staircase led to the upper floor. A kitchen could be seen through an arch to the left.

Still in handcuffs, Clarissa was escorted to the back of the room, to a steel-plated door with fresh mortar around the frame. There was a hefty shiny steel deadbolt that looked new.

The officer in charge let go of Clarissa's arm, and then handed his gun to the first officer, who stepped back two paces and pointed the weapon squarely at Clarissa's chest.

When the cuffs came off, the unarmed officer shoved her through the open door. As soon as Clarissa was inside, the door slammed shut, followed by the sound of the deadbolt being thrown.

Looking around, she saw micro-cameras mounted in all four corners near the ceiling. A red spot glowed beside each lens.

A narrow wooden door was set into the back wall. Behind it she discovered a small bathroom with a shower, sink, toilet, and a towel on a wooden rack. The back wall was rock-and-cement and looked impenetrable.

She returned to the bedroom, where there was a single bed with a thin mattress, a wooden table, and one chair. Light came from a frosted glass rectangle in the plastered ceiling. The floor was set with red ceramic tile. She briefly studied the cameras, and had no doubt that surveillance would be continuous.

On that first day the sounds which came from beyond the metal door were minimal. A few muddled words, the front door opening and closing, occasional boots clunking across the floor. But never the commotion of people going about normal lives.

When evening arrived, Clarissa smelled food cooking.

After a few minutes, while she was sitting in the chair at the table, there came the sound of the deadbolt being thrown. The door eased open and a man cautiously entered with a tray.

He was maybe twenty-five, and wore tight-fitting headphones. Immediately after he entered, the door closed behind him. He avoided looking directly at her, quickly stepped to the side of the table opposite where Clarissa sat, and placed the tray on the table. He then retreated to the door, always facing her but never looking directly into her eyes.

They have been well trained!

He rapped on the wood three times. The door opened, and as he stepped out Clarissa caught a glimpse of the officer who had been in charge of her capture. He now wore gray slacks and a simple white shirt unbuttoned at the collar. He held a gun at the ready.

Dinner turned out to be a lamb stew with carrots and onions, a slice of freshly baked bread, cubes of cantaloupe and green melon. There was no beverage, but there was an empty glass. Clarissa filled it with water from the bathroom sink.

Four hours later the light behind the glass rectangle in the ceiling dimmed for a few seconds. A minute later it went off, leaving her in darkness except for a sliver of light coming from beneath the door. In a few minutes even that was extinguished.

She slipped off her shoes and lay down on the bed, hoping the next day would hold answers.

Sleep came hard.

The following morning proved to be the start of a continuing disappointment. The light came on at what Clarissa guessed was around seven a.m. Then the smells of bacon and eggs, and shortly afterwards the same man, again wearing headphones, with an armed officer outside the door for backup. He entered and placed a breakfast tray on the table and carried the old tray out.

There was no lunch.

Clarissa decided to put her captors to a test. She pulled the chair over next to the door when she smelled cooking in the evening (lamb stew again) and waited. The man didn't appear. After several minutes Clarissa moved her chair back behind the table.

Unfortunately, it seemed her captors had also decided to put her to a test. No dinner arrived. By morning she was quite hungry. She sat at the table on the far side from the door.

Breakfast arrived on schedule.

After she had finished eating, the man returned, carrying some basic toiletry items, plus a pair of white cotton pajamas and a larger bath towel. A reward, she assumed, for her good behavior.

He placed the items on her bed, together with a sturdy paper sack. Clarissa took the hint, and later put her used towel in the sack and left it beside the door. When her next meal came, the paper sack went out with the old food tray. As the days wore on the routine never varied.

CHAPTER 16

Charlie drove Frank to Wenatchee, finding it hard to hold the Sentra's speed under sixty.

At the front desk of the Confluence Health hospital, the receptionist directed them to the surgical ward. When they entered the surgery foyer Charlie said, "You go ask. I'll find a seat." He glanced at a line of chairs along one wall, empty except for one elderly man. Frank nodded agreement, and Charlie walked to the furthest chair and sat down.

As Frank approached the counter, a woman wearing blue scrubs behind the low glass screen said, "May I help you?"

"I understand you have a Mister Spindler in surgery?"

"And you are?"

Frank handed her his business card.

She studied it briefly, and then said, "Please give me a minute. I'll need to get someone to help you with this." She turned abruptly and disappeared down the hallway that led toward the operating rooms.

Shortly, a man wearing blue surgical scrubs walked briskly down the hallway. His face said there were more important things that he should be doing. As he came to an impatient stop behind the glass, he glanced down at Frank's business card which he held in his right hand. Then his eyes came up and met Frank's.

"Mr. Miller?"

Frank nodded.

"I'm told you have a question about one of our patients."

"Yes."

"And your reason for asking?"

"I may be representing Mister Spindler in regard to a shooting incident that took place a few hours ago in Omak."

The man nodded with a solemn look. "He's in *two* right now. I expect he'll be there for a while."

"Any guess as to how long?"

The man studied Frank's face. "Do you know him very well, Mr. Miller?"

Frank knew any hesitation would make it easy for the man to assert medical privacy laws. He replied with the confidence of a lawyer who absolutely needed to know how his client was doing.

"I've been working with him on a separate legal matter. This shooting . . . well, it came as quite a shock."

The man took a long slow breath, came to a decision, and explained in a carefully measured voice that left no doubt.

"I worked admitting on this one. You ask how long he's going to be in surgery. The truth is he may not make it out of surgery. He's lucky to have lived for as long as it took them to get him here. If he survives, he'll be transferred to intensive care. For the long term he's probably going to be looking at substantial rehab in a nursing facility."

"Oh." Frank's lawyer mind was calculating the possibilities. A dead Gunther would tell no tales. But a murder investigation would present a new set of problems. And if Gunther did make it, Frank wasn't sure what surprises his "recovery" might hold.

"Where should we wait?"

"We?"

There was no avoiding that Charlie was going to be a part of this. His name and phone number had been on a slip of paper in Gunther's pocket. The detective assigned to the investigation might want to interview him.

The man in blue scrubs began to look impatient.

"There's a friend with me who also knows Mister Spindler." Frank pointed to Charlie on the far side of the reception area.

The man's look now left no doubt that the flow of information was at an end.

"There's a cafeteria downstairs. We can call the cell number on your business card when there's something to report."

"Thanks," Frank said.

He left the counter and walked back to Charlie and sank onto a chair beside him. "He says Gunther might not make it."

Charlie's face turned grim, and Frank was a little surprised.

"I thought you didn't care for him all that much."

"I don't," Charlie said softly. "At least not while he's in a position to make trouble. But a guy who lives for over two hundred and fifty years, when you hear maybe he's going to die, well, it makes you think how fragile life is and how quickly it can end. Even for one of *us*."

CHAPTER 17

After two weeks of worrying about not just her own future, but also about what her capture might mean for the safety of Nina, Clarissa grew desperate enough to try and communicate with the man wearing headphones. When the breakfast tray arrived, she opened her palms and spread her hands wide, while sitting behind the table in a non-threatening posture.

"Is there someone I can speak to about why I'm here?"

The man ignored her, set the tray down, and left quickly.

Dinner was a no-show. Clarissa gave up all hope to communicate.

Three more weeks passed before she finally felt a slight tingle of resonance as she waited for breakfast. At first she thought she must be imagining. But the tingle quickly resolved into the resonance of a member. *Someone* was here.

She hadn't bothered to dress beyond the cotton pajamas that morning. Her street clothes were neatly folded under the bed. She stripped off the pajamas and hurriedly dressed in the brown slacks, yellow blouse, and flat-soled shoes she'd worn at the time of her capture.

There came voices from beyond the metal door, and for the first time one was a woman.

Could it be Livia?

Finally, there was the sound of the deadbolt being thrown, and then the knob turning. The door swung wide. And there stood Liesel Hartkorn.

"Hello Clarissa," Liesel said, her smile more like an apology than a greeting. "May I come in?"

"Of course." Clarissa stood beside the table, well away from the door and the guard.

Liesel entered and the door swung shut. The sound of the deadbolt being rammed home confirmed she was still a prisoner.

After an awkward moment, Liesel opened her arms and they embraced.

"I can't tell you how happy I am to see someone I know," Clarissa said. As they separated, she voiced what seemed to be the logical explanation for her imprisonment. "So, it was the Council that ordered me kidnapped?"

"No," Liesel said. "The Council has no idea you are here."

Clarissa's face betrayed her surprise. "Do you know who is behind this?"

"I was contacted through an anonymous note that asked if I still valued your friendship and whether I might want to come and see you."

"And you don't know who sent it?"

"Not with any certainty. It was left at our Zurich office by a messenger. I was directed to come to San Sebastian, where I was met by a man at the airport." Liesel paused. "Do you mind if I sit? It's been a long day."

"You're welcome to the chair," Clarissa said. "I've already sat in it enough."

Liesel sat down, and then gazed around the sparsely furnished room. "How long have you been here?"

"Five weeks."

Liesel shook her head in disbelief.

Clarissa settled on the edge of the bed, folded her hands on her legs, and looked at Liesel with hope. "So?"

"I was told to ask you some questions." Liesel reached into a pocket of her slacks and pulled out a small folded sheet of paper. "The man who drove me here guaranteed I could leave at any time, but said there's no certainty you will be released. I suppose it depends upon your answers." She unfolded the sheet.

57

Clarissa glanced up at one of the cameras. The little red light assured her that *someone* was watching, and almost certainly listening.

"Okay," Liesel said. "First question. Why did you come to Spain?"

There was no point in lying. Before her capture, she'd asked too many questions of locals to think the target of her mission had remained a secret.

"I came to find out if Livia is still alive."

Liesel's look of surprise confirmed she hadn't known.

Clarissa couldn't tell if the next question was written on the paper, or if Liesel was simply curious.

"What did you want from her?"

And here, finally, was Clarissa's chance to communicate directly with her captor. She didn't bother to mince words.

"I hoped she might be persuaded to help me hide Nina from the Order. Since she was so efficient at keeping herself concealed from us for eighteen centuries, I thought she might have some good pointers."

Liesel paused a moment to digest what she'd heard. She then glanced back to the sheet. "Who is helping you?"

Clarissa now faced a choice. Be honest, and put those on her side at risk. Or refuse, and risk further detention. She knew where her loyalties had to lie. And it was an easy choice.

"I feel uncomfortable answering that question. It requires me to violate the trust others have placed in me, and I'm not willing to do that." She glanced up at the camera, as if to confirm that she was fully committed.

Liesel nodded slowly. "That was the last question. Now I suppose we wait." She refolded the paper and shoved it into her pocket.

In a minute, there came the sound of the deadbolt being withdrawn. After three sharp knocks on the door, it swung open. A guard entered and handed an envelope to Liesel.

She took the envelope and handed it to Clarissa.

The door had not shut. The guard stood his ground, still blocking the way, but his hand had at least not shifted to the pistol at his waist.

Clarissa tore open the envelope and withdrew a note, noticing there were also two wooden matches in the envelope.

The note was handwritten in a lovely, flowing script.

You may leave with Liesel Hartkorn, but you must fully comply with her directions. I may contact you later. Please burn this immediately. Livia.

Clarissa looked up at Liesel. "Do you know what it says?"

"No."

Clarissa looked up at the camera and realized this was no time for hesitation. She stood up, withdrew a match from the envelope, bent down and struck it on the red tile floor. She held the flame to one corner of the note and watched as flames licked through the handwriting. She dropped the last fragment and watched it curl into cinders on the floor.

She turned to face Liesel. "It seems I'm to be your guest."

"Is that what it said?"

"More or less."

"Meaning everything?"

"Not quite."

"Do you care to share what else it said?"

"No." Clarissa glanced up at the camera. "But I would like to leave here before someone changes their mind."

CHAPTER 18

Selena was so disgusted with her little brother that she didn't even want to be in the same house with him. Ernesto and Maria readily agreed to a sleepover at the Millers to preserve the peace.

"I'll bring her back tomorrow after breakfast," Anna assured Maria, as she led the girls out to the Volvo, all the while wondering when Frank might be coming home.

After retreating into the house to take the call, he'd come to the back door and signaled to her, his face grave with concern. "Charlie is on the way to pick me up. Gunther's gotten into some kind of trouble and he's in surgery down in Wenatchee." Then he turned away and walked back through the house and went out front to wait for Charlie. The two of them left just before the piñata incident.

As the girls climbed into the Volvo, Chantha asked Anna, "Where's Dad?"

"He had an emergency with a client," she said, trying to sound calm. "Someone came to pick him up. He'll be home later."

It wasn't the first time her small-town lawyer dad had had an urgent client problem on a weekend. Chantha knew his job sometimes required meetings on short notice. Still, it sucked. She wanted her father.

When Anna reached the house and pulled into the garage, the girls scrambled out and went inside. When they reached Chantha's bedroom, she pulled off Selena's bulky tee shirt and sweatpants and slipped into a pair of jeans and a cotton top.

Selena was still fuming about her brother.

"I'll kill him," she raged. "I'll poison his oatmeal. I'll strangle him with a zip tie when he's asleep, real slowly, until his eyes bug out and his tongue turns purple."

"Selena," Nina said softly. "Please give it a rest." She looked at Chantha, who appeared to have mostly recovered from the terror of the afternoon. Then she sat down beside Selena, on the edge of the bed, took her hand, and said in a somber voice, "Look at the bright side. It's one birthday we'll never forget."

Had she said it loudly, or insistently, it wouldn't have been funny. But in soft pedal it struck a chord. The girls simply fell apart, doubling over with laughter, breaking up whenever they looked at each other.

When they finally paused to catch their breaths, Selena looked from Chantha to Nina, and in a totally serious voice said, "Yeah, well, I'm still gonna strangle him."

Which provoked another helpless round of laughter.

When the joyous mood finally faded, Chantha said, "Mom's got a pitcher of lemonade in the refrigerator."

The girls headed for the kitchen and poured drinks with lemon wedges, and then went out onto the deck.

Chantha was the first to push through the French doors. "Hey," she said. "What's that?"

In the middle of the table lay a small blue plastic toy shovel, no more than six inches long. Nina picked it up, examined it, and said, "It must be another present from our mystery invader." The girls stared at the shovel, at each other, and Chantha realized there might finally be an answer. "The cameras!" she shouted.

They dashed inside, nearly colliding with Anna as she came from the laundry room where she'd taken Chantha's dress, now safely wrapped in plastic to await delivery to the dry cleaners.

"What's got you girls so excited?"

Chantha said, "Mom, there was another *thing* on the deck!"

Nina held up the shovel.

Anna stared at the little blue shovel, thinking it oddly incongruous with the earlier keys and gold wedding band.

"We need to replay the security recorder," Chantha said. "C'mon!"

They all crowded into Frank's study, where Chantha took charge, running the program backwards at high speed until there came a momentary flash of black. Chantha stopped the replay, and then started it forward at regular speed.

"A crow?" Selena puzzled, as a large black bird flew into view, holding the shovel in its beak.

"A raven," Nina corrected. "See how its beak is curved? Crows have a straight beak."

"Raven, crow, what's the difference?" Selena was clearly disappointed. Where was the excitement in a bird for heaven's sake!

"A raven is perfectly fine," Nina said, thinking it was a lot better than some nutcase obsessed with teenage girls.

"I guess," Selena conceded.

Anna was relieved. "Well," she said, "I guess this solves the mystery."

Selena remained puzzled. "But why is a crow—sorry, I mean a 'raven'—bringing stuff to your deck?"

"I don't know," Nina said. "But if it wants to bring us presents, maybe we should give it presents too."

Chantha thought for a moment. "What would a raven want from us?"

"Food," Anna said. "We've got peanuts in the kitchen."

The girls soon had a small bowl of peanuts in the middle of the deck table. They retreated to the family room, pulled up a couch just inside the French doors, and began a vigil, staring through the beveled glass panes. They didn't have to wait long.

Raven came swooping down, landed beside the bowl, picked up a peanut, and flew away.

"Cool," Chantha said, as the bird soared beyond the trees.

"I guess," Selena added.

Nina said nothing. She was thinking that the raven looked exactly like the one she'd seen in the neighbor's tree at the birthday party. And the new present—a shovel, even if it was only a toy—was precisely what she'd told Benny to use to dig a hole to crawl into. It seemed too much of a coincidence. And totally weird to think that a raven had somehow heard her, and that he was now attempting to signal his agreement!

CHAPTER 19

Frank and Charlie headed downstairs at the Confluence Hospital for a long overdue lunch. They paused in the hallway just outside the basement cafeteria, and Frank finally had a chance to pull out his cell phone and call Anna.

"Gunther's still in surgery. They say he may not make it. I'd like to stay here with Charlie for a while."

Anna considered telling Frank about the piñata misadventure, but decided against it. There was already plenty on his plate. In what she hoped was a cheerful voice, she said, "The girls are fine. Selena's come for a sleepover tonight. And I do have a bit of good news."

"I could use some. What's up?"

"We've solved the mystery about things being left on the back deck."

"Who is it?"

"It's not so much a *who* as it is a *what*. It's a raven."

"A raven?"

"A big one. It brought a toy shovel to the table earlier this afternoon. The girls replayed the surveillance video and there it was, dropping off a child's blue plastic sand shovel."

"Well, that's a relief," Frank said, glad for one less thing to worry about. "Please tell the girls I'm sorry I missed the rest of their party. I'll find a way to make it up to them."

"I don't think they minded too much, honey. They know you have obligations that sometimes happen on a weekend."

"Did you tell the girls why I left?"

"No. It would have upset Nina. And even if she knew about the shooting there is nothing she could do about it. Whether he dies or recovers, we can deal with it as it happens. Don't you think that's the best way to handle it for now?"

"Yes," Frank said, feeling a surge of gratitude for the wonderful woman he was married to. "I'll try not to be home too late."

As the call ended, Charlie said, "I agree it's not wise to tell Nina about Gunther before we know if he'll live. She's formed some kind of bond with him, and there's no doubt she'd want to come down to the hospital. And that's *not* a good idea."

"I agree," Frank said, as they entered the cafeteria. "As for the bond, it's called the *Stockholm Syndrome*." He grabbed a tray at the end of a long steel counter. "People who are taken prisoner sometimes form an emotional attachment with their captors."

Charlie grabbed a tray and pushed it along the counter, reaching for a tuna sandwich wrapped in cellophane, doubting Nina's attachment to Gunther had anything to do with what regular people experienced when they were held hostage.

They found a table at the back, and with no one close enough to overhear, Frank finally had a chance to ask what was foremost on his mind.

"If Gunther makes it through surgery and survives, what can we expect? Does the healing happen the same as it would with someone who's 'normal'?"

"Yes and No," Charlie said. "Blood still clots and tissue still heals. It all looks ugly and damaged at first. But with regular people there can be impaired organ function and long-term weakness. For Order members, the healing continues until everything returns to exactly like it was before. And we heal quickly."

"How quickly?"

"I once broke my arm when I was thrown from a horse. It was serious enough that a doctor had to reset the bone and put on a cast. I wore it for a couple weeks before the itching stopped. The doctor said I should keep it on for at least another month. But I cut it off, and not only was there no pain, there was no swelling. Within a few hours the skin, which was white and wrinkly when I pulled off the plaster, looked just the same as the skin on my uninjured arm."

"Gunther has more serious injuries," Frank said, sounding hopeful. "He's at least going to have scars, right?"

"No. Like I said, everything heals up. Where those bullets entered, there won't be any marks. Where the surgeon cut him open, it will look like it never happened."

Frank groaned in frustration. "Then we're going to have to find some way to get him out of the hospital before his body does the impossible." His face was grim, eyes squeezed shut in frustration.

"What's wrong?"

Franks' eyes snapped open. "You said the deputy who called you has Gunther's passport."

"Right."

"When they learn it's a forgery, they're going to place him under arrest, and eventually turn him over to Immigration for deportation."

"So . . . that takes him off our hands, right?" Charlie sounded relieved.

"The problem is that both Immigration and the Germans will cooperate with the local police if Gunther is subpoenaed to be a witness. The shooting was a big-time felony. Okanogan County will certainly want to prosecute. A case like that can take up to three months, maybe longer if the shooter waives the speedy trial rule. How long do you think it will take for Gunther's wounds to heal?"

"Not three months," Charlie said grimly. "My guess is he'll be up and walking around within a week. Three months from now, you'd never know it happened."

"Then we're going to have to come up with a 'Plan B'," Frank said.

"Unless he dies?"

"Yeah," Frank agreed. "But somehow I don't think we're going to get that lucky."

Frank was right. His cell phone rang an hour later.

When they reached the ICU, they were directed to a small conference room. A minute later a surgeon walked in wearing fresh blue surgical scrubs, with a stethoscope around his neck, looking tired but upbeat. Both Frank and Charlie stood to greet him.

"Which one of you is his lawyer?"

Frank stuck out a hand, "Frank Miller," he said. "And this is Charlie, one of—" he'd almost said "Gunther" and in that nervous moment he forgot the name on the passport. He had nowhere to go, but Charlie saved the moment with—"

"—I met Mister Spindler for the first time a few weeks ago."

The surgeon glanced at Charlie, and then back to Frank. "Do you know if he goes by his first name?"

Frank was clueless.

Charlie remembered the name the deputy had given on the phone. "It's Wolfgang," he said, realizing this might become a problem when Gunther came awake. "But he has a nickname. His friends call him 'Gunther'."

Frank coughed, and raised a hand to his mouth to cover the half-smile.

Charlie eased the conversation away from names with, "It's horrible what happened to him up at the Stampede."

"Yes," the doctor said. "But he's one tough fellow. It's a miracle he didn't bleed out on the way here. We went through several bags of blood, but every time it seemed like the bleeding might take off, the flow slowed down for some reason I can't explain. He's lost his left kidney, and we took out a slug lodged near his heart. He'll have scar tissue near the aorta that may require further surgery. Where the third bullet tore through his right thigh was the easiest procedure, but he'll be hobbling around for quite a while, and there'll likely be some permanent impairment. There were a couple of other superficial wounds. He's stable now, and we've got him heavily sedated and plan to keep him that way at least through the night."

Frank asked, "When do you think he might be discharged?"

"Two weeks at a minimum. And then he'll need rehab. We'll be discussing that with Mr. Spindler when he's in better shape."

"Could you possibly let me know when he's awake? I think he'll want some legal advice about going after that fellow who shot him."

"Certainly," the surgeon said. "But you should know that we've already contacted the German embassy. They'll be sending a lawyer they use on politically delicate matters like this. But I can certainly have whoever they send call you if you would like."

"Sure," Frank said, feeling the opportunity for damage control slipping away.

A beeper went off in the surgeon's pocket. He checked the message, and said, "If you gentlemen have no more questions, I need to go. We've had a busy night and I'm scheduled for another surgery."

"I think we've got all we need," Frank said, reaching out to again shake the surgeon's hand.

"Well," Charlie said after the surgeon was gone, "it looks like it's Plan B. Got any ideas?"

"Not at the moment," Frank said. "Right now, I just want to get out of here." He reached out to pat Charlie on the shoulder. "That was a nice catch with the name."

Charlie just smiled.

CHAPTER 20

Benny Hernandez was a scared little boy. Scared to sleep because of the nightmares about being buried alive. Scared that Nina might come to the house and cast another spell on him. And particularly scared by the shovels which appeared in his dreams, just enough out of reach so that he could never grab one to dig himself out of the cold earth where he was buried up to his chin.

Seeing a real shovel made him sick to his stomach. So much so that he refused to go into the big shed alongside the house where his father stored equipment for the yard care business. In the shed there were plenty of shovels. And other tools, like hoes and picks, which also might be used for digging.

He was mostly scared about misbehaving. For a boy about to turn eleven, who had always loved making mischief, never again doing something "wrong" seemed impossible. Benny knew he was eventually going to mess up. And when that happened there would be one terrible and unavoidable consequence. He would have to go find a shovel, hike up into the hills, dig a hole, crawl in, and never come out again.

As the days passed, Ernesto and Maria grew more concerned. Not because Benny was causing trouble. Just the opposite. He was suddenly *too good*. At supper his behavior was perfect, saying "Please" when he wanted something passed, making sure his sister was served first, volunteering to say grace. And at the end of each meal he was immediately up to help clear the table before his mom could even ask, running the sink full of hot water for washing dishes, insisting upon drying each dish and carefully putting it away. And when he wasn't doing everything possible to be helpful around the house, Benny stayed in his room, quiet as a stone.

Ernesto was so worried, that on the fifth day after the piñata debacle he knocked on Benny's bedroom door. When Benny called out "Come in" Ernesto discovered a room that was spotless. No shirts or underwear on the floor. Not a speck of dirt *anywhere*. A bible lay on the little stand beside the bed, open to the chapter Benny had last been reading, searching for an answer on those thin pages.

Benny had dark circles under his eyes. His skin looked waxy and pale.

"Benny? Are you feeling okay?"

"Yes, Father. Is there something you need me to do?"

"No." Ernest sat down on the edge of the single bed. Benny continued to stand, almost at attention. "Sit down, Son," Ernesto said, patting the mattress beside him. Benny obediently sat, staring straight ahead, almost as if in a trance.

"Your mother and I are worried about you."

"Why? I haven't done anything wrong, have I?" A sudden panic filled Benny's face.

"Of course not," Ernesto insisted. "In fact, you've been perfect these past few days."

Benny relaxed just a little. He'd tried so hard. The suspension his parents had put him on had actually made his life easier. Since he couldn't go outside without permission—and he most certainly hadn't asked for it—there weren't many opportunities for getting into trouble. He'd also completely stopped playing computer games, because sometimes when he lost a soldier, he'd say a bad word. Swearing might fit into the category of misbehaving. Instead, he spent his time cleaning his room, and doing whatever chores his mom or dad asked.

Ernesto now tried to encourage a reaction that was more like the old Benny.

"I have decided to take you off suspension. You can go outside if you want to play." He looked at Benny, hoping for some sign of relief. Instead, what he saw was fear. He began to wonder if a visit to the family doctor might be necessary. And then he had a sudden inspiration.

"Let's go for a drive. I want to get you out of the house for some fresh air. I need to pick up some stuff downtown. How would you like to come along?"

How would he like to come along? It was a minefield! Beyond the safety of the house there were a million chances to say or do something wrong. But telling his father "No" was an immediate "bad." So instead of making up an excuse (lying was certainly a form of misbehaving) Benny said, "Okay."

"Great!" Ernesto figured he had finally broken through. "I'll go grab my list of 'to do's' and meet you at the truck." He pushed up from the bed and walked to the door, leaving Benny wishing he were paralyzed. But there was nothing he could do now that he'd agreed. He stood up, carefully retied his sneakers, and went to join his father.

At first it seemed like everything might turn out okay. Ernesto drove to the gas station and filled the tank, while Benny sat in the passenger seat and stared out the window, watching a man washing the windshield of his Lexus. And then a lady, who walked into the station and came back out licking an ice cream bar.

The next stop was equally unthreatening because Benny again didn't need to leave the truck. Ernesto had recyclable cardboard and metal in the bed of the pickup. He drove a mile out of town to the transfer station, where he said, "You can stay in the truck, Son. This will just take a minute." He got out and dropped a sack of crushed soda cans into one bin, shoved a packet of cardboard into another, and then he climbed back into the truck. "There," he said, sounding satisfied. "I think we've earned a reward, don't you?"

Benny didn't think he'd earned anything since he'd done nothing. But disagreeing with his father might be considered misbehaving, so he said, "Sure."

"Good." Ernesto paused, scratched his chin, and said, "You know, there is one thing I should do before we go to the drive-in. I need to pick up something at the hardware store. It'll just take a minute or two." He smiled at his son.

71

Benny tried to smile back. But his heart was thumping, and his guts had turned to jelly.

CHAPTER 21

When Tina stepped off the propjet at the East Wenatchee airport, Anna was waiting with all three girls inside the small terminal. Anna turned to the excited teenagers and gently reminded, "Please remember that she's done a lot of traveling today, so don't bombard her with questions. Give her a chance to get to know you. There will be plenty of time later on to talk about your project."

The girls returned impatient looks, before Chantha finally said, "Okay, Mom. We'll give her a chance."

Nina nodded in agreement.

Selena forced a smile.

As they watched Tina cross the tarmac toward the double glass doors, Chantha blurted out, partly in shock, partly in awe, "Check out the hair!"

Tina's short, spiky locks were today dyed golden yellow at the tips, at the end of electric blues strands. Her short, jelled hair stuck straight out from her scalp. Something her stylist had called, "the match flame look."

Anna wondered aloud, "They sometimes do things a bit differently in California." While thinking, *Please don't let my girls become interested in something like this.*

"Way cool!" Selena said.

"Yeah," Chantha agreed, "but if you went home looking like that, your mom would ground you for a year!"

Nina laughed, and offered, "She'd probably shave your head too!"

Anna felt relieved.

73

"I wasn't thinking of actually doing it," Selena protested. "I just said it *looked* cool."

Tina passed the security rope and spotted them immediately. She walked up and dropped her bag on the floor. "You must be Anna," she said, and instead of reaching to shake hands, she lightly embraced Anna, giving her a French air kiss on each cheek.

Caught off guard, Anna just let it happen.

The girls' eyes grew a little wider.

"It's so nice of you to come," Anna said, recovering quickly.

"I'm totally excited about what the girls want to do," Tina said. "But you should thank Valerie. It was her idea to send me." She turned from Anna, and spoke to each girl in turn.

"You must be Chantha," she said, with a generous smile.

And then to Selena, "You're the girl who posted the bunny on the Internet. I love what you've done with your Facebook page, Selena. Nice job!"

Selena appeared ready to burst with joy.

Finally, it was Nina's turn.

"Valerie wished she could come and meet you, Nina. She asked me to tell you that she'll try and come up soon to get to know you in person." She reached out and gave Nina's hand a gentle squeeze. As they touched, it felt like a spark passed. Nina saw Tina's eyelids flutter a little, but no one else appeared to notice.

Tina turned back to Anna, who had by now picked up her bag, and said, "Please let me get that." Anna reluctantly handed the bag over, and then led the way out to the Volvo.

On the drive home, Anna's cell phone rang. She normally ignored calls in the car, but when she saw it was Selena's home number, she took it. While holding the phone to her ear, her face turned serious. After listening for a moment, she said, "I'll do it." She hung up, and said, "Selena, I'm going to need to drop you off at the hospital when we get to Langston. Something's happened to your brother."

Selena's face went slack. "What?" she asked.

Anna's reply was grim.

"I'll need to let your parents explain it to you."

74

♦

As Ernesto pulled up in front of Toomey's Hardware, he said to his son, "Why don't you come in with me, Benny?" He was hoping to see some small hint of joy, but instead a sudden hopelessness etched his son's face.

Benny couldn't say "No." But he didn't want to say "Yes" either. He looked dumbly forward, through the windshield, eyes unfocused.

Ernesto reluctantly took silence as a yes. And when Benny didn't immediately open the passenger door, Ernesto walked around, pulled it open, and said, "C'mon, Son. Let's get this done and then we can go have burgers and milkshakes." He stood patiently in the hot sun while Benny uncoiled from the seat and climbed out.

The hardware store was an old-fashioned family-run business that had somehow survived the big-chain invasion. Scuffed black linoleum covered the aisles; yellowed acoustic tile on the ceiling. Fluorescent tubes bathed everything in a flat white light.

Bolted to one wall were racks holding rifles, shotguns, fishing poles, and high-tech archery equipment. A long glass-topped case beneath the racks displayed dozens of pistols.

Ernesto led Benny back through the store, past camping supplies, camouflage vests and hats, flashlights, jackknives, kitchen supplies, drills, bits, wrenches, screwdrivers, saws, and every kind of power tool.

As they trudged down the wide center aisle, Benny kept his eyes narrowly focused on his father's back. This strategy worked until they reached the last side aisle. Ernesto now turned right and headed for a wall filled with long-handled tools.

Benny froze, eyes firmly focused on the black linoleum at his feet. It was only when Ernesto hollered impatiently, "Son!" that Benny felt compelled to look up. And there stood his father, holding a wood-handled shovel with a broad metal blade. Nina's face swam up in Benny's mind. She might as well have been standing beside him in the aisle, screaming in his ear, *"If you can't behave . . ."*

Benny fell to his knees, placed his palms on the worn linoleum, and threw up.

Ernesto dropped the shovel and ran for his son, even as Benny rolled over onto his right side, puke soaking into his shirt from the chunky pool of barf on the floor, curled into a fetal position, eyes glassy. The last thought that drifted through his retreating mind was that he had puked in a public place, and that was undoubtedly misbehavior of the highest degree. Now the only safe place to go was down into the darkness.

By the time the ambulance arrived, Benny was catatonic. The doctor in the emergency room thought it might be a *hysterical coma*, and was entirely puzzled over what might have caused such a reaction in a hardware store.

CHAPTER 22

Frank and Anna treated Nina, Chantha and Tina to dinner at the fanciest restaurant in the valley, the Cordon Bleu Steak House. What should have been a fun meal was made somber by the news of Benny's sudden hospitalization. When Tina asked if the girls wanted to talk business, Nina said, "I think we should wait for Selena."

"But what if she can't come tomorrow?" Chantha said. The news about Benny was grim. He might not awaken from his coma. And if he did, he might have brain damage. Selena coming to the house the next morning was very much up in the air.

Nina was insistent. "If she can't come, then we'll move ahead without her. But let's at least give her a chance."

Frank and Anna exchanged smiles across their sizzling steak platters. They couldn't have been prouder of how their girls were handling the situation.

Tina nodded in agreement, thinking it might be a good idea to order a second glass of wine.

The following morning, Maria arrived at the Miller's house with Selena. When the girls and Tina were gathered at the kitchen counter for breakfast, Maria and Anna walked out to the privacy of the living room. The anxious sharing of information between mothers came quickly and quietly.

"How is Benny?"

"They took him by ambulance to the Confluence hospital in Wenatchee last night."

"Will he be okay?"

"This morning the doctor called and said he was responsive. I'm not sure exactly what that means, but I think he's awake." Maria crossed herself. "Ernesto left for the hospital an hour ago, and I'm driving down now. Is it possible that you could watch Selena for us today?"

"Of course. You can leave her here for as long as you need."

"Thank you," Maria said, taking a shaky breath. Anna reached out and they embraced. Sudden tears coursed down Maria's cheeks. After a few seconds she pulled away, hastily wiping her cheeks with a shirt sleeve. "I don't want Selena to see me like this. She and Benny, they have fought a lot this summer, but last night Selena cried herself to sleep. I don't want her to worry."

Anna held Maria's hand as they walked to the front door. "I'm sure Benny is going to recover."

"We have faith in God," Maria said. "He will answer our prayers." But she sounded uncertain, and crossed herself.

Anna returned to the kitchen, where Selena was finishing her last pancake, trying to sound excited as she talked about the bunny project. But the extra makeup she had applied that morning didn't fully hide the dark rings under her eyes. And there was heaviness in the way she held herself.

"Selena, your mother asked if you could stay with us today, and I said we'd love to have you. I hope that's alright with you."

"Sure," Selena said bravely. "The doctors say Benny's going to be okay, and besides, I don't think he'd want to see me standing over him in a hospital bed."

Nina sensed Selena's pain and fear, and knew it was time for a distraction. "Tina," Nina said, walking to a red plastic canister on the counter. "Do you want to see something cool?"

"Sure," Tina said, watching as Nina pulled the cover off the canister and scooped out a few peanuts.

"Peanuts?" Tina was puzzled.

"Come out to the deck," Nina said, turning for the family room without offering an explanation. Everyone followed, with Tina wondering if maybe there were tame squirrels. Chantha, Selena and

Anna seemed to be enjoying the moment, which confused Tina even more.

From his favorite watching place in the neighbor's oak tree Raven saw a flamboyant newcomer walk out onto the deck with the princess. What amazing hair this female had! Colors in hues Raven had never before seen on a human. He assumed she must have entered her breeding period for such wonderful plumage to be on display.

For the past five days, Raven had flown down to eat peanuts left on the table, always bringing a present in return. Today, he carried nothing in his beak, having decided it was time to take the next step.

The four females had just reached the table, with Nina placing the bowl of peanuts in the center of the table, when Raven launched from his branch and soared toward the deck.

Nina was about to explain to Tina what this was all about when something black flashed down out of the sky. Raven landed beside the bowl, his dark eyes peering up at each of them in turn, hopping on scaly talons in a slow pirouette.

Raven finally faced Nina, opened his beak, and in what sounded exactly like Frank Miller's voice, he said, "*Nina.*"

Everyone took a step back from the table.

"Wow! Tina said. "Does it always do this?"

"No way!" Chantha was wide-eyed.

Selena looked as if she'd seen a ghost.

Anna wondered how the bird had learned to imitate Frank. And for the first time she wondered if this strange creature was safe to be around the girls.

Nina was trying to puzzle out how the raven knew her name. She remembered only one time when Frank had spoken her name when the raven was nearby. *It was at the birthday party.* Which implied that the same bird *was* keeping track of her!

Raven felt the strong emotional reactions of the humans, and realized he should have waited until just the princess was on the deck before uttering her name. Without taking a single peanut he launched into the air and disappeared beyond the oak where the tree swing hung.

"Wow!" Chantha said. "It said your name." She looked at Nina, wanting an explanation.

Nina just shrugged. How does someone explain what seems to be the impossible?

CHAPTER 23

The dominoes began to fall for Gunther. A Seattle attorney called Frank and asked him to meet her at the hospital.

When he arrived, the woman at the reception desk told him, "Mr. Spindler was transferred to a regular care unit yesterday. He's in room two-oh-six."

Frank thanked her and headed for the elevator.

At the second-floor station he asked the nurse, "Is Mr. Spindler receiving visitors?"

"He is," she said. "You're the second one this morning. There's already a lady in his room." She pointed down the hallway. "Third door on the right. It should be open."

Frank had hoped to speak with Gunther before the Seattle attorney arrived, and felt a knot in his gut as he approached the room and heard words being spoken in German. When he pushed the half-open door, he saw a woman sitting beside Gunther's bed. She wore dark blue slacks, a matching blue blazer, and a white blouse. A yellow silk tie hung loose around her neck. She paused mid-sentence and turned to see who it was.

"You must be attorney Frank Miller," she said, rising and offering a handshake that was firm and brief. "I'm Cynthia Travers, with Crestwell, Bergman and Jones. I'm basically their immigration law department." She chuckled at this observation, and said, "I've been chatting with Mister Spindler," immediately correcting herself, "With *Goon-tuh*," giving the correct German pronunciation. "It seems he's having something of a remarkable recovery."

"That's great," Frank said. He turned to Gunther, who lay contentedly on the bed, wearing a blue-and-white striped hospital robe half opened at the chest. A single gray monitor line was taped to his skin. It led to a wall-mounted flat screen that was tracing a blue line of regular-looking peaks and valleys.

"How are you feeling, Gunther?"

"Fine, Mister Miller. How are you today?" There was amusement in his voice.

"I'm well, thanks." Frank immediately returned his attention to the attorney. "Would you like to have a cup of coffee, Ms. Travers?"

She gave a broad, perfect smile. "Absolutely. It was a long drive over the mountains and I could use some caffeine." She flashed a reassuring smile at Gunther, and said, "I'll be back to finish up our interview after I've visited with Mr. Miller."

"I'll still be here," Gunther replied with a chuckle that conveyed an unmistakable hint of irony.

Cynthia Travers laughed.

Gunther laughed.

And Frank knew they were laughing about different things. He managed a quick, secretive look of disapproval at Gunther, before he walked out with Travers in tow.

Once safely in the hallway, Frank said, "There's a cafeteria in the basement, or there's an espresso stand near the main entrance. Your choice."

"Definitely espresso. And please call me Cynthia. May I call you Frank?"

"Certainly," Frank said, surprised at the informality. *Crestwell-Bergman* was a top Seattle firm, and Frank had expected nothing but a big city attitude from one of its attorneys. That was a big reason he'd chosen a rural practice. In Cascade County, nearly all of the attorneys were on a first name basis. He would have never thought to call any of his local colleagues "Mister" or "Ms."

Once they were settled in upholstered chairs opposite the espresso stand, Frank decided to encourage Cynthia's personal courtesy by offering one of his own.

"Would you like to know my view of what happened?"

"Absolutely." She gave a demure look, and took a sip of her latte.

Frank kept it simple, describing how a friend named Charlie, who was staying in the valley for a long vacation, had met Gunther quite by accident a few weeks back, and mentioned the Omak Stampede. Gunther went up to Omak, got shot during a scuffle with a few drunken cowboys, and the sheriff had called Charlie, who had in turn called Frank in case Gunther needed legal help.

"That's about all there is to it. Gunther got into an argument with the wrong bunch of rednecks, and now here we are at the hospital. Do you have any questions?"

She did. And the first was the one Frank feared most.

"Do you know why Gunther is here in the U.S.?"

Treading lightly, since he had no idea what Gunther might have told her, or what the German embassy knew, he said, "I suppose he's here on vacation?"

There was the briefest of pauses.

"That squares with what he told me. But to be honest, I think there's more to the story. Don't you get that sense as well?"

With the German embassy undoubtedly doing a background check, it seemed wise to agree that Gunther didn't appear to be your average tourist.

"He is a bit of a strange one," Frank said, sounding mildly perplexed, but not overly concerned. "I suppose if there's more, you'll find out soon enough. Is there anything you know that I should know?"

Cynthia paused, as if considering what information might be safe to reveal. This made Frank feel a little uncomfortable, and he now wondered if she might actually *want* him to feel uncomfortable.

"There may be a problem with his visa, but until I talk with the assistant to the ambassador in D.C. that's all I can say."

There was obviously was something else on her mind. Frank nudged her a little.

"And?"

"Do you intend to ask Gunther if he wants you to help him in the criminal matter? Or in a civil damages action?"

Frank continued to distance himself from any legal entanglement.

"If the German government is paying you, it wouldn't make much sense for me to be billing him for what you can do for free. And the prosecutor's staff will take care of the criminal matter. As for a personal injury case, it's not the kind of law I practice."

Cynthia now did a little distancing of her own.

"I'm just here to help Gunther get the ball rolling in the right direction, and to let him know his options."

Which confirmed, in polite *lawyereze*, that she owed her true allegiance to the German government.

Each attorney now knew precisely where the other stood. Frank saw it was time to gracefully end the dance.

"I'm sure Gunther will be grateful for any help you can give him. Right now, he's probably got more important things on his mind."

"Absolutely," Cynthia agreed. "Speaking of which, I'd better get upstairs and finish my interview."

"Are you staying in Wenatchee tonight?"

"No. But I'll be returning in a few days, when he's feeling better. The embassy can help with medical expenses and for travel back to Germany if he needs it. I'm the 'go to' person for stuff like that."

After Cynthia left, Frank headed for the cafeteria.

Nursing a fresh cup of coffee, he settled at a table, wanting to think through what might lie ahead, and how he could safely navigate the involvement of the Germans and their lawyer.

Half an hour later, just as he was about to head back upstairs, he was surprised by a familiar voice.

"Mister Miller?"

He turned, and there stood Selena's father, looking angry.

"Ernesto?"

"That girl. That *Nina*. She has placed a curse on my son!"

Nearby diners glanced in their direction.

"Please sit down," Frank said, gesturing to a chair on the opposite side of the table.

Ernesto looked confused for a moment. But finally, he sat, repeating the accusation. "She cursed my Benny." He pounded a fist on the table, rattling Frank's coffee cup, and drawing startled looks from nearly everyone in the cafeteria.

"Ernesto, *please* calm down. What makes you think Nina placed a curse on Benny?"

"You weren't there to hear it. But I will tell you."

Ernesto described what Nina had said to Benny at the party, and how it had felt like a gust of wind had practically blown Benny off his feet. His son's behavior had entirely changed from that moment on.

"He is awake now, here in the hospital. And all he says is, 'I'm sorry father. I have been a bad boy. I have misbehaved. I'm sorry.' And then my boy cries and cries. I am so afraid for him."

It was the first time Frank had heard exactly what Nina said to Benny. He recalled what Clarissa had told him about Nina's potential skills, one of which was exercising control over others' minds.

But that isn't supposed to be possible until she grows up.

Ernesto now cradled his face in his palms, elbows firmly planted on the table, tears leaking between his fingers. He began to sob deeply, uncontrollably.

Two nearby tables quickly cleared of diners. Those who were further away spoke in hushed voices.

Frank pictured a ten-year-old boy faced with only two options: to be perfect . . . or to go off and dig his own grave. And one thought rose up in his mind.

Where is Clarissa when we most need her!

CHAPTER 24

When the small private jet flew out of San Sebastian, Clarissa hoped for a short stay in some large German city before catching a flight back to the U.S. Instead, the jet landed at Innsbruck, where a Mercedes limo carried her and Liesel up into the Austrian wilderness.

The journey ended at a mansion with thick stone walls, protected by men who carried machine pistols, guarding a large compound bordered by a weathered split rail fence.

Clarissa confronted Liesel the moment they entered the mansion and were alone together. "So now I'm *your* prisoner," she said in a bitter voice.

"Please try to understand," Liesel pleaded. "I have obligations . . ."

"Of course," Clarissa seethed. "Fairness must seem like a terrible inconvenience for someone who chairs the Council."

"Clarissa, you have no idea how much of a threat you present to our people."

Our people?

Clarissa had of course known that her actions would topple centuries of tradition, and . . . *Let's face it: destroy most, if not all, of the members' privileges.* It still hurt that her old friend was so deeply entrenched with the conservatives that she was unwilling to consider an alternative to locking her up in the Austrian Alps.

Our people!

Liesel's position only continued to harden. After two hours of increasingly heated argument, she stood up, marched to the front door, and with total frustration said, "I was tempted to eventually let you return to the girl. But now that I see you are determined on just one course of action, I'll need to think it over some more." And with that proclamation, she slammed the door and was gone.

CHAPTER 25

The three girls and Tina spent Saturday afternoon in the living room, going over details for manufacturing and selling the bunny. Tina's advice was, "Take the design to an established toy manufacturer. That way you'll get a consistent, quality product, and you won't have to worry about shipping, sales tax, and all of the other details that business folks are good at. They'll have an established distribution pipeline for putting bunnies on store shelves. And since you already have a list of potential customers from Selena's Facebook account, I'm certain you'll have your pick of companies to work with. You'll just have to negotiate and decide which one offers the best deal. And you should also consider making an expensive collector's edition."

Nina was about to ask what the difference between a "regular" bunny and a "collector" bunny might be, when she got that funny "stepped on my shadow" feeling. In a few seconds the front door opened, and she heard a single set of footsteps coming through the house.

Frank entered the room.

"Are you girls making some progress?"

Nina sensed he was worried. Still, she joined in the round of "Yeses."

Frank's lips pressed together in approval before he turned to her.

"Nina, may I please have a word with you in private?"

"Sure," she said, rising from the couch, still sensing the "shadow" feeling and wondering who was nearby.

Selena and Chantha exchanged guarded looks as Frank led Nina from the room.

Once inside the home office, he closed the door and asked her to please sit, while he remained standing.

"Charlie is outside in my car. Would it be okay if you took a short break from your girlfriends and Tina to talk with him?"

"What does he want to talk about?"

"I think I should let Charlie explain that," Frank said, painfully aware that he could no more tell Nina what Charlie intended to say than he could walk on the ceiling.

"Okay." Nina folded her hands in her lap.

"You two can meet in here."

Nina nodded in agreement.

Frank returned a minute later with Charlie, and said, "Call me if you need anything. I'll explain to the girls and Tina that you will rejoin them as soon as possible." He pulled the door shut as he left.

Nina knew something important must have happened, and didn't wait for Charlie to begin.

"I want you to tell me the truth about what's been going on with Clarissa and my kidnapping."

Charlie settled in his chair and said, "Okay. But first I need to tell you that you should know that I can never lie to you."

"Why not?"

"If I lied you would know it. You have that ability, to know if someone is lying. You've surely realized that about yourself, haven't you?"

Chantha had often said that she had a "psychic ability" when it came to outing liars. But this couldn't be what Charlie had come to tell her.

"So why are you really here?"

"Because a problem has come up."

There was a moment of fear. "Is it Clarissa?"

"No," Charlie said.

"Where is she?"

"In Europe."

Why hasn't Frank told me this?

89

"Where?"

"I don't exactly know."

For a long moment Nina considered how strange it was that Charlie didn't know exactly where Clarissa was. Then she moved on.

"If it's not about Clarissa, what's it about?"

"It's about Benny."

"What about him?" She had come to the conclusion that Benny's sudden "illness" was an act. A childish attempt to defend the terrible thing he'd done to Chantha. He deserved whatever had happened.

Charlie was watching her closely. "Before I can explain about Benny, there are some things you need to know about yourself."

"Okay," she said, feeling defensive. But also very curious, and just a little excited.

Charlie settled back in his chair. He couldn't possibly tell her everything. The totality of what it meant to belong to the Order would be overwhelming. Still, there were certain things she needed to know.

♦

Upon learning from Frank about the confrontation between Nina and Benny at the birthday party, Charlie had given Frank the bad news.

"If she's somehow found the power to reach out and control the kid, then he's toast. There's no way a boy of that age can behave for the rest of his life."

"You mean the spell, or whatever it is, won't wear off?"

"If it does, it will likely take years."

"Can't you do something to reverse it?"

"Me?" Charlie had laughed. "I'm just a warrior. I can physically force someone to do things, but that's completely different from putting a suggestion into their mind that *compels* them to act. For that you'd need someone like Clarissa."

"Dang it!" Frank eyes momentarily pinched shut. "Isn't there some way to break this . . . spell?"

"I'm afraid not. That would require Nina understanding her power and what she's done."

"Then we need to tell her!"

Charlie had dug in.

"That's not what we talked about, Frank. If Clarissa doesn't return, I was only intending to tell Nina a few basic things. She shouldn't be told about her potential abilities until she is ready to handle them."

Frank shouted in frustration, his voice rising half an octave. "We absolutely must tell her everything she needs to know about herself so that she can fix this!"

"You mean *I* must tell her."

"Yes, *you* must tell her."

Charlie gave a chilling assessment of the situation.

"I don't mean to sound cruel, but in the overall scheme of things, the life of a ten-year-old boy doesn't really amount to very much."

Frank's reply was scalding.

"It's not about the boy. It's Nina you should worry about. Someday she'll learn what she is, and she'll know that she doomed Benny Hernandez to a horrible death. I don't know very much about people who belong to the Order, but I do know a lot about kids. Nina has a big heart, and if she learns that she inadvertently killed a boy, and that *you* passed up the opportunity to try and help her undo the spell, not only will she live with that guilt for the rest of her very long life, she'll also be righteously angry with *you*. And please correct me if I'm wrong, but from what Clarissa has told me, *you* don't want to be on the wrong side of a righteously angry Nina who has come into the full possession of her powers. So, *you* had better be enormously concerned about what happens to Benny Hernandez. Am I not right?"

Charlie hadn't thought of it that way. And what Frank said made sense. But there still remained one point Frank had overlooked.

"Just because I explain what she might someday be capable of doesn't mean she'll immediately be able to master mind control. She can be told of her potential, but what she did to Benny was spontaneous and unintended. Learning control of it is altogether different, and far more difficult than you might imagine."

"Okay," Frank conceded. "But at least we will have tried. And Nina will have been given the chance."

Charlie grumbled, sighed, and offered one last concern.

91

"Once she knows about the mind control power, she'll want to know about everything else."

"I know." Frank again closed his eyes. When he opened them, it was with a look of resignation. "I guess we're just stuck between a rock and a hard place."

Charlie smiled, and said, "We Indians have a different saying."

"What's that?"

Charlie's rueful smile faded as he spoke.

"We are caught between the bear and the cliff."

CHAPTER 26

Nina listened with growing excitement as Charlie described the Order as a lucky group of people who were gifted with perfect health, some even having the ability to exert a degree of control over "regular people." He told her that even though she had been born into this group, it might take many years before she could expect to fully control the ability. But somehow, through her anger, she had been able to place the thought inside Benny's head that he must behave, or else go off and dig a hole, crawl into it, and never come out.

He finished up with, "I'm sorry it has to come to you like this. Clarissa was hoping to ease you into knowing about your potential." And then he fell silent, hoping he hadn't freaked her out.

Nina didn't say anything at first. She just closed her eyes, picturing the meadow that often appeared in her dreams. A place filled with colorful tents and young people. She was certain this was a part of the secret world Charlie was describing.

She also sensed that Charlie wasn't telling her everything. *Clarissa already told me everything up at the ski lodge, didn't she? I know this because I dream about it. So why can't I remember most of it when I'm awake?*

She opened her eyes and studied Charlie for an uncomfortably long moment, before asking, "Why can't you just tell Benny he doesn't have to behave? Why does it have to come from me?"

"I don't possess the ability to reach into Benny's thoughts. I wish I could, but I can't."

Nina shifted in her chair, folding one leg under her bottom to sit on it. Her left hand bunched into a fist, then relaxed, then bunched again. "Why is it you telling me this? Why didn't Fra—why didn't *Dad* explain this to me?"

"Because he can't," Charlie said.

"Why?" She leaned forward. Charlie imagined a bear and a cliff.

"Because Clarissa put a block on his ability to talk about the Order."

Nina considered this for a moment, and then decided there was no point in getting mad about Clarissa messing with Frank's mind. She slid her leg out from under her bottom, settled her hands in her lap, and relaxed. "Okay," she said. "What is it that I need to do?"

Charlie felt the knot in his gut relax a little.

"Can you think back to the moment when you confronted Benny?"

Nina closed her eyes. She remembered the smell of fresh mown grass, the heat of the sun, pictured the piñata coming down, the odor of dog poop from the exploded baggie, Ernesto dragging his son across the lawn. She spoke with her eyes still closed.

"Chantha was crying. Maria was trying to wipe off the poop with a towel." Nina suddenly remembered the raven. *He saw what happened. And he was interested! But I'm not telling Charlie about that. Not yet. Maybe never.*

"I told Benny that if he couldn't behave, he should go off and dig a hole and climb in and never come out." Her eyes remained closed.

"How did you *feel* when you said that?"

"I was angry."

"I mean physically. Do you remember feeling anything inside?"

Nina's eyes moved rapidly behind her eyelids, as if she were watching a movie. "I felt warm," she said. "Warm and tingly." Her eyes flew open. "And it felt like a gust of hot wind came out of my chest." She gave a quizzical look. "I never remembered that until just now. But there was definitely a feeling of some kind of force surging out of me. And it went straight at Benny. I think he even took a step backwards."

"That was the moment," Charlie said.

"Wow! Can I really do something like that?"

94

Her sudden enthusiasm was a little scary, and Charlie knew he needed to rein it in. Wanting to steer her away from practicing on some unsuspecting person.

"Obviously you can, because you did it. But it's obviously something you have no real control over. Later in your life you'll be able to use it whenever you want, but it's going to take a lot of practice and learning. For now, all we need to do is to find some way to reverse what you did to Benny, or he'll go off as soon as no one's watching, find a shovel, and . . . well, you know."

"Yeah," Nina agreed.

Charlie still needed to confirm one important thing.

"Do you truly want to fix it?"

Nina's reply was indignant.

"Of course! I'm not a monster. And besides, he's just a little boy. A mean little boy. But he's also Selena's brother, and I know she'd miss him terribly." As an afterthought, she added, "Even if they do fight a lot." A sharp concern filled her eyes. "But how do I 'undo' this, Charlie? I didn't even know that I did it in the first place. Do I need to get angry again? Or can I just explain it to him and make it all okay?"

Charlie didn't mince words. "To be honest," he said carefully, "I simply don't know."

CHAPTER 27

Frank needed permission from one of Benny's parents to get Nina past hospital security. Ernesto finally agreed, but only after Frank practically begged him on the phone, asking what was the risk in having Nina apologize directly to Benny. That was how he framed it: as an apology. He didn't dare tell Ernesto what they really intended.

Frank didn't mention Charlie during the call. But without him, there was no hope of gauging whether or not the intervention had been successful.

When the trio entered the hospital lobby, Ernesto was stubbornly posted up at the information counter. He threw one suspicious glance at Nina, before saying to Frank, "My son's been moved to the pediatric ward." He then stared at Charlie. "Who is he?"

Frank spoke in an easy voice, as if he knew exactly what he was doing. "Ernesto, this is Charlie Dozen. He's a close family friend, and he's had some experience with this kind of thing. We thought he might be able to help."

"Nice to meet you," Charlie said, confidently extending a hand.

Ernesto cautiously shook hands, wondering what Frank meant by "experience with this kind of thing." This was the most "Indian" looking Indian he'd ever seen. Charlie reminded him of the legends he'd heard as a child in Mexico about native shamans and their magical healing spells. All of which was condemned by the Church as the work of the devil. He felt a chill and crossed himself, silently promising God a hundred Hail Marys every day for the rest of his life if this Indian found some way to help his boy. "This way," he said, mostly to Frank, turning for the center hallway.

As they waited for the elevator, a funny look crossed Nina's face. Charlie saw it and nudged Frank, who whispered to her, "Is something wrong?"

Nina's head was dipped at a slight angle, her face slack, as if she were listening to something faraway. She looked up at Frank. "Why is Gunther here?"

Ernesto turned from the elevator doors. "Who is Gunther?" He glanced around to make sure he hadn't missed someone approaching. He then threw a quizzical look at Frank, then Charlie, and finally, reluctantly, at Nina.

"*Who is Gunther?*" he demanded.

As both men struggled to come up with a believable lie, Nina spoke up.

"He's a family friend I just learned is in the hospital." Her jaw was now set tight.

The elevator doors hushed open and Ernesto stepped inside. Without looking back, he practically shouted, "My son is the point! Not someone named 'Gunther'."

Charlie and Frank nodded in agreement as they entered the elevator. Nina just stared down at the floor as the elevator doors closed.

When they reached the pediatric ward the woman at the counter told them, "Dr. Ginsberg wants to talk to you before you go in to see the boy." She smiled at Ernesto. "Of course, you don't need permission if you want to visit your son, Mr. Hernandez. But hospital protocol requires a doctor's clearance if non-family want to visit a child with . . . this kind of problem."

Ernesto gave a satisfied grunt.

They had barely sat down in the small conference room when a wiry woman with brown hair loosely tied up pushed through the door. She wore a long white lab coat, and appeared to be in a hurry. A stethoscope swung from her neck. She carried a medical chart in one hand, which she scanned even as she said, "I understand you want to see Benny Hernandez. May I know why?" Her eyes left the chart,

97

sizing up Charlie and Frank. A quick glance at Nina said a youngster wasn't entirely welcome.

"Attorney Frank Miller," Frank said, offering his hand. Dr. Ginsberg studied it for a second before reaching to give it barely a touch.

"Are you representing someone in this matter Mr. Miller?"

"No. I'm the foster father of Nina, the girl who was involved in the confrontation with the boy." Frank nodded to Nina.

"Hmmm," Dr. Ginsberg said, looking back and forth between the two. "I've heard about this 'incident' from Ernesto. I'm very skeptical that a girl saying something to a ten-year-old boy at a birthday party would later cause him to go into convulsions and fall into a hysterical coma." She paused to look at Nina, who smiled politely. "Is there some specific reason why you think she had such a dramatic impact?"

Frank volunteered, "Well, the confrontation came at the same time as the dog poop falling out of the piñata. I'm sure the boy felt bad about that. Maybe the two events are somehow connected?"

The doctor glanced at her chart again, then once more at Nina, who now decided to test her own supposed powers. Not knowing exactly what she should do, she simply thought as hard as she could, while looking at Dr. Ginsberg. *You really should let us talk to Benny!*

Dr. Ginsberg took a deep breath, let it out quickly, and then reached nervously into her right jacket pocket, as if fumbling for something. She looked momentarily irritated, took a short, sharp breath, and as the air rushed out, she withdrew her hand from her pocket and said, "Well, I don't see how it could do much harm, so long as his father is present. But please try not to stay more than a few minutes."

And then she turned and walked out the door!

Nina felt a surge of confidence.

When they reached the door to Benny's room, Ernesto turned and said, "Please let me go in first and make sure he's awake."

"Of course," Frank said.

Ernesto pushed the door halfway open and slipped inside.

Charlie gave Nina a suspicious look and seemed about to ask her something.

"Not now," Frank whispered, nodding toward the half-opened door. "Listen."

They could hear Ernesto speaking softly.

"Son? Are you awake?"

The boy's reply held a dreamlike quality.

"Yes, Papa."

"You have visitors." Ernesto sounded nervous, uncertain.

There was no reply.

"Nina wants to apologize for something she said to you."

Silence.

After a few seconds Ernesto came to the door. "You can come in, but I think they have given him something. He may not recognize you."

Benny was tucked beneath a thin blue blanket, his dark hair neatly combed except for one tiny tuft that stuck up in back. His skin was pale. Nina saw a kid who was *broken*. She looked across the bed at Ernesto and saw pain and desperate hope. Frank, standing at the foot of the bed, nodded for her to begin.

"Hi, Benny," Nina said in calm voice. "How are you feeling?"

Benny's eyes wandered away from his father, past the two men at the foot of the bed, to finally settle upon Nina. As they focused on her face his head jerked away to look back at his father.

Ernesto placed a gentle hand on Benny's shoulder. "It is okay, Son," he insisted. "She wants you to be well."

Benny's eyes reluctantly returned to Nina.

"I want you to get better, Benny," Nina insisted. "And I'm terribly sorry for what I said about going off and digging a hole. I apologize for that."

Benny's eyes remained fixed upon her, but the fear remained.

"You don't ever have to do that," she continued. And now she tried to focus and direct her thoughts at Benny, just as she had done with the doctor.

You were just being a little boy. It's okay. You don't have to find a shovel and go off and dig a hole and climb in if you ever misbehave again. I order you to never go off and find a shovel and dig a hole and climb in! Never do that!

99

Nina searched for some sign of success. But Benny just looked away, back to his father.

"I'm tired, Papa. Can I sleep?"

"Of course you can." Ernesto gave Nina a hard, uncompromising look. "You should go." He then looked at Frank. "I want to stay until my boy is asleep. I will call you later."

They retreated down the hallway, past the nursing station, reaching the elevators before anyone spoke. It was Frank who finally said to Charlie, "Well, what do you think?"

Charlie spread his hands in surrender. "No clue," he said, turning to Nina. "Did you feel *anything?*"

"I don't know," Nina said. "I just . . . I . . . don't know." *It worked with the doctor. Please let it have worked with Benny!*

"Well," Frank said, trying to sound upbeat. "You certainly tried your best, Nina. And who knows? Maybe it did have an impact."

As the elevator doors swooshed open, Nina asked, "Can we go see Gunther now?"

Frank reached out and put a hand on her shoulder, and said, "Let's go down to the cafeteria and talk about it first."

Back in Benny's room, Dr. Ginsberg returned and found Ernesto sitting patiently at bedside, gazing at the peaceful face of his sleeping son.

"Mr. Hernandez?" she said softly.

"Hello, doctor," Ernesto said.

"How did the visit go?"

Ernesto shrugged. He almost spoke, appeared to reconsider, and looked back down at his son.

"I'm sorry I had to leave," the doctor continued. She reached into her pocket and withdrew a silvery pager. "It's designed to vibrate silently. It went off with a high priority signal when I was with you and the others. It was something I had to respond to. I apologize."

CHAPTER 28

Nina sat alone on the back deck, bathed in sunlight, entirely frustrated. The previous afternoon in the hospital cafeteria, Charlie had revealed another piece of the puzzle about the Order.

"If we don't sneak Gunther out, the doctors are going to see things that just don't happen."

"Like what?"

"His wounds will heal rapidly, and there won't be any scars. And his kidney will begin to re-grow."

Nina remembered what Charlie had said about members being very healthy. But organ re-growth?

"Really?"

"Yes."

"So why can't I visit him?"

Frank had cut in.

"Because we can't have you connected with him in any way. Gunther entered the U.S. on a fake passport, and it's possible he might be arrested. I've already met with an attorney who works for the German government, and she thinks I barely know anything about Gunther. If it got back to her that my foster daughter was visiting him in the hospital it would raise questions."

"Will I ever see him again?"

Charlie offered, "When we smuggle him out, we might be able to arrange for the two of you to have a brief visit."

She had reluctantly agreed to leave the hospital without seeing Gunther.

Later that afternoon, Nina and the girls had met with Tina one last time, and agreed to let her and Valerie negotiate a contract with a toy manufacturer. Frank had then driven Tina back to the airport in East Wenatchee. Anna was at work so the girls were alone.

Selena had earlier called her father to come and pick her up. When they heard his pickup pull up out front, she had dropped the bomb.

"My father doesn't want me to come here anymore."

"Why?" Nina asked.

"Because of the curse," Selena said.

"Oh, that's just a bunch of crap!" Chantha protested. "You don't really believe Nina hexed your little brother, do you?"

"I guess not. But my father thinks she did. He calls her evil, and says I shouldn't be around her. I'm sorry." She appeared ready to cry. Nina tried to comfort her.

"Don't worry, Selena. It's all going to work out. We can still see each other at school, can't we?"

Selena looked uncertain.

There came a pounding on the front door, immediately followed by, "*Selena!*"

Selena impulsively hugged Nina, and then Chantha, and ran for the door in tears.

"Well, that's a crock," Chantha said, walking to the front window to watch Selena and her father climb into his pickup and speed off down the road. She turned back to Nina. "I can't believe they're so superstitious!"

In that moment Nina desperately wanted to tell Chantha everything. But Charlie had stressed how important it was to keep the "Order thing" under wraps. Nina wasn't certain she agreed about the need for secrecy, especially with Chantha. But how do you tell someone you have a miracle ability, when you have no clue how to *use* the miracle ability?

Nina had pleaded with Charlie to tell her more about what she might be able to do later in life, but he had insisted, "These are things we should leave for Clarissa to explain." And when she asked when Clarissa might return, all Charlie could offer was, "Soon, I hope."

And now, as she sat alone on the back deck, it all seemed hopeless.

Anna had taken Chantha to shop for some last-minute school supplies, and asked if Nina wanted to come, but Nina wasn't in a mood to do anything.

She was about to go back inside and maybe watch some television when she heard the beating of wings.

The raven landed on the table. He seemed perky today, and hopped to within easy reach. Then he gave a funny little screech that sounded like a can opener cutting a rusted can. Followed by, "Nina" in that eerie voice which sounded so much like Frank.

Nina thought she understood, and smiled down at the big bird.

"If that first sound was your name, there's no way I could repeat it."

The raven dipped his head, as if in acknowledgment.

In that instant, something popped into her mind. "You sure are a different kind of bird, aren't you?"

The raven screeched, and seemed excited.

"Do you want some peanuts?"

The raven did a little hop, and then pecked twice on the table. Nina took this as a "yes" and headed for the kitchen.

But after she returned and laid several peanuts on the table, he just stared up at her.

"What?"

To which the raven answered with the rusty can opener sound.

"I told you I can't make a sound like that," Nina said. "So why don't I just call you 'Raven'."

She felt strange for a second, as if a shadow had fallen across her mind.

The bird was staring up at her. "Nina," it said. And then, "Raven!"

CHAPTER 29

Gunther disappeared from the hospital near the end of August. Frank arrived home to report the news, and found both girls in the kitchen. Nina was holding an electric mixer with both hands while its blades churned up creamy yellow batter in a steel bowl.

"Hi, Dad!" Nina and Chantha said in unison.

Frank's face softened. "What are you two characters up to?" He loosened his tie and removed his suit coat and draped it on the back of one of the captain's chairs, pleased to have a moment of peace before delivering the bad news.

"We're making cornbread," Chantha said, pointing to a greased muffin tin on the counter beside the stovetop. "Mom's doing fried chicken for dinner." Chantha studied the churning batter, and then said to Nina, "I think that's enough."

Nina lifted the blades and let them fling the last yellow bits onto the sides of the bowl before flicking off the switch and carrying the mixer to the sink. Frank watched Chantha carefully pour the batter into paper cups in a muffin tin, while Nina washed the beater blades.

Chantha pulled the oven door open and slid the muffin tin onto a rack, closing the door quickly against the heat.

"Something bad has happened," Frank finally confessed.

The girls turned to face him.

"Gunther's run away from the hospital."

The girls glanced at each other in a way that said Nina had already shared at least a few details about Gunther.

"Why?" Nina asked.

"The lawyer for the German's called me yesterday to say she'd be meeting with him to ask questions about his citizenship. She wanted to know if I would be there on Gunther's behalf and I told her no. After she hung up, I called Gunther to warn him. I didn't expect him to run. I just wanted him to be prepared." What Frank had really wanted was for Gunther to work with him and Charlie on a disappearance. Gunther taking things into his own hands felt like an invitation to disaster. The look on Nina's face said she agreed.

"Where do you think he's gone to?"

"I don't know, Nina. He didn't have much money. U.S. immigration has almost certainly been alerted, so even if he had enough cash to buy a plane ticket, they'd never let him get on a flight. If I had to make a guess, I'd say he's still somewhere nearby. But with Gunther, who knows? He could have stolen a car and be in Colorado by now."

Chantha was upset that Frank didn't seem more concerned.

"Is he well enough to be out on his own? I thought he was hurt pretty bad."

"He was healing quickly," Frank said, seeing a look on Nina's face that said she'd now be telling Chantha about the recuperative abilities of an Order member.

Nina said, "Shouldn't we be looking for him?"

"If Gunther needs our help, I'm sure he'll figure out a way to get in contact with us." But Frank knew Gunther was used to doing things on his own. He'd probably find some rough neighborhood to hide out in. Frank doubted it would last for long. "Girls, I'm tired," he said. "It was a long day. I'd like to get out of my work clothes and into some sweats and run a few laps around the neighborhood before dinner."

After Frank left, Nina said to Chantha, "Let's go out on the deck." She reached for the peanut canister and grabbed a handful of nuts.

A few minutes later Raven came swooping down. As he pecked at the red-skinned unsalted nuts (Anna had suggested he probably didn't need a big daily dose of salt, and had bought a bag of raw peanuts at the health food store) Nina was already filling in Chantha on Gunther's ability to heal quickly.

105

"Charlie says that members of the Order heal really fast. Even though it's only been two weeks since he got shot, Charlie says he's going to be okay."

"But he lost a kidney, didn't he?"

"Charlie says it will re-grow."

"Really?"

"Yeah."

"I didn't think that was possible."

"It is for people in the Order."

"Wow," Chantha said softly, thinking for a moment. "Does other stuff re-grow too?"

"What do you mean?"

"Like if you cut a finger off, would it grow back?"

It was Nina's turn to think. Did bones also re-form? Finally, she said, "I'm not going to chop one off to find out."

This provoked nervous laughter from Chantha. "I wasn't suggesting that."

"I know," Nina said. "They wouldn't let me talk to him in the hospital. But now, if I could find him, there are all sorts of questions I want to ask."

"Can't you just ask Charlie?"

"He doesn't want to tell me very much."

"Why not?"

"He says I should wait for Clarissa to return." Clearly frustrated. "I think I could get Gunther to tell me everything."

"So how do we find him? School starts next week, and that doesn't leave us much of a chance to do any looking."

Nina shrugged. "I wouldn't even know where to start."

"Maybe Dad was right about Gunther contacting us if he gets into trouble."

"But if he contacts Dad or Charlie, they may not tell me. And they still wouldn't let me ask him questions."

Raven had devoured three nuts, and was now trying to follow the conversation between the girls. As the princess spoke, he focused on her emotions and caught flickers of images. As she used the name *Gunther,* he was certain she was talking about *Dark Soul.* There was a

106

strong emotional longing when she said that name. Raven puzzled over why the princess would long for *Dark Soul's* presence. But if that was what she wanted . . .

Nina was about to say something when Raven interrupted.

"Goon-tah!"

Nina and Chantha stared down at the bird.

"Goon-tah!" Raven repeated, insistent.

Nina thought she understood. "Wait right here," she said to Raven. "Don't leave, please!" She stood up and backed away from the table, holding her palms out as if to signal *stay*. "Keep him here," she pleaded to Chantha.

"I'll try," Chantha said, looking at the bird with absolutely no idea how to keep it from flying away.

Nina quickly returned with the gifts Raven had brought and laid them on the table. The gold band, key ring, toy shovel, a beach-tumbled nubbin of blue glass, a silver hoop earring, a bottle cap, and a little ball of tinfoil.

Nina sat down facing Raven, the gifts now piled between them. She pointed at the little pile, and said, "Gifts," then moved her finger so that it pointed at her own chest. She repeated "Gifts" again, pointing to herself while Raven watched. He cocked his head to one side, eyeing the little pile.

"Gifts," Raven said.

Chantha said, in barely a whisper, "This is totally amazing."

Nina ignored Chantha and continued to concentrate on Raven. "Gifts," she said carefully, pointing to the pile, then at her chest. And then she said, "Goon-tah." Again pointing at her chest.

She was about to repeat the action, when Raven interrupted.

"Gifts," he said. "Goon-tah." Triumphantly followed by the rusty can opener sound that Nina knew must be his name.

"It's talking to you!" Chantha said, staring at the bird in awe. "And you're asking him to go find Gunther?"

"Yes," Nina said. She stared hard at Raven. "Please find Goon-tah for me."

"Goon-tah," Raven said, stretching his wings.

The girls watched him beat his way up into the sky and disappear beyond the tree line.

"Totally cool," Chantha said.

"Yeah," Nina agreed. *"Totally!"*

CHAPTER 30

Raven caught a powerful thermal and climbed inside the rising column of air until the updraft could lift him no further. The scent of a distant fire teased his horny nostrils, as the magnificence of autumn spread out below, with oaks, maples and birches along the lakeshore tinged with the first hints of orange and yellow. Vast stretches of foothill grasses toasted golden brown were spotted with sagebrush faded to khaki.

When he finally reached the large human settlement at the base of the lake, Raven tucked his wings and dove, leveling off not far above the ground, zooming along with great purpose.

As he approached the pink building, he ruffled his feathers and bled speed. His wings came up for a final brake, and Raven settled nicely onto a window ledge.

It was here that *Dark Soul* had come after the fireworks. The window was pulled up to admit an afternoon breeze, and Raven hopped inside.

He immediately knew that someone different lived here. The scents of mingled sweat and alcohol were clearly not *Dark Soul.*

Still . . .

Raven hopped down onto the floor and began to search. He finally found what he wanted, tucked against the wall beneath the bed. A forgotten sock.

Raven thrust his beak inside the sock, confirmed it held the essence of Dark Soul, and then tucked it over twice, picked up the neatly packaged prize in his beak, and hopped out from under the bed. Three quick beats of his wings and he was again perched on the windowsill.

The worn metal knob on the door rattled, turning with a little squeal. Raven dropped a damp gray lump on the sill as he launched into the air.

He flew south along the highway. Near the top of the slope, he spotted his Road Kill family gathered alongside the asphalt. They were now over two dozen, with the spring-born chicks having grown enough to leave their nests and join in food hunts.

They were huddled around a deer that had wandered onto the road and been struck by a car. It lay bloated in the ditch, where someone had dragged the carcass out of the path of traffic.

Raven landed in a sagebrush bush and draped the sock over a branch. He would join the feast before asking his comrades to smell the sock and then spread out in search of *Dark Soul*. Human food was all well and good, especially coming from the hand of the princess. But a warm and rotting deer carcass? Oh! So much better!

CHAPTER 31

School clothing was an emotional issue. Nina's previous foster parents had set a stingy budget of two hundred dollars for back-to-school purchases. Anything over that amount she'd had to buy with her summertime job earnings.

Frank and Anna insisted she not worry about the cost. But for a girl with a history of frequent foster parent changes, not being intimidated by price tags proved to be impossible.

For the first day of school Chantha bought a red Ralph Lauren dress and shiny black patent leather loafers. Nina chose off-the-rack black cotton slacks, a yellow blouse, and a pair of budget-brand white sneakers that she insisted were the most comfortable shoes she'd ever put on. Frank and Anna grudgingly accepted that it was going to take some time for her to adjust, and said nothing more about school clothing.

Far more important was the issue of safety. Frank would be driving the girls to school in the mornings, while Anna shortened her workday to pick them up after the final bell.

As Frank pulled into the visitor's parking lot on the first day of school, the number one item of business was a meeting with the principal.

When he and the girls walked into the principal's office, they were surprised to see Vice-principal Boyd Nedrickson sitting in one of the four chairs lined up before the massive wooden desk.

Behind the desk sat Vernon Rumsey. At six and a half feet in height, his imposing presence sent a message to all who entered.

Vernon cared about every child entrusted to his care, and tolerated nothing less than total respect for "his" kids.

"Nice to see you, Frank," Vernon said in a booming baritone. He got up and purposefully walked around the desk to shake Frank's hand.

"Thanks for taking the time," Frank replied.

As Vernon retook his seat, Frank looked to his left. Working hard to sound polite, he nodded to the vice principal, who had remained seated. "Good morning, Boyd."

"Good morning, Mr. Miller," Boyd replied stiffly.

Vernon eased back and said nothing. Boyd's attitude could be dealt with later. Now he needed to get straight to the problem at hand. It was the first day of school and his "to do's" list was endless. Still, a kidnapping threat would always take priority.

"Did they ever catch the guy?"

"No," Frank said, hoping he wouldn't be pressed to elaborate.

"That's too bad," Vernon said. "Do they have any leads?"

"I'm told the FBI is still looking, but I doubt they'll find out who it was."

"That's a shame," Vernon said. "What would you like us to do to protect your girls?"

Frank settled in his chair.

"Anna and I will be picking them up and dropping them off. If you could adjust Nina's and Chantha's schedules so that they are always on school grounds, like if the kids go for a PE run around the neighborhood our girls should be exempted, it would be much appreciated."

Boyd Nedrickson cut in with, "We can certainly do that." But his tone of voice said it was a bother.

Vernon again ignored Boyd's attitude, and smoothly carried on with, "What you're asking is understandable. We can also call if there are any field trips to make sure you are comfortable with the girls going. And we always make sure there are plenty of chaperones."

"Good," Frank said, satisfied.

After the meeting ended, Frank walked to the front door with the girls. A line of yellow busses had pulled up out front. Students were streaming in through the double doors.

"Remember to wait inside until you see Anna's car this afternoon. Do you both have your cell phones?"

"Yes, Dad," Chantha said, sounding impatient. Nina patted her back pocket where her new cell phone was jammed.

"Good," Frank said. It took every bit of self-control not to give the girls a hug, but he knew it would be mortally embarrassing in front of their teenaged classmates. He turned and began to dodge his way through the steady stream of kids.

As they turned for their lockers they passed a group of girls, one of whom broke from the others and confronted Nina with, "I heard you got kidnapped this summer." She stood waiting for confirmation.

Nina cautiously asked, "Who'd you hear that from?"

"Who cares? Did it happen?"

Chantha stepped up. "Our summer business teacher tried to take her somewhere, but Nina got rescued before anything bad went down." She stood protectively by Nina's side.

"Wow!" the girl said. Then, almost reluctantly, "I'm glad you got saved. Welcome back to school." She returned to her three friends. As they walked off, she could be heard loudly confirming this delicious bit of gossip.

"Oh, that's just great," Nina said.

With frustration, Chantha said, "It must have been Selena."

"Yeah. I thought she might have a hard time keeping it a secret."

"We should tell her to keep her big mouth shut."

"No. That would only make her father mad if he found out."

"I don't care. She doesn't have the right to go around telling everyone."

Students now filled the halls, and several gave Nina extra looks. For the first time in her life, she was the center of attention. But as she and Chantha walked to their lockers, she wished there were some way to make everyone forget. She didn't want to be the center of attention. She desperately wanted to be just one more girl entering ninth grade.

CHAPTER 32

By the time of the October meeting, Pieter Silberhof had already been ejected from the Council. The first matter on the agenda would be the election of a new chairperson. Next would be bringing the total number of councilors back to seven. And finally, there was the vexing problem of what to do about Clarissa and Nina.

Liesel felt particularly vulnerable as she entered the ancient oak-paneled sanctuary on the third floor of the Order's Zurich headquarters. It was no secret that she and Clarissa had once been best friends. If anyone discovered that she now had Clarissa sequestered at her Austrian villa, she would be gone from the Council in a heartbeat. She needed her colleagues to remain clueless, and keeping a low profile seemed the best strategy.

When Isaac Onejeme made the surprise announcement, "I would like to nominate Liesel to be our new chairperson," she was stunned.

Liesel wasn't the only one who couldn't believe what she'd just heard. Trisha Peterson stared at the tall Nigerian as if he'd just nominated the Pope. Even the usually demure Francois DeVaux was wide-eyed.

Liesel fought back a feeling of panic, staring at Isaac while trying not to look shocked.

Hiroshi Nishikura, a man most comfortable with plants and their uses, and not so much with humans and their failings, raised a polite hand.

"Yes?" Isaac asked.

Hiroshi glanced nervously between Liesel and Isaac, and then around the table at his surprised colleagues. "Uh . . . meaning no disrespect," he glanced again at Liesel, almost as if in apology, then back to Isaac with a more determined look. "But given her close friendship over so many years with Clarissa, your nomination is difficult for me to understand." He shifted uneasily in his seat.

Isaac glanced at each of the other Council members in turn, focusing last upon Sandro. "And you, our charming Italian? Do you feel she is inappropriate because she was a close friend of our foe?"

Sandro at least didn't squirm. But he didn't appear to be particularly happy. It took him a moment to find words that, if not especially charming, were at least not outright offensive.

"I would like to hear your reasoning, Isaac, before I make a decision." He gave Liesel a brief smile, hoping to confirm that she hadn't been offended. She returned a forgiving look, and Sandro felt a little better.

"Does anyone else wish to add something to the discussion?" Isaac inquired politely. No one spoke. "Good. I will now tell you my reasons for asking Liesel to take the helm." He cleared his throat, intertwined his fingers and flexed them outwards as if stretching for battle, thick black knuckles popping.

Enough Hollywood Liesel thought. *I'm as puzzled as the others for why you've put my name forward.*

"As you know," Isaac began carefully, "Liesel and Clarissa were for many years the closest of friends. However, when Clarissa decided over a decade ago to become a proponent for taking the Order public, Liesel was faced with a difficult choice: stay with us, or join Clarissa. Her decision at that time was to remain loyal to the Order. And to this day she has held to her promise."

He paused just long enough to confirm that no one wanted to clear a throat, cough, or offer any other signal that they thought what he was saying was a mound of elephant dung. Seeing no sign of dissent, his voice assumed a tone of certainty.

"Because of that friendship, Liesel possesses the clearest understanding of Clarissa's way of thinking. I believe she will be the

115

best judge of what Clarissa might be capable of, and what her next move might be."

Sandro threw one last punch, and this time his words weren't meant to mollify or soft pedal his concern. "It's the former friendship that still bothers me," he said, with a challenging look at Liesel. "How can we be certain that you are one hundred percent in favor of keeping the Order a secret?"

Isaac turned to Liesel, and nodded. "Perhaps you would like to address Sandro's question?"

Liesel didn't feel like addressing anything. But speaking was required if she wanted to become the chairperson. And in the space of two minutes, while Isaac had made his remarkable presentation, that desire had blossomed.

She now glanced from face to face, searching for what each of them might be thinking. *And walk the line and do it well, or this one perfect window of opportunity will be forever lost.*

"It is true that Clarissa and I have been close. And I do understand her plan for exposure to the rest of humanity. I personally believe it is not governments or the scientific world that we should fear most. It is the extremely wealthy who, if they knew our secret, would stop at nothing to explore the possibilities for acquiring what we have, either for themselves, or for their children. We know our longevity has never been passed down. But it would be impossible to convince normal people of this. It is crucial that we maintain a wall of secrecy." Liesel paused, saw three slight nods of agreement, and more importantly no frowns or headshakes.

"I feel honored that Isaac thinks me worthy of leading the Council. After listening to his reasoning, I think he may be right. Perhaps I am the best one to move us forward."

She shut up.

"I have one final thought," Isaac said, before anyone could voice dissent. "If we reach a point where we are able to negotiate with Clarissa, I doubt she would trust any of us except perhaps for Liesel."

"She won't negotiate," Trisha said abruptly.

"Why not?" Isaac asked.

Trisha looked around the room, wondering if they might not yet fully understand. "She holds real power in controlling this child. The girl is like a nuclear weapon. Don't you see what she might become?"

"I do," Sandro said quietly, remembering his encounter with Nina at the American high school.

"And she's not the only one on Clarissa's team," Trisha continued. "There's a math genius from San Jose, the Indian, and *Gunther*." This last name spoken with pure venom. "She's got her little team in place. And she believes she is right in what she is doing."

"Does that mean you oppose Liesel for chairperson?" Isaac asked, on the verge of losing patience.

"No," Trisha said. "She was with us on the jet. She saw the girl. She saw the Indian. She saw what Clarissa is capable of. I just want to be very clear about what is at stake. I want Liesel to understand that she can't take halfway measures."

"I believe she fully understands." Isaac nodded to Liesel, who nodded back, as if in full agreement. "Are there any other questions?" There were none. "Then I would like a show of hands in favor of Liesel becoming our new chairperson."

Five hands were raised, while Liesel's remained demurely folded on the table. "It's unanimous," Isaac declared. He turned to Liesel.

"Madam Chairperson, I turn this meeting over to you for the election of a new member of the Council. And with your permission, I would like to submit a first name for consideration."

Liesel was so happy it didn't occur to her that Isaac might be up to something. "Please tell us who you have in mind," she said, followed by an easy and inviting smile.

And that was when the meeting, from Liesel's perspective, went straight into the crapper.

CHAPTER 33

School began to feel very much like a game of hide-and-seek. Nina and Chantha were signed up for the same classes, but Selena wasn't in any of them. And when Selena saw Nina in the hallway, she purposefully turned away.

"What should I do?" Nina pleaded to Chantha.

"It's her dad who's behind this. She'll come around. Give her some space."

Good advice. But it wasn't a solution, just a delay.

When word came from Tina at the end of September that a deal had been struck for the manufacture of the bunnies, Nina finally had a good excuse.

When the buzzer sounded for lunch, Nina posted up at the end of the hallway. When Selena went to open her locker, and while her back was turned, Nina walked up from behind.

"We have a contract for the bunnies," she said to Selena's back, trying to sound excited.

Selena nearly dropped the two books she was holding. Nina was afraid she might run off without saying a single word, even an angry one. But as Selena turned around, her face was softened by curiosity. She glanced nervously at the floor.

"We do?"

"Yes," Nina said, hopeful. "She said we might even start getting checks before Christmas."

Selena looked around to see if anyone had seen them together. When she saw no one was watching, she settled down.

Nina didn't care if someone was watching. What she cared about was mending a friendship.

"How have you been?"

Selena turned to lay the two books on the upper shelf in her locker. "Fine, I guess."

There was one question Nina couldn't resist asking. Something she'd lost sleep over.

"And Benny?"

Selena turned back to face Nina, her face freshly troubled. "Mom and Dad decided to home-school him for a while. He's got books and lesson plans and there's stuff online to watch. But he never leaves the house. You should see his room. It's like . . . clean. Like you could probably eat right off the floor. It's like he's not even the same person."

"I'm sorry," Nina said.

Selena impulsively reached out to envelop Nina in a vast hug. Nina thought Selena might cry, but when she let go Selena's eyes were dry. "It's not your fault," Selena said. "I'm not sure it's anybody's fault. He did something terrible, and now I guess he's paying the price."

It was now Nina who wanted to cry. She held back the tears, just barely, and offered, "Do you want to have lunch with me and Chantha?"

After the briefest of hesitations, Selena said, "Sure," and immediately reached to slam her locker shut.

As they walked down the hallway, Nina wanted to take Selena's hand and tell her how much she wanted their friendship back. But that was too much, too soon. It seemed far easier to talk about what had been going on in her new life with the Millers.

"The raven's been coming back every day. Sometimes he brings me a gift, but nothing as neat as the ring. Mostly it's shiny stuff like bits of glass or a bottle cap. Except for three days ago when he brought a dead mouse."

"Ewww!"

"Yeah, it was really nasty. I yelled when I saw it and I think it scared him. But at least he hasn't brought any more dead stuff."

Nina was tempted to share that she'd asked Raven to find Gunther. But Selena might wonder why she thought she could ask a bird to find a person. And this could easily lead to her thinking that maybe Nina did have special powers. She kept the conversation on safe ground.

"I haven't heard anything from the Torgersons."

"That's strange."

"Yeah."

"Do you miss them?"

"I miss Evelyn a little. She tried so hard to be a mom. And she was absolutely the best in the kitchen. But Dan, I don't miss him at all. I'm sorry she's stuck with him."

"Yeah," Selena said, remembering times when Nina had reported something mean or dumb Dan Torgerson had said or done. As they walked down the hallway, she was feeling more comfortable, and it suddenly seemed a good time to ask something she was curious about.

"I don't see you and Chantha getting off the bus anymore."

"No," Nina said, pleased to learn Selena had been watching. "Frank and Anna thought it would be safer if they dropped us off and picked us up from school."

"You don't think those people who kidnapped you will come back, do you?"

"I don't think so. But for now, we just want to be sure we get to school without having to worry about it."

"Right," Selena agreed.

When they entered the cafeteria Selena became excited. "There's Chantha!" She grabbed Nina's hand and led her through the maze of tables, to a table along the back wall.

Nina let herself be pulled along, praying that Chantha wouldn't challenge Selena about starting the kidnapping rumor.

CHAPTER 34

Raven shared the sock and its unique scent pattern with the Road Kill family, and asked for their help to search the valley for Dark Soul. After two luckless days, the conspiracy gave up the search, and returned to hunting for animal carcasses along the highways, leaving Raven to carry on with what none of them had been too keen on doing in the first place.

As the reds and oranges of autumn faded into the yellows and browns that signaled winter was near, Raven spent many afternoons visiting different spots around Lake Cascade, but Dark Soul seemed to have vanished. Still . . . he'd made a commitment to the princess. So even when frost began to appear in the valley, and snow sketched the mountain peaks, he would find new out-of-the-way spots to look for a trace of Dark Soul.

After each day's search he would return to the place where the princess lived, sometimes bringing a gift.

The princess had a new schedule. She now left each morning with the other girl and the adult male; returning in the afternoon with the girl and the adult female.

The adult female could often be seen watching through one of the windows as he met the princess, lingering for a long moment before returning to whatever it was that humans did in their vast dwellings. Sometimes the other girl came out onto the deck. But mostly it was just the princess who came through the double doors to greet him. The words she spoke were a challenge to understand, but the emotions behind her words were now coming through clearly.

There had only been one awkward moment, when she screamed and then shouted angrily upon seeing the mouse he had dropped on the table. Raven flew away with the soft little gray-backed, white-bellied critter in his beak, landing just beyond the line of trees at the back of the yard, safely out of sight.

This marked the end of his bringing any offering of food. Not that Raven minded. Mice were one of his favorites.

CHAPTER 35

October brought snow to the Austrian Alps, first crowning the peaks, then gradually creeping down the slopes.

Clarissa was pacing in the front hall of the chateau, having given up any hope of being released in the foreseeable future, when Liesel stomped in, threw aside her hooded jacket, and collapsed into an overstuffed chair. Liesel's head was bent forward for some time before it finally came up.

"What?" Clarissa asked, fearing the worst. Had Pieter again taken matters into his own hands? Had the Council sent someone after Nina? Had they tracked down Valerie in San Jose? She settled into a chair opposite Liesel, and waited.

When Liesel finally spoke, her face was flushed with anger.

"I had been considering giving you a chance to plead your case to the general membership. I thought it the fairest way, both for you and for them, to put everything on the table. But near the end of the Council meeting yesterday, our colleague from Nigeria . . ." Liesel paused, her words now sizzling with contempt, "*Mister Isaac Onejeme*, made an off-hand suggestion that it might not be the worst thing if you or the girl were to meet with 'an unfortunate accident'." Liesel's body shook with rage, eyes riveted as if staring into some other dimension.

Clarissa knew she had angered the membership. *But has it truly come to this? Is our one inviolable rule now to be cast aside?* "How did the others take it?" she asked cautiously.

123

"Francois and Hiroshi were their usual quiet selves, acting like little children who've been told to behave or they might get slapped. Sandro just shrugged, as if he'd already decided. I think he's still frightened from that walk-by encounter he had with Nina at her school. I doubt he'll ever recover from the shock of discovering a teenager who is so much more powerful than himself."

"And Trisha?"

"She was perfectly content to go with the flow."

"And the person who replaced Pieter on the Council?" Clarissa hadn't yet learned who the newest director was.

"Umberto Gonzalez," Liesel said, as if the name produced an instant headache. "He was actually excited by the idea of harming, or even killing, one of our own."

"That maniac was promoted to the Council?" Clarissa stared at Liesel in disbelief.

"His nomination was sprung on me by surprise. Isaac had obviously planned it all along, knowing I'd object if he didn't time it perfectly. The monster was already in the building. As soon as the nomination was made, Isaac summoned him upstairs."

Everyone in the Order knew of Umberto's penchant for hooking up with religious zealots. His stints with groups like the Inquisition usually lasted just long enough for him to get in his sadistic kicks. He would then manage to disappear long enough to be forgotten, before reemerging to join the next crusade, jihad or pogrom that promised torture, mayhem, murder.

Clarissa began to feel a little desperate.

"What do you intend to do?"

"I've been pondering that question ever since you told me about the girl's mother."

Several years had passed since Clarissa had first told Liesel about an undiscovered member who had borne a special child. No member had ever had children who lived beyond the regular human lifespan. Nina's mother was the exception. And this child was not merely a member. She held the potential for developing all of the skills; a level attained in the history of the Order only by Clarissa, Livia, Eustachus, and Amon. That the mother had died in a car accident was a tragedy.

124

That her daughter had not been in the car when it crashed was a miracle.

Liesel now laid everything on the table.

"Do you still believe that Nina will bear children like herself?"

"Yes, I believe she will."

Liesel leaned forward in her chair. "Then I will help you to protect her. But for now, I need to work from within the Order, as the chair of the Council."

"They elected you to be the chairperson?"

"Yes," Liesel said, smiling. "It was the one thing that went right."

For the first time, Clarissa felt the ordeal she had gone through since arriving in Europe might have been worthwhile.

"I need to get you back to your precious Nina," Liesel said.

"Nina Bea," Clarissa corrected. "That's what I call her. It's like a secret code name she and I agreed upon. If you and she ever meet, that's what you should call her. It will confirm you're on our side."

"Nina Bea," Liesel said thoughtfully. "I've got a jet waiting at Innsbruck to take you back to your Nina Bea."

The two women stood and embraced. As Clarissa pulled away, she asked, "Are you certain you want to remain in Europe? Maybe you should come and join us. You might be safer."

"Safer, perhaps," Liesel said. "But I wouldn't be nearly as useful in America as I will be if I stay here."

Later that day, standing on the rain-soaked tarmac at Innsbruck's airport, Clarissa once more embraced Liesel, saying, "Be careful. And if it gets dangerous, don't hesitate to come. Please promise me that."

"I promise," Liesel said, wondering how she might ever be able to keep it.

CHAPTER 36

Gunther had no choice. The attorney from Seattle made it clear he was in trouble with both the German and American immigration authorities. He snuck out of the hospital in the middle of the night, hoping to travel across the country and find a freighter headed for Europe that would welcome a free deck hand. But after several hours on a Greyhound bus, the wound near his heart began sending shooting pains through his chest.

Sweating profusely, and starting to feel dizzy, he got off the bus in Yakima. After asking three people on the street where a homeless person might be able to spend the night, he was directed to an old storefront with peeling white paint and plate glass windows painted black. The shelter was not an ideal place to recuperate, but Gunther couldn't risk a hospital. He staggered in through the front door on a blazing hot afternoon, welcomed by a cool wash of air.

The woman at the counter started to explain that they had a dorm style room for men, but quickly realized he was in bad shape. She then offered a small private room that was reserved for "special cases," not bothering to explain this usually meant someone needing to sleep off a drunk, or who was ill with something that might be contagious.

After she watched him collapse onto a cot, she went to tell the manager that they had a problem.

Florence "Flo" Talley had run the shelter for three years. During that time, she had witnessed a parade of drunks, illegals, drug users, the mentally challenged, and the just plain poor. But rarely had she come across someone as puzzling as the man she briefly interviewed, who called himself "Gunther."

The shelter always tried to assess a newcomer's needs, find them work if possible, and move them into more permanent accommodations. But the man with the German accent obviously needed time to recover. Flo considered calling the free clinic and asking them to send a nurse to check his medical condition. But a little voice in the back of her head hinted this might not be well received by her new guest. She decided to wait and see how it played out, hoping it wasn't a mistake.

After one week the woman who changed his sheets reported that the bedding was no longer soaked with sweat.

Gunther was moved to a bunk in the men's dorm room. He came to communal meals, and sometimes watched television in the dayroom, although he showed no interest in socializing with other residents.

It was time for a talk.

When Gunther entered the small office, he half-expected to find a police officer waiting. But there was only the petite manager lady with short-cropped brown hair and piercing green eyes. She sat calmly behind a small desk, and waived with one hand for him to sit. As he settled down, she opened with, "Are you feeling better?"

"Yes," Gunther said, resting his elbows on the chair's metal arms. "Thank you."

"You were in tough shape when you came to us. I almost called for an ambulance." She paused, her eyes studying his.

Gunther dipped his head in agreement. "*Ja*," he said, immediately correcting himself. "I mean *yes*, I was in bad shape. But I'm better now."

Flo reached for a mug on the desk and took a sip of tea. "With your accent I am assuming you are German?"

There was no point in a denial, "Yes," Gunther replied calmly.

"Were you intending on staying in the area?"

"Why do you ask?"

Flo was committed to helping those with legitimate needs. And despite Gunther's strangeness, there was a feeling of destiny about the man.

127

"If you want work, I might know of a possibility."

Gunther was still thinking about the east coast and a ship's passage to Europe. But he'd also been thinking a lot about the girl. She was in his dreams. He worried for her safety.

"I might be interested," he said cautiously.

"Well," Flo said, equally cautious, "I know someone who owns a vineyard. He immigrated to the United States from Germany as a teenager, so the two of you might have things in common. That was forty years ago, but Walter Bremmer might still be interested in giving a fellow German a chance. What do you think, Gunther? Should I give Walt a call?"

CHAPTER 37

Walter Bremmer had gone on vacation in America as a teenager with his parents in 1975. The family's visit began in Seattle, where they rented a car and headed east, crossing the Cascade Mountain range into the dry eastern interior. Werner and Verena were so impressed by the vitality and beauty of the Yakima valley that upon returning to Germany they applied for immigration visas. Werner was a physician, and fell into a category of need under U.S. immigration quotas. Their request was approved, and the family moved to Yakima the following year. Werner joined the staff at the local hospital, and the family applied for citizenship soon afterwards.

Everything seemed perfect, until both Werner and Verena died from pneumonia during the winter of 1979. At nineteen, Walt suddenly found himself alone.

He'd recently enrolled in an agricultural program at Yakima Valley Community College, and had enough money from his parents' savings to complete his education. Having no particular desire to return to Germany, Walt remained in school and earned his AA degree.

After graduation, Walt considered his options, and decided that growing grapes held promise. He bought his first twenty acres in 1981, planted Riesling vines, and never looked back.

He'd met a girl while in school, and they married at the time of the land purchase. One child was born of that marriage, a boy named Jurgen, who went to live with his mother in Seattle when the couple divorced in 1990.

Jurgen attended college and became a schoolteacher, but still came to Yakima on summer breaks to work for Walt in the vineyard. It was on one of those visits, in 2007, that a rollover tractor accident took his life.

Walt's world crumbled. For a while he just wanted to die.

After months of grieving, he began to think he might survive. He buried himself in his work, discovering a new level of devotion to his Hispanic workers. He bought more land, planted more grapes, and never spoke about the loss of his son.

By the time Gunther showed up outside the corrugated-metal equipment shed, Walt's three hundred acres comprised one of the largest vineyard operations in the valley.

On a hazy autumn morning, a beat-up Chevy pickup ground to a stop in Walt's dusty work-yard just long enough to deposit Gunther, before speeding back down a graveled road framed by trellised vines heavy with ripening grape clusters.

Walt came striding out from the shed, wearing brown coveralls, leather boots, and a black Stetson wedged firmly on his head. As he approached the stranger, he half-shouted, "You the fellow Flo Talley sent my way?"

"Yes, sir," Gunther said, taking a couple steps and extending a hand, finding Walt's grip strong, calloused, and oily from the harvester transmission he'd been working on.

Walt gave Gunther a good look-over before asking, "Done any farm work?"

"I have," Gunther said.

"What kind?"

Since his birth in 1744 he'd done plenty of physical labor in the fields of Europe, in between the times he was fighting as a mercenary. Gunther shrugged, and said, "Vegetables, hay, wheat, orchards, lots of different jobs."

"Huh," Walt said, unconvinced. The newcomer's body didn't have the physical signs of a laborer. He looked to be in his late twenties or early thirties. The face was smooth with not even a sun freckle. The hand he'd shaken had no calluses.

Still . . . the man's German accent reminded Walt of his own roots.

"Ever worked in grapes?"

"No," Gunther confessed.

"How's your health? Flo said you came to her shelter real banged up. What happened?"

By now the gunshot entry and exit wounds had completely healed. With no scars, claiming he'd been shot wasn't going to convince anyone outside of the Order. Gunther gave what he hoped sounded like a reasonable answer.

"I was beaten up by some cowboys at a rodeo. I went to a clinic and they said my kidney and stomach were bruised." That was as inventive as he wanted to get. If Walt insisted on him seeing a doctor, Gunther knew what an exam would reveal. He could already feel his kidney re-growing. That didn't happen in the regular medical universe. The pain beside his heart was gone, but there might still be damaged tissues that would show up on an MRI. Doctors wouldn't be able to make much sense of all this without bullet entry scars.

"Do you think you're ready to go back to work?" There was caution in Walt's voice.

"I think maybe light work at first," Gunther said. "I'd be grateful."

Walt chewed this over for a moment, seemed to almost reach a conclusion.

"What part of Germany do you come from?"

"Wilhelmshaven," Gunther said. "Do you know it?"

"Sure," Walt said. "My folks and I went there on vacation a couple of times when I was a kid."

"And where do you come from?" Gunther asked.

"Have you ever been to Munich?"

"Yes. It is a beautiful town."

"We lived in Regensburg, not very far from Munich, before we immigrated to the States. Do you know Regensburg?"

"I've taken the train through it a couple times," Gunther said.

In truth, mention of the town brought back vivid memories.

In April of 1809 he had participated in the Battle of Ratisbon—the old name for Regensburg—as a mercenary for the Austrians. On the other side of the lines had been none other than Napoleon. It was particularly memorable because it had been Gunther's first major fight since he'd learned that he belonged to a peculiar group of people who, he was assured by the Watcher who had found him, lived long lives and healed quickly and completely.

The French had soundly whipped his regiment and taken Gunther prisoner. He was later released, after he demonstrated some fluency in French, albeit with a German accent.

This was certainly not something he could share with Walt. Gunther just smiled, as if recalling a pleasant-yet-distant memory.

"I've not been back to the old country since we left in nineteen seventy-six," Walt said, with a distant look that hinted of an unpleasant memory. He quickly shifted gears, now businesslike. "Let's talk about what I need here on the ranch. I mostly sell to wineries who buy in bulk. They come in with trucks to pick up flats of grapes. The picking we do for most of our customers is done with mechanical harvesters. But we've got a few winemakers who insist on hand picking certain blocks that we grow to their custom specs." Walt paused to see if Gunther understood. When Gunther nodded, he continued.

"The lightest work we have is sorting out the leaves and the other junk the mechanical harvesters pick up, plus cleaning the equipment with brushes and a pressure washer. Do you think you could handle either of those jobs?"

"Yes," Gunther said.

"Good. I'll put you together with one of my Mexicans to show you the ropes. After that, if you've got any questions, just ask one of the amigos, or come around and see me. We'll get you started first thing tomorrow morning. We get going at six." Walt paused to see if the early time appeared to bother Gunther.

"Where do I stay?" Gunther asked, not looking at all concerned.

Walt was pleased, and made a mental note to call Flo and tell her things had begun well. "We've got a bunkhouse on the south side of the vineyard. I don't suppose you'll mind sharing showers and a kitchen with my regular boys?"

"I've got no problem with that," Gunther replied confidently.

"Good." Walt said, even more pleased. The new man had cleared the necessary hurdles. "Maybe later on, after you get settled in and have a few days of work under your belt, we can sit down and talk about Germany."

"That would be fine," Gunther said, giving a broad smile.

Walt returned a smile, and then waved to a man wearing a straw hat who was raking up grape leaves and stems into a pile on the far side of the hard-packed yard.

"Juan!"

The man's head turned in their direction, and he hollered back, "Si, Señor Bremmer?"

"Can you take a few minutes and run our new hand down to the bunkhouse?"

"Of course, Señor Bremmer!" The man laid down his rake and pulled off his leather gloves, tucking them into his belt, and began walking their way.

Walt turned to Gunther, and with a steady look said, "Are you certain you've got no problem working with Mexicans?"

"Of course not," Gunther replied. Wishing he could tell Walt that he belonged to the planet's smallest minority, which brought a unique understanding of what it was like to be an outsider.

"Good. Because they're the best workers I've got. I couldn't run the place without 'em." His face softened as he reached out to again shake Gunther's hand. "Welcome aboard, amigo!"

CHAPTER 38

Charlie felt a strong resonance as a car pulled up outside the Bosecker Inn. He wondered if Frank had brought Nina, but that made no sense. They had agreed to keep her away from Portage to prevent a chance meeting with her former foster parents. Frank would have certainly called first to let him know if they were coming.

He rolled off his bed, and was walking through the dayroom, on his way to the front desk, when he heard the front door open, and then the receptionist's excited voice.

"Mrs. Cumberland! Welcome back."

"Thank you, Iris," came Clarissa's tired reply.

When Charlie stepped into the foyer, and Clarissa saw him, she immediately dropped the bag she was carrying, and walked up to him and pressed her cheek into his shoulder, wrapped in his embrace.

When she finally pulled away, Charlie studied her face with concern.

"You look exhausted."

"I am," she said. "The jet was a small one and we had to stop for fuel in Iceland and Chicago. I left Austria thirty-one hours ago."

"Austria?"

"It's a long story." She glanced at Iris, who was listening intently. "Is my room still available?"

"Of course, Mrs. Cumberland. Charlie kept it paid up."

Clarissa smiled at Iris, before saying to Charlie, "Could you please come upstairs and give me an update?"

Half an hour later, Clarissa sat alone in her room, contemplating Charlie's news. Nina knew of the Order. She knew she had fledgling abilities. She still didn't know how long she would live. And most importantly, she was unaware that her children might carry the genetic trait. But the reality was that she knew far more than Clarissa wanted her to know.

Benny Hernandez was the urgent problem, and there was only one way to fix it.

But for the moment, Clarissa desperately needed rest. She took a shower, and then slid under the old-fashioned quilt on the queen-sized bed, falling asleep almost immediately.

CHAPTER 39

Nina had given up hope of helping Benny by the time of Clarissa's return. Benny remained isolated at home, so even if she managed to recapture the feeling she'd had at the party, she would have had to ask Selena to either smuggle her into the house, or convince her little brother to come outside. Neither of these could happen without telling Selena why it was necessary. And the very idea of revealing that she might possess the power of mind control was out of the question.

When Clarissa showed up at the Miller home on Saturday morning, Nina's frustration came pouring out.

"Can't you just undo it?" Sounding as if it were all somehow Clarissa's fault.

And it is my fault. I gave her the dreams. I started her down the path. I just didn't expect it to happen so quickly.

"I can't," Clarissa said, clearly anguished.

"Why not?"

"Because it's personal between you and Benny. When you locked up Benny's mind with your command, your thought patterns became the key. I could give him a different command, but I can't remove the command you gave him."

"Then give him a command that says he can be a regular kid again."

Clarissa shook her head. "People's brains form unique rules of behavior. These rules must be consistent. If I gave Benny a command that conflicts with your command, such as telling him that he's free to misbehave, it would set up an inference pattern in his brain. Having two conflicting commands competing with each other would tear him apart. He'd either lapse back into a coma, or he'd have a brain hemorrhage and die."

Nina's eyes hinted at panic. "What can we do?"

Clarissa hesitated, before offering in a careful voice, "I can try to teach you how to do this . . . mind control."

The fear on Nina's face vanished. To be replaced by a look of curiosity that made Clarissa nervous.

They began working on it during the evenings, after Nina came home from school. But after three weeks, Nina still couldn't get the hang of reaching out with her mind. That rush of energy she'd experienced at the party simply wasn't ready to return.

CHAPTER 40

As Gunther's strength returned, he began to tackle more strenuous jobs, and before long he was able to do anything Walt asked. Life at the vineyard settled into a comfortable routine.

After many weeks of hard work, the harvest finally came to an end. It was time for a celebration.

On a Saturday in November a pig was bought from a local rancher and hauled in one of Walt's pickups back to the vineyard. It was butchered out behind the bunkhouse, cut into large pieces, and the fatty meat was rendered in a huge copper kettle set over a crackling wood fire.

As the sun fell behind the hills, calloused brown hands eagerly shredded the pork *carnitas*, spreading the succulent morsels on fresh flour tortillas, adding chopped tomatoes, lettuce and green chilies, doused with hot sauce, ready to be washed down with cold Mexican beer.

After dark, Walt arrived at the campfire wearing his Stetson. With a huge grin he said, "Well done, boys! We've had a great year and I'm giving all of you a bonus!" This was met by a round of cheers. Walt then walked amongst the only family he knew, slapping some on the back, shaking hands, always calling a man by his first name, promising he'd find work for anyone who wanted to stick it out for the winter.

When he'd finished individually thanking each man, Walt turned to Gunther. "It's time we had a talk," he said, pointing to an empty bench alongside the bunkhouse.

After they were settled on the hard wood, with their backs comfortably leaned against the rough wall, Walt asked in a fatherly voice, "What are you planning to do now?"

This question had come to weigh heavily on Gunther's mind. He still had a strong desire to return to Germany, which was now a real possibility because of his earnings. But there was something troubling him deeply.

Walt sensed something was wrong, and asked, "Something's gnawing at your guts, isn't it?"

Gunther nodded, and then stared out across the trampled ground, toward the men with whom he'd lived with for many weeks.

Walt followed his gaze to the men, who were now comfortably seated around the blazing campfire, drinking beer from longneck bottles, gossiping in Spanish.

Gunther found the courage to be honest, both with himself and with Walt. "There was someone I left in a hurry," he said, struggling to keep his emotions under control. "I had no choice at the time. And I'm not even sure it's safe to go back." He swallowed hard. "But I think I need to say a proper goodbye."

Walt was now remembering the son he'd never had a chance to say goodbye to, and offered a bit of wisdom borne from that crippling loss.

"There comes a time when we all have to face up to the truth. I think you'd better take the risk and do what's right."

Both men fell silent.

They sat side by side on the bench for a long while, each lost in his thoughts. Gunther about Nina. Walt about his son, and also about the country he'd left as a young man; a country he now thought it was perhaps time to visit and bury a ghost or two. He eventually reached over and put a gentle hand on Gunther's shoulder. "What say we have a beer with the boys before we turn in?"

Gunther smiled.

The two men stood up and walked over to join the farmhands gathered close around the campfire.

CHAPTER 41

The kidnapping rumors finally began to die down in the hallways of Langston High. Nina caught an occasional glance, but Chantha was usually at her side to return a defensive stare, while Nina looked away. "Just keep ignoring them," Chantha insisted. "Don't do anything to encourage it."

The girls' friendship with Selena continued to be awkward. One afternoon, as the three huddled in a corner of the empty music room, Selena lamented to Nina, "My parents can't know that I'm talking to you. They still think you're responsible for what's happened to my brother. If they found out about us meeting, I'd be grounded forever."

Chantha objected, "It's just plain crazy to think Nina made that happen." But by now she knew the truth. She quickly shifted the conversation to a safer topic.

"Dad says we should be getting our first checks from the bunny sales next week."

Selena had already picked out several things she wanted to buy, including a new computer for Benny. Not one as nice as what Trisha had bought for their project, but much better than the old family computer, and easily fast enough for online gaming. It would be a vote of confidence from a sister who had taken center stage. She eagerly asked, "How much do you think we'll get?"

"Dad says we'll get several hundred dollars each."

Selena's disappointment was clear. "I thought we were supposed to become rich!"

Chantha shrugged.

"There'll be more," Nina said. "Don't worry. With all those names we got off your Facebook, it's just a matter of time."

Selena's shoulders slumped. Nina reached out and put one arm around her. Chantha joined with an arm from the other side.

The girls sat in silence until Chantha volunteered, "It's almost lunchtime. I'm going to head for the cafeteria."

"I'll come with you," Nina said.

"I'll see you later," Selena said gloomily.

As they walked down the hallway toward the cafeteria, Nina said, "I wish all of this had never happened."

"No, you don't," Chantha said, coming to a stop and staring hard at Nina.

Nina stared back, confused. "What?"

"No, you don't," Chantha insisted. "You've got a chance at something incredible. It's not going to be easy, like the A's you get in school. But if you do it right, I'll get to see you do something extraordinary with your life, and there's no way I'm going to let you back away from it."

Chantha was flustered when she saw Nina didn't fully understand.

"I'm the sister of someone who is incredible. You just need to keep on learning whatever it is you're supposed to be learning and let it all happen." She turned for the cafeteria and began to walk.

Nina was stunned, and trailed Chantha in silence, realizing she had somehow missed how important this was to Chantha.

When they reached the food line, Nina loaded her tray with a sandwich, an apple, and a carton of milk, and followed Chantha to an empty table where they sat down side by side.

"Empty" didn't last long.

As the girls began to eat, a boy's voice challenged them from behind.

"I think you made up the whole kidnapping thing just to get attention."

Nina turned, knowing exactly who it was before she saw him towering above their table.

There stood John Bradley, a junior, and more importantly the quarterback of Langston's football team. Beside him stood the team's star receiver, Josh Anderson, six-foot-three with curly blonde hair. Their wide grins spelled trouble.

"Care if we join you?" John said, walking around the table without waiting for an answer. He slid onto the bench. Josh settled in beside him, thumping his tray down hard.

The noisy chatter which had filled the lunchroom sank to an expectant hum.

As Chantha began to lift her tray, intending to move to another table, John casually reached out and grabbed one corner and pushed it back down onto the table. "What's the rush?" he said, eyes bright and mean.

Nina's eyes narrowed, and her words were cutting.

"*Let go of it.*"

John's reply left no doubt where this was all headed.

"Who's gonna make me?"

Josh planted his elbows on the table, interlocked his fingers, and settled his chin on his now-fisted hands. "Yeah," he said. "Who's gonna make us?"

Chantha feared what might happen if Nina spun out of control. She stood up, abandoning her lunch.

"C'mon, Nina. Let's leave the goats to their pasture."

But as Nina shifted her legs out from under the table, John jumped up and raced around to confront Chantha. "You take that back," he said, glaring down at Chantha's defiant round face.

"Stuff it," Chantha replied, dark eyes cold and unblinking.

Nina pushed in between the two. "Leave her alone," she said.

Josh, still seated, was becoming uncomfortable. These were, after all, ninth graders. And they were girls. He stood up, calmly walked around the end of the table, and said to his quarterback, "Let's get out of here and leave the table to the kiddies." Followed by a snort of laughter.

"No," John said, unwilling to let Chantha go unpunished. "I want her to apologize. And I want her slug girlfriend to get out of my way." He reached out and pointed his index finger straight at Nina, stabbing until he was nearly touching her chest.

Nina felt the same tingling she'd felt at the piñata party. Several thoughts came about what she might say, but the consequences were more than she wanted. So instead of giving a command that she knew would have to be obeyed, she simply spit into John Bradley's face—thinking, as she saw her spittle strike his forehead and cheeks, his eyes blinking wildly—*You have no idea how lucky you are.*

Had Josh Anderson not lunged to grab and pin John's arms behind his back, he would have no doubt flattened Nina.

"Let me go!" John screamed, struggling to break free. "I'm gonna teach her a lesson she'll never forget!"

Chantha jumped up and grabbed Nina by the arm.

"Nina, come on! We need to get out of here!"

Nina's entire body continued to tingle as she let Chantha drag her backwards, all the while glaring at John.

The eyes of every student in the room followed the girls as they moved toward the double doors at the far end of the cafeteria.

John Anderson's angry words echoed off the high ceiling.

"You'd better run you little bitches! This isn't over! You're both dead meat!"

Like all student fights, everyone wound up in the principal's office, each claiming it was entirely the other side's fault. But the spitting tipped the scales for who got punished.

"We can't have that kind of behavior on school grounds," Vernon Rumsey said, his voice inviting no disagreement. "I'm going to suspend Nina for three days. And she'll have to take some anger management counseling to ensure something like this will never happen again."

Nina now wished she *had* given John Anderson a command. Maybe that he would never again be able to pass a football. Or better yet, that he would always throw the ball to someone on the other team.

She would serve her suspension, only to return to a school where classmates now viewed her as someone who might at any moment spin out of control. As winter approached, she came to understand exactly what the word *pariah* meant.

CHAPTER 42

Liesel opened the annual fall meeting by urging the membership to keep an open mind for possible solutions to the *Nina Problem*. This was met by stiff lobbying from the conservatives. The result was an almost mob-like mentality, in which a consensus quickly emerged: the ruling Council should deliberate, but not dally. No one believed Clarissa's threat of an Internet dump of their identities was real. A second kidnapping was overwhelmingly favored.

On the day after the tents that had dotted the alpine meadow were all packed up, and the roughly two hundred members who had attended were headed home, Liesel took one of the Order's jets to the French city of Rouen, close to where fellow Council member Francois DeVaux maintained a country estate. She had asked if he would be willing to meet with her privately, and he had reluctantly agreed.

The cab from the airport deposited her on a cobbled drive, in front of a restored nineteenth century chateaux with red-tiled roofs, yellowed granite walls, heavy blue window shutters, and a circular turret.

Before she could knock, the massive oak door swung open. Francois appeared beneath the stone arch, and in a cheery voice asked, "Have you been to Monet's gardens at Giverny recently?"

"No," Liesel said, puzzled.

Francois turned, speaking over his shoulder as he walked across the parquet floor into the reception hall. "It's such a nice day. Let's go to the gardens."

"Alright," she said, disheartened by his unwillingness to simply sit down and talk.

"Pierre!" Francois shouted.

A door at the back of the hall opened and a muscular man in his 30s appeared.

"Sir?"

"We will be taking the car to Giverny. Please bring it around."

"Yes, sir."

As Pierre retreated, Francois called out after him, "And please tell Marcel to get a picnic lunch packed up!"

The "car" turned out to be a vintage Rolls Royce. There was no soundproof screen between driver and passengers, so Liesel was forced to endure small talk during the time it took to reach the gardens. For the better part of an hour, she listened to Francois drone on about current events in France—an impending rail workers strike, the odds of any meaningful success for the conservative National Front Party, and whether or not this fall's Bordeaux harvest would yield a vintage wine.

When they finally reached Giverny, Claude Monet's gardens were bursting with color. Red ivy crept up the walls of the late painter's stone cottage; trees held brilliant mantles of yellow and orange; rose bushes drooped with fat year-end blossoms.

Francois led her down a meandering trail to a bench near the Japanese footbridge. After they brushed away a few fallen leaves from the wooden slats they sat down, the picnic basket nestled between them. Liesel finally had her chance.

"I need to know where you stand on physical action against Clarissa and her supporters."

Francois crossed his legs and gazed out across the lily pond, chewing on what suddenly seemed to be a tough bite of ham-and-cheese croissant. When he finally swallowed, he said, "I haven't entirely made up my mind." Followed by a nervous smile.

Liesel doubled down. "Are you willing to yield control to someone like Umberto?"

Francois appeared hurt by the accusation.

"Of course not. Everyone knows what a monster he is."

"Do you think Isaac will be any better?"

"I don't know . . ."

"Of course, you know." Liesel reached out, placing a hand on his arm. "Francois . . . if it's left to Umberto and Isaac, it won't be long before someone winds up dead. We have always respected the lives of our members, no matter how they act. Even someone like Gunther. If we abandon that commitment, what kind of monsters does that make us? How can we claim to deserve our privileges if we are willing to kill to preserve them?"

Francois placed a hand atop hers, now very warm on his arm. "But none of us has ever proposed revealing our secret. Don't you see what that would mean? We would be hounded out of our sanctuaries. Everyone would hate us."

Liesel countered with Clarissa's argument.

"Exposure is inevitable, Francois. The world's security agencies are already trying to account for every person on the planet. And they have new tools, like facial recognition, iris patterns, and DNA tracing, all managed with increasingly powerful computers. They might even begin to require people to get an electronic chip imbedded under their skin just to be able to buy things."

"Do you agree with Clarissa's approach of using the girl to establish a bridge?"

"I don't reject it outright. If we were to move toward a gradual release of information to the right people, we might maintain some kind of control."

He lifted his hand from hers, stretched his legs, and closed his eyes. When he finally reopened them there was a hint of compassion.

"Alright, I will support you by voting against anything that suggests violence toward Clarissa or her supporters. As for a kidnapping, well, I'm still undecided. And I reserve the right to change my mind on any of this, at any point in time. Is that fair?"

It wasn't exactly what she had wanted to hear, but it was probably as much as she could have hoped for.

Best to put a smile on it.

"Yes," Liesel said, leaning to give Francois a light kiss on the cheek. "Thank you, old friend," she said softly. "I was beginning to feel very alone."

They spoke no more about *The Problem*.

After lunch they strolled back to the Rolls, along a path strewn with colorful leaves. As they approached the limo, Francois invited her to stay for dinner.

"I wish I could, but there's someone else I need to talk to."

"May I ask who?"

"I'd rather not say." Liesel gave a lighthearted laugh. "But you can strike Isaac and Umberto off the list!"

This brought a chuckle from Francois.

Pierre stood waiting by the Rolls. As they climbed in, he asked, "Home, sir?"

"No. Take us to the airport. My friend has a flight to catch."

Later, as the small private jet climbed above the green fields of Normandy, angling east toward Zurich, Liesel had a dark moment. She'd just finished a phone call with the Japanese member of the Council. To her thinking, it was Hiroshi Nishikura who seemed most likely to lean in her favor. But he had refused to meet.

That left just Trisha and Sandro, and neither seemed promising.

CHAPTER 43

Professor Mitchell Young was about to betray a trust, and he felt horrible for it. Mitch had been Valerie Chun Li's PhD thesis advisor at Stanford. Since then, they had sporadically remained in touch. Near the start of summer Valerie had called, sounding upset. She'd asked if he could meet with her to discuss a problem.

Mitch drove from Stanford to her office in San Jose, and listened to a description of a meeting with someone she identified only as "Clarissa." This woman had informed her that she was for all practical purposes an immortal. The encounter had ended with Clarissa's remarkable summoning of a bird from a tree, which flew in through an open window. Valerie had been frightened to the point of fainting. After she came to, she'd ordered Clarissa out of the building, and then struggled to understand what had happened.

Mitch was skeptical at first, but Valerie backed it up with convincing facts. She never remembered being sick. She still looked late teens, even though she was now thirty-four. Every cut or bruise or scrape had healed quickly and completely. There was not a single scar on her body, not a single gray hair on her head, not a single wrinkle on her face.

Clarissa had also told her that every member of the Order was exceptional at something. For Valerie, it was math.

Mitch knew about the math. Valerie had entered Stanford at the age of sixteen, was later assigned to Mitch as her thesis advisor, and graduated with a PhD *summa cum laude* at twenty-two. If she had not chosen to open her own company, specializing in statistical analysis for businesses, she would have had her pick of the world's finest universities at which to teach.

As he had studied her face, he realized she still looked young.

Too young.

She asked him what she should do, upset at not having found some mathematically precise solution. His advice had been simple: Go talk to Clarissa. Learn more about this "Order."

Curious about how it had gone down, Mitch had made a follow-up call to Valerie in late June.

"How did it go up in Washington?"

Her reply was hesitant, defensive.

"There was some excitement. I'm okay, but I'm terribly busy at the moment. Would you mind if I filled you in later?"

"Sure. But I'm really looking forward to hearing the story when you have the time."

And that had been the sum total of their communication until this chilly November morning.

His finger was trembling as he touched the numbers on his cell phone.

"Mitch," Valerie said warmly. "I'm sorry not to have gotten back to you earlier. I guess it just slipped my mind."

He nearly hung up, ashamed for what he wanted to ask. He swallowed hard, and said, "May I come and see you about something?"

"Sure," she said. "What's wrong? You sound stressed."

Stressed wasn't the half of it. But over the phone wasn't the right place.

"I'll tell you when I get there. Is an hour from now okay?"

"I can make that work. I'll clear some time on my schedule."

When his Prius entered the underground parking garage of Valerie's building there came a fresh surge of embarrassment. It grew stronger as he stepped from the elevator and pushed through the glass door into Valerie's reception. The embarrassment he was prepared to deal with. His fear was what Valerie's response might be.

The young woman behind the front desk, with spiky yellow hair that ended in lime green tips, immediately reached for the phone. "Dr.

Young has arrived," she said into the handset. After a few seconds she cradled the phone and said, "Ms. Li is on another call but she'll be out in a bit. Would you like anything . . . tea, coffee?"

"No, thank you," Mitch said.

Too jittery to take a seat, he backed away from the desk. He was standing in a corner, fighting the urge to pace, when Valerie entered.

"Mitch!" She held out her hands in greeting.

He walked over, took her hands, and burst into tears.

Valerie's smile vanished. "Come," she said, leading him down the short hallway. When the door to her office was safely closed, he collapsed into one of the chrome-and-leather chairs.

"What's wrong?" she demanded.

"It's my grandson," Mitch said, wiping away tears with the sleeve of his shirt. "He's been diagnosed with acute lymphoblastic leukemia."

Valerie remembered the boy she'd met two summers ago on the Stanford campus. He was six then, a slim kid with brown hair. Curious and energetic. Mitch had introduced Tommy as "My first and best possible grandson!" A few minutes later, when they were alone, he'd confessed, "Tommy is also likely to be my only grandson. My son's wife, Annie had some complications during the birth, and she won't be able to get pregnant again."

Valerie was now close to tears herself.

"When did you learn of his cancer?"

"A month ago. He'd been feeling tired, and they finally took him to the family doctor. The blood tests indicated something more serious so they referred him to the Stanford hospital. I was present when the oncologist delivered the verdict."

"Is he getting treatment?"

"He's been through chemo, and they're searching for a bone marrow donor, but so far there's been no match."

Valerie began to suspect what he might want from her. Mitch didn't let her twist in the wind.

"Do you know what your blood type is?" He sounded hopeful.

"Why?"

His reply poured out with an ease that said he'd practiced the delivery over and over.

"A hematologist we consulted last week said there was an outside chance they might be able to find someone with a close enough match to try an experimental whole blood transfusion. He asked if my son and daughter had saved any of Tommy's birth cord blood, which would be the best possible match, and would contain a high concentration of T-cells. They weren't even aware of the possibility of saving the cord blood when Tommy was born. Then I remembered you saying that Clarissa told you that members of the Order have T-cells that never go away. Honestly Valerie, I wouldn't ask if there were any other options. But now the docs say Tommy may not have much longer, maybe a couple of months. And I'm desperate . . ." He sounded entirely broken as he mumbled, almost as if to himself, "I'm sorry. This is just pure grasping at straws, and I never should have come to ask you this."

"No," Valerie said. "You have every right to ask. I'm your friend, Mitch. And if I can do this for your grandson . . . if my blood can possibly save his life, I'll gladly give you some. And in answer to your question, no, I have no idea what my blood type is. But there's a day-surgery clinic not too far from the office, and I'd guess they can do the test."

Half an hour later they had the answer. Valerie's blood was B positive. Tommy's was O-negative. A whole blood transfusion was impossible.

CHAPTER 44

The Road Kill conspiracy had found a dead coyote in the roadside ditch where the highway crested through Turner's Notch. As the sun edged above the horizon on a late autumn day they were partying-down on the half-frozen carcass.

Raven was digging his beak into the tasty rotting flesh when he felt the same peculiar sensation he sensed with the princess. He looked up from his perch atop the carcass and saw a pickup with Dark Soul at the wheel speed past.

Without hesitation he launched into the air.

The other birds watched him fly away, amused that their trickster was willing to give up such an excellent meal for the pursuit of a human vehicle. A young raven immediately hopped up to take his place.

The highway was posted at fifty miles an hour, a speed somewhat faster than Raven could match. He barely managed to keep the pickup in sight, but as it slowed upon entering Langston he finally caught up.

He soared on a cold wind until the pickup stopped at a familiar place. Humans came here at certain times of the day to eat. In the alley out back was a dumpster. If the lid was left open there were often easy pickings for a hungry bird.

Raven pushed away the thought of the dumpster, landing instead atop the building across the street. He watched Dark Soul exit the pickup and enter the eating place.

Once he was certain Dark Soul would be staying for a meal, Raven took to the air and headed for the large building where the princess came most days to gather with other young humans. He'd never made contact with her here because intruding where young humans gathered in large numbers could sometimes be dangerous.

Today he was willing to take the risk.

Nina was listening to Mr. Preston's final comments about Shakespeare's play *Romeo and Juliette* when she saw several students turn to look out a window. Then she heard a noise, *tap, tap, tap* on the glass. Perched on the ledge was her raven.

Mr. Preston eyed the bird that was interrupting his class, and was inspired to recite a famous bit of poetry. "'Quoth the Raven, nevermore', to borrow a phrase from Edgar Allen Poe. It seems our newly arrived friend is in disagreement with my interpretation of the Bard!"

Laughter filled the classroom.

The raven tilted its head and looked at Nina.

Tap, tap, tap. Now more insistent.

Mercifully, the buzzer rang a minute later. A few students went to the window to stare at the bird. Some tapped back with fingers on the glass. Most hustled out of the room, intent upon a hot lunch in the cafeteria. Raven briefly stared back at the human gawkers before taking flight.

Nina first ran to her locker to get her coat. Then she dashed down the hallway and out the front door. The raven was nowhere in sight. She was ready to go back inside when she heard the soft beat of wings.

Raven had launched from the school roof, and now landed at her feet.

Nina glanced back at the school. No one appeared to be watching, so she looked down at Raven.

"What are you doing here?" she asked.

To which Raven replied, "Goon-tah!"

"You found him?"

Raven hopped furiously, and then flew out to the sidewalk that fronted the street. "*Goon-tah!*" came his urgent cry.

There was a moment of fear about leaving the school without telling anyone. But if she told a teacher without a good excuse, or even worse, that she was chasing after a bird, they would probably take her to the school nurse for an examination. And then they would call Frank or Anna.

Nina considered texting Chantha. But Chantha had never been overly keen about the bird. Telling her that she was going to follow Raven wasn't going to draw support. More likely a protest.

Nina began to walk with increasingly swift steps away from the school. When she almost reached Raven, he again took flight, this time landing halfway down block.

Nina followed.

By the time they reached Langston's central business district, Nina was beginning to have serious doubts. And then she felt the resonance.

Raven was now perched atop the hood of a car that was angle-parked in front of a building where *Sam's Place* glowed in bright orange neon behind a plate glass window.

Raven offered a guttural "Goon-tah."

At which point the restaurant door swung open and there he stood: the man who had kidnapped her five months ago. The man she'd handed a fabulous black pearl to just before he turned her over to Trisha Peterson. The man who had switched sides and assisted in her rescue.

Gunther let the door close behind him, took three steps, and stopped. He glanced at the bird on the car hood.

"Goon-tah," Raven said. Followed by, "Nina." He spread his wings and launched from the car hood and flew around the near side of the diner and was gone.

The door opened behind Gunther and two women, bundled in heavy coats, their breaths fogging, dodged around the German and hurried to a nearby car, giving Gunther and Nina only the briefest of looks.

Nina was shivering.

"It's warm inside," Gunther said.

Nina knew she'd come too far to turn around. "Okay," she agreed.

He led her inside, to a corner booth.

A waitress with blonde hair piled up in a bouffant, her nails painted a blistering red, hustled over to their booth.

"You two want some lunch?" She gave Gunther a look that said something didn't seem quite right.

Nina focused on the waitress and felt something like a shiver run up her spine. "No, thank you," she said. "I'm just here to visit with my uncle." *And would you please leave us alone!*

"Oh," the waitress said, confused for a second. "Okay, then. Give me a shout if you want to order something, Hon." She left, looking satisfied.

Gunther was impressed. "You've come a long way," he said.

Nina was amazed that it had actually worked. Or at least it had *seemed* to work. "I don't understand it yet," she confessed.

Gunther nodded. "It's easier when it comes naturally. When you simply let it happen, like you just did with that woman."

Nina wanted to forget the waitress. She had found Gunther, and now the questions came pouring out.

"What happened to you? I knew you were in the hospital, but they wouldn't let me come and visit you. Are you okay?"

"Yes, I'm okay. I got into trouble with some cowboys up in Omak and ended up in the hospital."

"What did those cowboys do to you?" Her words were protective, and Gunther felt special in a way that burned down to the core of his soul.

"Nothing serious," he said. But even as he spoke, he realized Nina would know he was lying.

As she stared, he came to an easy decision.

"I was shot several times. One bullet smashed through my left side, and the surgeon had to remove a kidney. Another came close to my heart. The rest weren't quite as bad."

Nina's eyes glistened at the corners.

"Are you okay?"

"I'm fine now."

"Are you sure?"

"Yes."

Nina settled in her seat, abandoning her plan to sneak back into school at the start of the second-class period. Her next question would forever change her view of the world, and her place in it.

"What should I know that Clarissa and Charlie haven't told me?"

CHAPTER 45

Nina returned to school a few minutes after the buzzer had gone off for her last class, and found a police cruiser parked out front. An Amber Alert had been issued after she didn't show up for three classes in a row. She was sent to the school counselor's office, where she was interviewed by Sergeant Paul Crenshaw. They faced each other across a small metal-legged table, while Tony Farnham watched from behind his desk, taking notes, occasionally glancing up with a scowl for what he was hearing. He'd earlier told the sergeant about the quarterback-spitting incident, concluding with, "She's a very troubled child."

Crenshaw's immediate goal was to figure out if there was something truly wrong, or if this was just a teenager acting out.

"You say you went for a walk to sort things out. What things were you 'sorting out' Nina?"

She was tempted to say it was none of his business. But that might just get her suspended again. She instead said something that made Farnham sit up straight in his chair.

"I've been ostracized because no one likes it that I didn't kowtow to the high school quarterback like he was some kind of hero."

"Are you referring to the spitting incident?"

"Yes. John and his football buddy Josh were harassing me and my sister at lunch, and he started poking a finger at my chest, so I spit in his face. He had it coming."

Farnham couldn't resist making a comment that was purely calculated to upset Nina.

"It's not her real sister she's talking about. And that's certainly not the way everyone else described how the confrontation went down."

Nina's face grew warm. She could feel the blood pounding in her temples.

Crenshaw saw the flush come up in Nina's cheeks, and immediately raised a hand to stop the counselor. "I only want to hear her side of it right now, Mr. Farnham."

Farnham's eyes returned to his pad, and he scribbled something down.

"So," Crenshaw said to Nina, trying hard to ignore the counselor. "What form does this ostracizing take?"

Out of the corner of her eye Nina saw Farnham scribbling away on his yellow pad, and decided that if he wanted a war, she'd give him one.

"Kids stare at me in the hallways like I'm some kind of freak. They don't sit at my table at lunchtime. And some of the staff, especially the ones who coach sports," she paused just long enough to make certain Farnham was getting the message, "are mean to me. They ignore me in class, and even when I get all of my homework done and it's perfect, they still find some way to criticize me."

It wasn't the first time the sergeant had seen child abuse surface as misbehavior at school, and he wanted to make sure he wasn't missing something.

"Is everything okay at home?" he asked.

Nina bristled. The color in her cheeks was redder now. "Of course everything's okay at home. I've got the best parents in the world. And the best *sister* in the world!"

Farnham cleared his throat.

Nina focused on the officer, knowing it would irk Farnham that he'd not succeeded in getting a reaction.

"Alright," Sgt. Crenshaw said, impressed at the girl's self-control. This was obviously a good kid who was having a rough stretch during her adolescence. The school and the family would work things out. "I think we're nearly finished. Is there anything you want to add, Nina?"

"No."

"Mr. Farnham?"

"Not for now." He stabbed at the tablet with his pen, as if to communicate the depth of his frustration.

Crenshaw smiled at Nina. "The important thing is that you're safe. We've called your parents and your mother is coming to pick you up."

Upon hearing the word "mother" Farnham slammed his pen down in utter frustration.

"Okay," Nina said, feeling better. Someone had finally taken her side, and it felt good.

For several minutes she sat alone in the room used for student detentions, happy to be out of range from Tony Farnham.

Just before the final buzzer, Anna pushed through the door.

"Nina, are you alright? You had us all so worried!"

"I'm fine, Mom. And I'm sorry."

"Where did you go?"

"Just for a walk."

It was clear Anna didn't believe this, and Nina felt a sudden urge to confess. But she'd promised Gunther she wouldn't tell anyone he was in town. A promise was a promise.

"Please don't do this again. We were worried sick you might have been kidnapped."

"I won't, Mom. I promise." Nina noticed a hint of redness around Anna's eyes, and it made her want even more to tell her about Gunther, and how Raven had led her to him. She swallowed hard.

"Let's go find Chantha," Anna said, relieved.

They were standing just inside the front doors when the final buzzer sounded and the rush of kids began. Nina's absence hadn't been broadcast to the student body, so her disappearance couldn't have been the cause for the panic that filled Chantha face.

"What's wrong?" Anna asked.

Chantha's eyes welled with tears, as she said, "Selena says Benny has disappeared."

CHAPTER 46

Valerie knew the odds for obtaining usable Order blood were low. But she'd promised Mitch she would try. Still, when she arrived in Langston, she had no exact game plan.

She found Clarissa at the Bosecker, and explained her impromptu visit as wanting to get to know Nina better. Clarissa was too focused upon the boy's disappearance to question this, and Valerie took advantage by pushing the conversation in a safe direction.

"What happened?"

"He just walked away from the house in the middle of the night. A shovel is missing from the garage. The boy's sleeping bag and backpack are also gone, so he must still have some sense of self preservation. There's hope he'll survive outdoors for a while, if the weather doesn't turn too cold."

"How is Nina taking it?"

"I don't know."

Valerie was stunned. "You haven't spoken with her?"

A look of defeat crossed Clarissa's face. "Something odd happened yesterday. She went missing from school for two hours, and when she returned the police interviewed her and she said she went for a walk to, as she put it, 'sort some things out.' When I reached the house that evening, she went straight to her bedroom and refused to come out." Clarissa's voice held a ragged edge. "I'm afraid I've completely lost her trust."

"Has she said anything to her foster parents?"

"No, and that's very worrying. She was doing so well with the Millers."

Valerie saw an opportunity.

"Maybe I could talk to her alone, try to gain her confidence, and try to find out what's wrong. What do you think?"

"You could certainly try," Clarissa said. "But you'll have to be careful what you say. She doesn't know everything yet."

"Like what?"

"The big ones are longevity, and that her children are likely to carry the trait."

"Do you think she knows you've held something back?"

"She must have discovered more about herself, although I'm at a loss to know how. Something's got her upset." Clarissa sighed. "I fear I've made a mess of it."

Valerie pressed on.

"Should I call first? Or just go over?"

"Just go. I'll call Frank and tell him why you're coming. And by the way, I released him from the command not to discuss the Order with outsiders."

CHAPTER 47

Nina was in her room with the door closed, lying in bed staring up at the ceiling, when she felt the resonance of someone coming to the house. She knew it must be either Clarissa or Charlie. No way would Gunther take the risk; and besides, they had arranged for a different way to meet.

A couple minutes later there came a gentle knock, then Anna's voice, "Nina . . . there's someone here to see you."

"Go away!" Nina shouted.

"It's not who you might think it is," Anna said softly. "And I think you will want to meet this person."

Not who I think it is?

Nina rolled off the bed. She cracked open the bedroom door, hand resting securely on the knob. "Who is it?"

"Do you remember us telling you about the woman from California who helped to rescue you?"

"The one from San Jose?"

Anna heard a spark of curiosity.

"Yes."

"Is she here?"

"Her name is 'Valerie' and she's flown up specially to meet you."

"Why?" Nina's hand remained firmly on the knob.

This attitude would have warranted a scolding if she'd been speaking with Chantha. But Anna was uncertain how far she could go with Nina. Frank had just shared how unique and special their new daughter was. In a casual tone of voice, Anna said, "I don't know exactly why she's come, but I suppose it must have something to do with the Order."

Nina was surprised. Had Clarissa finally opened up and told Anna the secret? Was Frank's block gone? "Okay," she said, slowly pulling the door open, releasing her grip on the knob. "I'll meet her."

When Nina and Anna emerged from the hallway, Valerie was standing alone in the living room. Frank and Chantha had already retreated to the master bedroom; the sound of a television came from the far end of the house.

"I'll leave the two of you to talk," Anna said.

Nina watched Anna disappear down the hallway. Fiercely holding her emotions in check, she turned to face Valerie.

"So," Valerie said, "we finally meet." She stood still, letting the moment unfold.

Nina didn't mince words.

"Why are you here?"

Valerie knew she had to be honest.

"I came to meet you and to get to know you. But mostly, I came to ask a favor."

"What?"

"Can we save that for a moment?"

If Valerie needed help, Nina figured she might be willing to do something in return. And there was only one thing that truly mattered. "Okay," she said.

"You're upset about something," Valerie said.

"Is that what Clarissa told you?" Nina crossed her arms, eyes uncompromising.

"It's what I see in your face right now. But to answer your question, yes, Clarissa told me you were upset. So did Anna. But no one knows why. I'd like to help."

"Okay," Nina said, followed by a question that caught Valerie off guard.

"How old are you?"

Does she know?

"I'm thirty-four," Valerie said, expecting a barrage of questions.

Nina didn't disappoint.

"You don't look thirty-four. You look more like twenty."

"I know."

"Isn't that strange?"

"I suppose it is."

"Are you sure you're thirty-four?"

"Yes, I'm certain I'm thirty-four."

"Do you have any scars?"

"No," Valerie said.

"How long do you think you'll keep looking twenty?"

"For a long time."

"Ten years?"

"Probably."

"Longer than ten years?"

"Probably."

"You know I can tell when someone is lying, don't you?"

She knows! But how much? And how did she find out?

"Yes."

"Then you know that 'probably' isn't anywhere near to the whole truth."

"Yes."

Valerie knew what needed to be said, but the words still came hard.

"I'll probably look twenty a hundred years from now."

"Like Charlie?"

"Yes, like Charlie."

"How old is Charlie?"

Valerie didn't know his birth date. Just that he was born on a reservation in Wyoming before the masses of white settlers had arrived.

"I don't know exactly, but I'd guess somewhere between a hundred and fifty and two hundred years."

Nina's face betrayed no shock. Not even a hint of disbelief.

Who told her? Did the Order send someone?

Nina's next question was relentless.

"How old is Clarissa?"

Valerie tried to sound rational as she said, "Around two thousand years." It still sounded ridiculous.

164

Nina didn't flinch. She finally uncrossed her arms, relaxed a bit, and said, "What was the favor you wanted to ask?"

CHAPTER 48

The Zurich headquarters wasn't just a place for meetings. Inside the Council's chambers were stored the records of the Order, including the names and histories of its members, in hand-written volumes dating back three millennia. For this reason, security was tight. To enter the building, one first had to pass through a checkpoint manned by armed guards. The Order used retired soldiers who understood the value of secrecy. Men who could look forward to a comfortable retirement in some faraway place when their two-year hitch with the mysterious employer was completed.

Once past the guards, a locked steel gate barred the stairwell. Then up three flights of steps to the conference room door, with both a manual lock, and a digital fingerprint scanner set to accept only current members of the Council. No outsider had ever tried to penetrate this far, but if someone did manage to reach the inner sanctum without entering the correct code on the scanner, there was one final precaution in place.

In a concealed space directly above the ancient volumes was enough fuse-primed thermite to incinerate the records within seconds. And shortly after the thermite inferno, fifty kilos of C-4 plastic explosive would detonate and level the building.

The Order took no chances.

The November Council meeting took place on a dreary Wednesday afternoon, with rain pounding against the cut crystal panes of the chamber's windows. Down at the edge of Old Town, the Limmat River flowed like a shadow in the gathering darkness. Cars crept along the frontage road, their gleaming headlights mirrored on the wet pavement like melting strands of pearls.

A few minutes after Liesel's arrival, she heard the echo of conversation as Isaac and Umberto climbed the stairwell. When the tall Nigerian and the troublesome Spaniard entered and saw Liesel seated at the conference table, they fell silent, shucked off their raincoats and hung them on wall pegs by the door, careful not to make immediate eye contact.

Liesel had kindled a fire in the old *klatchoffen,* a long-standing tradition for a winter meeting of the Council, despite there now being plentiful heat from a central gas furnace. The green enameled stove was crackling pleasantly, scenting the air with hardwood smoke. The men stood in front of it for a minute, warming their hands against the radiant heat.

An unpleasant tension began to build.

Isaac eventually turned away from the stove, finding a chair at the end of the table. "Good afternoon," he offered as he settled on the time-worn leather.

"Good afternoon, Isaac," Liesel replied politely.

Umberto now left the stove, and chose a chair directly across from her. She nodded politely as he settled in.

The curt dip of his head appeared to take some effort. They had never liked each other, and now seemed the most unlikely of times to pretend otherwise. He cleared his throat.

"Is there any news from America?"

"Nothing new," Liesel said.

"Then perhaps we still have an opportunity to make amends for Pieter's terrible mistake."

There's always someone else to blame, Liesel thought. *And in this, we are no different from the rest of humanity.* She turned her head and stared out the window, watching rivulets of rain trace the glass.

It wasn't long before Sandro arrived, wearing his usual straw fedora. He hung his rain slicker on a peg and moved to the table, seeming ready to tackle whatever needed to be done. *"Ciao,"* he said crisply, tipping his hat to the two men, and then to Liesel, before taking a seat beside her.

As he settled in, Liesel searched his face for a clue as to how he might vote. He returned a grin that hinted he might be on her side. Or, perhaps it was just a show of sympathy for the seemingly impossible political mountain she was trying to climb? Liesel looked away, toward the window and the rain, remembering their last meeting.

Following her Monet Gardens meeting with Francois, she had arranged to meet with Sandro in Zurich. They had rendezvoused by the lake, sitting on a bench, at first awkwardly quiet, watching children pitch bread to the ducks and swans along the seawall.

The autumn sun reflected off the pavers. A gentle breeze off the water brought a refreshing cool and the rustle of dry leaves in the yellow canopy of chestnut trees lining the cobbled walkway.

"Well, here we are," Liesel had finally offered.

"Yes," Sandro replied, sounding melancholy. "We face a challenge none of us wanted." He gazed out across the water, adding, "I suppose it was inevitable."

His blue eyes reminded her of Vincent Van Gogh's face on rough canvas, painted by his own hand, pain flowing out in swirled strokes of blues, yellows, greens.

Sandro smiled, and the illusion was shattered.

"I do regret that your elevation to leadership of the Council was accomplished by a trick pulled by Isaac to bring Umberto onboard."

"Yes. It was perfectly timed. Any chance I might have had to object was gutted by his generosity in nominating me to be the chair." It still rankled to remember how easily she'd been manipulated.

"And now he will want to launch another attempt at the girl."

Liesel stared hard into Sandro's face.

"Would you be willing to take my side in objecting?"

"Possibly. It depends upon how the meeting goes. I don't want to risk losing face by voting for a hopeless cause." Realizing how tactless this was, he quickly added, "Not that I think your cause is hopeless. But . . . it would be helpful if I knew of some good alternative."

And there was the crux of it. Liesel had nothing to offer that might be acceptable to the conservative faction. She could only restate her fear about the consequences, and no one seemed ready to buy into that vision.

"With Isaac and Umberto calling the shots, we may well end up with a disaster on our hands."

"Possibly," Sandro said.

And that was pretty much where they had left it.

Now in the conference room, with Francois and Hiroshi having just arrived, she began to wonder how Trisha would play out.

She had tried to arrange a meeting with the American, only to have her calls go unanswered. She wasn't even certain Trisha was still in Zurich. All Liesel knew for sure was that Trisha was incommunicado. It seemed an ominous sign.

The paneled oak door swung open and the tall blond hurried in, peeled off her gray wool coat and hung it up, stripping off her gloves and tossing back her hair to shake away the rain.

"Sorry I'm late," she said, taking a seat to Umberto's right. "Have I missed anything?"

"No," Liesel said, scanning the faces. Sandro and Francois looked apprehensive. Isaac and Umberto appeared comfortable and determined. Hiroshi, across the table and seated beside Umberto, seemed more-or-less resigned.

Outside the rain continued. Up in the Alps snow was pounding down.

Five thousand miles away, in the Cascade Mountains of Washington State, a bitterly cold dry snow had begun falling shortly after dawn. By mid-morning several inches of fluffy white flakes covered the ground.

The search for Benny Hernandez was turning desperate.

CHAPTER 49

Valerie's favor was simple enough. Nina figured that if her blood could save a boy's life in California, it might make up just a little for the curse she'd cast on Benny. She immediately agreed to be tested.

Valerie pulled a plastic bag from her purse. "I'll need to prick your finger," she said, as she tore open the bag and pulled out a card with four quarter-sized circles, then four white plastic applicator sticks, a lancet in a green-and-white plastic cartridge, and an alcohol swab.

"Have you done this before?" Nina asked, eying the lancet.

"No. But in the video, it looked fairly straight forward."

Nina wasn't entirely happy that a video had been Valerie's source of instruction.

Valerie ripped open the foil packet and plucked out an alcohol swab.

"Which finger do you want me to poke?"

"None?" Nina gave a nervous laugh.

"I'm sorry," Valerie said, offering a sympathetic smile.

Nina extended her left index finger. Valerie swabbed it and pressed the cartridge firmly so the lancet would penetrate deep. When she pulled it away, a drop of blood welled up. Selecting an applicator stick, she collected the droplet and smeared it inside the first circle on the card.

There were soon four smeary red smudges on the card.

Nina tried to ignore her stinging finger, and asked, "What now?"

"We wait for patterns to form."

And then came an unexpected knock on the bedroom door.

Valerie looked for some place to hide the evidence.

"It's Chantha," Nina whispered. Then in a clear voice, "What is it, Chantha?"

"Your bird is back." Chantha sounded impatient. "He's hopping all over the deck table. It's kind of creepy."

"I'll be right out," Nina said. "I'll meet you in the family room."

"Okay," came Chantha's uncertain reply. There was a long moment before they heard footsteps walking away.

Valerie whispered, "I thought we were in trouble."

Nina glanced at the red smears on the card. Nothing had changed. "How long will it take?"

"Probably a few more minutes. Why don't I stay here while you go and see what's up with your bird?"

Nina headed for the deck.

Raven had flown in just before dark the previous day. She had given him a scrap of raw sirloin, which he attacked with gusto, tearing off bites while holding it with one claw, gobbling down each small piece and then twisting his head in joy, looking up at her with first one eye, then the other.

When he had finished the special meal, Nina began to concentrate, trying to send a message.

I need help finding Benny.

Raven had cocked his head to one side, as if listening.

I need help finding Benny. Nina pictured in her mind's eye the fiesta party in August, when Raven was sitting in the neighbor's tree. She pictured Selena's brother; a slim boy with short brown hair, a pug nose, malevolent eyes. Sitting alone at the back of the yard.

"Benny," she said, concentrating.

Raven did a little hop, and again tilted his head.

I'm not getting through to him.

And then she had an inspiration.

"Stay right here!" She backed away from the table and sprinted for her room. When she returned, she held the tiny blue shovel. When the bird saw it he perked up.

"Find Benny," she said, holding out the shovel. "Find out where he dug his hole and come and tell me." She concentrated, picturing

Benny in a hole in the ground, and made digging motions with the shovel.

"Please!"

Raven hopped up and down just once, before spreading his wings and flying away.

Now he was back, strutting around the deck table, making tracks in the fresh snow.

"It's gone absolutely nuts," Chantha said. "Maybe it's caught some kind of disease."

"No," Nina said confidently. She pushed wide the door. Her shoes crunched snow as she walked up to the table.

"Benny!" Raven proclaimed. "Benny! Benny! Benny!"

"Alright!" Nina said, stifling a laugh. "Calm down." And then she saw a problem.

How will I be able to follow him?

When Raven had led her to Gunther, all she'd had to do was follow him along the sidewalks of Langston. Now, unless the boy was somewhere nearby, she would have to follow a bird in flight. And Benny was likely to be exactly where she had commanded him to go: up in the hills. He could easily be miles away.

But she had to try. The first part would be getting the bird inside. It was too cold to stay out on the deck.

She reached out with her left arm, and Raven hopped up from the table with a quick beat of his wings and landed halfway between her hand and elbow. She felt his talons grip through her shirt. He seemed aware of how sharp they were, because his clench was firm enough to hold him steady, but not strong enough to penetrate her skin. He was surprisingly heavy, and shifted nervously to maintain his balance.

"Benny . . ." Raven said softly, and then he closed his eyes for several seconds. They opened briefly. "Benny," he repeated, again closing his eyes.

Nina was shivering.

Raven's eyes opened again. "Benny," he said once more, and this time his eyes remained open.

Nina realized what Raven wanted. She closed her eyes, and instead of brown-blackness she saw a burst of blue light—a million dots of glitter, swirling like a blizzard. The light was shooting around and through a huge creature that stood in front of her.

The blue glitter-haze began to swirl in tighter and tighter, and as the light collapsed, a twisting double helix leapt from the creature's chest, pulling her inwards. For a moment she fought the sensation. And then she let it happen. As she drew close, she realized—

I'm looking at myself through Raven's eyes!

Nina's eyes snapped open. The bird, perched on her arm, was staring straight back at her. "Benny!" Raven said, with a slight squeeze of his talons on her forearm.

CHAPTER 50

It seemed the Council debate would never end. There were occasional harsh words, and Liesel even found it necessary to call for a timeout at one point, during which the affable Francois was heard to mutter, "I feel like I'm being strangled."

In the end they took a vote, and despite her plea for more time to consider alternate solutions, everyone sided with the hardliners to approve another kidnapping attempt.

It now became necessary for her to confirm that she would accept the result. Otherwise, a motion would quickly follow to appoint a new chairperson, followed by her ejection from the room.

"With a majority agreed, I turn the floor over to Isaac for a discussion about how this should happen."

Isaac blinked in surprise, but recovered quickly, giving her a graceful nod. "I yield the floor to Umberto," he said, watching to see if she would flinch.

Liesel remained focused, giving no sign of resistance or discomfort.

Isaac gave Umberto a brisk nod.

"The problem as I see it," Umberto began, in a smug voice, "is that if we again send a member, as we did with Trisha, we run the risk they will sense our resonance and have an opportunity to take defensive action. For this second attempt we must involve someone who is not of the Order."

He paused to make sure no one intended to object. His gaze was met by six attentive faces. Enjoying the moment, he continued with the carefully scripted outline he and Isaac had agreed on.

"You all know about my hobby of joining certain religious movements. A while back I had the opportunity to hook up with a small-but-powerful Catholic faction."

Everyone in the room, except Isaac, felt a little uneasy. This was the darker side of an already unappealing man.

Umberto stood up and sauntered over to the klatchoffen. He addressed the group with the stove pleasantly warming his backside.

"I will make use of my Vatican connection to recruit the priest Sandro met on his first trip. When the time is ripe, this priest will lead the effort to seize the problematic child so we can bring her back to Switzerland."

Umberto casually retook his seat, surveying their faces. "Any questions?"

There were none.

"Good." He turned to Liesel. "Shall we take a vote, Madam Chairperson?"

Liesel remembered Sandro's words of caution at their Lake Zurich meeting—about not doing something stupid and losing *face*. The war was still there to win, so long as she remained a player. Liesel knew it was necessary to swallow hard, and take her lumps with grace.

In the end, all hands were raised in favor of Umberto's proposal.

CHAPTER 51

Nina pushed through the French doors and hurried into the family room with Raven on her arm. "We're going to follow him to where Benny is!" she declared, immediately turning to Chantha. "Benny's going to be cold so we'll need blankets." She turned to Anna. "Could you please run some hot water and fill a thermos with tea. He's going to be dehydrated and really cold—"

"Woah! Just a minute," Frank interrupted, staring at the bird on Nina's arm.

As if on cue, Raven launched from Nina's arm and landed on the back of the sofa.

Frank took a deep breath. "You're going to have to explain this," he said to Nina, throwing another hard look at the bird.

Nina thought about the swirl of blue energy, knowing there were no adequate words to describe it. She settled for something simple.

"If I close my eyes and concentrate, I can see things through the raven's eyes."

"Huh," Frank said, unconvinced.

Nina knew time was precious. Raven had conveyed that Benny was rapidly failing.

"He knows where Benny is," Nina insisted. "All I need to do is close my eyes and I'll be up there in the air with him. Except I'll still be able to talk to you in the car and describe where he's flying to."

At that moment Valerie walked in, having heard the commotion. She volunteered, "I remember what Clarissa did at my office, making a bird fly in through a window. And you should have seen the flock of birds she summoned to keep the Order's jet from taking off. What Nina is describing may actually be possible." She paused, and gave Nina a sad little smile.

Nina instantly knew that her blood wasn't O-negative.

Valerie nodded in confirmation; a gesture entirely lost on the others.

Raven interrupted with, "Benny!"

Frank threw the bird an exasperated look, and said, "Okay . . . Chantha, can you please go and get a couple wool blankets from the spare bedroom." He turned to Nina. "So how does this work?"

Nina's enthusiasm spilled out.

"We go to the car and the raven flies up into the sky and I describe where he's headed."

Frank let out a long sigh. "Okay," he said. "What've we got to lose?"

After two heavy blankets were retrieved, and the thermos of tea was ready, Nina carried Raven out to the Volvo and sat him on the hood. She climbed into the back seat. Valerie sat in front. Frank turned the ignition key and the engine purred to life.

Nina closed her eyes, and like magic there she was, perched on the hood of the car, looking at three auras. The one in the back seat (herself) was surrounded by a blue storm. The human behind the steering wheel had a red aura. The human in the other seat was swathed in a soft blue aura.

Alright Raven, let's go.

But when Raven lifted into the air and the ground fell away, Nina's sense of placement in space completely vanished. She felt an intense vertigo—of falling *upward* at a frightening speed.

Stop! Come back!

?????

I'm not used to flying. I'm getting sick!

Inside the car, with the engine running and the vents finally beginning to blow warm air, Frank was waiting for directions from Nina. When the raven swooped back down and landed on the hood, Frank turned around and saw Nina's eyes were wide open, her face pale, her expression desperate.

"What happened?"

Nina sounded panicked.

"When he took off it felt like I was falling up into the sky. I looked down and I had no idea of what it was I was looking at. Everything was moving so fast. And I felt his . . . body . . . flying." She shivered, remembering hugely strange muscles pulsing in her torso and shoulders. "I'm not ready for that."

Frank turned the car engine off, thinking the search had ended before it had even gotten started. And feeling relieved. Seeing things through a bird's eyes still seemed more than a little crazy.

"Wait," Valerie said, turning to Nina. "When the raven is on the ground are you okay with that? Can you tell what he's looking at?"

Nina closed her eyes, and again she saw the three of them sitting inside the car. Blue and light blue and red.

Raven. Can you look at the house?

Raven turned his head, a jerking motion that threw Nina off balance for a second. And then she recognized the front door, and off to the right the large bay window of the living room. Through the glass she saw a small pinkish figure standing beside a taller pinkish figure.

Chantha and Anna. Thank you, Raven.

She opened her eyes.

"When he's not moving, I can tell what he's looking at and I don't get dizzy."

"Okay," Valerie said. "If you ask him to fly in the direction of Benny, we can watch which way he goes and catch up to him wherever he lands. And then he can do another flight. It'll be like hop scotch. Do you think that might work?"

Nina looked at Raven on the car hood. What other option was there?

"Let's try it."

"Good."

Nina closed her eyes.

This time, instead of thinking in words, Nina visualized what she wanted, picturing him taking off, flying toward where Benny was, landing at some human-made place to wait for them to catch up. There was a flash of thought from Raven that Nina knew to be downtown Langston. And then she opened her eyes.

At which point Raven launched into the air and flew off in the direction of Langston.

Nina said to Frank, "He's headed for Langston. When we get there, you'll need to stop and I'll try to reestablish contact." She sounded worried. "I don't know how far this mental connection works from. I just hope we don't lose him."

Frank turned the key and pulled out of the driveway.

Snow had fallen earlier but was now melted off the road's surface. He made a right at the end of the cul-de-sac. As he sped down the West Lake Road he looked up into the sky, but the raven was already out of sight.

Ten minutes later they reached Langston's city limits. Frank pulled off to the side of the road, and Nina closed her eyes.

Her fear of losing Raven vanished as she found herself looking at what seemed to be Raven, but with something behind him that was strangely familiar.

Where are you?

Where the young humans come.

Nina realized she wasn't seeing Raven; she was seeing his reflection.

"He's on a window ledge at the school!"

"Okay," Frank said. He pulled back onto the road.

When they reached the high school there was Raven, perched on the second-floor window ledge, exactly where he'd come two days ago to find Nina to lead her to Gunther.

"Where to next?" Frank asked, starting to believe that maybe miracles *could* happen.

The bird took flight, and this time it headed in the direction of Turner's Gap. Frank raced through the downtown and onto the East Valley Highway, speeding toward the summit.

When they were two miles beyond the city limits, he again pulled the car over to the side of the road. Snow from earlier in the day still covered the breakdown lane this far off the valley floor. Only the main lanes of travel were bare.

179

"Try it again," Frank said.

Nina took a deep breath, hoping Raven wasn't still up in the air. As she closed her eyes there was a moment of nothing except brownness. And then she was

there . . .

She began to describe what she was seeing.

"Benny's sleeping bag is in a shallow hole. I'm standing at the edge, on a pile of dirt, and there's a shovel stuck on top of the dirt pile. The ground is mostly white around the fresh dirt."

Please can you move around?

With a brief beat of his wings, Raven was now perched on the rounded end of the shovel.

"*Whoa*," Nina said.

"Is something wrong?" Frank asked.

"No," Nina said. "It's okay." The world had stopped reeling as soon as he landed. And the disorientation of flying hadn't been quite as bad this time. She concentrated on what Raven was now seeing.

"There's lots of sagebrush. Clumps of yellow grass. Snow underneath. No buildings. No roads."

There was something else that was disturbing. Nina was seeing the world *as the Raven saw it.* The sagebrush was *a place where you could land and search for food. Something tasty.*

She felt suddenly nauseous and had to open her eyes. Valerie was watching closely. Frank was also studying her face.

"You were breathing pretty fast there for a moment," Valerie said. "Was something wrong?"

"He was thinking about a mouse," Nina said, her stomach queasy. "He was thinking about eating a mouse."

"Ooh," Valerie said.

Frank gently eased her back on track. "Nina, can you ask him if he's near the highway?"

She closed her eyes and found Raven was still perched atop the shovel handle. *Can you look in the direction where the cars go?* She pictured Frank's Volvo, and was rewarded by a quick head jerk to the right. But there was still nothing familiar. Without opening her eyes, she said, "I think I'll have to risk him flying. Valerie . . . can you please hold my hand?"

"Of course." Valerie twisted around and reached to intertwine her fingers with Nina's. "How's this?"

"Good."

Now . . . I need you to fly up into the air so I can see where the road is. But please go slow, if that's possible. And if you could please try to hover for a few seconds so I can get my bearings?

Raven pushed into flight. He climbed until the place where the cars traveled came into view. For a moment he wondered if the deer carcass had been entirely eaten. Maybe it had already been removed? Humans sometimes took the food away.

Can you find something else 'human' to show me? And please stop thinking about dead things.

Raven focused his eyes into the distance, searching along the road, and found an object from the human realm.

"The sign! I can see the sign!"

"What sign," Frank asked.

"The one that says, 'Turner's Gap'."

Thank you, Raven. She opened her eyes. The dizzy feeling of being detached from the ground eased, and she released Valerie's hand.

Frank shifted into gear and pressed down on the gas pedal. As the Turner's Gap sign came into view, he asked, "Do you know which side of the highway he's on?"

"No. But I know how to find out. Can you pull over?"

Frank braked to a stop. Nina pushed open the Volvo's door and stepped out into a cold wind. The sun was low on the western horizon and no longer a source of heat. She closed her eyes.

Raven. We need to know where you are. Can you make a loud sound?

By now Valerie and Frank had joined her alongside the car. As Nina opened her eyes, there came a distant *Qwark! Qwark! Qwark!* From the snowy field on the northern side of the road.

It took two minutes of pushing through the sagebrush and tromping through several inches of fresh snow before they saw the shovel with the bird perched on top, his wings outstretched in greeting.

Raven settled his wings back into the warming position alongside his body, shifting in the breeze to keep his balance.

The hole was just deep and wide enough to hold the sleeping bag. It was drawn shut at the end, with a boy-sized lump curled up inside. A knapsack was wedged between the bag and the frosted dirt wall.

"Benny!" Frank shouted.

There was no movement.

Frank said to Valerie, "Take the other end." He straddled the near end of the hole, his boots dislodging clods of frozen earth as he reached down and grabbed one end of the sleeping bag. Valerie got a grip on the other end of the bag and together they lifted it free and gently laid it down on the snowy ground.

"I think I felt him move," Frank said, pulling open the end of the bag.

The top of Benny's head emerged, hair and forehead grimed with sweat-caked dirt. There was also a smell. Benny had soiled himself.

"Good Lord," Valerie said, as the stench hit her.

At which point Benny's eyes opened. He began to push, weakly, with his left arm, as if fending off an attack. As his eyes focused, he saw Nina standing behind the two adults. "No!" he cried, both arms coming up to shield against the evil one. He struggled to get back into the hole.

Frank reached out and grabbed Benny's arms, now clawing pathetically, and held them until Benny stopped trying. At which point the boy began to cry, snot running from his nose. He next tried to bang his head against the ground, but Frank put a protective arm around his head and held him. He looked up at Nina. "Is there anything you can do to make him stop trying to hurt himself?" He glanced up at the raven, still perched on the end of the shovel.

She closed her eyes.

Raven, can you help me?

Raven's eyes shifted from the princess to the boy. There was barely any redness coming from him, and for a brief instant he thought of,

Food.

No! Not food! We must help him!

182

Raven's eyes shifted back to Nina. Slowly, the threads of blue light that wove in and around and through her body began to stretch out like taffy, reaching out to the boy, still wrapped and held in the arms of the red/man.

Tell him, came the thought from Raven. *Tell him to stop trying to become food.*

The blue threads of light now reached Benny, dancing around his face like flickers from a campfire. Benny suddenly relaxed in Frank's enveloping arms.

"It's working," Frank said.

But Nina knew it wasn't enough. Not yet. She still had to find a permanent fix. Her eyes remained shut tight.

What do I say to him?

There came an image of soaring in the clouds, and the thought: *freeeeeeeeeeee!*

With her eyes still closed, Nina began to speak, seeing her blue energy wrap tighter and tighter around Benny's head.

"Benny," she said.

He opened his eyes, face now calm. Where the blue touched him, it immediately shifted to red.

"I ordered you to go and dig a hole if you misbehaved. You have dug the hole and you have fulfilled your obligation." She paused, wondering if these were the right words.

There came an insistent thought from Raven.

Free!

Nina continued in a steady voice. "I now *free* you from the obligation. You will again be a normal boy and you may do whatever you want to do, with no penalty for misbehaving. Do you understand?"

There was a nervous moment, still with her eyes closed, watching her blue energy transform into red energy as it danced around the boy's head and shoulders. And finally, "Yes," Benny said. And then he slumped unconscious in Frank's arms.

Qwark! Raven proclaimed triumphantly. He launched from the end of the shovel, and before Nina could open her eyes, he pushed one last thought in her direction: a vision of a rotting deer carcass.

CHAPTER 52

Umberto stood on the cobbles of St. Peter's Square, reminiscing about an execution on the very spot on a hot August day in the year 1617.

The offender had been a minor official in the papal hierarchy who'd been caught reading Galileo's pamphlet that described a radical proposition about the solar system. The Catholic mainstream, which at that time was the equivalent of saying anyone who didn't want to have the Inquisition come calling, was appalled by the Copernican heresy that the Earth orbited the sun. This heretic theory of *heliocentrism* had been wholeheartedly adopted by Galileo in his treatise, set forth in a pamphlet distributed far and wide. It placed the sun, and not the Earth, at the center of everything. The Catholic Church was located on the Earth, not on the sun, and the leadership in Rome was obsessed with the need to literally *be* the center of everything, Copernicus and Galileo notwithstanding.

Recognizing both the brilliance and the popularity of Galileo, and knowing that his execution would garner bad publicity, they had merely imprisoned him for life. For others who professed to believe in such radical teachings, the holy fathers were less inclined to suffer their continued presence amongst the living.

Was it cypress wood we used that day? No . . . it was cured pine logs, brought in especially for the event from the countryside, stacked squarely beneath the post we tied him to.

Umberto's pleasant reverie ended when he saw Bishop Giuseppe Assante hurrying down the front steps of the great basilica, weaving past gawking tourists who were braving the cold to visit one of Rome's great attractions. The bishop cut a path directly toward him.

Please don't let this fool sink to his knees or try to kiss my hand!

Assante was laboring as he approached, breath fogging in the cold air, and for a moment it seemed that he might actually fall to his knees.

"Not here," Umberto said softly, as the bishop skidded to a halt. Umberto moved to place one arm around the bishop's shoulders. "Let's walk and find someplace to sit."

"Yes, Your Holiness," the priest whispered, stunned by the intimacy of Umberto's unexpected embrace.

Umberto had warned Assante not to call him *Your Holiness* in public places. But his mood was too good, and the day too important, to lay into the bishop. As they walked, he asked in a politely quiet voice, "How long has it been since I last saw you in person, Giuseppe?"

The bishop shuddered with pleasure at being addressed informally. *So personally!* Umberto had rarely used his first name in the forty years since his initiation.

"Five years and three weeks, Domine."

Well at least he now remembers to use that *term.* "Domine" was Latin for *master*—the Roman *pater familias* or head of the household. The senior male who held absolute power over his family and his slaves. Including the power of death.

They were near the edge of the square, and Umberto paused. He studied the priest's face closely, as if cataloguing every feature. "You have white hair now, Giuseppe. And so little of it." There was a touch of regret, as if anticipating a loss in the not-too-distant future.

"Yes, Domine. And you . . . have not changed." Another involuntary shudder. "As always."

Umberto lifted his arm from around the bishop's shoulders and pointed toward a small bench. "Please sit. We must talk."

Several pigeons gathered near the bench cooed nervously, and then reluctantly strutted aside. The bishop obediently sat. Umberto continued to stand directly in front of him. Assante gazed up with adoration.

185

"I need your help on a mission to the United States," Umberto said. "It concerns a teenage girl, and the priest of a small congregation in the northwestern corner of the country, near the city of Seattle. Have you ever been to Seattle?"

"No, Domine."

"Me neither. I understand the seafood is excellent."

Giuseppe didn't bother to respond to the comment about seafood. During their infrequent meetings, Umberto sometimes made observations that weren't connected to the subject at hand. Giuseppe had always interpreted this as the sharing of a tidbit of personal information—a special insight into the Master's mind. This was one of those tidbits. Giuseppe knew that his own opinion about whether or not there might be good seafood in Seattle was irrelevant.

Umberto was fully enjoying the moment, and despite the biting cold he was in no hurry.

"How is our new Pope working out?" He arched his back and rolled up on the balls of his feet, jamming his hands into the pockets of his tweed jacket.

Giuseppe searched for some reason why this might be important, came up with a zero, and finally offered, "Most of the common people love him more than they did the German. Some in the clergy are nervous, especially those who have lived in luxury." He fell silent, hoping this was the answer Umberto wanted.

Umberto couldn't have cared less about the new Pope. He simply wanted to bring the conversation to a point where the bishop was more settled. To place him in an emotional state where he could absorb the necessary information about the mission, and also to prepare him for a very special bit of drama.

"Good. I'm glad the people like him. I like him as well."

Giuseppe smiled. He had apparently said the correct thing.

"Do you think *il Papa* might let me borrow you for a few days?" Umberto's jovial tone left little doubt as to what he expected.

"I do not think I would be missed. I am, after all, only the curator of the museum. We have no new exhibitions to prepare for in the coming weeks. And I can always make some excuse if there is a conflict. How long will you need me for?"

"I think three or four days would suffice. But you must also return to help me again in the springtime. Can you arrange that?"

"Certainly, Domine."

"Good."

Umberto finally sat down on the bench beside Giuseppe. He looked across the courtyard at the great dome of St. Peter's, sensing the power radiating from its marble and granite, lamenting that he would never have a chance to occupy the chair of St. Peter. But that was enough of daydreaming. It was time for the surprise. He leaned close to Umberto and softly said, "I never did tell you which of Jesus' disciples I was. Would you like to know?"

Giuseppe was stunned. The Master had alluded to being personally acquainted with important religious figures, but he had never said he was actually one of them!

"I was the one they called 'Matthew'." Umberto fought back a smile as he continued with, "The accounts of my death were highly exaggerated."

Giuseppe couldn't help himself. He bent to kiss the ring on Umberto's right hand.

It was undoubtedly the most profound moment of the bishop's life, so Umberto let it happen. He waited a long moment before he continued.

"Have you brought the relic?"

Giuseppe's head came up, his face now awash with tears. And for a moment he was uncertain what to call the Master. Was *Domine* still appropriate? Should it instead be *Matthew*? *Saint Matthew*? Giuseppe had no clue. So instead of making a choice, he held his silence and reached inside his coat to a deep pocket and withdrew a six-inch iron rod, with a wooden knob on one end. On the opposite, rounded flat end, roughly an inch in diameter, the letter "C" was raised with a tiny cross inside.

"Good," Umberto said. "When we travel, you must bring it. We shall be initiating a new soul into the fold."

CHAPTER 53

Valerie called ahead to the hospital. When they pulled up to the emergency entrance, two paramedics were waiting. They lifted the boy from the back seat, wrapped in the wool blanket, laid him on the gurney, and hurried him inside.

As Frank stood with Valerie and Nina at the entry doors, a doctor came out and asked Frank if he knew the boy. Frank said he did.

"If you could please come inside for a few minutes Mr. Miller, I'm sure the police will have questions. I'll be in surgery with the boy."

They followed the doctor inside, and after he left, Frank said to Valerie, "I think it best if you and Nina find a spot to hang out while I take care of this."

"Good idea," Valerie said, turning to Nina. "I'll bet they have a cafeteria. Let's do a bit of exploring." They left quickly.

A few minutes later a middle-aged cop, with three gold chevrons on his sleeves, found Frank in the waiting room.

"Are you Mr. Miller?"

"Yes," Frank said, holding out a hand.

"Ben Crenshaw," the cop said, shaking Frank's hand, followed by a shrewd look. "Your name sounds familiar. Have we met before?"

Frank recalled Anna mentioning that a police officer named *Crenshaw* had interviewed Nina at school. He wasn't keen on the sergeant making the connection, and deflected the question with, "I'm an attorney, so you might have seen me down at the courthouse. But I don't handle criminal matters, and I don't think we've met. My practice is mostly estate planning, real estate, and the occasional divorce . . .so long as the client doesn't walk into my office with a black eye." Frank offered a wry grin.

The sergeant chuckled in a way that said he'd seen his fair share of domestic abuse.

Crenshaw now glanced at the only other person in the reception area—a woman watching TV with the volume turned down. "This is no place to talk. There's a coffee shop upstairs, if you've got a few minutes?"

Frank figured that was probably where Valerie and Nina had wound up. He countered with, "Let's see if they have an empty room we can use. There's a better chance for privacy."

Crenshaw shrugged approval.

They were directed by the receptionist to a small room furnished with a conference table and chairs, an oil painting of mountains, and an end table heaped with dog-eared copies of *Time*, *Sports Afield*, *National Geographic*.

The sergeant pulled out a chair. "Tell me what happened," he said, settling down in a way that said it had been a long day.

Frank took a chair across the table, hoping he didn't look as nervous as he felt.

"We have a friend visiting from California, and I was showing her around the valley. She wanted to see some of the wildlife down by the Columbia, and when we reached Turner's Notch, I saw a flock of crows circling. I'd heard a boy was missing, and wondered if it might be him the crows were interested in. You might call it a lucky hunch. I told our friend I wanted to go and check, and, well, I found him."

Frank now remembered the advice he gave to clients before they took the witness stand. *Answer the question. Don't volunteer anything. The more you say, the flakier you sound.*

Frank shut up.

Crenshaw listened intently, and now politely asked, "Would this friend be available if I wanted to ask her a few questions?"

"Sure," Frank said, instantly regretting the mention of a friend. "Should we make an appointment for her to come down to the station?"

189

Crenshaw paused, and said, "Let's wait and see," in a *no big deal* tone of voice. "After all, this was something the kid did to himself, so it's not like there's going to be a criminal investigation." And then he got a funny look. "This woman . . . what's her name?"

"Valerie," Frank said.

"She must still be here at the hospital?"

Frank's courtroom instincts took over. His response came out smooth as silk, with no sign that his mind was racing a million miles an hour.

"She came into contact with the kid's poop, and headed for the bathroom when we got here. I don't know where she is right now, but I could certainly go and look for her if you want to talk to her right away."

The sergeant considered this for a moment, gave a tired look, and said, "Nah. Let her get cleaned up. I'll call you later if I need an interview." He stood. "You did something good today, Mr. Miller. You saved that kid's life. If they gave out medals, you'd be first in line as far as I'm concerned."

"Thanks," Frank said, standing up, shaking the officer's hand, relieved.

As he listened to the sergeant's heavy footsteps recede down the hallway, Frank realized his armpits were damp.

CHAPTER 54

Valerie and Nina found the third-floor café deserted except for a middle-aged Hispanic woman in a green uniform who was busy wiping down a stainless-steel counter. She looked up as they entered. "We're closed for lunch," she said. "But there's coffee and tea." She pointed at two silvery air-pots on the counter, and added, "There are sandwiches in the case." A refrigerated case with glass doors sat beside the pots. "It's the honor system. Just put your money in the box." Beside the case sat a wooden box with a slot in the top, no lock, just a latch.

The woman took a few last swipes at the counter, while Valerie and Nina found chairs near the windows. A minute later, as the woman left, she called out, "There'll be someone come up to serve dinner at five. It's mac and cheese with green salad tonight." She pushed through the door and was gone.

Nina got in the first question.

"My blood's not O-negative?"

"You're A-positive."

"Are you planning to ask Clarissa if she'd be willing to donate?"

"It's hard to imagine her agreeing."

"Yeah," Nina said flatly. "It's not a part of her grand plan to help some kid in California, is it?"

Valerie shook her head.

"What about Charlie?"

Valerie had been tempted, especially after she learned that most Native Americans have O-type blood. But there was one big hurdle.

"He'd tell Clarissa for sure."

Nina turned to stare out the window, and in a thoughtful voice said, "What if there was someone else?"

With that question, Valerie knew how Nina had learned about the Order. Knowing that Frank might show up at any moment, she didn't waste time.

"Do you mean Gunther?"

Nina kept staring out the window, and without looking back at Valerie, she said, "What if his blood was the right type?"

"If he was willing, I could take it back to California without telling anyone."

Nina turned to look squarely at Valerie, and her words came slowly, carefully. "Will you absolutely promise not to tell anyone?"

"Yes, I promise."

Nina nodded in approval. "He was the reason I skipped class. Raven came to the school and tapped on the window, and when I went outside, he led me to Gunther."

"Where is he?"

"At a motel here in Langston. I've got his cell number."

There remained one problem. What reason could she give for driving off with Nina for an hour or two so they could meet up with the German? And then she saw a possible solution.

"Let's see if Frank and Anna will let me pick you up from school tomorrow to take you Christmas shopping."

A conspiratorial grin spread across Nina's face. Valerie returned the grin, knowing she'd cemented a friendship.

CHAPTER 55

It isn't every day that one gets a call from the Vatican! This thought had ricocheted around Father Thomas Clark's mind for the past two days.

The man his parishioners called "Father Tom" had been roused from a lovely dream about trout fishing in a high mountain lake when his bedside phone began to ring in the middle of the night. After trying to ignore the insistent caller for what seemed like an eternity, he finally reached over and turned on his bedside lamp, with a less-than-humble thought.

It's probably some fool who's broken up with his girlfriend.

As he reached for the handset, he was fully prepared to remind whoever it was that a priest wasn't necessarily available at 3am unless it was a true emergency.

And if this isn't truly urgent, you can plan on going straight to the confessional!

"Yes," he said sharply.

"Am I speaking to Father Thomas Clark?"

The voice sounded . . . *Italian?*

Father Tom cleared his throat. In a voice now more polite, he replied, "Yes. This is Father Clark. May I ask who is calling?"

"My name is Giuseppe Assante. I am with the office of the Holy See in Rome."

Father Tom sat upright in bed, now fully awake. He reached to flick on the bedside lamp, and fumbled for words.

"Father Assante . . . may I ask the purpose of your call?"

"Actually," the voice replied crisply, "it's *Bishop* Assante."

Father Tom felt a sudden urge to pee. He began to dig a fingertip at the crusty sleepers tickling the corners of his eyes

Assante continued in a dry tone.

"A matter of great concern to the Church has arisen. This will involve you, Father Clark. Is this a convenient time to talk? I know it is late at night in your time zone and I could certainly call later . . ."

"No, no please." Father Tom swung his feet off the bed, stared briefly at the cross hung on the wall, Jesus nailed to the wood. *Forgive me Savior for I am an impatient man.*

Assante was all business as he continued.

"Are you familiar with what must be confirmed before we canonize a saint?"

It seemed a strange question. "Yes," Father Tom said hesitantly. "Miracles must be confirmed." And now suspicion edged in. Why was a bishop from Rome calling him at 3am to discuss canonization? It seemed absurd. So . . . was this a gag call? A hoax? If so, it was in terrible taste.

There won't be enough Hail Marys to say in a lifetime if this is some Catholic's idea of a prank!

But the man on the other end of the line hardly sounded like a prankster.

"I have been appointed by His Holiness to be the postulator for a potential candidate for sainthood. It is a most unusual case, and will require unprecedented steps to ensure the veracity of the claim."

Father Tom's suspicion of a hoax strengthened.

Why would someone from the Vatican be calling a rural priest in the far reaches of the American West with something like this? Sorry about being such a doubter, God. Really truly sorry. Especially if this is legit. But how can it be?

It seemed as if Assante had read his mind.

"I presume you are wondering why the postulator for a prospective saint might be calling you."

"That thought had occurred to me," Father Tom said warily.

Assante launched into the explanation Umberto had outlined.

194

"Do you remember a visit you had this past summer from an Italian by the name of Guido Androcelli?"

A face swam up in Father Tom's mind. *How could I have forgotten that remarkable man?* And then he remembered telling Mr. Androcelli what Selena had revealed in confession. Violating the sanctity of the confessional was a major mistake. "Yes," he said meekly.

How could I have been so stupid? So reckless. So unworthy! And who is this really?

The priest sounded upset. Hoping he hadn't somehow tripped up, Assante continued in a brisk voice.

"Mr. Androcelli was an agent of the church, sent to determine your worthiness."

"I had no idea," Father Tom said, feeling relieved it wasn't about the confessional. But the conversation still seemed crazy.

"Of course, you had no idea. But have no fear. You were found to be worthy."

"Worthy of what?"

"Of being appointed, under my direction, to the most sacred task that might be asked of someone in the priesthood. You have been nominated to judge whether or not a living candidate for canonization can perform a miracle."

Father Tom felt his cheeks begin to burn. The man who claimed to be a bishop had just described an impossibility. There were no *living* candidates for canonization. It took decades, even centuries, following a person's death before they could ascend the ladder toward sainthood. Growing angry, he found himself wishing he'd hung up. Or not answered the phone in the first place.

Assante continued as if it were a done deal.

"I will be forwarding the details fora visit I shall be making to discuss this matter in detail with you. Do you have any questions?"

"No," Father Tom said flatly.

"Fine," Assante said.

A tone signaled the call had ended.

Father Tom stared at the little screen on the handset for the number of the caller. It read: *Out of Area.*

195

He stood up, heedless of the need to pee, and walked swiftly to his computer in the study and turned it on, anxiously waiting for the browser to load. He then keyed into his account with the Church and went to the roster of employees in Rome. And there, listed as *Curator of the Vatican Museum*, was *Bishop Giuseppe Assante.*

At which point Father Tom involuntarily peed just a little.

CHAPTER 56

On the day after Benny's rescue, Nina and Chantha found a quiet spot at the back of the school cafeteria. Nina finally had a chance to begin reporting the events surrounding the rescue. This was unfortunately cut short when students began pouring in for lunch.

Chantha's curiosity was totally stoked. There remained so many unanswered questions about the Order, Valerie, Nina's growing powers, and even the raven. Not knowing was driving her crazy. When Nina told her at the end of the school day that she needed to spend the balance of the afternoon with Valerie, Chantha was devastated.

As they stood just inside the school's front doors, awaiting Valerie's arrival, Chantha pleaded, "Why can't I come with you? I need to know the rest of it!"

Nina was hoping not to draw attention, but the probing eyes of departing students fell upon her. News that she had somehow been involved in Benny's rescue had spread like wildfire. She spoke softly, barely above a whisper.

"I'm sorry. You just can't. Valerie and I have private things we need to talk about."

Chantha turned away, upset.

"Please don't be like this," Nina pleaded.

Chantha turned back. "It's not fair," she protested.

Nina reached out and put a hand on her arm. "I'm sorry. I promise this evening you can ask me all the questions you want."

Chantha shrugged off Nina's hand and turned away, eyes glistening with near-tears. "It's just not fair," she said.

Valerie finally arrived, and Nina was temporarily off the hook.

As the three walked out to the guests' parking lot and climbed into Valerie's rental car, Chantha was sullenly quiet the whole time.

When they pulled to a stop in front of Anna's accounting office she finally spoke, to remind Nina, "Remember, you promised." She pushed the car door open, got out, slammed the door shut, and didn't bother looking back.

"What did you promise?" Valerie asked, as she drove from the parking lot.

"That I'd answer all of her questions about what happened with Benny."

But Nina knew it wouldn't just be about Benny. And she couldn't possibly tell Chantha everything she'd learned from Gunther.

My life has become a closet of secrets. And I hate it!

Valerie was concerned. But what she needed to accomplish in the next few hours might mean life or death for a boy in California. So instead of exploring the dicey subject, she focused upon what needed to be done.

"Where do we go?"

Nina pulled out her cell phone and dialed the number Gunther had given her. "We're on our way," she said, and hung up. She looked at Valerie. "He's in unit two-oh-seven at Mom's Parkway Motel. It's up near the city limits just off the main road."

Valerie drove two blocks and then turned onto the East Valley Highway.

Nina settled back, remembering what Gunther had asked when she'd called earlier.

"Why is this necessary?" And the message was clear. *I need to know you have considered all the possible consequences, and weighed them against what you might stand to lose.*

Her first point was, "I did something bad to Selena's brother and it made me feel terrible. I want to do something to make up for it."

Gunther was unconvinced. "Is that all?"

"No. You told me Clarissa intends to use me as a bridge between the Order and the regular world. I don't know if that's a good idea, but if it happens, there are going to be a lot of people who will expect miracles. For instance, our blood curing sick people, like this kid from California. If our blood can do to something like that, wouldn't it be a really good thing to know ahead of time?"

There was a long silence on the other end of the line, and she began to worry. "Doesn't that make sense?" she finally insisted.

"Yes," Gunther agreed. And then a little more positively, "That is good thinking. I will meet with this Valerie and hear what she has to say."

Now, as they reached the outskirts of Langston, Nina got that tingling feeling. "He's there," she said, pointing to a black-on-white sign posted up alongside the highway that read: *Mom's Parkway Motel*.

"I don't feel his resonance yet. Are you sure?"

"Yes," Nina said. "And that means he can feel me too."

Valerie turned into the driveway fronting the motel. Snow from the previous night had been plowed from the parking slips and was pushed up in dirty mounds.

The room numbers facing the highway were all in the one hundreds. Valerie rounded the first building and found a second building, separated by a wide access lane with angled parking slots. And finally, she sensed Gunther's resonance.

A door opened near the middle of the building and Gunther stepped out. Valerie pulled into a space directly in front of him.

As soon as the car came to a stop, Nina pushed open the passenger door and ran to him. He protectively wrapped his arms around her, while Nina's right cheek buried into his chest. Over the top of Nina's head, Gunther was glaring at Valerie.

She pulled the trunk release, got out, and walked around to retrieve the test kit. She had decided not to retrieve the full blood collection kit from the Bosecker. There was no point in risking an encounter with Clarissa unless Gunther's test was positive.

As she approached the pair, he waved her into the room, closed the door firmly, and demanded, "Why are you doing this?"

199

She laid the test kit on an end table, and said, "When Clarissa first told me about the Order, I was so upset that I reached out to the only person I felt I could trust. Mitch Young was my mentor and math professor when I was at Stanford. I told him everything Clarissa told me, hoping he could help me piece it together."

Valerie was embarrassed by the admission, but she was stuck with what she'd done and there was no getting around the consequences.

"His eight-year-old grandson has fallen ill with a very aggressive and hard-to-treat cancer. Mitch learned about an experimental whole blood therapy that might be a cure. The problem is that the blood must have lots of active T-cells. Mitch remembered what I'd told him about the recuperative powers of members of the Order, and he thought our blood might work. We had mine tested, but I'm Type A. The boy is Type O-negative."

Gunther's expression remained dark. "Have you tested Nina?"

"Yes, but only after she agreed. I didn't force her. She's A-positive, the same as me."

Gunther stared hard at Valerie.

Nina reached out and took his hand. Her slender fingers wrapped around his thick ones. "You agreed," she said.

The tenderness with which he answered surprised Valerie.

"Yes." He looked back to Valerie, finally softening just a little. "You may do your test, and if my blood is the right kind, you can call this Mitch in California and tell him you have a match."

Valerie gestured toward a chair. "If you don't mind?"

Gunther sat down and began unbuttoning his right shirt cuff so he could peel back the sleeve.

"That's not necessary," Valerie said. "I just need to prick one your fingers." She ripped open the plastic sack and laid out the kit's contents while Gunther re-buttoned his cuff.

Nina sat on the edge of the bed, watching as Valerie carefully smeared blood inside each little circle on the test card. Fifteen minutes later they had an O-negative confirmation.

And now Gunther had one final question.

"If this works, do you really think your professor will keep our secret?"

"He promised that if I hold up my end of the bargain, he'll never tell anyone where the blood came from."

This appeared to amuse Gunther. "And you believe him?"

As much as Valerie wanted to insist that Mitchell Young was an honorable man, she couldn't be absolutely certain. But she was convinced of one thing. If the transfusion wasn't attempted, and Tommy died, Mitch would lose the most precious person in his life. And what might be the fallout from that?

"As much as I can believe anyone for something like this, yes, I believe him."

Gunther shrugged. This was for Nina. Not for Valerie. And certainly not for someone's grandson.

It was fully dark by the time Valerie dropped Nina off at the Millers and headed back to the Bosecker to retrieve the collection supplies. She had called a private jet service in Seattle to dispatch a Cessna Citation to the Wenatchee airport, and if her luck held, she would be handing the chilled blood bag to Mitch before midnight.

But a new problem now arose.

Snow was beginning to fall as Valerie turned her rental car onto the West Lake Road. Feathery flakes swirled across the asphalt. The rental car's headlights painted an empty road rapidly turning white. She turned on the radio, and caught a weather report. Up to ten inches were expected by morning.

Can I make it to the airport? I'm used to driving on warm California freeways in a Maserati, not icy rural roads in a Ford Fiesta.

Mitch had told her that properly cooled blood would be good for at least twelve hours. But it couldn't be allowed to freeze. That would destroy the red blood cells. If she had trouble reaching the airport, and was forced to hole up in a snowbound car until emergency services could rescue her, she might lose the blood.

She briefly considered waiting until morning.

But I might not be able to get out of the valley if it snows heavy tonight.

201

And what if the Citation got snowed in at the airport tomorrow morning? What if Gunther lost his nerve and backed out because she had waited too long?

It has to be now.

Still . . . as fresh snow covered the road's surface, Valerie was compelled to ease her foot off the gas pedal.

CHAPTER 57

Like all of the Order's long-range jets, the Gulfstream 550 carrying Umberto and Bishop Assante was configured for maximum comfort. It was rare for more than one member to be on a flight, and even rarer for a member and a non-member to be onboard together—the exception being the pilots, who were always "normals."

Umberto presently occupied the stateroom at the back, with the comforts of a bed, toilet and shower. A solid door separated him from the rest of the aircraft.

The bishop was relegated to the main cabin, which didn't involve much of a sacrifice. There were four leather seats, a couch which made up into a bed, an entertainment system, and a galley stocked with gourmet food and beverages.

Not that Assante took advantage of everything. Concern about disturbing the man whom he now revered as *The Disciple Matthew* translated into planting his rear in one of those comfortable seats, and getting up only to raid the refrigerator or to use the forward lavatory.

Contact between a member and the crew on any of the Order's flights was practically nonexistent, except when a member entered or left the jet. So when a knock came on the door to the private stateroom just two hours before the jet was scheduled to land at Wenatchee, Umberto pushed back the down-filled comforter, pulled on a bathrobe, and was ready to punish the fool who had disturbed his sleep.

It turned out to be the captain, dressed in black slacks, a white shirt, a black jacket with captain's bars, and a black hat with golden fern-fronds on the bill.

"Yes," Umberto said, eyes focused unmercifully upon the captain.

The captain politely averted his eyes from the robed man. "Sorry to disturb you sir, but the weather at our planned destination has deteriorated into a blizzard. I need to file an alternate flight plan that will take us into Seattle instead of the central part of Washington State."

The captain fell silent. He'd flown many times for this peculiar group of clients, but never for this man. The chief of operations had cautioned him, "Don't do *anything* beyond standard procedure. Don't speak directly to him unless you are first spoken to. Keep your words to a minimum. And *never, ever* disagree."

Umberto glanced over the captain's shoulder. The bishop was exactly where he should be; the top fringe of his white hair was just visible over the back of a forward-facing seat. Umberto refocused on the captain's face, whose eyes were still averted toward the floor.

"Is it dangerous to land where we intended?"

"Yes, sir." The captain wanted to explain that there were also mountains near the airstrip. The main runway was only a little over a mile long. There was no advanced instrument landing system in place. And the weather was reported to be truly awful. But he remembered his boss's advice and kept his mouth shut. His total deference was not lost on Umberto.

"How long is the storm supposed to continue?"

"Until around mid-morning tomorrow, sir."

"If we fly into Seattle tonight, you are telling me that tomorrow afternoon we can take a short hop over the mountains into Wenatchee and we can be there no later than, say, two o'clock?"

The captain's eyes came up briefly, just long enough to reassure the passenger that he was certain of his information.

"Yes, sir."

"Good," Umberto said. "Do what is necessary."

The captain obediently turned, and was walking briskly up the aisle when Umberto's voice boomed out.

"*Bishop Assante!*"

The captain kept walking past the bishop, who pulled the buckle on his seatbelt and jumped up.

204

"Yes—" *Father protect me, I almost said Domine!* "—my son?"

"Would you call the gentleman we were scheduled to meet this evening. Tell him we are delayed and will instead arrive tomorrow at 2pm *sharp!*"

Umberto was pleased when he saw the captain half-stumble at the word "sharp."

Within seconds Assante was on the satellite phone.

CHAPTER 58

Valerie felt Clarissa's resonance as she parked the rental car on the street in front of the Bosecker. Her shoes left snowy drag-marks on the cement walkway as she approached the porch. She climbed the three steps and then paused, her gloved hand nervously grasping the brass doorknob. After three frosty breaths, she pushed open the door and stepped into the reception area.

The rich aroma of roasted chicken flooded her nostrils. Muted conversation came from the dayroom, where the communal dinner was being served. Mercifully, there was no one in sight.

She quickly climbed the stairs, half-expecting Clarissa to be waiting on the second floor. Relieved to find the short hallway empty, she continued to climb, reaching the third floor and the safety of her room.

Mitch had briefed her on blood drawing procedures, and given her two different kits. The first was the type-test kit. The second kit was more involved, with a butterfly needle and tubing, two five hundred ml collection bags, and a strip of latex rubber for tying off the upper arm to raise the veins. Everything contained in sterile plastic packaging.

She had stashed the collection kit beneath clothing in her suitcase—a safe enough place to prevent housekeeping from spotting it. She now dug with one hand under a sweater, expecting to feel the plastic bag.

And felt nothing.

She began pulling clothes from her suitcase until everything was strewn across the bed. And still there was no kit.

And then she heard the soft rattle of a door knob. And an instant later, "We need to talk."

She turned, and there stood Clarissa. The look on her face left no doubt about who had taken the kit.

"You had no right to go through my luggage," Valerie said, sounding both angry and embarrassed.

"I had every right," Clarissa replied calmly, as if reprimanding a slow student. She stepped inside and closed the door and took steps until they were practically face to face.

Valerie's words tumbled out. "Why do you think you have the right to control everyone around you?"

"I don't," Clarissa said, eyes steely. "But I think that whatever it was you intended to do is not in Nina's best interests. Did you plan to go back to the Miller's tonight and take her blood? And what do you want it for in the first place?"

Valerie still wasn't ready to concede anything, and countered with, "Do you make a habit of searching other people's luggage?"

"No," Clarissa said, stepping back from Valerie. She turned and walked to a chair set against the wall. Once seated, she said, "I only did this because I was warned that something was wrong."

"Warned?"

"Yes, I was warned. Frank called and said he'd noticed that one of Nina's fingers had been punctured on the tip. Apparently, he has some familiarity with blood testing, and that's what it looked like. He went into her room after the two of you left and found the test strip and the lancet, both wadded up in tissue paper in the garbage can." A critical smile fleetingly crossed her face. "If you are going to engage in subterfuge you really should learn to hide the evidence better."

Valerie sat down heavily on the edge of the bed.

Clarissa prompted, "Why do you want her blood?"

"I don't," Valerie said. "She doesn't have the correct type. She's A-positive. I need O-negative."

"So why did you come back here for the kit?" Clarissa suddenly *knew*, and now she uttered a single word, "Gunther?"

207

There was no point in denial. No need, really, even to speak.

Clarissa's face came alive as the pieces fell neatly into place. "So it was Gunther who told Nina about herself and the Order?"

"Yes."

"And he must have O-negative blood?"

"Naturally."

"Where has he been hiding out since he left the hospital?"

Valerie shrugged. "I've no clue."

"How long has he been back?"

Valerie again shrugged, and then offered, "It was he that Nina went to meet when she left school last week, so I'd guess he's not been back much longer than that."

"So why do you want some of Gunther's blood?"

Valerie explained about Mitch's grandson.

Clarissa grimaced. "And so it starts," she mused. "I thought we might have had years, but turns out we just had months."

"I'm sorry. I shouldn't have—"

"No," Clarissa interrupted. "I moved too quickly. If I'd found a way to handle things more diplomatically, maybe we wouldn't be where we are at today. I'm willing to accept part of the responsibility for this crisis. But you should have come to me first."

Valerie tried to defend her decision.

"I don't believe it is a crisis. I trust Mitch not to betray us. And besides, wasn't it a part of your plan to begin contacting people in the scientific world? Can't we just use this brilliant mathematician as our first contact?"

Clarissa's blue eyes were unsympathetic.

Valerie offered what she thought was her strongest point.

"Everything that happened was Nina's choice," she said. "She offered to give some of her own blood, if it had turned out to be the right type, to try and save the boy."

Clarissa sat still, listening.

"She told me that she felt terrible about what she'd done to the Hernandez boy, and that she thought this would be a fair thing to make it 'evens'."

Clarissa didn't look concerned, and countered with, "Well of course, she's just fourteen, and at that age you feel responsible for everything."

"I agree. But that wasn't her only reason."

Clarissa nodded for her to continue.

"Gunther told her that you intend to use her as a bridge for bringing the Order out of the closet. Nina thinks one of the first questions scientists will want answered is whether or not her blood, or for that matter any member's blood, can, as she put it, 'work miracles.' She wants to know if that's possible. If it is, then it's going to make a huge difference in the risk to all of us."

Clarissa settled back in her chair; her face shadowed by a thoughtful look of concern.

Valerie waited, staring out the window at the snow. The powdery stuff was gone, and in its place huge flakes now fell. The street lamp on the corner was dimmed to a soft blur through a curtain of white.

Clarissa cleared her throat. "Perhaps . . ." she began slowly, knowing she needed to make a concession if she wanted any chance of regaining Nina's trust. Stuck with the reality that Valerie was her only solid bridge for making that happen. "Perhaps she is right. Are you still willing to take Gunther's blood to California?"

"Yes."

"And I imagine you have made arrangements to get it down there quickly?"

"I have a jet arriving in East Wenatchee this evening."

"Well then," Clarissa said, rising from her chair. "You had better get going. And just in case you run into trouble, I'd like to send Charlie along, maybe with a shovel to dig you out of a snow bank if necessary." Her face softened; her mouth curled into a forgiving smile. "You have a good heart, Valerie. I'm sure that's an important reason why you and Nina have hit it off so well. I'm too ancient in my thinking, and I forget what it's like not having my own way."

Valerie now had a new worry to deal with. "If I take Charlie, how do you think Gunther might react?"

"If he's doing this because of his fondness for Nina, I doubt Charlie's presence will make any difference."

There was no time to argue. "I need to leave," Valerie said. "It's not slowing down outside." She glanced out the window.

Clarissa didn't bother to look. Instead, she said, "I'm still very worried about how your friend Mitchell Young is going to handle the result of the transfusion."

"Do you mean if it fails?"

"No," Clarissa said carefully. "I'm worried what he might do if it works."

CHAPTER 59

On the morning following the big snowstorm, Chantha stood just inside the French doors, surveying a deck covered with a foot of fresh powder snow. The radio said school was cancelled for the day. She turned to Nina, sitting on the sofa, and said, "Let's go skiing."

Frank stood beside the sofa, holding a fresh mug of coffee. Nina looked up at him, and asked, "Can we?"

"Of course," Frank said, taking a sip.

"Are you going to ski too?"

"I think I'll pass," Frank said, wanting some private time to mull over a new problem. Clarissa had called the previous evening with bad news.

"I heard from my contact in Switzerland that they're sending a man named Umberto Gonzalez."

"When?"

"Soon."

"Do we need to worry?"

"I'm told there will be another kidnapping attempt."

Frank's frustration came pouring out.

"I thought the computer program Valerie designed was supposed to scare them off. Don't they believe we will use it?"

There was a long pause on the other end of the line, before Clarissa confessed, "They have apparently decided to call our bluff."

"Our bluff?"

She sighed, and offered, "One doesn't burn down the house just to get rid of the termites."

"He's really going to attempt another kidnapping?"

"Not personally. He gets other people to do the nasty stuff."

"Who's it going to be this time?"

"He apparently plans to use the Catholic Church in Langston. Umberto has a history with religious movements, especially the Catholics. He burned people at the stake during the Inquisition, Frank. And now he's been elevated to the ruling council and tasked with completing the job where Trisha failed."

Frank had hung up, utterly frustrated.

As he now watched Chantha and Nina load skis and poles into the Volvo, he thought the best option might be to send her some place the Order would never think to look. But sending her away would cause collateral damage. She finally seemed to be settling in, despite the challenges at school, and Frank was worried about her mental health.

Should all of us leave?

But that would raise other problems.

I'd be giving up my law practice. Anna would lose her accounting clients. We'd have no way to make the kind of living we have now. And if the Order has the tools Clarissa says they have, finding our family would be no great challenge. The first time we cashed a check or used a credit card, they would have us. Finding four people wouldn't be nearly as difficult as finding one girl who won't be employed, won't have a bank account, and won't be writing checks.

There was, of course, one other big problem with sending Nina away.

She won't want to leave Chantha behind.

CHAPTER 60

Shortly after dawn on Monday the storm passed out of the valley, leaving a foot of snow in its wake. Valerie and Charlie had been lucky to even reach Mom's Parkway Motel, where they were forced to hole up for the night. Even if they had been able to continue on to East Wenatchee, a text message arrived saying the jet had turned back to Seattle when the Pangborn Airport runway was closed by the blizzard.

Gunther grumbled about the delay, but remained committed. His blood draw finally took place just before noon, after the local TV news reported that snowplows had reopened highway 97. A full bag of warm blood went into a slurry of snow and water in a small ice chest.

When Charlie walked out to Valerie's rental car to start it up, and discovered that the plow which had cleared the parking lot had also nicked the right rear tire, leaving it flat. There was no spare in the trunk, and with the jet scheduled to land in less than two hours there was no time to call a repair shop.

Only one other vehicle was readily available, and Gunther insisted that if they wanted to use his pickup, he would need to be the driver, since Walt had lent it to him on the condition that he be the only one behind the wheel.

They agreed, and Gunther went out to scrape the ice from the heavily frosted windshield. He then gunned the engine to life, layering the parking lot with a thin cloud of blue tailpipe smoke.

Valerie and Charlie left the warmth of the hotel room and climbed into the still-frigid cab, Valerie occupying the middle of the worn gray velour bench seat, her arms crossed against the cold. Charlie, to her right, had the little chest containing the precious bag of chilled blood safely nestled between his booted feet.

Gunther drove cautiously down the East Valley Highway, easing off the gas as he crossed icy patches on the road. When they reached the Columbia River, where the air was warmer and the highway was finally free of ice and snow, he relaxed behind the wheel and began to ask questions, starting with Charlie.

"How did you and Clarissa meet?"

"I first saw her in Berlin during the summer of eighteen ninety-three," Charlie said. "And we became romantically involved."

Gunther's eyes left the road for the first time, glancing at Charlie. "Like boyfriend and girlfriend?"

"Yes."

Gunther's eyes shifted rapidly between Charlie and the highway.

"What were you doing in Berlin?"

"I was working as an Indian savage for Buffalo Bill's Wild West and Congress of Rough Riders of the World. Clarissa came to the show, sensed my resonance, and approached me afterwards."

Gunther's curiosity was stoked. "Did you already know what you were?"

"No. But I was forty-five, and I still looked like I was in my early twenties. I knew something was wrong. Other performers were openly calling me the 'Ageless Indian.' When Clarissa came along and explained why I wasn't looking any older it made perfect sense."

"I never heard anything about you. Why didn't you come to Zurich and join up?"

"I already felt like an outsider, being an American Indian. To me the Order was just a bunch of freaks. Joining up would have separated me that much more from the regular run of humanity. I kept my distance, and later on, when Clarissa and I broke up, I headed back across the Atlantic."

"Do you still think of the Order as a bunch of freaks?"

"More or less," Charlie conceded.

Gunther thought for a moment, before saying, "I don't think that's too far from the truth." He settled back, contemplating what he'd heard.

It felt like the win Charlie had been hoping for. A bond, of sorts, by sharing personal details about his life that Gunter could relate to. At the very least it was a step in the right direction. Being on a more personal footing with Gunther might easily translate into being on better terms with Nina.

Gunther was too curious to stop asking questions.

"So why did Clarissa seek your help with Nina if the two of you broke up over a hundred years ago?"

"We kept in touch," Charlie said. He might have added that even though the romance had faded for Clarissa, his love for her had barely dimmed. But that would have revealed a pain he wasn't keen to share with anyone.

Gunther had heard enough from Charlie, and now turned his attention to Valerie.

"How did you first get tangled up with her?"

Valerie had to admit that *tangled* was an appropriate way to put it.

"She ran across me by accident at the L.A. County Art Museum a few months ago. Then she came to my office and confronted me with what the Order was all about. After that, well, things just kind of took a natural course."

Gunther seemed satisfied. He settled into driving. The remainder of the time passed with just small talk.

When they reached Pangborn Field, a small Citation jet was parked beyond the chain link fence in front of the pilots' lounge, its left engine roiling exhaust. Gunther pulled up alongside the building and kept the engine running. The old heater was on its last legs, and the inside of the cab had never gotten very warm. Valerie stepped out, clutching the small blue-and-white ice chest with both hands.

A bitter wind was keening, driving bits of snow across the freshly plowed tarmac, pushing the orange windsock straight out. Charlie walked her to the jet, his body partially shielding her from the wind. Once she was safely aboard and the hatch sealed, he trotted back to the pickup.

"I hope this doesn't turn out to be a mistake," Gunther said, as Charlie climbed into the cab and slammed the door.

Charlie rubbed his hands, holding them against the tepid air blowing from the dashboard vent. "Me too," he said.

They watched the Citation taxi toward the south end of the runway, where it paused just before the threshold, holding its position for what seemed like too long. Charlie was about to wonder aloud if there might be a problem, when Gunther spoke.

"We've got incoming," he said, pointing to a bright dot that quickly resolved into a jet descending from the Southwest. "It's a big one," he said, adding, "A Gulfstream by the look of it."

CHAPTER 61

The lower runs at Kearney Ridge were groomed, but there was plenty of virgin powder on the higher slopes. As the girls rode the lift to the top, Nina looked over at Chantha, all bundled up in matching light blue nylon pants and a down jacket. A blue ski cap was snugged over her ears. Wide goggles framed her face.

"You go first," Nina said.

"Okay," Chantha readily agreed. "But you're first on the next run."

When they reached the top, they pushed off the T-bar and slid to the edge until the tips of their skis were nudging into fresh powder. The sharply angled winter sun had turned the gently undulating slope into a glittering sea of white snow diamonds. They looked at each other, and Nina nodded *Go!*

Chantha launched off the edge and began carving graceful S-turns in the powder.

For one precious moment Nina felt totally at peace with the world. She gazed out across the wintery land, to where the old forest began. Embedded somewhere in the tall pines lay the glade where she had first met Clarissa in early May, while hunting for mushrooms.

Has it really been seven months? It seemed like years had passed.

She pushed the thought aside, shoved with her poles, and began cutting a mirror track to Chantha's. The lazy figure eights now resembled the double helix of a DNA molecule.

Even as she flew down the mountain, a thought intruded.

On the drive up she had noticed that Frank was distracted. He'd worked hard to conceal it, and Nina didn't think Chantha was aware that her father had something of considerable weight on his mind. But Nina had seen it clearly. In the way he held himself—sometimes gripping the steering wheel a little too tightly; occasionally biting the inside of his lip; a breath held a little too long and let out too slowly. He hadn't said much, and that, too, was uncharacteristic.

There came a moment, as they were unloading, when she turned away from Frank and saw his face reflected in the car window. His look of fear lasted just a second. When she turned around, he gave her a sad little smile, eyes crinkling at the corners.

Even as he paid for their lift tickets, telling them he would be in the lodge to watch how beautifully they skied, he seemed . . . *tight.* As if struggling to figure out a puzzle that might not have a solution.

And how do I know all of this?

The answer came easily.

Because it's a part of what I am.

As she reached the bottom of the hill and slid up beside Chantha in the lift line, Nina knew she needed to ask Frank what was troubling him.

Like it or not, I've grown up in a terrible hurry. There are people who are hundreds of years old who want to control me. The only way to defeat them is to think like an adult. And I can't win unless I take control and do whatever is necessary.

But what can *I do?*

CHAPTER 62

The Citation sat on the ramp as the Gulfstream came in fast and flared for a landing. The tires hit the concrete and gave off little puffs of bluish smoke. Gunther read the identification markings stenciled on the engine as it sped past. "That's a Swiss registration number, and I'm sure—"

"It's the same jet they came for Nina in," Charlie finished.

"If they see us . . ."

"Right. We need to get out of here."

Gunther pushed the clutch and shifted into gear, backing the pickup away from the fence. And in that moment, the door to the pilots' lounge opened. Out walked a tall man, clean cut, wearing black gloves and a gray topcoat with a red wool scarf wrapped tight around his neck.

Gunther floored the clutch pedal and pressed the brake. The pickup rolled to a stop.

The newcomer seemed not to notice them as he walked briskly out onto the tarmac. His brown hair was pushed around by the wind, but he remained focused on the Gulfstream as it taxied in his direction.

Charlie looked at Gunther. "We need to find out what they're up to."

"Agreed."

"How about we go to the main terminal and wait for this guy to drive by?

Gunther saw three vehicles parked in the lot. One was a white Lexus SUV; the other two were beaters. "It's got to be that SUV," he said. "It won't be hard to spot when it goes past." He lifted his foot from the clutch and brought the pickup around in a tight turn.

By the time the Gulfstream eased to a stop in front of the pilots' lounge, Gunther's pickup was sheltered amongst dozens of cars in the public parking lot in front of the main terminal. Valerie's Citation had finally taken off, and was a dwindling speck on the southern horizon.

As the pickup's engine thrummed a slow rhythmic beat, Gunther turned to Charlie.

"Should we call Valerie and let her know?"

"She's already got plenty to think about."

"How about Frank?"

"What would we tell him?"

Gunther reluctantly added, "Clarissa?"

Charlie settled back against the seat. "Let's see how it unfolds before we get her all excited," he said.

CHAPTER 63

Father Tom sat in the private pilots' lounge for nearly an hour, thankful it was empty. Fifteen minutes ago, when the Citation landed, he'd thought it must be the bishop. But when he walked out, the pilot who came to the hatch told him they were here to pick up a woman.

Later, Father Tom saw a slender young Asian woman escorted out onto the tarmac by a tall Native American with a ponytail. He'd been curious about the unusual pair, and what might be in the ice chest she clutched. But a few minutes later, when he saw the Gulfstream coming in for a landing, his attention shifted completely to the arrival of the bishop.

Assante had called yesterday, after the blizzard descended, with very specific instructions. "We must land in Seattle to wait out the storm. We will arrive at your local airport tomorrow afternoon at two pm. Please don't be late!"

"Yes, Your Excellency."

"When you come, you should be driving a decent car, but nothing that would draw attention. No limousines. And please no chauffeur or anyone other than yourself. Understood?"

"Yes, Your Excellency."

"After you meet us at the airport you will drive us to Langston. Please try to hold your questions of our guest to a minimum. You can talk about ordinary things, like the weather, or how your parish is getting along, but you must avoid any inquiries about the ceremony. It will all be made clear at the appropriate time. Do you have any questions?"

"No, Your Excellency." Which was purely a lie. Father Tom had plenty of questions. His follow-up call to the Vatican had confirmed the bishop's identity, and he knew well enough to shut up and let things unfold until he was certain of his ground.

"Good. I'll call if there is a change in plans."

Father Tom had immediately contacted an affluent parishioner for the use of a white Lexus RX 350, explaining he wanted it to pick up a "special guest" and that he might need to keep the car for a day or two.

He now began to walk toward the Gulfstream. The wind stung his ears and cheeks, but he held his head high, fully determined not to let physical discomfort cause him to appear as anything less than dignified.

When the hatch opened and the steps were extended, Father Tom forgot the bitterly cold wind.

A man appeared at the cabin door and waived him up. As he began to climb, Father Tom wondered if this could be the bishop. He hadn't exactly expected the bishop to be wearing a mitre cap and vestments, but this man wasn't wearing anything to identify himself as a member of the clergy. Instead, he wore black slacks and a dark blue jacket.

When he reached the top of the steps, the man reached out to shake his hand. "Father Clark, I presume?"

Father Tom nodded.

"I'm Bishop Assante. Please come inside so I can introduce you to our guest."

The bishop led him into the cabin, where a man who appeared to be in his early thirties immediately rose from his seat. He was thin, with neatly combed dishwater blond hair and a closely cropped beard. He stood three inches shorter than Father Tom, and had a demeanor that oozed humility and modesty.

As they shook hands, what might have been a fuzzy electric shock seemed to travel up Father Tom's arm.

"It is such a pleasure to meet you, Father," the man said, in a heavy Italian accent. "I'm not a member of the clergy, so please call me by my first name, Umberto." He flashed a smile that seemed to light up the cabin.

Father Tom felt his knees almost buckle. "Thomas Clark," he replied in a shaky voice. "It's a pleasure to meet you. And please, call me 'Tom' if you are comfortable with that. It's what the boys call me when we get together for our Tuesday poker night."

The admission that he gambled was something he would have never thought of sharing with a stranger . . . until now.

"Calling you 'Tom' would please me very much," Umberto said, as he released Father Tom's hand.

"Well," the bishop interjected, with some urgency, "perhaps we'd better get on with the drive to Langston."

"Certainly, Your Excellency," Umberto said in a deferential tone of voice. Followed by the briefest flicker of a smile for Father Tom. And a gentle mental nudge: *It's you and I who are the important persons. He's just a stuffed shirt from the Vatican.*

A few minutes later, as Umberto and Father Tom sat beside each other in the front of the Lexus, with the bishop stuck in back, there remained only one question Father Tom wanted to ask.

What's this "miracle" that's supposed to happen?

CHAPTER 64

When the girls came off the ski hill, Frank gave Nina a grim look Chantha didn't see. Nina knew he must have come to some decision. It was equally clear that Chantha wouldn't be included in the conversation. The drive home seemed to take forever.

After they unloaded their ski equipment from the Volvo, Frank said, "Chantha, would you please go and ask your mother when dinner will be ready?"

"Sure, Dad." Chantha turned to Nina. "Come on, let's see what Mom's got cooking."

Frank quickly said, "I need to talk with Nina for a minute, Chantha." When she continued to stand beside Nina, Frank reluctantly added, "Alone."

Chantha was about to protest, but Nina said, "It's okay. I'll be there in a sec."

There was nothing Chantha could do. She turned abruptly, giving Nina a look that said she expected an explanation later on.

As Chantha pulled the door into the house shut, Nina turned to Frank, who now leaned tiredly against the driver's door of the Volvo.

"What's happened?"

"They've sent someone new."

Nina's heart began to pound.

"Should we be doing something?"

"Not yet. It's more complicated this time."

"How so?"

Frank had long since accepted that Nina wasn't your average fourteen-year-old. Finding Benny by using the raven as her "eyes" had driven that point home. But his instinct was still to shield a child from the adult world, both as a father and as a lawyer." Nevertheless, she had to be told.

"Charlie and Gunther saw one of the Order's jets arrive when they took Valerie to the airport. Two men got off and were driven away by someone who fits the local Catholic priest's description. By the time they called Clarissa, she'd already been contacted by someone in Europe to warn her someone dangerous was coming."

"Who is it?"

"A man named Umberto Gonzalez."

"Do you know who called Clarissa from Europe?"

Frank had been curtly told by Clarissa that it was better if he didn't know.

"She didn't say."

Nina's mistrust of Clarissa now had one more reason to fester.

But I can afford to be stubborn because of what Gunther told me. She no longer has the option of keeping me in the dark!

There would be no compromising.

"We need to have a meeting," Nina said, leaving no doubt that this wasn't a request. It was a command.

CHAPTER 65

As Father Tom drove his distinguished guests north along the Columbia River, Umberto waited until he was certain the priest was comfortably under the full sway of his charm, before saying, "We will be returning to Rome tomorrow, so checking into a hotel seems like more of a burden than a convenience. It's a shame we couldn't stay with you at the rectory tonight, Tom."

"You certainly can stay at the rectory!" Father Tom said, elated at the prospect.

Umberto shifted in his seat to look back at the bishop. "Would that be acceptable, Your Excellency?"

Assante had been listening to the casual banter between the two, wishing he could tell the priest just who it was he had the privilege of being in the presence of, much less *chitchatting* with. This was, of course, impossible. Even after the initiation, the disciple's true identity would remain a secret. Umberto had been clear about this.

He now leaned slightly forward, remembering Umberto's instructions. *You must maintain the pretense that you are in charge.* In a lightly dismissive tone of voice he said, "I'm sure we can make do with whatever the good Father might provide."

Father Tom now remembered there were unwashed dishes in the sink. Sheets on the spare beds weren't so fresh. *Have I enough food in the refrigerator to cook a decent meal?* Not that he was hungry. He could have easily gone without eating until tomorrow's delivery of the bishop and Umberto back to the airport. He anxiously said, "Maybe I should stop at the grocery store and pick up something for dinner? Or would you prefer going out? We have several good restaurants here in Langston."

Umberto politely said, "I have no special needs."

Assante begrudgingly offered, "We can make do with whatever you have on hand. After all, it's only for one night."

CHAPTER 66

Valerie stepped from the Citation into a pleasant California afternoon, gripping the ice chest's handle as if she were carrying a small nuclear device. Six hours had passed since the blood draw at the motel, and even though the pouch had been kept cool, and the blood should be fine, it had occurred to her that there might be some component in Order blood which made it incompatible with the rest of humanity. They were planning to pump this into an eight-year-old. Maybe it would cure his cancer, but it might also kill him. She couldn't dispel the fear that this wasn't going to work. The idea of curing cancer with blood from a virtual super human seemed too much like science fiction for it to be real. The more distance she could put between herself and what was about to happen, the better she would feel.

She saw Mitch exit the terminal and walk quickly toward her, and she hurried to meet him. As the distance closed, he seemed only able to stare at the ice chest. "Is it in there?" he asked, as they met halfway on the wide asphalt tarmac.

"Yes," Valerie said, handing over the chest, feeling relieved. Now all she wanted was to head for her condo, and a long hot shower.

Mitch took the ice chest, and then offered a pained look.

"What?"

"There's a problem."

The worst thought occurred. "Has he died?"

"No. Tommy's alive. Sick, but still alive."

"What's wrong?"

The look on his face morphed from pain to guilt.

"Mitch," Valerie said, with a directness usually reserved for her more stubborn Chinese clients. "We had a deal. I've delivered on my end of the bargain, and this ends my involvement."

"Valerie," he pleaded, "please just hear me out."

She wanted to sprint for the lobby and order a cab. Mitch's stubborn face said it was already too late for that.

"Okay, tell me."

"I'll fill you in once we're in my car." Mitch stared down at the chest. He was gripping the handle so tight his knuckles were turning white. "We haven't any time to waste."

She almost said no. But he turned for the terminal without giving her a chance to protest. She trailed him all the way to the parking garage, growing angrier by the moment.

His Prius was parked on the first level. He popped the trunk and put the ice chest in, slamming the lid. Then he came around to where Valerie stood at the front bumper.

"Come on," he said. "It's not too far."

She was fuming mad, and determined to resist.

"Why must I come with you?"

"They need to meet you."

Valerie suddenly found herself screaming, *They aren't supposed to know who I am!*"

Mitch's confession spilled out.

"I had no choice. At first, my son didn't accept the blood as special. When I told him a doctor at Stanford was willing to take the risk, he said I was crazy. He refused to agree to an 'experimental' transfusion. I had no choice but to show him the pictures of you. I'm so terribly sorry Valerie. There was just no other way."

For a moment, the only sounds in the garage were the roar of a jet taking off, the distant rush of cars on the 101, and the squeal of tires as a car came down the ramp.

Valerie now wished she had never agreed to go for the blood. Her trusted friend had placed her in the greatest imaginable danger, and now she lost the last bit of restraint.

"I'm sorry Mitch, but the world's going to come to a fiery end before I'll meet up with some doctor I don't know and tell him all about who and what I am." She was shaking, fists clenched.

"You have to come," Mitch pleaded. "We can't do the transfusion unless there is proof of how unique it is."

"And I'm supposed to be your proof? What am I supposed to do to convince them? Are they going to cut me and watch me heal? But we don't have time for that, do we. And if you'll recall, my 'gift' is *math*, Mitch. I can't force birds to fly in through windows. I can't reach into someone's mind and force them to do something!" Valerie paused to catch her breath. And then an entirely new fury erupted as she realized what it might take to prove what she was.

"Am I supposed to take off my clothes so a stranger can examine me? To see that I have no scars? No moles? That my skin is perfect? And when I come up flawless, then they'll be convinced?"

Mitch stood speechless, her words ringing in his ears.

"I trusted you, Mitch. And you've betrayed me!"

Tears began to stream down his cheeks. "You're right," he said, slowly collapsing onto the ground. "I'm sorry," he bawled, rolling onto his left side, his face now pressed senselessly against the pavement.

As hard as she tried to fight it, a vast wave of pity rose up inside her. She looked around the parking lot and was relieved to see that no one was watching. At least not yet. But this was a busy place. Very soon someone would walk or drive by, stop, and want to help. Or they would simply call the police.

And there was that blood in trunk . . .

She bent down and put her hands on his shoulders, tugging him into a sitting position. She eventually got him onto his rear, with his back leaned against the Prius, legs straight out, tears still flowing, chest still heaving.

"Okay," she said. "Please look at me."

He took a hesitant breath.

In that fractured moment Valerie found herself saying, "So who is it that I have to meet?"

CHAPTER 67

Nina and Frank sat in his home office with the door shut, the aroma of pot roast drifting in from the kitchen.

"I want to set some ground rules for tomorrow's meeting," Nina said, arms stubbornly crossed. "The first one is that Clarissa needs to stop calling me 'Nina Bea.' That 'Bea' thing, plus her giving me that stuffed bunny, were just ways to trick me. As if I were some child she could control with a 'secret' present and a special code name.''

"Okay," Frank said. "I'll call and tell her before she comes." He was unsure how Clarissa would react, but what choice did she have? He even found himself agreeing. To a woman of Clarissa's age and experience, a girl barely turned fourteen would indeed seem immature and ripe for manipulation. But was treating her like a child wise? Now that Gunther had filled her in on much of what Clarissa had held back, Nina had good reason to be upset.

But she still doesn't know that her mother passed the genetic trait to her. Frank was in full agreement about keeping that a secret.

"Is there anything else?"

Nina began to relax, uncrossing her arms, letting her hands slink slowly into her lap.

"Both she and Charlie must treat Gunther with respect. They treat him like he's unimportant, and that's not right. I'm going to listen to what he has to say just as much as anyone else."

Frank nodded for her to continue.

Nina seemed pleased with this, and offered, "I think what you and Mom and Chantha have to say should carry equal weight too, don't you?"

Hearing Chantha's name concerned Frank. "I'm not sure Chantha should be included," he said.

Nina's face turned stubborn. "She has a right to participate. Whatever we decide to do is going to affect her just as much as it will everyone else."

Frank saw she wasn't going to budge. But he had one condition, and on this he was unwilling to negotiate. "Alright," he said. "But if the meeting takes a bad turn, I reserve the right to ask her to leave the room."

Nina paused, before conceding, "Okay."

"Is that all?" The smell of pot roast was making his stomach grumble.

"No. There's one more thing. After we all meet, I want to talk to Clarissa alone. I want her to tell me everything she knows about my mom and dad."

"That sounds fair," Frank said, trying not to telegraph what he was thinking. *If she asks the genetics question, there's no way Clarissa will be able to lie.*

Nina stared back as if she were reading his mind. Before she could speak, there came a knock and then Anna's voice from the other side of the door.

"Frank? Are you and Nina about done? Dinner's ready."

"Are we done?" Frank asked.

"Yes," Nina said, willing to let Frank off the hook.

CHAPTER 68

Father Tom ordered out for pizza. A pimply faced teenager, wearing a dingy brown jacket and a faded blue baseball cap, arrived shortly after six, carrying a large flat insulated bag. "Where do you want me to put the pie?" the boy asked, appearing ready to step inside.

"There's no need to come in," Father Tom said. "I'll take it."

The boy pulled a flat cardboard box from the bag and handed it over.

"Hang on for a minute," Father Tom said. He carried the box inside and set it on the kitchen table. When he returned, he handed over two twenties. The boy made change, and when Father Tom passed back a five, the boy accepted it with a huge grin.

"Thanks, Father."

Father Tom didn't recognize the boy in the dim porch light, and he was curious. "Are you one of my parishioners?"

The boy looked a little embarrassed. "No. My manager told me it was for the Catholic priest." There was a moment of hesitation. "I'm not a Catholic," he said, sounding apologetic. "Have a nice evening, Father."

Father Tom watched the boy dash back out into the snowy night and climb into a Chevy Vega parked under a street lamp. There was a big dent in the passenger door. A plastic pyramidal sign strapped to the roof glowed with the words ALDO'S PIZZARIA.

He thought about the boy as he walked back to the kitchen. This was the kind of kid he always hoped would come to church. Someone with limited opportunities, lucky to have graduated from high school, maybe coming from a broken home, and likely to have tried drugs. And likely to get some girl pregnant before he could even legally buy alcohol. A soul ripe for redemption. He sighed at the loss of an opportunity.

There were already plates and silverware set out on the kitchen table. He opened the box, and the aroma of hot cheese and pepperoni flooded the room.

The bishop was drinking a can of pop.

Umberto held a longneck bottle of beer. When Father Tom had asked earlier if the two men wanted wine, the bishop had shaken his head and said, "Soda, if you have it."

Umberto had seemed eager for alcohol.

"Do you have beer?"

Father Tom kept a stash of brew for those nights when the men came to play poker. He said to Umberto, "I've got a six-pack of Budweiser and a few bottles of a local ale."

"The ale sounds nice," Umberto said. "I'll have two if you don't mind. It'll help for later on." He hadn't offered a reason for what that meant.

By the time the men were pulling slices of pizza from the box, Umberto was already popping the cap off the second bottle. He took a swig, and gave a little burp. "Sorry about that" he apologized. He gazed at Father Tom with appreciative eyes. "Might I possibly have one more?"

"Of course," Father Tom said, worried that his special guest might have a drinking problem.

After they finished the pizza, and a third beer had been guzzled down, the bishop politely asked a tipsy Umberto, "Would you like to tell Father Clark your story now?"

"I suppose it is time," Umberto said, in a reluctant and noticeably slurred voice. "Can we possibly go into the living room where it is more comfortable?"

"Of course," the bishop said. "But first I need to retrieve something from my luggage."

When he returned, he carried a leather pouch, eight inches long, with a drawstring pulled tight at one end. He said nothing about the pouch, just nodded that they should follow him into the living room.

Father Tom and the bishop wound up seated beside each other on the couch. The bishop reverently laid the pouch between them on the blue velour fabric. Umberto continued to stand. The bishop suggested, "Maybe you should begin with the vision?"

"Yes," Umberto agreed. He seemed to fumble with his thoughts for a moment. Then he stood up straighter, as if prompting himself to have courage.

"I am a simple man, Father. I live in a small town in Italy. I am now forty and I have been working in carpentry ever since my father agreed to let me study under him as an apprentice at the age of fifteen." He paused, as if seeking his bearings. Father Tom wondered how much the alcohol might be affecting him and considered suggesting that he sit down, but Umberto began to speak again before he could make the offer.

"As I said, I am a simple working man. Last year I was chiseling a notch in a board at our workshop, when the room seemed to dissolve around me, and I found myself in a strange place." Umberto took a deep breath, as if reliving the moment.

"I saw a girl, maybe fourteen years old. And behind her there stood something evil. A black wraith with red eyes that glowed. Its claws were resting on her shoulders, as if it was guiding or controlling her. I was quite scared, but found myself unable to move." Umberto shivered. He blinked his eyes hard as if to dispel the memory.

"As I said, I had been working on a board. I was holding a chisel in my left hand and a hammer in my right. When the vision came, I forgot entirely what I was doing. I no longer felt the tools in my hands."

Father Tom was now sitting up straight.

"I sometimes work out in the shed with my shoes off. My father says it is a bad practice, but I have always thought it made me be more careful. When you are working in a woodshop, being careful is important. If you might step on a nail, or something sharp, or even catch a sliver, you are more likely to watch where you are stepping if

235

you are barefoot." Umberto chuckled a little, as if at his own foolishness. "Besides, I like the feeling of walking without shoes." And for a moment there was silly grin.

Umberto's face rapidly returned to serious.

"I dropped the hammer and chisel out of fear for the beast standing behind the girl, which I have no doubt was either Satan or one of his minions. The chisel fell with the blade straight down and it chopped off the little toe on my left foot."

Umberto saw Father Tom wince, and wished he could smile. But that would ruin everything. He kept a straight face and continued with his story.

"At that moment, I thought chopping off my little toe was a good thing, because with the pain the demon's spell was broken and the vision was gone. But there I was, with my foot bleeding all over the floor, and my little toe lying in a puddle of blood. I found a rag and made a tourniquet to stop the bleeding, and then I drove to the local doctor, carrying my little toe, and feeling very stupid. He told me the toe could not be sewn back on. He then sutured the skin to prevent more bleeding, and gave me some pills for the pain."

Umberto saw that Father Tom's eyes were now focused on his left foot. It was time. He took a deep breath, sat down on the floor, and began to untie his shoelaces, speaking as he pulled off the left shoe, and finally the sock.

"As you can see," he said, extending his now bare left foot, "the toe has re-grown."

Father Tom stared. He could not see a scar, or even so much as a bunion or a callus, marring the smooth white flesh. The foot not only looked whole; it looked perfect.

"I thought it might be a miracle, so I went to consult my local priest. But when I told him the story, he scolded me, saying I shouldn't make up such rubbish." Umberto was now staring at his own bare foot, as if it were some foreign object not even attached to his body. He looked up at Father Tom, his thin angular face filled with conviction, eyes beginning to tear up.

"Our priest is an old man, already in his eighties, so I don't blame him for questioning my story." Umberto dashed away the tears with the back of his hand. "I was convinced that something miraculous had happened. But this accident occurred when a vision of evil was in the room, and I didn't know how to interpret it. Had the devil caused me to injure myself and then healed me? Was I now cursed? Or had it been God who delivered me from wickedness and cured my wound?" Umberto paused, his face a mask of worry.

"These questions kept me from sleeping much for many days, and I found it difficult to eat. I lost weight, and I knew if this continued, I would waste away and maybe starve to death. Finally, I went to someone higher up in the Church, and eventually they took me to meet Bishop Assante." Umberto looked at the bishop, who now took over the story, just as he had been instructed.

"When Umberto first came to me, I too thought he must have concocted a tale. Or maybe he'd had some type of delusion? We at the Vatican hear tales of miracles on practically a weekly basis. Few of them are credible. But Umberto was insistent that he'd had this vision, lost his toe, and that it had grown back. He persuaded me to call the doctor in his home town, and sure enough, the doctor confirmed that Umberto had come into his office and had lost a toe."

The bishop's face betrayed a growing excitement.

"What I am about to tell you must remain a secret. And what we are about to do must be told to no one until it is time to disclose the results to those in Rome who will sit in final judgment. Do you promise this, Father Clark?"

If a bomb had suddenly exploded in the front yard of the rectory, Father Tom would not have heard it go off. He nodded dumbly in agreement.

"Then we shall proceed with the next step. And for this we shall be using a holy relic."

The bishop reached for the pouch that lay between them on the couch. He pulled at the knot, and worried the leather drawstring until he could withdraw an object. It was mostly iron, tapered in the middle until it was no thicker than a pencil, with a wooden knob on one end. The opposite end flared into a disc about one inch in diameter. He held it up so that Father Tom could see what was on the flat end. A stylized "C" raised in the metal, roughly the size of a quarter, with a tiny cross in its center.

"I have never been a strong believer in the righteousness of the crueler periods of our church's history. But as the museum's curator, I have come across many devices that come from those dark times. This particular relic dates from the time of the Inquisition. It is documented to have first been used in the year thirteen-ten to determine if certain Knights Templar were true to the cause of Christ, or if they were heretics." The bishop paused, seeming pained by what he was about to relate.

"Fifty-three knights wound up being put to death after none of them passed the test." He held out the relic. "Would you like to examine it, Father?"

Father Tom was horrified, and could only stare with revulsion at an instrument for determining life or death.

"Yes," the bishop said, pulling it back. "I, too, was at first repelled." He looked at Umberto, who was now retying the laces of his shoe. "But it does have its uses, being a blessed and holy object. When a decision had to be made about whether or not to test the man who now sits on the floor before us, to learn if he has been graced with a healing by our Lord . . . or, has been captured by Satan's spell, this seemed an appropriate way to seek the truth."

Father Tom's questioning look was met with a solemn declaration.

"We will be using the relic to sear a mark on Umberto's body. For any normal person, such a wound would result in a scar. If it was the work of the devil that healed his toe, then we will expect evidence of a scar, made by a holy relic of the Church, to be visible after the burn has healed. If, on the other hand, the wound heals and no scar is visible, we may assume that it was an act of our Savior that caused the healing. Once this is established, we will need to consider whether or not to move on to the second concern, that being the girl from Umberto's vision."

Father Tom had momentarily forgotten about the girl, and in puzzled voice asked, "Why is she important?"

"Because," the bishop said, gravely, "Umberto's vision carried more information." He looked to Umberto, whose response left no wiggle room for doubt.

"As I stood in the workshop, feeling the agony in my toe, it came to me that I knew where the girl lived." He stared straight at Father Tom. "That place is here, Father. In this valley where you tend to your flock. And in my vision, I also saw your face, as clearly as I see you now."

Father Tom became aware of a ringing in his ears.

The bishop said, "That is why we sent Father Androcelli this past summer, to confirm that Langston existed as it was seen by Umberto in his vision, and to confirm that you were in fact the priest for the local church. But we are getting ahead of ourselves." The bishop fingered the relic for a moment, caressing the raised "C" with the tip of his index finger, almost lovingly.

"First, we must be certain of a second miracle. Only then can we concern ourselves with what might be done about the girl, who, if this test holds, must be believed to be under the power of Satan Himself." He paused, to be certain that Father Tom was not overwhelmed.

When Father Tom nodded for him to continue, the bishop said, "May we use the stove in your kitchen?"

CHAPTER 69

"You're too upset to be driving," Valerie insisted. "Give me the keys." Mitch handed them over, his face awash with uncertain hope.

As she pulled onto the 101 and merged into rush hour traffic, Valerie began firing questions.

"What's his name?"

"Who?"

"The doctor doing the transfusion."

"Actually, it's a 'her'," Mitch said. "And she already knows you."

Valerie turned to stare at him, momentarily losing track of the blue Mercedes she'd been tailgating at seventy-five miles an hour. "She knows me? How is that possible?"

A nearby car's horn blared and Valerie's eyes snapped back to the road. The right wheels of the Prius had drifted across the divider line. Once the car was re-centered in the middle lane she kept her eyes forward, demanding, "Who is it?"

"I doubt you'll remember her," Mitch said. "She was a pre-med student when you were doing graduate work. She took one of the courses where you filled in as my TA. Do you remember an Angela Cornish?"

"What class did she take?"

"Inferential statistics."

"And the year?"

"Oh-four."

"Which semester?"

"Spring."

Valerie thought back, picturing the faces. How many students had there been? *Twenty-five.* And how many were women? *Just five. Two sat together in the back, and their names were . . . Liz and Trudy. The others were scattered amongst the males. Mary, in the third row, was a rich undergrad whose parents were Stanford alums. She hadn't lasted long, dropping out in the fourth week. Then there was Judith in the middle of the front row. And . . . Angel, in the second seat from the right in the front, a sophomore with a full ride scholarship because her folks were poor and she was brilliant. An Alabama beauty who had jokingly called herself "Angel from Montgomery" after the John Prine song.*

Valerie had liked her because she asked really great questions. Tall and willowy, with auburn hair cropped seriously short. And a southern drawl that sounded pleasantly like Dolly Parton.

"Do you mean Angel? The tall one who always wore black slacks no matter what the weather?"

Mitch didn't have a clue what Angela Cornish had worn fifteen years ago. These days it was a long white coat. When they met, he'd been far too worried about his grandson to notice what she wore beneath that coat. "That's her. But I'll have to take your word on the black slacks."

"How'd you find her?" Eyes still forward, but focused upon extracting as much information as possible about someone who might become an adversary.

"I called the hematology department and asked if they had a woman doctor on staff, figuring that might go down better with you."

Valerie was in no mood to reward him for choosing a female doctor.

"And?"

"There were three women MDs in the department. I asked if any were Stanford grads. Angela was the only one. I made an appointment. When we met, I asked her if she knew anything about using whole blood transfusions in the treatment of leukemia, and it turned out to be the focus of her current research." Mitch paused, remembering what had taken place next. It was amazing how connected things could be, and how strongly coincidence could play a role.

He'd been nervous. Angela Cornish took a long look at him, and laughed with a mischievous grin that said there was something he wasn't getting. After a few seconds, she said, "Don't you remember me? I was in your stats class, Doctor Young." She laughed more freely when she saw he still didn't remember her, adding, "That is whenever you bothered to grace us with your presence. Most of the time you sent this Chinese math whiz to torment us poor undergrads. By the way, whatever happened to . . . Valerie? Wasn't that her name?"

"I was stunned she remembered you. But then, you're a very memorable person."

Valerie saw the sign for Sand Hill Road, jockeyed into the right lane, and took the exit headed east, now just a few blocks from the campus. She pictured Angela, recalling the near-perfect test scores aced by the brilliant southern girl. *And now she's possibly going to deliver a cure for a boy's cancer. How appropriate that it might come from someone called Angel.* She glanced at Mitch.

"You told her everything?"

"No. I just told her what I thought would be enough for her to understand the situation. And then she said to me, 'Doctor Young, I don't mean to sound disrespectful, but isn't it possible that you are reaching just a little too far in hopes of finding a miracle to save your grandson?' And I agreed that it sounded nutty. And we laughed, and then I showed her the pictures of you. She was intrigued and said she'd at least like to meet you."

The Stanford campus loomed ahead. Valerie glanced at Mitch, holding back her anger. There was no point in raging. She was committed.

"Where do I go?"

Mitch pointed to a four-story glass-and-white structure with STANFORD MEDICINE in red and blue lettering at the top. "It's probably too late for valet parking, but there's an underground garage if you turn over there."

242

Valerie made the turn and slowed for the ramp. She found an empty space near the elevator.

After the engine was off, she looked hard at Mitch before reaching for the door handle.

"Did she promise to keep this a secret?"

"I'm not sure she even halfway believes what I told her. To make that kind of a promise, she's first going to have to believe you're for real."

Valerie shook her head in frustration, unable to see a way out of what Mitch had gotten her into. Her sarcastic reply cut deep. "I doubt *believing* will be much of a problem once she sees me again."

"Right," Mitch conceded, too scared to feel relieved. He was still half-expecting Valerie to suddenly balk and insist upon leaving.

Instead, Valerie got straight to business. "Where's your grandson now?"

"He and his dad are in a room at the Westin. They'll come on a moment's notice." Mitch reached into his suit coat pocket and pulled out a cell phone. "All I have to do is make the call."

Getting his son to bring the boy for an experimental treatment had been a struggle, even after he'd seen the photos of Valerie. But Tommy had been slipping deeper into his illness day by day, rapidly growing thinner and paler. Art was ready to grasp at straws. He'd finally agreed that if a Stanford doc would accept the risk, he was willing to take the chance. Both had cried at that point, and then they held each other until the crying stopped.

Valerie's voice brought him back to the present.

"And Tommy's mother? What was her take on this?"

Mitch nervously confessed, "She thinks he's brought the boy down to the hospital for more tests, and that 'daddy' wanted to give him a fun night in a fancy hotel as a reward for being a good boy."

"Mitch . . ."

"I know, I know. It's wrong. But Annie's a cautious person. Art and I agreed she'd go ballistic if she learned what we were up to." He stared out the passenger window, across a row of cars, speaking almost as if he were alone. "I had so many hurdles to clear. I couldn't risk one more."

He turned back to her. "Does it really make any difference whether or not she's given her consent?"

Valerie rolled her eyes, before saying, "I suppose not." She pulled the handle and pushed open the driver's side door. "C'mon. Let's not keep the good doctor waiting."

CHAPTER 70

After dinner Nina cut a juicy sliver from the fatty end of the roast and went out onto the deck. She swiped fresh snow from the wood railing and laid the morsel down.

Raven now came every morning, usually just before she and Chantha left for school. Nina would stand behind the French doors, awaiting his arrival. He would give a cry of greeting as he landed and saw her behind the glass, and then he would gobble down whatever meat she'd left.

After his meal, Raven would fly to the front of the house and wait until Frank backed the Volvo from the garage with the girls inside. He would then soar above the car until it turned from the *cul de sac* and sped down the West Lake Road.

Tonight, after she laid out his treat, she went straight to Chantha's room.

As soon as the door closed, Nina said, "We're having a meeting tomorrow evening. Everyone's invited, including you."

"Me?"

"Yes, you. You're my sister and this affects you as much as it does everyone else."

"What's up?"

"The Order has sent someone new to try and kidnap me."

Chantha sank down onto her bed.

Nina sat beside her and took her hand, gently molding Chantha's fingers into the cup of her own palm. "Don't worry. We'll figure out how to stop them."

"Why can't they just leave you alone?"

Nina felt extra warmth flowing in Chantha's hand. Her heart rate had picked up. Her breathing came shallower and faster. Her pupils were slightly dilated.

"Because Clarissa wants to use me to take the Order public, and they don't want that to happen."

"How would they know that?"

"It was the bunny and that crest on its chest. When Selena put it up on the Internet, they recognized it as belonging to Clarissa, and they knew there must be a connection between her and someone here. They sent that guy we saw with Mr. Farnham to investigate, and he sensed my resonance there at the front doors to the school."

Both girls glanced at the shelf above Chantha's desk. On it sat the bunny, its chin drooping over the edge, floppy ears hanging, eyes apologetic. The black pearl now sewed back inside its chest.

"They think kidnapping me is the best way to stop her."

Chantha was angry.

"This was all Selena's fault. If she hadn't put that rabbit up on Facebook and asked everyone in the whole world where she could get one, nobody would have a clue about you."

"Let's not blame Selena," Nina insisted. "She had no idea about the consequences of what she did. She's already suffered enough." She still felt at a loss for the damage to her friendship with Selena. "I miss her," she said, closing her eyes in pain. And in that moment, she felt her consciousness slipping out in Chantha's direction.

Nina opened her eyes and let go of Chantha's hand, fearful that she might accidentally find herself inside Chantha's mind. She wasn't ready for that.

And probably never would be.

CHAPTER 71

Langston's Catholic Church was an imposing structure in a neighborhood otherwise filled with ordinary homes. It had a gabled roof with a tall bell steeple crowned by a white cross. The rectory was separated from the church by an alley.

A white Lexus SUV now stood in the rectory's front driveway.

Half a block up the street was a micro-park where kids could shoot hoops on a cement half-court; a perfect place to burn off extra energy after having to sit through a Sunday morning service. Gunther's pickup was parked there beneath the snowy limbs of a leafless maple. From this vantage, the cross and steeple of the church were visible over the rectory's roof.

As darkness settled in, Gunther and Charlie sat in the cold cab, waiting for something—anything—to happen. Gunther's arms were tightly crossed against the cold. The windows had begun to fog up, forcing them to wipe the glass every few minutes.

"Do you think we should we start the engine?"

Charlie shook his head, recalling his summer encounter with a local sheriff's deputy who had stopped and hassled him. "Nah," he said. "This time of the night we'd be noticed for sure."

A minute later, as Charlie was once again wiping the front windshield, he said, "Hey. We've got some action."

A blue Chevy Vega braked to a stop in front of the rectory. A teenage boy got out, yanked open the back door, and pulled out a flat padded case.

"Pizza delivery," Charlie said. "It appears they wish to dine in."

The boy walked swiftly to the rectory and knocked while holding the padded case on one extended arm in a precarious balance. A porch light came on and the door opened. A man stood framed in the yellow light.

"There's our priest," Charlie said.

The kid pulled out a large flat cardboard box from the insulated bag. The priest took it and disappeared for half a minute, returning to hand over money. The kid practically skipped back to the car before he drove away.

"Wish we had some pizza," Gunther grumbled, watching his breath swirl and fog the windshield yet one more time.

"Later," Charlie said. He settled back against the seat, replaying what he'd learned from Gunther.

Earlier that afternoon, as they'd driven back from the airport, he'd gotten the German to reveal where he'd disappeared to after fleeing the hospital.

"I took a bus and headed south. I began hurting, so I got off in a city called Yakima and found a homeless shelter. The gal running it put me onto a job after I recovered."

"Doing what?"

"Working in a vineyard."

When Charlie asked who he'd worked for, Gunther shrugged. The man had been kind. The least he could do was protect his identity.

"Why'd you come back here?"

Gunther looked at Charlie as if he'd just asked the strangest of questions. "To see Nina, of course. I couldn't leave without telling her goodbye."

"But you didn't just say goodbye. Why did you decide to stick around?"

"Because she asked me to," Gunther replied gruffly.

"And all of that stuff you told her about the Order? Did she ask for that too?"

"Of course," Gunther said, indignant. "She's got a right to know, doesn't she? After all, it's her life. She's the one who's got to live it."

And he's right about that. I warned Clarissa, but she didn't believe me. So now we're dealing with the consequences.

248

Sitting in the dark, watching the rectory, Charlie realized nothing was going to happen tonight. "Let's go get something to eat," he said. "I don't think they'll be going anywhere before morning."

Gunther immediately reached for the key. The straight-six beneath the hood reluctantly turned over and chugged to life.

CHAPTER 72

Pieter Silberhof sat in a Vienna coffee shop, gazing out the window at a drift of new snow banked against the far side of the cobbled street. The scene brought back memories of an encounter with Mozart, during the holiday season of late 1766.

In that desperately cold winter, Pieter had struggled through deep snow to reach the opera house, hoping for a distraction from a troubling problem. At the age of 42 he had recently learned that he belonged to a group of long-lived people who called themselves the Order. He was finding it difficult to accept that he would outlive everyone he knew, and would soon need to leave his beloved Vienna.

Music seemed like a perfect diversion.

The ten-year-old Mozart had lived up to his billing. Playing a harpsichord, accompanied by two violins and a cello, the boy's self-composed melody had simply soared. The sonata made Pieter's heart speed up and his mind slow down, and for one precious hour he'd forgotten everything except the ethereal music.

The boy's father, Leopold, stood with a protective hand across his son's shoulders as Pieter approached after the performance. Surely this level of genius signaled that he *belonged*. That he too was a *member*. But there was no resonance emanating from the slim youngster, dressed in a waistcoat with gold embroidery, a white silk scarf, elevated by high-heeled shoes, and topped by a powdered wig which made him seem much taller than he actually was.

Years later, when Mozart was in his twenties and early thirties, Pieter would occasionally visit Vienna to see the prodigy all grown up, conducting his magnificent symphonies and operas. He would sit in the back of the hall, wearing a disguise so that old friends wouldn't recognize him and wonder why he still looked twenty-two when he was in his sixties. Pieter always left lamenting that this brightest of flames would eventually gutter and be extinguished.

Mozart's death came far sooner than expected, at the age of 35.

Pieter now retreated from the memory, returning to a disturbing present. Since his ejection from the Council at the end of September, he had become a troubled man. Not for having been thrown off the Council. He figured he'd had that coming for sending Gunther to America without prior Council approval. Over the course of a very long lifetime, an occasional misstep was to be expected. With centuries to look forward to, punishing yourself for every mistake was pointless. You simply took things in stride and moved on.

But after retreating to Vienna, he'd had plenty of time to think about the girl. As winter descended, what Liesel had first said to him in the Council's chambers in April kept coming back to haunt him.

"She may have found The One."

At the time she said this, Pieter had assumed Liesel was merely reporting that Clarissa had finally found a tool to train for eventually taking the Order public. The girl was nothing more than a ticket to make it happen.

When Sandro traveled to Langston, and then returned to report to the Council what he'd learned about the girl, the stakes increased. The girl's impressive potential made her a very *capable* tool. But still *just* a tool.

Now, Pieter wasn't so sure. What kept swirling around in his head was how Liesel had phrased it. Not *Someone*. But *The One*.

The Order had kept track of the troublesome Clarissa in the decades before she arrived in eastern Washington, where she had unexpectedly settled down for 13 years. It wasn't uncommon for a member to live in one locale for a while. A constantly changing address was tedious.

But why central Washington? Clarissa had seen Caesar's legions on the march, witnessed the Renaissance, and attended Shakespeare's plays when The Bard himself had acted on stage. So why had she chosen to live in the middle of nowhere for so long!

No member had ever sensed a "new" member's resonance before they entered their teens. If resonance occurred at birth, one would have expected its detection, at least once or twice before now. If the girl had been a baby when Clarissa first moved to this desolate region, she should have been effectively invisible to someone capable of sensing resonance. Could it have possibly been just a coincidence that Clarissa remained for years in one tiny geographical region, where a baby was maturing into a girl who carried the most powerful of gene configurations?

The scenario made far more sense if one of her parents had been an undiscovered member who had drawn Clarissa's attention. With this thought in mind, Pieter began to search for an answer. And what he discovered supported his suspicions.

According to the local newspaper, the girl's parents—Jon and Betty Haas—had died in a car crash when Nina was still in the cradle. One particular paragraph in the obituary caught Pieter's eye.

Betty was employed by the United States Forest Service. "A true loss to science," her supervisor said. "We have lost a modern genius and she will be sorely missed."

Pieter continued to dig.

The father appeared to be a rather ordinary accountant. But the mother had graduated summa cum laude with a degree in botany from a prestigious local school, Whitman College. She was the student body secretary. A star player on the Lacrosse squad. And after she was hired in a research position by the government, she had authored four peer-reviewed papers on conifer forest diseases, before her untimely death at 26. In short, she appeared to be remarkable at whatever she chose to do.

Pieter looked out across the snowy cobbled Vienna street and finally reached a conclusion. When Liesel had called her The One, she had truly meant *The One*. A child born to a member, who was herself a member. And if this were true, and the longevity trait had finally found its genetic footing, then as her progeny multiplied upon the Earth, the current population would find it difficult to compete with this new species of human. Just as Neanderthals had gradually become extinct and been replaced by Homo sapiens thousands of years ago, so would ordinary humans be replaced by Nina's descendants.

The One!

Pieter wanted to get back in the game before it was too late.

CHAPTER 73

As they climbed out of the Prius, Mitch said, "Pop the trunk and I'll get the chest."

"I'd rather carry it myself," Valerie said, reaching to pull the release. She walked around to the back without waiting, and gingerly lifted the blue chest.

Mitch followed, and now reached up to slam the trunk lid shut. "Wait a minute," he said. "I owe you something before we go in."

"What?" Valerie gripped the handle a little tighter.

Mitch stared at the ground, carefully focusing on what he wanted to say. Finally, his eyes came up to meet hers. His voice was shaky.

"Up until now I've been forcing you to do this. But I owe you what I'm about to say. And I truly mean it."

"Mitch, you don't have to—"

"No. Hear me out." His eyes remained fixed upon hers, committed.

"Okay." The ice chest suddenly felt heavy.

"If you told me, right now, that you wanted to get back into the car . . . I would drive you to San Jose, and I would call my son and tell him this was all a mistake. Then I'd call the doctor and tell her I was confused and she should forget what I said." The last few words choked up in his throat.

"Is that all?" Valerie asked, indignant.

"Yes," Mitch insisted. "I mean it. I truly do. You can back out of this right now if you want to."

Valerie was tempted, picturing how wonderful it would be to disappear into the comfort of running her business. But as quickly as this fantasy materialized, it vanished. And not because she felt compelled to save Mitch's grandson. She simply didn't believe it *could* be undone. How long would it take before Angel got curious enough to drive down to San Jose to look her up? And if her former student saw someone who looked *exactly the same* as she looked twelve years ago? Someone who'd purposefully evaded a meeting?

Valerie let out a long breath. "We've come too far."

Mitch's face flooded with relief.

She reached out with her free hand and patted him on the shoulder. "C'mon. It'll be alright." But that was a lie. Valerie had never been more unsure about something turning out right.

The night was softened by a warm breeze hinting of bay trees and saltwater, making the walk through the complex of medical buildings quite pleasant. By the time they reached the "F" clinic, where Angela Cornish's office was located, Valerie felt ready. Mitch had called as they walked, and they found the doctor waiting just inside the clinic's front door.

Valerie immediately recognized the tall, willowy southerner. Except now there were a few gray hairs amongst the auburn, and the doctor wore glasses. A long white lab coat, with her name embroidered in Cardinal red above the lapel, didn't extend far enough to conceal the black slacks.

"Told you about the pants," Valerie whispered to Mitch, trying to lighten the moment. But it wasn't going to be that kind of night. Mitch appeared not to have even heard what she'd said.

The doctor stared at Valerie as they approached. Out of politeness, she briefly shifted her attention to Mitch, offering a sympathetic smile as she reached out to shake his hand.

"Dr. Young."

"Dr. Cornish."

And just as quickly the preliminaries were over.

Angela released Mitch's hand and shifted her attention to Valerie. For a long and uncomfortable moment she studied Valerie's face, as if cataloguing every pore, follicle, the perfect skin. She glanced down at the blue ice chest Valerie still held tight. "Mitch told me the most intriguing story," she began, struggling to sound objective. "I'll

255

confess I wasn't ready to believe. But . . ." Her eyes came up, and now she found it impossible to finish, staring at exactly the same face she remembered from her undergraduate math class.

There was no one else around to witness what was happening. But it wouldn't last if Angela continued to gape at her. "Maybe we should go to your office?" Valerie suggested.

Angela heard her own voice as if it were coming from another dimension, saying, "Yes. Certainly. This way, please."

When they were safely behind a closed door, Angela sank into a chair behind her desk, while Frank and Valerie settled in chairs opposite. The ice chest now sat safely on the floor between Valerie's feet.

"How is this possible?" Angela began, unable to keep from staring at the remarkably young face.

For an instant Valerie imagined herself wearing a niqāb. *Wouldn't it be great to be a Muslim right now. She wouldn't be able to see anything but my eyes.*

"I don't know the exact science of it," Valerie began, pushing the niqāb thought aside. "The way it was explained to me is that one in roughly twenty million people are born with a body that doesn't lose its ability to produce stem cells, and so the immune system never weakens. And when there is damage, the repairs come very fast, and consequently, 'we' live a very long life."

"Are either of your parents like this?"

"No. My parents are aging normally."

"So the trait isn't passed down?"

"Not that I'm aware of."

"Are you . . . healthy?"

"Perfectly," Valerie said, wary of what might be coming next. "I've never had a cold. If I get cut, it heals and there's no scarring. Would you like to check?" She steeled herself, willing to undress—after Mitch left the room, of course—so Angela could confirm what she was saying. It was the best proof. A perfect body with no scars at the age of 34 would be an impossibility unless what Mitch had told her was true.

Angela saved her the embarrassment.

256

"No. I can see you're not making this up. And the person who donated this blood? Is he the same as you?"

"Yes," Valerie said. "He's the same as me."

"And he's in his mid-thirties too?"

"Older," Valerie said.

Angela wanted to ask how much older, but before she could find the words, Mitch cut in with a hopeful, "Can we do the transfusion?" His hand was already in his jacket pocket, fingering the cell phone.

"I'll need to do some testing first," Angela said. "Would you mind if we took some of your blood and ran it through the lab?"

"Sorry, but that's not going to happen," Valerie said.

"What?" Mitch was stunned.

Angela was quick with, "We need to make certain it's the right type. There are also HLA factors to determine. It would be reckless to begin a transfusion without proper lab work."

"Here's the deal," Valerie said firmly. "First of all, we have just one donor and his blood is all you're going to get. It doesn't matter what the HLA factors are because there's no way they'll change. Mitch's grandson is O-negative, and that requires O-negative blood for a transfusion. I ran a test on the donor and it came up O-negative. If you want to bring in a kit and do a type test here in your office, fine. But there is no way a sample leaves this room, because you and I both know what would happen. You wouldn't be able to resist the temptation to preserve some of the blood and do a whole lot more than just testing for transfusion compatibility. You'd do a full genotype and try to figure out what makes it different from everyone else's, right?"

Angela smiled. "Okay," she said. "If it works and saves the boy's life, we would certainly pull it apart and see if we can figure out what makes it tick."

"Even if it didn't save the boy's life—and by the way, his name is *Tommy*—you would still analyze it down to the last fragment of DNA."

Angela steepled her arms on the desk and rested her chin on the double-fist. "I suppose you're right."

"It's Nobel Prize type stuff, isn't it?"

"I hadn't thought of it that way . . . but yes, it might possibly be."

She has no clue that we of the Order have the ability to detect a lie. And the message had come through loud and clear. Angela knew the Nobel Prize was hers if this worked. But she still had to prove it, and for that she needed the blood, and she probably also needed a little boy to live.

"The deal is this: you can run the basic tests here in your office. If it passes muster, you can do the transfusion. Bring in whatever you need from the lab, but I get to take away everything that comes into contact with blood. The needles, the tubes, the bag. All of it. I can't take Tommy, so I'll just have to hope his father has the good sense not to let you take some of his son's blood later on. Do we have a deal?"

"Yes," Angela said immediately. "We have a deal."

And this time she was telling the truth. Valerie turned to Mitch. "Do you want to make that call now?"

The weight of eternity having just lifted from his shoulders, Mitch reached into his pocket and grabbed the cell phone.

Angela stood up. "Shouldn't we wait until I run the typing tests?"

"Go get your kit," Valerie said. "You should have enough time to test the blood before Tommy and his father arrive."

CHAPTER 74

When Art Young pushed open the glass door to the clinic, holding his eight-year-old son's hand, Valerie was shocked. The boy wobbled like a toddler as he walked into the foyer. His pant legs billowed; his shirt hung loose. His eyes were sunken and dark. And he looked *wary*. Tommy was coming to yet one more place where people in white coats had so far failed to slow his illness. A place where guarded looks told a far different story than the doctors' hopeful words. A place without real hope.

Worst of all was the look of submission. He knew he was going to die.

Valerie wanted to weep. But instead, she broke from Mitch and Angela and met father and son halfway.

When Art recognized who she was, it was with the same surprised look as Angela's. Here was a woman he'd not seen in years, yet her face was unchanged.

Before Art could speak, Valerie crouched down, her eyes now level with the boy's.

"Hi, Tommy. I'm a friend of your grandfather's. My name is Valerie."

After a few uncertain seconds the boy said, "I call him 'Papa'."

"Well," Valerie said, struggling to remain calm and positive, "I call him Mitch, and I've known him ever since I started college at Stanford."

Tommy just stared back.

Angela came up behind Valerie and touched her on the shoulder to let her know she was there. She then squatted down beside Valerie and gave the boy a reassuring smile. "I'm Doctor Cornish," she said. "But I'd like it very much if you would call me by my first name, Angela. Would you like that?" She held out her hand. Tommy studied it for a moment, before reaching out and limply closing his fingers around hers.

"Okay," he said, immediately withdrawing his hand. Then, "Dad says you can help me. Is that true?"

Art Young, standing behind his son, had a sudden tear streak his left cheek. He quickly wiped it away with his shirt sleeve, bit his lower lip hard, willing the tears to stop. Tommy hadn't seen, which was all that mattered.

Angela continued to hold Tommy's gaze. In a firm and certain voice, she said, "We're going to do our very best, Tommy. I promise."

Tommy now peeked over Angela's shoulder at Mitch, who had walked up until he was just a few feet away. "Hi Papa," he said, offering the most loving of pale smiles.

Mitch reached down and lifted him. The boy nestled his chin securely against Mitch's left shoulder, cheek pressed into the warmth of Papa's flesh, skinny legs dangling.

"How's my big boy?" Mitch whispered into Tommy's ear.

"I'm okay, Papa," Tommy said, resigned, but happy in the moment.

Angela stood and said in as professional of a voice as she could muster, "Let's go to my office."

She led the group down the hallway, and once they were inside, she turned to Valerie and said, "May I speak with you for a moment?"

Valerie followed her out into the hallway.

After she had gently closed her office door, Angela's voice turned coldly practical. "There's one last hurdle we must clear before we can begin a transfusion."

Have I missed something?

"What?"

"We need to draw a small amount of blood from the boy and mix it with an equal amount of blood from the bag. It won't take long. Five minutes, tops. Just to make sure that clotting doesn't occur."

Valerie looked as if she'd been slapped. This was exactly the fear she'd had on the flight down. Some secret blood component that might be deadly.

"Why didn't you tell me this before?"

"We couldn't do it without the boy. And if you hadn't gone rushing up to him and his father, I could have handled it in a more diplomatic way. So now we're stuck with what we have." Her eyes fixed on Valerie's, as if to say, *You're in my ballpark now so please don't be difficult!*

Valerie remembered what she'd said to the boy. Her cheeks began to flush. "How could we ever tell Tommy that we can't help him?"

"We won't," Valerie said coldly. "I'll also bring in a bag of saline, and if we get clots, I'll begin a simple drip. The boy won't know the difference. It will be up to you to take Art out of the room and tell him why he's getting saline instead of blood."

Valerie pictured Art's face upon being told there would be no "miracle cure." Not even an attempt at one.

Angela gave her a moment to process the reality, and then said, "So . . . are we agreed on the procedure if it becomes necessary?"

"Yeah," Valerie said, knowing exactly what Art's reaction was going to be if things went south.

"Good. Then I'll go get a bag of saline and the clotting test and I'll be right back." She turned and walked briskly down the hallway.

Valerie returned to the office.

Art looked nervous as she entered. "What did she want?"

"Nothing important. She's gone to get something, and she'll be right back."

Art couldn't ask. Not in front of his dad or his son. But he was certain that whatever had been said out in the hallway held his son's life in the balance.

When Angela returned, she held a small syringe and a red-rubber-capped test tube in one hand. In the other hand she carried a white paper sack with a heavy bulge. She sat the sack on the desk alongside the ice chest, and then turned to Tommy.

"I'll bet you've had a doctor do a blood test before, haven't you?"

"Yes," Tommy said, gamely. "They stick you with a needle."

"Well, I have to take a little bit of your blood before we can start. Do you think that would be okay?"

"Yeah," Tommy said. "Papa says I need to be a big boy." He held out both of his arms, palms up. There were little red dots in the crooks of both elbows. "Which one do you want?"

Angela chose the right arm, and quickly swabbed the bluish skin with an alcohol pad. "Now there's going to be a little stick," she said, deftly inserting the needle before Tommy had a chance to think about it. She drew a small amount of blood and then withdrew the needle and wrapped tape over the puncture fast as you please.

"You're really good at that," Tommy said, adding, "I know, because I've had a lot of experience."

"I'll bet you have, Tommy," Angela said, careful not let emotions muddle her words. "You handled it like a real pro." She walked around the desk and injected the blood into the test tube. Then she pulled a second syringe from her lab coat pocket and lifted the ice chest's lid. Without removing the blood bag to where Tommy could see it, she drew some blood through the bag's needle trap and injected it into the tube with Tommy's blood. She shook the tube briefly before placing it inside the chest and closing the lid. She walked back around the desk to face Tommy.

"Before we get going, I'm going to need use the ladies' room. Would you like me to bring you back something to drink?"

Tommy thought for a moment. "Do you have any grape pop?"

Angela's face was truly angelic as she said, "I'll bet I can find you some." She looked at Art, then Mitch. "Gentlemen? Anything?"

Both shook their heads. Something was going on, and neither had figured it out. Angela made a little prayer that she wouldn't have to run the bluff. "I'll be right back," she said, closing the door softly as she left.

Valerie had never believed in a personal God that you asked favors of. But in the five minutes that Angela Cornish was gone, she somehow found it in herself to pray. It didn't seem to matter whether her audience was real or imaginary.

Please Lord. Just this one time.

When Angela returned, she held a can of Welch's grape soda. She pulled the tab and handed it to Tommy before walking around her desk. Careful to block Tommy's view of what she was doing, she lifted the lid to the ice chest, grabbed the tube, and studied it for a moment. She placed it back in the ice chest and turned around. A smile spread across her face.

Valerie closed her eyes, and her heart whispered, *Thank you.*

CHAPTER 75

As Raven flew over the Catholic Church, he spotted Dark Soul and the Indian sitting in a human vehicle. Their presence was curious enough to hold his interest, so he roosted in a tree and took up watch.

Later, when the men finally drove off, Raven flew onto the roof of the house. He waited for a long while but no one came out. With his curiosity unsatisfied, Raven eventually left to join the Road Kill mob in a large pine they had chosen for the night.

Raven returned the following morning. As a weak winter sun peeked over the southeast horizon his curiosity was rewarded. Three men came out and walked toward a white vehicle parked on the street.

Raven launched into flight and landed at the edge of the yard. They ignored him as they passed. He expected this. It was only children who usually recognized the arrival of a bird.

One of the strangers was of the new breed, but his aura was the darkest of blues, moving tight against his body with bits of scabby brown embedded in the matrix—looking very much like dead leaves in oily water swirling down a gutter. Raven's name for this newcomer came easy.

Evil Soul.

There was a white wrap on one of Evil Soul's hands. A heavy bandage covered the skin from the knuckles all the way back to his wrist. There was also a smell, easily detectable to Raven's sharp olfactory sense. It was not a smell unique to humans. All flesh gave off this odor when it came too close to fire.

CHAPTER 76

Burnt flesh.

As Father Clark drove his two distinguished visitors away from the rectory, he couldn't shake the image of what had occurred last night.

Umberto began to shiver as soon as they entered the kitchen. He stood mute beside Father Tom as the bishop twisted the dial to *Hi* on the electric range, and then stood the relic with the "C" resting on the black spiral of the stove element.

After two minutes the element was glowing orange. The bishop turned to Father Tom. "Do you have a hot pad?" he asked with chilling calm.

Father Tom went to a drawer and nervously grabbed a quilted pad with the words "JESUS CARES" embroidered in blue on creamy fabric. He handed it to Assante, who folded it in half and then used it to grab the wooden knob.

"The time has come, Umberto. Are you prepared?"

Umberto reluctantly unbuttoned the right cuff of his long-sleeved shirt and rolled it back to his elbow. He moved to the counter and laid his hand palm downwards on the tile, nervously glancing at the bishop before closing his eyes. "I'm ready, Your Excellency," he said stiffly.

Assante moved quickly, pressing the hot metal to the back of Umberto's hand. It sounded like hamburger slapped on a BBQ grill. Umberto's face twisted in a grimace of pain, but he somehow kept from shouting out.

Father Tom was instantly nauseous. He'd expected the branding to be a light touch, not this crippling assault. The torture seemed to go on forever, and he finally shouted, "That is enough!"

The bishop lifted the hot metal from Umberto's hand to reveal a searing wound almost to the bone. Blood was oozing from the circle of curdled flesh.

"My God!" Father Tom said, lunging to turn on the cold water in the sink. He then gently took hold of Umberto's arm and thrust the burned hand beneath the steady stream. "Hold it there," he said, in a voice that sounded much kinder than were his thoughts. "I'll go and get bandages and some antibiotic cream." He glanced at the bishop with such ferocity that Assante thought the priest might strike him. Instead, Father Tom hurried off to the bathroom for the medical supplies.

When he came back, he didn't trust himself speaking to the bishop without unleashing a flurry of obscenities. So as soon as he'd doctored the damaged hand, he poured Umberto a double shot of Scotch, and then politely said "Goodnight" and went upstairs immediately to his bedroom, where he knelt on the floor and prayed, asking the Lord for forgiveness for having taken part in such a barbaric act. He then collapsed into bed, emotionally exhausted.

At breakfast, Umberto said he felt much better. But his face was pale and his eyes were reddened.

There was something else that made Father Tom's morning a personal torment. On the drive to the airport, his thoughts kept returning to a confession made by one of his parishioners, Ernesto Hernandez, many days ago, during which he'd called a local orphaned teenager a witch. "That Nina is a caster of spells, Father. I witnessed her placing a curse on my son. She is the devil's spawn!"

Is this the girl from Umberto's vision?

If Assante was willing to sear the hand of a true believer, what might his intentions be for dealing with a witch? Father Tom shuddered at the thought.

By the time they pulled into Pangborn Airport's civil aviation lot, Father Tom was repeating a silent prayer, over and over: *Please*

Father, help me with this burden. Let those in Rome find a way of dealing with this without involving me further.

The bishop was upbeat as he and Father Tom walked across the windswept tarmac to the jet. "It should only be a month or two before I call you to report on what has happened with Umberto's hand." He paused at the base of the stairs. Umberto was already onboard. The Gulfstream's engines were whining in the cold morning air. The captain now appeared at the open hatch.

The bishop waved that he was coming, before turning to Father Tom to give one final warning. "Remember that you are to tell no one of this."

He offered a final smile as he turned away from the priest to climb the steps. But Assante was worried. Father Tom's reaction had been more negative than he'd expected. If he were pushed too hard, Assante thought it possible he might even involve the police.

Perhaps he was not a good choice?

But that decision was best left to Umberto. The disciple would know the proper course to take if the priest became a problem.

CHAPTER 77

The couches in the family room were shoved up against the walls and the curtains on the French doors drawn shut. Seven chairs formed a circle.

When Clarissa and Charlie arrived, just after dark, Frank asked Nina to step out of the room with him for a moment.

Once they were in the spare bedroom, and with the door closed, he said, "Are you still certain you want Chantha to participate?"

"Yes," Nina replied firmly. "Like I already said, this is going to affect her, and she deserves to know what's going on."

Frank didn't mince words.

"I will do everything in my power to protect Chantha. It was never a part of the bargain that she would be involved in something like this. It's not fair to you either, but you have no choice."

Nina protested, "Don't you think she'll be safer if she knows everything? And remember, she's not like me. She doesn't radiate this resonance thing, so it's like she's invisible to *them*."

Frank realized she'd missed something, and here was where experience in life did count for more than Nina's awesome potential.

"By *them* I presume you mean members of the Order. But this time they could send someone who doesn't have resonance. If it's people like the Mafia, kidnapping Chantha might be the easiest bargaining chip to exchange for you."

Nina realized Frank was right. And it reinforced a decision she'd already made.

I have to leave.

They returned to the family room and took seats with the others in the circle. Frank got things started with, "Let's begin with a report from Charlie."

Charlie coughed lightly, looking from face to face.

"After we put Valerie on the jet to San Jose, we saw one of the Order's Gulfstreams arrive. We hid out in the main terminal parking lot about fifty yards off the exit road. When the SUV passed, Gunther recognized Umberto. The driver was the local Catholic priest. There was another man with them."

Clarissa asked, "What did he look like?"

"White hair, in his late sixties or early seventies."

"Then he's not a member," Clarissa said with relief. She nodded for Charlie to continue.

"The SUV wound up here in Langston, parked in the rectory's driveway."

"And this morning?"

"Gunther waited in his pickup near the rectory, while I drove to the airport."

He nodded to Gunther, who continued with, "They came out shortly after dawn, and I got pictures of all three." He sounded proud.

Clarissa begrudgingly gave him a smile.

Charlie wrapped up with, "The priest walked Umberto and the old guy out to the jet shortly before noon."

Frank said, "So what now?"

Everyone looked to Clarissa.

"Umberto has obviously chosen to recruit the priest. He might be used to get local help, or simply to act as a spy. My bet is the latter. They may fly agents in from Europe for the actual kidnapping attempt. If we knew who that third man was it would be helpful." She turned to Charlie. "Can you email Gunther's photo of him to Valerie? Ask her to try and match his face with a name. Also ask her to check the flight records for the Gulfstream. If it came from Rome, it's likely he's with the Catholic Church."

"Will do," Charlie said. And then he switched gears. "I think we need to set up a better line of defense. I'd like to begin by moving Gunther closer to Nina. He's not much use to us where he's at now."

269

Gunther looked pleased.

Charlie turned to Frank. "Are there any vacant houses nearby?"

"I can check. But I'm not sure anyone would be willing to rent on a short-term basis. It's a fairly exclusive neighborhood."

"Frank," Anna said hopefully, "We've got an extra bedroom. What do you think?"

Frank had already considered the possibility. But things were complicated enough without bringing the German into his home. Now that Anna had offered, he didn't particularly want to alienate Gunther. Especially since Nina had taken such a liking to him. He turned to Clarissa. "What do you think?" he asked, hoping she still distrusted Gunther enough to nix the idea.

Her answer came as a surprise. "I think it's an excellent idea."

Upon hearing this, Nina smiled for the first time that evening.

CHAPTER 78

When the family meeting ended, the real meeting finally took place. With the door to Frank's home office closed, Nina and Clarissa sat facing each other, and for one very nervous moment neither looked at the other. And then Clarissa opened with, "What would you like to know about your mother?"

"What was she like?"

"A lot like you," Clarissa said, remembering the precious few minutes she had spent with Betty Haas in the mall. "You have her light brown eyes. Her hair was the same brown as yours, but she wore it longer, almost to her shoulders. It held a lot of curl, and yours is nearly straight. How tall are you now?"

"Five foot nine."

"Your mother was about three inches taller."

"What else?"

"Her voice was pitched lower, but I think that's just because she was older. I think you'll end up sounding much like her."

"Did she say anything about my father?"

"She mentioned you were with him that afternoon."

"Is that all?"

"I'm afraid so."

"Where did you first meet my mom?"

"In a mall."

"Like . . . a shopping mall?"

"Yes," Clarissa said evenly. "That's where we bumped into each other."

And now came the big question.

"So how was it that you met my mom out of all the people who were there that day?"

And here it was. Clarissa knew there was no avoiding the truth. "I think you may have already guessed what drew me to your mother."

Nina's heart was beating fast. "Do you mean she was one of *us*?"

"Yes. Your mother had resonance. There was no mistaking that she was a member of the Order."

"Did she know?"

"No."

"Why didn't you tell her?" There was a hint of anger in Nina's voice.

Clarissa defended with a logic that centuries of experience had taught.

"Your mother was only twenty-six. We've always tried to wait until new members are at least forty before we approach them. Not aging in a normal way makes it easier for someone to believe, and to accept the reality of what their future will hold."

Nina's head tilted forward; eyes momentarily unfocused. When she came back, her questions were rapid fire, and the anger was now real.

"When would you have told her?"

"When she was ready."

"And when would that have been?"

"I would have waited at least a few years."

It seemed completely unfair that her mom had possessed such an enormous gift, and had zero chance to learn of its existence. If she'd been told, she might have been more careful. She might still be alive today.

There was something else that made Nina angry, and now seemed the right time to bring it up.

"Do you still want to groom me to tell the world about the Order?"

"Is that what Gunther told you?"

"Yes."

"The answer to your question is . . . no."

This caught Nina by surprise. Other questions she had intended to ask suddenly became irrelevant. She paused, collected her thoughts,

272

and in a puzzled voice asked, "Are *you* planning to tell the world about the Order?"

"I once thought I might do that, because I once thought that was the right thing to do."

"But you don't think that way now?"

"Something changed my mind."

"What?"

This was the final threshold. Clarissa would now learn whether or not what she wanted to do was even possible.

"It was *you* who changed my mind, Nina."

"Me?"

"Your mother was very special, and by 'special' I mean special *like me*. She had the potential to have all of the abilities, and that only happens once in a very great while. I felt I at least owed it to her to ensure that you were looked after. I hired a private investigator, and he found your foster home. Frankly, I didn't expect anything other than a normal baby. But when I drove by the house, and I felt your resonance coming from inside, I *knew*."

"You knew what?"

"I knew that a child who was a member had been born to someone who was also a member."

"And?"

"You are the first," Clarissa said.

As the reality sank in, Nina cautiously asked, "Does this mean that my children will also be members?"

"The odds are high."

"How high?"

"I'm as certain as I can be that your children will be the same as you and your mother."

Nina rocked back in her chair.

Clarissa brought the point home, needing to know that Nina fully appreciated the consequences.

"Nina . . . do you know what anthropologists think drove the Neanderthal people into extinction?"

Nina remembered watching a National Geographic special on modern man that told the story of the evolution of mankind and all of the earlier species that preceded homo sapiens. "Wasn't it modern humans? Didn't we just out-compete them?"

"Yes. And in the same way, your descendants may replace the current human race. This would present an enormous threat if the normal population found out."

Nina's eyes and the firm set of her mouth said she understood.

Clarissa plunged on.

"When people discover what you truly are, they will fear you. We can't let them know until you are ready to defend yourself. I'm hoping to take you some place where no one can find you, at least for a few more years."

"Where would that be?"

"Spain."

"Why Spain?"

"Do you remember when I got stranded in Europe?"

Nina nodded.

"I went to the Basque Country to see if I could find the only person who has ever successfully avoided the Order. I'd hoped she might help me make you disappear. Instead, I was captured and held prisoner."

"How did you escape?"

"I didn't. One of her people contacted a woman from the Order, who is a close friend of mine, and after several weeks she came and picked me up. Livia has recently contacted my friend again to set up a meeting. I'm hoping she is going to offer to take you in."

"Do you trust her?"

"I don't think we have much choice."

To Nina it seemed like there was plenty of choice.

"What does Charlie think about me going to Spain?"

This question opened a door for Clarissa. Something she hadn't quite known how to approach. And here was an opportunity.

"He'll go along with whatever I want."

"Why?"

"Because I've told him that I don't have long to live."

Deceiving Charlie seemed totally wrong, and once again Nina found herself growing angry.

"Don't you think that's being unfair to Charlie?"

"Nina . . . it's not about what is *fair*. None of this is *fair*. It just *is*."

Nina suddenly remembered that members couldn't lie to each other.

"Are you really sick?"

Clarissa tried to explain something she still didn't fully understand.

"I ache in my joints, and I have bad headaches. I sometimes have a shooting pain in my left arm. It's not an option for me to go to a doctor for tests. If I could consult with one of our members who knows about plants and their healing properties, I could probably get some form of treatment, but that's not available at this point."

And this is the real reason I need Livia. I can't pursue my original plan to use Nina as a bridge to scientists and government leaders, because I might not have enough time left to see it through. She's too young to trust her being able to do it on her own. But I can't come out and tell her this. Not yet.

Nina leaned forward in her chair; her face filled with sudden concern. "What are you going to do?"

"There may be nothing I can do about my own condition. But it shouldn't prevent me from trying to get you to a safe place until you're ready to make your own choices."

CHAPTER 79

The Banhofstrasse cut through the heart of Zurich's economic and shopping district, paralleling the Limmat River as it flowed between steep concrete-and-stone walls. This wide boulevard was now decorated for the winter holiday season, with a splendor to rival New York's Fifth Avenue, Rome's Via Veneto, the Champs-Élysées in Paris, and Oxford Street in London.

Christmas trees were wedged in everywhere, bedecked with tinsel and colored bulbs, and ornaments of every imaginable kind—some dazzling with gold and silver; others in old-fashioned painted-wood simplicity. For the length of one block, hundreds of light globes hung like giant strands of pearls. The patisserie shop windows were loaded with honey cakes and chocolate truffles, éclairs and strudel, hard candy and Luxemburgerli macaroons.

The outdoor Christmas Market at the far end of the street was crowded with shoppers dressed in wool coats and ski jackets, wearing scarves and knit caps pulled tight against the frigid air, jostling for bargains on tables set out by day-vendors.

Trisha wasn't in a holiday mood as she exited the main train station. With only a few blocks to go, on a clear day she might have chosen to walk and enjoy the festive atmosphere. But light snow was drifting down, making the sidewalks treacherous. A wind swirled amongst the buildings, lifting powdery gusts that stung her face until she was able to climb aboard one of the blue-and-white trams.

Half a year had passed since the aborted kidnapping. Her Council colleagues had reassured her that it wasn't her fault, saying her plan had been good; that she couldn't have possibly foreseen Gunther switching sides. But despite the support she received, Trisha still felt mortally embarrassed. She was determined to do whatever possible to atone and make things right. Even if it meant working with someone who made her feel *unclean* each time they met. But the Council had entrusted a sleazebag with the task of capturing the girl, and so it was to Umberto whom Trisha now reported.

The exclusive club where the meeting would take place was tucked away on a side street. She exited the tram after seven blocks, turned right at the corner, and walked twenty yards down the snowy sidewalk before pushing through a heavy wooden door that opened into a small reception room.

The doorman, dressed entirely in black except for a white bow tie, met her with a polite "Bitte?"

"Trisha," she replied. "I'm here for a meeting."

He gave a brief smile of understanding, and immediately escorted her down a softly lit wood-paneled hallway to a private dining room.

When she entered, she found Pieter Silberhof sitting at a table with Umberto, each with a half-drunk glass of red wine.

"Greetings," Umberto said, gesturing toward an empty third chair, with no apparent interest in rising.

Pieter immediately stood and pulled back the chair to seat her. As he eased the chair up behind her, and then retook his own seat, Umberto reached for an empty wine glass, lifted a bottle of Lafite Rothschild, and began to pour. She watched the deep ruby liquid splash into the cut-crystal glass.

Umberto said in a mocking tone, "I hope it wasn't too much of an inconvenience coming here today?" He set the bottle down and then shoved the glass toward her across the white linen tablecloth.

She lifted the glass, ignoring him for a moment, pretending to study the fractured light in the crystal. "Why would it be an inconvenience?" she said, taking a sip of what turned out to be a truly outstanding vintage. She took two more appreciative sips before setting the glass down.

"Well, the shoppers. The snow. And it's quite cold."

"I managed," Trisha said, tempted to say she wasn't a fragile flower. She held her temper in check, returning a bland look.

"Good," he said, obviously not caring how she felt. "I hope you don't mind that I invited Pieter to our meeting?"

"If you thought it was necessary, I'm sure you had good reason." She gave the briefest of smiles to the Austrian.

Pieter's mouth briefly formed a little "O" of approval.

Trisha's eyes returned to Umberto, and for the first time she noticed the back of his hand. The skin was badly mottled from a burn.

Umberto grinned and said, "An injury in the kitchen a few days ago, but as you can see it's healing nicely. Another few weeks and you'd never notice."

Both men laughed.

Trisha knew the joke. Members always healed, and never with residual scarring. If you saw a member who'd been recently injury, the standard line went something like, "Oh, that looks horrible! How will you ever live with it?" Followed, of course, by laughter.

Trisha gave a polite chuckle, while contemplatively tracing the rim of her wine glass with one finger. "What do you have in mind?"

"We will again use a warrior when we go for the girl," Umberto said. "Do you have any objection to Pieter?"

Trisha shot a hard look at the Austrian, as if to remind him that it was he who had sabotaged her effort to capture the girl. "Only if he agrees to let us know everything he's doing."

Pieter was about to protest, but Umberto held up a hand to cut him off. "He has given me every assurance that he will follow my directions to the letter, and that there will be no independent decision making. Isn't that right, Pieter?"

"Absolutely," Pieter said, defensively. "I understand you being upset with me, Trisha, and you have every right to be. My fault was in trusting Gunther. But I'm certain it will go better this time around." As if in apology, he reached for the wine bottle and added a bit of wine to her glass.

She managed a smile. Not a *bright and happy* smile, but a smile nonetheless.

"Good," Umberto said. "Now that you two have made up, let me tell you what I've got planned."

By the time he was finished, Trisha had concerns. The plan depended upon a priest being able to recruit normals. Time was another problem. It would be weeks before Umberto could return to show the priest that his wound had fully healed. Then, if the priest agreed to cooperate, it would require more work in Langston before they were ready.

Her greatest concern was that Umberto was enjoying the intricacy of his scheme far too much. *He fancies himself a showman, and he's relishing the staging of a performance. But this isn't Broadway. And we are not putting on a play.*

Both men were watching to see how she might react. *They are such incredible jerks!* But her only option was to join the circus, or leave. Trisha desperately wanted to prove herself a team player. It was time to suck up her pride.

And if Umberto fell short?

Then my failure may not look so awful.

"Okay," she said.

"Good!" Umberto beamed a triumphant grin.

"I'm hungry," Pieter said, relieved that the confrontational part of the meeting was done. "Let's order some food!"

CHAPTER 80

With the Road Kill conspiracy now encamped for winter along the Columbia River, Raven's flight up to the lake was a challenge even on the best of mornings. The princess still needed him, so each day Raven came, even if snow was falling and the wind was howling.

In the earlier seasons of his life, he hadn't discovered a single human whose aura wasn't some shade of red. Now he'd encountered five whose auras centered around the color blue. The princess, of course, with her beautiful blue tornado of light. The ancient woman, whose aura was a deep blue shading toward lavender—colors not so different from the iridescent sheen on Raven's own feathers. The man with a ponytail, whom Raven recognized as a member of the tribe that had lived here for many thousands of seasons, who sported an aura of purplish blue. Dark Soul's solid midnight blue. And just a few days ago the new man, *Evil Soul*, had arrived, radiating an aura the color of a blue-blackened scab.

Humans had at some distant time in the past lived in harmony with other life on the planet, but they had recently become detached. This had spawned a reckless disregard not just for other animals, but for plants, air, even the soil upon which they walked. They also fought amongst themselves, and not just to secure food, territory, or breeding rights. Too often the violence seemed purely for entertainment. In Raven's world such an animal would have been rapidly culled out by the others.

Since the rescue of the boy, Raven hadn't allowed the princess to reenter his mind. She had made many attempts, often closing her eyes and concentrating when he came for his morning treat, but he had blocked her thoughts. She certainly possessed the potential to bridge between the species. But without a teacher on the animal side there was no way for her to learn how to make the cross over.

Raven knew the time for that crucial lesson was drawing near.

CHAPTER 81

Father Tom was a worried man. Despite the Christmas season, when gifts of food—including homemade cookies, cakes and candy—were regularly left at the parsonage, he'd lost weight. On this first morning of the New Year, he stood on the bathroom scale and watched the number *167* appear in red numerals. It had read *183* on the day of Assante's and Umberto's arrival.

He ambled into the bedroom, pulled on a pair of slacks, and found it necessary to cinch his belt two extra notches. Staring into the mirror above the chest of drawers he saw dark circles under his eyes, hollowed cheeks, parchment skin. *I look like I've been in chemotherapy.*

And then there were the nightmares.

In one dream he saw the Italian carpenter's hand being seared by the relic, the hot iron melting through delicate bones as if they were wax, steam hissing from the wound, the stench of burning flesh.

In another dream the girl stood before him. For a moment she was beautiful. But then she suddenly morphed into a Gorgon, with writhing snakes for hair and black eyes that drew him down into the depths of Hell.

He would awake screaming, bed sheets soaked with sweat.

Falling asleep again often proved impossible. He would rise from his single bed and ramble around the house, wearing only boxer shorts, nursing a glass of Scotch in the hope it would dull the terror and help him find rest. But even if he did manage to fall back asleep after knocking back a couple of stiff shots, the dreams were relentlessly waiting.

Another problem loomed. The bishop and the carpenter might return at any time. And if Umberto's hand was perfectly healed? Father Tom knew he would then be expected to cooperate in some kind of action against the girl.

Father Tom was now certain he knew who she was. It could only be the one who had supposedly placed the curse upon Benny. Selena often mentioned this girl during weekly confessions, pleading for help to find some way to forgive her former best friend. Reporting—often in tears—that she was pressured by her parents to not give in to the temptation to make contact. Father Tom winced every time he heard this through the confessional screen.

And finally, there was the ideological dilemma.

Thomas Clark had grown up in the 70s and 80s. His seminary training began in 1994, and followed the new way of thinking. God was an infinite being, filled with compassion and understanding. The Old Testament's fire-and-brimstone missed the mark. All that was necessary for salvation was to recognize the Lord as your savior and to ask for His forgiveness.

An Umberto miracle would challenge that basic premise. If miracles could be directly observed, then God stopped being an abstract force. He instead became a God who got down to the bone. A God who personally recruited zealots for the war against evil.

This would mean the devil was real, which was a concept that Father Tom had never fully bought into. In this new miracle world, there would be an active devil who possessed people and made them do bad things. Father Tom didn't like that picture. Not one bit. Because it would shatter the way he looked at his fellow man. It would force him to begin to judge each person. To weigh whether or not someone who acted less than perfect had been corrupted by evil. And from Father Tom's observations of his fellow man, there were precious few truly decent people walking around.

It would also force an uncomfortable realization. If his entire understanding of God had been essentially flawed, then how unhappy might God presently be with Father Thomas Clark?

CHAPTER 82

On the last Sunday of the Christmas break, Nina went to Chantha's bedroom and closed the door.

"I'm leaving," she declared.

Chantha's eyes went wide.

"You have to keep it a secret," Nina insisted, grasping one hand and pulling her down to sit beside her on the bed. "No one knows about this except Gunther."

"Aren't you safe with him staying here in the house?"

"It's not about me. As long as the Order knows where to look for me, I'm putting all of you at risk."

"But we all agreed to take that risk. Isn't that our right?"

"Don't I also have the right to make a choice? Can't I decide to do something to protect all of you?" Still holding Chantha's hand, she gave a reassuring squeeze. "I'll be alright. Gunther won't let anything bad happen to me. And even if the Order catches up to us, Clarissa says there's no way they would ever hurt me. It's against their rules."

Chantha wasn't thinking about rules. She was thinking about how kids at school shunned her just as much as they did Nina. She pictured herself roaming the hallways and everyone turning away.

"What am I going to do without you? Nobody talks to me anymore. I'll be totally alone!"

"No," Nina insisted, squeezing Chantha's hand again, feeling the warmth of her skin. Sensing the pain. Determined to resist the urge to try and reach out with her mind and somehow make it all better.

"Once I'm gone, lots of kids will want to be your friend again. It's me they have a problem with, not you."

This logic failed to hold back Chantha's tears. Nina held her as the sobs came, still certain that most of the kids at school would come around.

But maybe not the two football jocks. I'll have to do something about them before I leave.

When the crying ended, Nina led Chantha to the bathroom, and with a wet washcloth did her best to wipe away the evidence that something had gone terribly wrong.

CHAPTER 83

When Liesel entered the atrium of the Order's Zurich headquarters on the fifth of January, one of the two guards, in a navy-blue suit with a slight-but-obvious bulge beneath his jacket, said in a polite voice, "Ms. Hartkorn?"

Before she could respond, he handed her a white envelope which bore her initials—*L.H.*—in flowing script. There was no return address. The guard nodded politely, and immediately returned his attention to the front door.

The fine linen paper and the handwriting were the same as on the envelope she had received back in August, summoning her to Zizurkil to pick up Clarissa. Upon being handed that earlier note, she had quizzed the guard on how it arrived.

"By bicycle messenger."

"And how did you know it was intended for me?"

"He gave a brief description of you."

It had been profoundly disturbing to learn that a bicycle messenger knew what she looked like.

Liesel left the atrium, passed through the first security door, and climbed to the top of the first flight of steps. Unable to wait any longer, she tore open the envelope and pulled out a single sheet of paper. The black ink looked as if it might have come from a quill pen. As with the earlier note, the words were minimal. But this time there was a name to confirm the source.

January 15, 2pm, Caen, Le Bouchon du Vaugueux. Come alone and tell no one. Livia.

She climbed the last two flights, clutching the note in her hand. Once inside the boardroom she laid the invitation on the conference table and stared at it.

Why Caen, rather than Spain?

The French town on the Normandy coast seemed a long way from where Livia presumably lived in Basque Country.

Is it because she wants to meet me on neutral ground?

Liesel remembered what Clarissa had told her many years ago, about a meeting she'd had with Livia toward the end of the second century.

"She said she wasn't a part of our club, and felt no obligation not to harm me."

Liesel walked to the back of the room where the historical volumes were kept, curious if there might be more information in Clarissa's entry about that early encounter.

Members had long debated the wisdom of keeping a written history. The volumes lining the back wall formed a virtual encyclopedia of everything pertaining to the Order. As such, they presented a potential threat to the Order's cherished secrecy. Custom had so far prevailed, and the volumes survived.

There were vast differences between the eighteen earliest volumes and the newer ones. The two oldest volumes dated from the time before Christ and were written in Greek on papyrus, loosely bound by thin cords of goat leather. The next sixteen were written in Latin on velum, covering the time period from Christ's crucifixion up until 700 AD.

All eighteen early volumes were preserved in a hermetically sealed glass case which required a fingerprint scan to gain access. Liesel pressed her right thumb to the small reader pad and heard a click, then a slight hiss.

The volumes inside the case were numbered "I" to "XVIII. She withdrew volume IV, which covered the last half of the second century.

Like most members of the Order, she was fluent in Latin. Carefully leafing through the loosely bound pages she found the entry. It was

287

dated in the system used during Roman times: *In the third year of the emperor Severus.* In modern terms that translated to 195 AD.

In my search for Livia, I journeyed to northern Spain to the Roman province of Varduli, a place inhabited by a people who call themselves the Euskaldunak.

Livia seems to have a favorable relationship with locals, as my inquiries were met by either denial of any knowledge about the woman, or anger and outright warnings to leave before it was too late.

We finally met in a field on the outskirts of a small settlement the locals call Zizurkil, a few miles up from the coast. There was no mistaking the strong resonance that identified her as one of the rare ones who hold all of the powers.

She is a beautiful woman with dark eyes and chestnut brown hair, straight white teeth, full lips, a feminine figure, slightly less than six feet in height.

My encounter was brief, due to her hostility, culminating in an attack against me by three armed native men who appeared to be fully under her command.

Liesel closed the volume and carefully slid it back onto the shelf, easing the door shut and pressing her thumb to the lock. A slight hiss confirmed it had sealed. The sound of a compressor motor assured that argon gas was being replenished inside the case.

She walked back to the table and sank onto one of the comfortable leather chairs. Staring out the window, she saw that fat snowflakes were beginning to stick to the red-tiled rooftops of Old Town.

CHAPTER 84

Chantha was right about being isolated. When school started up again in early January, kids in the hallways looked the other way as they passed. It was no better in the classroom. Like when Nina raised her hand in second period English, after Mr. Preston asked who knew the major forms of Shakespeare's plays. He called on a boy up front, who said, "Comedies." A girl in the fourth row added, "Tragedies." But Nina's hand was still up in the air when Mr. Preston said, "Well, I guess no one remembers that *histories* was his third form."

Slowly her hand came down.

On Tuesday she found Chantha standing in line at the cafeteria. She cut in to join her, which drew sharp looks from kids directly behind, but just as quickly the kids turned their heads away.

Even the server ladies refused to make eye contact as they spooned out tuna casserole, steamed green beans, and mashed potatoes.

They found an empty table, and as soon as they sat down, three kids at the next table got up and took their trays to the other side of the cafeteria.

"This is ridiculous," Nina said, stirring a mound of tuna casserole with her fork, surveying the room, hoping to see someone—anyone—looking back. Her stare was finally returned, though it wasn't what she'd hoped for.

Across the room, John Bradley was glaring at her as if he'd just spotted a plague victim.

"Oh great," Nina sighed. "Our star quarterback has taken a fresh interest in making my life miserable."

Chantha followed Nina's gaze. When John saw her looking in his direction, he slowly shook his head in contempt.

Seeing this, Nina pushed back her chair. "This is going to end," she said, standing up.

"No, Nina, don't!" Chantha pleaded, reaching to grab her arm. "You'll only make things worse. And then we'll have open warfare and you'll get suspended and I'll be here all alone."

Nina stared at John. He glared back. Chantha began tugging at her shirt, trying to get her to sit back down.

"Okay," Nina said, collapsing onto her chair. She lifted her fork and angrily speared a chunk of tuna, twisting noodles around it before lifting it to her mouth. But before she put it in, she said, "This is going to end."

"What do you mean?"

"I'm not sure," Nina said. "But I'll think of something."

"There's nothing you could do that wouldn't just make it worse. Please let it go. Please!"

But Nina couldn't let it go. She felt John's eyes on her for the rest of lunch. It took a supreme effort not to stare back.

When she and Chantha got up to leave, she didn't see John and Josh also get up. It wasn't until they reached their lockers—in a hallway that was nearly empty—that the two jocks suddenly appeared, walking purposefully in their direction. When Chantha saw them coming she turned to Nina and said in an urgent voice, "Please don't say anything!"

"What was that?" Josh asked, close enough to have overheard.

Nina stepped in between the boys and Chantha. "Nothing," she said, as Josh and John came to a stop.

"Didn't sound like nothin' to me," Josh said, mocking. "It sounded to me like little miss prissy was telling her girlie friend to keep her mouth shut." He looked to John for support. "Sounds like good advice to me. What do you think, John-o?"

"Definitely good advice," John agreed.

Nina felt a tingle deep in her gut.

"You both think you're pretty important, don't you?" Nina said, trying to push the tingling away. *I can't. Not here in the hallway.*

The boys edged closer.

John sneered, "We're a heckuva lot more important than you'll ever be."

The tingle became a throb. "Want to make a bet?" Nina felt herself beginning to lose control.

"Why bother?" Josh said dismissively. "You'd lose a hundred percent of the time."

At that moment a small miracle happened. Arnold Nott appeared at the end of the hallway, and saw what was going down. The clicking of his Oxford wingtips picked up speed.

"Nina," Chantha whispered, nodding down the hallway at the math teacher, now swiftly approaching.

Nina glanced at Nott, and then looked back to John and Josh, and in a soft but fierce voice said, "Meet me outside the library after the fifth period buzzer. That is, if you've got the guts." She turned away from the boys, and reached into her locker to grab a book.

"What's going on here?" Arnold Nott demanded as he practically slid to a stop.

"Nothin' Mr. Nott" John said, with a grin.

"Yeah," Josh added. "We were just trying to be friendly, since they don't seem to have many friends these days."

Nott groaned in pure frustration. "Let's just move along, guys. Okay?"

"Sure," John and Josh said together.

"No problem-o, Mr. Nott," Josh added confidently.

They walked off in the direction Nott had just come from.

He almost turned to follow, thought better of being openly rude, and said to Chantha, "Is everything okay?"

"Yes," Chantha said, trying not to sound as upset as she felt.

"Nina? You okay too?"

"Sure," Nina said, totally defiant. "No problem-o."

Arnold Nott thought of several things he might say, decided none of them would do any good, and hurried off down the hallway.

Chantha turned to Nina. "What on earth were you thinking?"

"Mr. Nott isn't going to do anything to us."

"Not *him*. I meant what you said to the boys!"

291

"Don't worry. I won't get in a fight."

"Nina! Please!"

"I won't get in a fight," Nina insisted.

Kids with curious faces were now drifting down the hallway. Word had gotten around about the confrontation between the "problem girls" and the school's star athletes.

Chantha felt desperate. "We need to talk."

"Okay," Nina said. But her mind was made up. She would now deal with John and Josh on her own terms. And she didn't intend for it to be pretty.

CHAPTER 85

An email to Valerie from San Jose signaled the beginning of the end for any peace of mind she might have hoped for.

Valerie, a miracle has happened! Tommy's white blood cell count has come up, he's got more energy, his doctor says there's real hope. I cannot put into words how much this means to me, to our family. I am in your debt forever! Mitch.

She was happy for a moment. Happy for Mitch. For the boy's father. And especially for the kid.

Then came an ugly thought.

A failure would have dulled Angela Cornish's interest in Order blood.

The euphoria vanished with a cruel realization.

Am I really that shallow?

And from the core of her gut, the answer was . . .*Yes, I am.*

The phone calls from Mitch began later that morning. Valerie told Tina to say she was extremely busy and that it would be a while before she could get back to him. But after the fourth call, she realized he wasn't going to go away. She begrudgingly took the fifth call.

In a busy voice she said, "Hi Mitch," hoping he'd take the hint she didn't want to talk.

"Did you get my email?"

"Yes. I'm happy for you."

Mitch seemed oblivious to her hint.

"I can't even begin to tell you how much we appreciate what you've done."

The word "we" was more than a little bothersome. Valerie knew it was futile to hope that "we" meant only Mitch and Art. There was also an eight-year-old boy who could have easily told his mom about the magical transfusion. And Dr. Cornish was almost certainly on the "we" list. Who else might there now be at Stanford? Fear began to bubble to the surface.

"Look, Mitch. I'm really busy right now. I appreciate you letting me know your grandson is better. I'm happy for you. But if that's all . . ."

"Well . . ." Mitch countered, sounding nervous.

Valerie knew something was wrong. "What's the problem, Mitch?"

"It's just that Dr. Cornish wanted to do some follow up—"

"Mitch!"

She had screamed, and now took a deep breath, fighting for composure. Still at a forceful volume, she said, "That was a one time thing, Mitch. We agreed to that, didn't we?"

"Yes, but—"

"There are no 'buts' in this. You promised, and I will hold you to that promise. Even if it means . . ." She had almost said *Even if it means I have to close up shop and move to some place where they'll never find me.* But that would have been a mistake. If she was going to leave, it was best not to let *them* know she was going. Valerie chose her next words carefully.

"Even if it means I never speak to you again. And I'd hate for that to happen. You've been a great sounding board over the years and I value our friendship. So can't we please just put it to rest?"

"Forgive me." Mitch sounded embarrassed. "I'm sorry. If it were just me, I'd never bring it up again."

Valerie knew there was more. "But?" she prompted.

"I'm not certain Angela Cornish is going to go away so easily."

"Do I have a problem?" She was now angry.

Mitch heard it, and backpedaled.

"I don't know. Maybe. Probably. She wanted me to set up a meeting with you. I told her no. I'm worried for you, Valerie."

The ensuing silence felt like a guillotine blade being hoisted up a scaffold. Mitch had tried to protect her and he had failed miserably, from the tone of his voice.

It's me who made the decision to get the blood. I knew the risks. Now I'm the one who'll pay the price.

"Okay," Valerie said. "If she contacts me, I'll make it clear I won't cooperate. What can she do? There's no law that says I have to give her blood."

"I agree. And if there's anything you need me to do, I'll do whatever I can to keep her off your back." But Mitch didn't sound hopeful.

"Thanks," Valerie said, stabbing to disconnect the call.

Two hours later, Tina buzzed. Valerie was working at the stand-up desk. She pushed the intercom button without looking away from the computer screen.

"Yes?"

"There's a Doctor Angela Cornish here to see you. She doesn't have an appointment, but she says it's urgent."

Valerie stood rigid, with one thought. *Why didn't I tell Tina to say I'm unavailable?*

"Ms. Lee?" Tina sounded nervous.

Valerie realized the doctor needed a message set in cement, face to face.

"Please show her in, Tina."

When the door opened, Angela Cornish immediately began to apologize.

"I'm sorry to come without first setting up a meeting. I was worried you wouldn't agree, and we definitely need to talk." She took a step toward the chairs around the Ming table.

"Don't bother," Valerie said coldly. "You won't be here that long."

Angela froze. Valerie took steps until they were face to face.

"I'll be perfectly clear so that you will never again feel the urge to come to my office, or to attempt any kind of contact with me ever again. What I did, I did for Mitch and his grandson. If I had known you would be showing up here, even if it was just to congratulate me upon being a wonderful human being, I would have let that little boy die. If you think that makes me a horrible person, then get it through your thick head that I can be a horrible person without a scintilla of regret."

"But—"

"Did I say you could talk?"

"No."

"Then we have a complete understanding. And now you will turn around and walk out that door and never return here again. Understood?"

"I'll leave. But on one condition."

"I don't accept conditions, and you have no right to set any." Valerie's pulse throbbed in her temples.

"It's a simple one," Angela countered, refusing to back down.

Valerie sensed fear not so deep beneath the surface. She studied Angela's face for a moment, and then said, "Alright. Spit it out."

"We isolated and sequenced the new blood. There doesn't appear to be anything unusual in the genome. What was unusual were the T-cells being present in such a large number. If we could learn how an adult's body generates so many restorative cells it could make an enormous difference in medicine. We might save millions of lives." She sounded enraptured, as if by a new religion.

Any remaining shred of patience now vanished. Particularly after Angela's repeated use of the word "we."

"That source of blood is no longer available," Valerie declared coldly.

"I assumed that to be the case."

The implication evoked pure outrage.

"You want to study *me?*"

And now there was more than a hint of terror in Angela's eyes. But still she persisted.

"I just want you to consider the possibility. That's my condition. Just think about it. If we could only explore how the T-cells get there in such numbers—"

Angela stopped when she saw Valerie's arm reflexively draw back. The fist remained raised as Valerie considered the possibilities. *They might arrest me for assault. But it could also give her a trace of DNA*

296

from my hand. Down came the arm. But what followed was nearly as effective as if she had beaten Angela to the ground.

"You will now leave. If you approach me again, I will have you arrested for stalking, and then I will then do everything in my power to alter the course of your life in ways that you will find extremely unpleasant. Am I making myself clear?"

"Yes," Angela said, trembling.

Valerie pointed to the door. Angela turned, took quick steps, grasped the knob, and shut the door carefully but firmly behind her.

Valerie stared at the door as a cold sweat chilled the base of her spine, dampening the white silk blouse where it tucked into her slacks.

A minute later, when the anger had subsided to a point where she could finally speak again, she punched the intercom button.

"Yes, Ms. Lee?"

"Tina . . . if that woman ever comes here again, I want you to call the police and tell them she is trespassing. Clear?"

"Yes, Ms. Lee."

Valerie sank into a chair and began to look around the room at the symbols of her life's work. A stand-up teak desk. Her Stanford diploma in a rosewood frame. Three inter-linked high-definition flat screens. A sixteenth century ink-and-wash landscape by Chen Chun. A feeling of defeat rose up inside her as she realized what was happening.

I'm already beginning to say goodbye.

One more thought flavored the misery of the moment.

How will I tell my parents that their only child needs to disappear forever?

CHAPTER 86

Nina asked the study hall monitor—a senior girl she'd not said a single word to in her two years at Langston High—if she could leave to use the bathroom. The tall blonde, who in a disturbing way reminded her of Trisha Peterson, gave a barely perceptible nod, not bothering to take her eyes off the book she was reading.

Once outside the room, Nina headed in the opposite direction from the girls' bathroom, hurrying down an empty hallway toward the library, wondering what would work best to set John and Josh straight.

Should I condition their football performance on good behavior? Make them puke if they even so much as think about mistreating Chantha? I could even blind them! But that seemed just a little too harsh. *What if I just ordered them to do everything in their power to protect her?*

She worried the boys might already be waiting, but as she turned the corner, no one stood in front of the library.

Two minutes went by, and her disappointment began to morph into frustration. As confidence began to dribble away, she found herself beginning to hope that John and Josh wouldn't show. But just as she decided it was time to return to study hall, the boys appeared at the end of the hallway. And they looked like they were coming to settle a score.

Her frayed confidence vanished.

Instead of standing her ground, Nina pushed open the heavy glass library door, looking for some safe place, and headed for a table close to the desk where the librarian was sorting a handful of index cards.

At the age of 63, Mabry Talmidge had spent 40 of those years working for the Cascade School District. Arthritis had recently become an issue. But today wasn't one of those achy episodes, during which she wished she'd take an early retirement and moved to someplace warm like California or Arizona. "Mabes," as everyone affectionately called her, was actually in fine fettle, despite the bitter January weather. And when her body felt good, Mabes was a delightful soul to be around.

She immediately recognized the girl—rumored to be perpetually in trouble—as she slipped into the room, quietly taking a seat for no apparent reason.

After a moment of pondering, Mabes carefully laid down the handful of index cards, and lifted the reading glasses from her nose to let them dangle from the slim cord around her neck.

"Excuse me, young lady?"

Nina looked up.

"Do you need help?"

"No," Nina said, having no desire to explain why she'd entered the library. A quick glance confirmed the boys were now standing just outside the door. They were laughing, as if they'd just shared a joke.

Mabes followed Nina's gaze and saw John and Josh. As soon as her eyes met theirs, they looked away. After a few seconds they disappeared. Her attention shifted back to the girl.

"It's 'Nina' isn't it?"

"Yes," Nina said, now wishing she could turn invisible.

"Is there something we should call the principal's office about?"

"No . . . please. It's okay." But Nina's face said otherwise.

Mabes thought hard for a moment. She had never been a fan of high school sports, firmly believing that school was a place for math, English and science. And maybe some history and music for electives. Football occupied no place in her vision of a proper education, and setting two cocksure athletes straight on how they should treat girls would have given her great pleasure.

"If those boys were bothering you, I would have no problem helping explain it to Mister Rumsey." She waited to see if the girl would take her up on the offer, and was disappointed when Nina stood up.

"I'm supposed to be in study hall," Nina said, apologetically. "I should get back."

Mabes watched her push through the door, and pause to look up and down the hallway. As the door began to close, Mabes heard the quickly fading *slap-slap-slap* of sneakers on waxed tile.

CHAPTER 87

Nina confessed the library disaster to Chantha, who told Frank. He knew Nina still distrusted Clarissa, but decided it didn't really matter if they were on poor terms. No one else was qualified to offer the kind of help she needed, so Frank called Clarissa, and she readily agreed to come over the next morning. He then called the school to report that Nina wasn't feeling well and would be taking a sick day. Gunther was told that he would have to leave the house the following morning so that Clarissa and Nina could have total privacy.

Nina barely slept that night. At breakfast, her reddened eyes betrayed she had cried.

After the family finished breakfast, she took a sliver of fatty ham out to the deck and laid it on the railing. When she came back inside, she settled on the couch in the family room to wait for the raven.

Clarissa arrived, Anna left for work, and Frank drove Chantha to school. Gunther had left earlier in his pickup, not mentioning where he was going or what he intended for the rest of the day.

Clarissa entered the family room and sat down beside Nina. After a nervous moment Nina's emotion poured out.

"I thought I knew how to do it," she said, twisting a sheet of Kleenex in frustration. "When the boys came up to us at our lockers, I felt the tingle and then it got all warm inside my chest. But later, when I was out in the hallway by the library, it was like everything had drained away and I was just *normal* again." She lifted the tissue and blew her nose in utter frustration.

"It takes time," Clarissa said. "You must be patient. I can help if you want me to."

Not wanting to say anything that might betray her plan to escape with Gunther, Nina decided it was best to pretend to accept Clarissa's offer.

"Would you?"

"Of course," Clarissa said.

Nina continued to push the conversation in what seemed like a safe direction. "How long did it take before you could use your powers?"

The question brought memories of Clarissa's early years.

She had been struggling to function in high Roman society, being the bastard daughter of Julius Caesar and thusly frowned upon by the elite. Her half-brother Octavian wasn't present to defend her honor. He was off across the Mediterranean fighting Marc Anthony and Cleopatra, where he finally won a decisive battle in 31 B.C., the same year that Clarissa turned 32. After routing the rebel navy near the Actium peninsula in Greece, and then eliminating Anthony and Cleopatra in Alexandria, he returned home, took one look at Clarissa from across the marble portico of the family mansion, and in a stunned voice said, "You still look like a girl!"

The following year her seemingly perpetual youthfulness was explained when she was approached by two men who appeared to be in their early twenties. They identified themselves as watchers, who represented a group of specially blessed people who were spread out across the Roman Empire and beyond.

Three years later, when she arrived in *Turicum,* which was a Roman trading post that many centuries later would become the city of Zurich, she finally began to learn to use her skills.

"I was forty before I really understood what I was capable of," Clarissa said.

Nina's eyes went wide. "I'm fourteen! That's twenty-six more years! I can't wait that long!"

Nina's panic seemed a bit exaggerated, but Clarissa reminded herself that even though she held vast potential, Nina was still an adolescent. She tried to reassure her, to calm her down.

"You shouldn't have to wait nearly as long as I did. I had no one to help me early on. You have a huge head start because you've already seen what's possible. You have much learning to do, but I promise everything will come in time."

Nina's frustration continued to play out the moment.

"Why can't I just do it right now?"

"What you did to Benny at the piñata party was driven by anger. Later, and with the raven's help, you acted in a desperate moment. In both situations, what you did was instinctual. It's much harder to use your powers in a fully rational moment. But I promise it will come. It's just going to take time."

Nina groaned. Turning away, she looked out the window and saw the sliver of ham was still lying on the snow-crusted railing.

Clarissa saw her sudden look of concern.

"Is something wrong?"

"It's Raven," Nina said. "He should have come by now."

CHAPTER 88

Liesel's train pulled into Caen on a cold January afternoon.

Spotty rain had fallen all along the route from Paris. A steady breeze was now pushing the coastal clouds inland. *Le Bouchon du Vaugueux* was half a mile away, in the heart of old Caen. With blue sky beginning to break across the ocean, Liesel decided to walk off her nervous energy.

She expected to at some point feel Livia's resonance as she strode briskly along the path that paralleled the *Quai Vendeuvre*, but was left disappointed by the time she spotted the restaurant's red doorframe and window molding, fancying up an otherwise drab block-and-mortar corner building.

She peered in through a window and saw a few customers, mostly couples, at a handful of tables. No one seemed to have noticed her arrival. She decided to wait inside where it was warm and left the window, stepping up to the entry stoop.

As she reached for the door handle, a voice startled her from behind.

"Ms. Hartkorn?"

Liesel spun around, confronted by a thirtyish man wearing black wool slacks and a black leather jacket. His hair stiffly gelled.

Upset at the unexpected greeter, her question came out sounding more like a demand.

"Are you with Livia?"

"Yes," he said, as if this were an obvious fact.

"Why didn't she come herself?"

His indignant look said there should be no need to explain.

"Would you please be so kind as to come with me down to the harbor?"

The harbor was six miles away. If this were a trap, the distance would serve to separate her from her own security people—*if* she had decided to ignore the warning to come alone. Which she hadn't.

"Why?"

"I've been given instructions." He was beginning to sound impatient. "If you would please just come with me in my car." He pointed to a silvery Peugeot, parked two spaces down the narrow street.

Liesel stood her ground.

"Will you guarantee that I am absolutely safe in coming with you?"

With obvious frustration, he said, "Yes. I guarantee that you are absolutely safe. And since you can tell if someone is lying, you will know that I am being honest in my answer."

Liesel wasn't happy. But she sensed he was being truthful. She turned abruptly for the car, saying over her shoulder, "I'm not happy with the way this is being handled."

By the time he caught up with her she had already reached the front passenger door, pulled it open, and started to climb in.

There was a fragile moment when it seemed he might demand that she get into the back seat. But after the briefest pause, he walked around to the driver's side, got in and started the engine. He pulled sharply from the curb without a word.

Fifteen minutes later, when they reached the frontage road along the seawall, she saw why he had brought her here.

During the winter there were rarely yachts of any size moored in these cold Atlantic waters. Today, a white mega-yacht rode the light swell. With three decks, it looked to be around fifty-five meters in length.

The man braked to a stop alongside the seawall, near where a tender was tied up at a pier that extended out into the bay. Two crewmen, in white uniforms and wearing black berets, stood waiting on the heavy wood planking.

Liesel waited until the Spaniard came around to open her door. As she climbed out, she asked, "Am I supposed to go out to the yacht?"

"Yes," he said.

"Are you coming?"

"I will stay here to drive you back to the train station."

That seemed hopeful, and for the first time Liesel smiled. The man's stony face said he didn't really care whether or not she was pleased.

As one of the sailors on the pier waived for her to come down, Liesel's excitement returned. For the first time in eighteen centuries a member of the Order was going to come face-to-face with the elusive Livia.

She scrambled down the gangway.

One sailor helped her into the boat, while the second briskly untied two ropes holding the tender to the pier. There was a light chop as they motored out into the bay. The high bow cut easily through the waves.

As they neared the massive yacht, Liesel began to feel resonance. The strength of it rose quickly as they approached. Except for Clarissa, she had never felt this level of power coming from another member.

A ladder was extended.

Once she was on deck a crewman escorted her out of the wind and into the main salon, where a woman stood waiting. She was perhaps fifty, with dark hair pulled back in a bun. It wasn't Livia.

"Welcome," the woman said.

"Thank you," Liesel replied, wondering why Livia wasn't present to greet her.

"Please come with me," the woman said, stiffly formal.

Liesel followed her down a short hallway that ended at a solid-looking door, which her escort reached to open.

She now expected to see Livia. But as the door swung wide, all she saw were teak paneled walls, a couch covered in green silk fabric, two matching overstuffed chairs, and a small secretarial desk.

An envelope lay on the desk.

She turned back to the woman and asked, "Is this where we are to meet?"

"I'll return once your conference is finished," the woman said, pulling the door firmly shut as she left.

In one corner of the room, just beneath the ceiling, a tiny red light winked on. Liesel recognized the miniature video camera as similar to those she had seen at the farmhouse near Zizurkil. A woman's voice issued from a hidden speaker.

"Welcome to the Esmerelda." Firm and reassuring. "Please make yourself comfortable."

Liesel remained standing, confused and beginning to feel upset. "Am I speaking with Livia?"

"Yes. I'm sorry, but we will be unable to meet face to face. Please accept my apology for this inconvenience. Will you accept this condition? Or should I terminate the meeting now? I will honor whichever choice you wish to make."

For a moment Liesel considered declining. But she had come so far
. . .

"Will we ever meet face to face?"

"That is doubtful. Do you wish to continue?"

What choice do I really have?

"Yes."

"Good. Before you sit down would you please go to the desk? There is an envelope for you."

Liesel walked over and picked up the envelope, recognizing the satiny paper as the same stock used for the two messages she'd received in Zurich. The envelope flap was unsealed.

"Please read the letter," the voice directed.

Liesel moved to the couch, sat down, withdrew a single sheet, unfolded it, and read the flowing script.

Dearest Clarissa:

I am willing to provide protection for the girl, if that is what you want of me. Liesel Hartkorn will be able to confirm she has come into contact with my resonance, although she and I will not have met in person. When you come to the rendezvous I am proposing, I will meet with you personally so that you may confirm she is in safe hands. Liesel will tell you the place where the girl can be delivered into my custody. It will occur this year at three o'clock Pacific Standard Time on the anniversary of your father's death.

With respect,
Livia

Liesel looked up at the camera. "You want to schedule a meeting on the Ides of March?" There was irony here. Clarissa's father, Julius Caesar, had been slain on the floor of the Roman Senate on the Ides of March, the "Ides" being the 15th day of a month in the Roman calendar.

"Yes," the voice confirmed.

"But that is nearly two months from now. Why will it take so long?"

"There are certain preparations I need to make. And it will also take some time for this ship to sail between here and the place where she is to bring the girl."

"Which is?"

"A marina they call 'Shilshol' in Seattle. A tender will arrive at the dock fronting a business called the Seaview Boatyard. My yacht will then sail immediately for Spain. Please don't mention the date and time during your telephone conversation with Clarissa. That is what the letter is for. You will need to mail it to her to convey that part of the message. Are you willing to do this?"

"Yes."

"Thank you."

The red light on the corner-mounted camera winked out. Within seconds the salon's door swung open. The woman who had escorted her appeared and beckoned with one hand.

Two minutes later she was back in the tender as it plowed through choppy water toward the dock, feeling enormously cheated for not having met the legend in the flesh.

CHAPTER 89

Raven flew over the rectory on his daily visits to the princess. On this particular morning, the large white car that had first brought Evil Soul into the valley was again parked on the street.

Raven landed on the car's hood and found it still warm. Today's flight had been against a freezing headwind, and the car's heat was most welcome.

After a few minutes he launched back into the air and briefly circled the building, landing atop a fence separating the rectory from the church. He settled in to wait and see who might come out.

CHAPTER 90

Frank had just begun what promised to be a long and busy workday when his receptionist buzzed. He picked up the hand set and glanced at his desk calendar, confirming that his first appointment wasn't until 11:00. "Yes, Penny?" he said, as he twisted in his chair and reached back to the credenza for a contract litigation file that needed interrogatories drafted.

"Mr. Miller, there are people here from Homeland Security and the FBI who want to talk to you." She sounded nervous, even a little frightened.

Any thought of working on interrogatories vanished. "I'll be right out," he said, placing the litigation file back on the credenza, reflexively straightening his tie as he stood. Trying to figure out which of his cases might have provoked a visit from either agency, much less both. He drew a blank on clients, leaving just one disturbing possibility.

When he reached the reception area there were three people waiting. The woman he recognized immediately. It was Cynthia Travers, the attorney with Crestwell-Bergman. She had called him just once after Gunther's disappearance, to ask in a slightly disgusted tone of voice if he knew where "that man who calls himself *Gunther*" had vanished to. Frank had told her he hadn't clue. Which at the time had been the truth.

Frank had long since concluded that she and the Germans must have given upon their search for the elusive "Wolfgang Arthur

Spindler." Now it was clear that she hadn't given up. To the contrary, she had called in reinforcements.

"Frank," Cynthia said warmly, as if they had been friends for forever, reaching to shake his hand.

"Cynthia," Frank replied, working hard to sound equally cordial, while his gut churned. "To what do I owe the honor?" He glanced at the men standing behind her. Both in their forties. Dark blue suits. One taller by a good eight inches. The short fellow a wide-body with the build of a bar bouncer.

"Is there someplace where we can talk in private?" she asked.

"Sure," Frank said. "Please follow me." He led them down the hallway and into the conference room.

Once the door was closed no one moved to sit down.

Cynthia introduced the muscle man first. "This is special agent Dirk Jones with the FBI's Spokane office."

Agent Jones reached to shake Frank's hand, seeming amused behind cold eyes that shouted ex-military.

Cynthia turned to the tall man. "And this is Homeland Security Agent Nathan Adams."

Adams gave a broad smile. "Call me 'Nate'," he said, faded blue eyes seething with reptile aggression.

"Frank," Frank offered, releasing the hand after one quick pump.

Adams turned serious.

"We're hoping you can give us an update on the whereabouts of the alleged German national who's been calling himself Wolfgang Spindler." He nodded to Cynthia. "Or, as Ms. Travers has informed us, the man who goes by the nickname of 'Gunther'."

Frank knew he could be indicted for shielding a criminal if he were to deny knowing Gunther's whereabouts. And since it was possible they had discovered Gunther was now living in his home, it took him just one second to reach a decision.

"He showed up recently and asked if I might know of someplace where he could stay for a few days. I didn't see any harm in putting him up, since I wasn't aware that he'd done anything wrong. Was I mistaken?"

Cynthia cut in before either agent could speak.

"I'm surprised you didn't call me. Did I somehow leave the impression that I didn't want you to get in touch if he turned up?" Clearly unhappy. But still polite, and offering Frank what amounted to an out.

It was his turn to be polite. And cooperative.

"I hadn't heard from you in quite a while so I figured you were satisfied with whatever it was you had discovered about the man. He didn't seem like he was on the run. The fact that he came back here, where he was known, said to me he was not in any kind of trouble. I actually thought he might have already contacted you." He paused, and said very carefully, "Was I wrong? Because if he is in some kind of trouble I'd very much appreciate knowing about it."

The agents were following the conversation back and forth between Frank and Cynthia.

"When we ran his passport we discovered it was a forgery, so we're not sure who he is. Out of caution, we contacted the FBI, and they pulled in Homeland Security just in case there's a terrorism connection. From the German Embassy's perspective we simply need to determine his true name and nationality so that he can be handled in an appropriate manner. If he is a German citizen, the likely solution will be deportation back to Germany, where the authorities can resolve any concerns about why he is traveling on a forged document."

Frank tried to sound apologetic. "Now I'm embarrassed that I didn't give you a call."

Agent Adams was clearly disgusted that the two attorneys were playing nice. "Do you know where he is at this moment?" he demanded.

"No," Frank said, trying to sound contrite. "But I could call the house and see if he's there. One of my daughters stayed home from school today. She wasn't feeling well this morning, and one of our friends is taking care of her."

"We'd prefer that you not make that call," Adams said quickly. "It might alert him to us being here."

Frank knew the unannounced appearance of two Federal agents would scare Nina. And who knew how Clarissa might react. But before he could protest, Adams continued.

"We'd prefer to go over to your house with you. We don't want to upset any members of your family, but we are very interested in questioning this man. I'm sure you understand, being a lawyer, how important it is that we have every possible chance of safely taking him into custody." The implicit threat that Frank needed to cooperate—or else—was clear.

"Of course," Frank said, knowing the pleasantries were over. "But would you mind if I called my wife and told her what's going on?"

Adams was having none of it.

"Mr. Miller, I thought you understood that alerting family members isn't something we can allow you to do."

"Okay," Frank said.

And now came the big worry. Frank was certain the agents were confident they could take Gunther down. Travers would have told them their target had had one of his kidneys removed. There was scarring from a bullet close to his heart. They were expecting a man crippled by internal injuries. An easy target.

As they escorted him outside to a black van in the lot, Frank prayed that Gunther had kept his promise to stay clear of the house.

CHAPTER 91

Clarissa and Nina heard tires crunching snow along the curb, and then a car's engine being turned off. Frank or Anna would have opened the garage door. Gunther's pickup had a finicky whine. And Charlie had called earlier to say he'd be hanging around the Bosecker all morning.

They exchanged looks as Clarissa rose from the couch and walked through the short hallway into the living room and then up to the front windows, where she saw four people exiting a black van and walking swiftly toward the house.

Nina had followed, and now stood behind her. Clarissa spoke without turning around, her entire attention focused upon the body language of the approaching group.

"It's Frank. There are two men and a woman with him. No one looks happy. Say as little as possible, and please take cues from me if you need to speak."

There came the sound of a key being inserted into the front door lock.

Frank entered, followed closely by the others. "Hello, Clarissa," he said, brows bunched for just an instant, clearly a warning.

The tall man and the stocky man immediately stepped to either side of Frank, scanning the room as if expecting trouble.

Clarissa felt enormous relief when their eyes didn't settle upon Nina.

Frank now sounded as though he'd been seriously prompted on what to say.

"Is Gunther here?"

"No," Clarissa said, looking perplexed. "He left just after you and Anna went to work."

The stocky man demanded, "Do you know where he went?"

"No," she replied, perfectly polite, but with a look that said she didn't appreciate the hostility. "I was here for only a few minutes before he drove off. We really didn't say much more than "Hi" to each other." She turned to Nina. "Nina . . . do you know where Gunther went this morning?"

Nina looked both confused and concerned. "He didn't say." And then she looked directly at the stocky man, and in a deadpan voice said, "What do you want him for?"

Clarissa was surprised by the raw surge of power. She couldn't have given a more focused command herself.

Dirk Jones' face went slack as he replied.

"He's in the U.S. on a forged passport, and we think he may have terrorist connections."

"Good lord, Dirk!" The tall agent looked ready to slap his colleague. Then he realized just how transparent he'd become. He gave Dirk a nasty look, and quickly shifted his attention to Frank.

"You told us he was driving an older dark blue Ford pickup?"

"That's correct," Frank said.

"Then we'll just have to go looking for him. Meanwhile, we'll need to have someone remain in your house for the next few hours, just in case he returns."

Frank was quick to protest.

"I can't agree to that unless you can produce a warrant."

Frank turned to Cynthia for support, but before she could weigh in, Adams said coldly, "I can get one of those, easy as pie." He reached into his pocket, pulled out a cell phone, and began punching in numbers.

Clarissa now surprised everyone, except Nina, who immediately saw what was coming.

"I think we will be just fine if someone sticks around the house for a bit. After all, I can't imagine we have anything to hide." She gave a perky "helpful citizen" smile. "In fact, I think it would actually make us feel a lot safer!"

Adams paused in his dialing and gave a hard look at Clarissa.

Frank now realized what Clarissa was up to. An agent left with her was an opportunity, not a problem.

"Are you sure?" he quizzed Clarissa.

"Of course, I'm sure, Frank," she said calmly, turning to Agent Jones. "Didn't he call you 'Dirk?' We haven't been formally introduced. I'm Clarissa." She reached out and shook his hand. Dirk's face morphed from *slack* to *surprised* to *pleased* within a few heartbeats. "I'm guessing you'll be the one staying with Nina and me this afternoon?" She threw an inquisitive look at Adams.

He stared back, sizing her up. "Fine then," he said. "Are we all agreed?" He threw one last challenging look at Frank.

"I guess so," Frank said slowly.

Clarissa gave a mental push. *What's holding you up?*

Adams obediently moved on.

"Mr. Miller, I expect you'll want to return to your office. I'm warning you not to make an attempt to tell this Gunther fellow that we're looking for him if he shows up. That would be direct interference in a criminal investigation. Do I have your promise to call me if he comes to your office or contacts you by phone?"

In a resigned voice, Frank said, "I understand my duty."

"Glad to hear it," Adams said, satisfied. He turned to Cynthia. "Ms. Travers, you know what this Gunther fellow looks like. I'd appreciate your coming with me to identify him."

Cynthia nodded, happy to exit the awkward situation.

After the three left, Clarissa turned to Agent Jones.

"May I call you Dirk?"

"Yes, ma'am," Dirk said. "And I'm sorry about all of this and the way it happened. I hope you can forgive us for interrupting your morning."

"We certainly can," Clarissa said smoothly. "We all know how important it is to pay attention to the possibility of terrorists these days. And who would have thought Gunther might be one! I've only been around him a little, but you'd never suspect someone as caring and gentle as that man might secretly be a violent criminal."

As Clarissa spoke, Nina had to cough to cover an involuntary laugh. And then she asked in a courteous voice, "Agent Jones, would you like me to make you a cup of coffee?"

"Why . . . that would be very nice," Dirk replied, as if speaking to a child. "And please, if you want you can call me 'Dirk.' I really wouldn't mind at all."

"Okay, Dirk," Nina said, feeling the power and enjoying the sense of control. "Do you take cream or sugar?"

"Both please."

At that moment Nina saw a flash of black outside the kitchen window, and shouted, "He's back!"

Dirk's right hand reflexively slid under the left lapel of his jacket. "Who's back!" he demanded, ready to draw.

"Raven!" Nina said.

Clarissa quickly explained.

"There's a raven that's taken to visiting the house. Nina puts out little bits of food for him in the morning. He was late in coming today and she was worried."

Dirk cautiously withdrew his hand from the butt of the revolver.

Clarissa turned to Nina and said, "Why don't you go out and say 'Hi' to your feathered friend." She turned back to the FBI agent, and with a helpful smile said, "I think I can handle brewing Dirk a fresh cup of coffee."

CHAPTER 92

Raven waited on the white picket fence for nearly an hour before the back door of the rectory swung open. Three men emerged and trudged through the snow, headed across the alley for the church, white breaths swirling in a stiff morning breeze.

Having identified the leader of the trio as Evil Soul, Raven beat his way up into the sky, cutting straight across the lake.

When he swooped down onto the deck, his first thought was of food. When the princess rushed out onto the deck, he was already gobbling down the frozen meat she had previously laid out.

Her violently swirling blue energy said she was upset. But when she spoke, he only recognized his own name and Dark Soul's. The rest of the human language made little sense.

"Raven," Nina pleaded. "You have to go and find Gunther and warn him not to return to the house. There are bad people who have come after him."

"Guntah?" Raven said, cocking his head to one side.

Nina wore only jeans and a tee shirt, and her ears were already stinging from the cold. She held out her arm, and pleaded, "We need to go inside!"

Raven saw the princess extended her arm, and without hesitation he lifted his wings and in two quick beats landed just below her elbow, talons biting just deep enough to hold him steady.

Dirk and Clarissa were watching from the kitchen.

"Now that's what I call amazing!" Dirk said to Clarissa, as the bird lit on the girl's arm.

"Yes," she agreed. "They've developed a rapport that's quite remarkable."

When Nina came inside, she walked up to Dirk and said, "He's very cold so I thought I'd bring him in to warm him up. Is it okay if I take him to my room?"

"I don't see a problem with that," Dirk said. And after a chuckle, "Just make sure he doesn't poop on your rug!"

"He's never pooped inside the house before," Nina defended, turning for her room. *But I'd love to see him drop a present down the back of your collar!*

"How sweet do you like your coffee, Dirk?" Clarissa asked, deflecting his attention.

"Lots of sugar," Nina heard Dirk say, before she closed her bedroom door.

She took Raven over to her desk and he hopped down, and then looked up at her.

For a moment they were both thinking the same thing: *Will we be able to communicate?*

Nina remembered how it had happened with Benny. She closed her eyes and began to concentrate. Gradually, images began to form. At first they were fleeting and ghostly. Slowly they took shape. Snow on the ground. A cold wooden ledge that her talons clung to. A shrill wind swaying her body. She saw a white cross and recognized the steeple at the Catholic Church.

Her head swiveled in a way that didn't seem possible, and now there were three auras coming toward her. Two were the red of regular humans. The third was an oily blue with bits of brown. At its center was a black core.

Raven, who is this?

Evil Soul.

Umberto?

???

Never mind. How long has he been here?

An image of the sun coming up and setting and coming up again flashed through her mind.

Nina got right to the point.

The man in my house has come to take Gunther away.
Dark Soul?
I wish you wouldn't call him that. He is my friend.
He is Dark Soul. Troubled human.
Yes, I know. But still a friend.

A sense of ambivalence. If she had chosen Dark Soul as a friend, so be it.

You must warn Dark Soul that bad people have come to take him away.
Can't you warn him?
No. This man, and another who has come with him, are watching me and my family.
Where is Dark Soul now?
I don't know. Can you find him?
Where do I look?
He is driving the blue pickup. Look for it.
How do I warn him? He is not like you. He is not capable of seeing my thoughts.

Nina opened her eyes and stared at Raven. She hadn't thought about that. And now her idea seemed hopeless. She was almost ready to give up when she had an inspiration. *Maybe Clarissa knows a way!* She considered taking Raven with her, but that would only complicate things. "You need to stay here," she said.

Raven appeared to understand, his head bobbing up and down.

Nina found Dirk and Clarissa sitting in the kitchen at the breakfast bar, captain's chairs turned to face each other. Dirk was slurping coffee as Nina walked in.

"How's it going with the bird?" he asked, cradling the mug in both hands.

"I think he's doing better," Nina said. She glanced at Clarissa, uncertain how to get her attention without alerting the agent.

Clarissa instantly understood that something was wrong. She turned to the agent and said, "You look a little tired, Dirk. Why don't you go into the living room and take a short nap on the couch?"

"You know, it has been a busy day," he said, yawning. "I think I'll do just that."

"Don't worry about your friends. I'll wake you if they come back."

"Thanks," Dirk said, offering a frank confession, "They're not really my friends." He put down his mug and slid off the captain's chair.

Nina watched him walk into the living room, before turning to Clarissa.

"Wait a minute," Clarissa said, nodding in the direction of the departed agent.

Nina climbed onto a chair and stared at the countertop, biting back words that wanted to pour out.

After a minute that seemed like an eternity, Clarissa said, "Okay, what's up?"

"Umberto is here," Nina said. "I think he's staying at a house behind the Catholic Church. There are two other men with him. I'm sure one must be the priest. I don't know who the other one is, but it's probably the one Charlie told us about."

"You got all of that from the Raven?"

"Yes." Nina said proudly. And then, in frustration, "I asked him to go and find Gunther and warn him about the government agents. But he says he can't communicate with Gunther like he does with me. Is there some way you know of to make that work?"

"You're over-thinking the problem," Clarissa said calmly. "We'll just turn your Raven into a carrier pigeon."

Nina's eyes lit up. "I should have thought of that!"

After Raven enjoyed a second piece of steak, Nina took a narrow slip of paper, wrote a note to Gunther, and taped it around Raven's left leg. Raven hopped back onto her arm, and she walked him out onto the deck. She closed her eyes.

Please try and find him. After you do, come back and I'll give you more food.

Raven flew off in the direction of Langston.

Clarissa was waiting just inside the French doors. As Nina pulled off her coat, Clarissa said, "I think we need to do something about Umberto before he becomes a real problem."

"What can we do with the FBI and Homeland Security watching us?"

"I wasn't thinking of *us* doing anything," Clarissa said, with a vengeful grin. She glanced in the direction of the living room. "The time has come for Dirk to do us a favor."

CHAPTER 93

Umberto and Bishop Assante followed Father Tom from the rectory, crossing the back yard on the path that led across the alley to the church. None of them noticed the raven that took flight from the white picket fence near the gate.

Father Tom still felt shaken by what he'd witnessed the previous afternoon, when he'd met the Gulfstream that had landed just minutes before, and was parked on the tarmac. When the cabin door opened, Assante appeared at the top of the steps and said, "Come inside and see what's happened."

Father Tom had entered the cabin, and witnessed the perfectly healed flesh in stunned silence, as the bishop declared, "The miracle is confirmed! Tomorrow we will hold a private Mass, and pray for guidance on what should be done next."

As Father Tom now unlocked the back door of the church he shuddered, remembering the account of Umberto's earlier vision: *"I saw a girl, maybe fourteen years old. And behind her stood something evil. A blackness, with red eyes glowing like coals on the darkest night. Its claws resting on her shoulders, as if they were guiding or controlling her."*

As they kicked snow off their shoes, Father Tom shut the door and then turned to Assante and said in an uncertain voice, "Should I dress in green?" That was the color for a regular mass. But today seemed anything but regular. He wasn't even certain whether vestments were appropriate. This felt more like a council of war.

"Green would be fine," Assante said.

Father Tom headed for the sacristy, while the bishop and Umberto went into the chapel.

Feeling sick to his stomach, Father Tom stripped off his black wool coat and draped it on a chair. From the wardrobe he lifted a coat hanger holding the Alb, slipped it off the hanger and pulled it on. He then took the cincture cord from a drawer and cinched the Alb tight around his waist. He lifted the green stole from where it hung on a wall bar and draped it over his left shoulder. And finally, he pulled on the green chasuble.

He stepped in front of the full-length mirror, just as he did before every service, and everything seemed right . . . except his face. The man who stared back had dark circles framing sunken eyes, skin pale as wax paper, and brown hair that lay flat and oily against the scalp.

Father Tom crossed himself, and asked God to guide him through this most difficult of days. After one hard swallow, followed by several shaky deep breaths, he left the safety of the sacristy for the uncertainty of facing a devil that now seemed altogether too real.

CHAPTER 94

Raven failed to return by the time Frank got home from work.

Nina became progressively more upset, despite Clarissa's repeated assurances that things would work out for the best. Nina was already picturing Gunther behind bars.

"They must have caught him. If Raven was able to warn Gunther, he would have already flown back to tell me."

Clarissa thought Gunther was quite capable of defending himself. He should have had no problem if he'd tangled with the officer, unless Adams had gotten incredibly lucky. She was far more worried that Gunther had injured or even killed the agent.

The forecast was for temperatures near zero, and Clarissa suspected the raven had been forced to return to his wherever his conspiracy had settled in for the night. If he hadn't flown to a lower elevation where the air was a few degrees warmer this would be a tough night for him to survive.

Anna had earlier declared she was too stressed to cook, and ordered out for pizza. The delivery guy finally arrived at the front door and handed over two large flat boxes. Frank carried them inside and set them on the dining room table.

Nina immediately asked, "Would it be okay if I ate in the family room? If Raven comes back, I want to know right away."

"Of course," Frank said. "Why don't you and Chantha take some slices and go there to wait."

"I'll be with the girls," Anna said.

When the girls and Anna were out of earshot, Frank turned to Clarissa and softly asked, "What happened to the FBI guy?"

"I sent him to pay Umberto a visit."

"You mean to arrest him?" Frank imagined the repercussions. There would be more agent visits to his office, his home. Federal prosecutors might be brought in to consider filing charges.

Clarissa gave a wicked smile. "Don't worry. I'm more subtle than that."

"How did the agent get to the church?"

Again, *that* smile. "I had him call the local police for a ride." She was clearly enjoying the moment. "Umberto is a coward at the core of his rotten little soul. Having an FBI agent show up would scare the shine off his shoes." She fixed Frank with a *get real* look. "You must have figured out that it was Umberto who sent the police after Gunther?"

"Are you sure?"

"Absolutely," Clarissa said, as she pulled a piece of pizza from a box and took a satisfying bite before continuing.

"I sent Dirk to the rectory and told him to specifically ask for the priest, and to tell the good Father that the FBI was canvassing the neighborhood looking for two foreign pedophiles."

"Huh," Frank said, picturing the panic Dirk's visit must have caused. This brought a smile, and a question. "What's the next step?"

"We hope that the raven found Gunther first. If so, Gunther is probably headed back to where he disappeared to last summer."

"And that would be?"

"I don't have an exact address, but he shouldn't be hard to find."

"How so?"

"Charlie wrote down the pickup's license plate number. Don't you attorneys have a way to find the address where a car is registered?"

Frank smiled, and nodded. Clarissa had found a way to make things right. Having her around now felt like the best kind of insurance.

"Do you want stay here tonight? We've got a hide-a-bed in the family room."

"No. I've gotten used to my room at the Bosecker. And I need to bring Charlie up to date. I can't risk doing that over the phone. I'll come back in the morning so we can work on a new plan."

"Agreed," Frank said. "We have a lot of thinking to do about what's best for Nina."

"And your family," Clarissa added, trying to sound generous, and largely succeeding.

"I appreciate that."

After they finished dinner, Clarissa went to check on Nina. She found the two girls ensconced on the family room couch, staring out the French door windows at a dark deck. Of Anna there was no sign, and Clarissa guessed she had retreated to her bedroom.

"I'm leaving now," she said, standing in the entryway. "Nina . . . has there been any sign of your raven?"

"No," Nina said glumly.

"Don't stay up all night. Ravens are very intelligent. If there is a way, I'm certain he's found it." But Clarissa doubted the bird had found Gunther. By "a way" what she really meant was a way to survive the night's brutal cold.

She left the house and walked to where Charlie's white Sentra was parked against the curb.

On the drive around the northern end of the lake she continued to worry. Every scenario she imagined held risk for Nina.

But when she reached her room and found a FedEx envelope slipped under her door and ripped it open, the options shrunk down to just one.

CHAPTER 95

The rectory's doorbell rang in the middle of dinner. Father Tom said to Assante and Umberto, 'It's probably one of my parishioners." With an apologetic smile he got up from the kitchen table and walked out to the living room. When he opened the front door, there stood a man in a black trench coat, holding open a leather wallet with a golden badge and a printed ID that said: *FBI Special Agent.*

In a stern voice the man said, "I'm Dirk Jones with the Spokane office of the Bureau. We're investigating a report of two foreigners who have sex slavery plans for children here in Langston. Do you have any knowledge of someone coming from Europe who might fit that profile?"

If Dirk Jones hadn't been programmed by Clarissa to just make the statement, and to do nothing further, he would have instantly recognized the shock and guilt that filled Father Tom's face.

"Nuh . . no," Father Tom stuttered. "Do you have a description of who it is you're looking for?"

"No, sir," Dirk replied, with military precision. "We're just going door to door and asking folks if they've seen anyone over the past few days who seemed unusual or suspicious. Thank you for your time." The agent nodded politely and turned away.

Father Tom watched him walk out to the police cruiser. For a moment he was tempted to run after the agent and tell him that yes, he did know of two men who'd flown in from Europe and who were interested in a local girl. It was only the mental image of Umberto's perfectly healed hand that stopped him.

As he closed the door and returned to the dining room, Father Tom decided there was a lot of thinking that needed to be done before he would give any more help to the bishop, or believe anything he was told by the Italian who claimed to be a carpenter.

CHAPTER 96

Raven found Dark Soul's pickup parked in back of Sam's Diner, safely out of view from the street. He was unable to spot Dark Soul inside the building. Since there was no way to signal his arrival, he settled down on the dull blue metal of the pickup's hood, and began what would turn into a long cold wait.

When Gunther finally exited the restaurant, the bird he discovered sitting on the pickup's hood looked almost dead. He climbed into the cab and started the engine, anxious to get back to the Miller's and check up on Nina.

The windshield had entirely frosted over. As Gunther waited for the reluctant heat from the vent to melt an oval of clear glass, he noticed that something was attached to the bird's leg. Curious, he got out of the cab and walked around and lifted the bird, which readily allowed itself to be picked up.

Once back inside the cab Gunther peeled the little strip of paper from the bird's leg, and then carefully laid the bird down on the passenger seat. After he'd read what was written on the paper he looked down at the raven with a mixture of pity and kindness.

"You must be the one who comes to visit Nina." He studied the raven, now reduced to a weary ball of black feathers with glassy eyes. "You look just about done in." Knowing the bird's death would hugely upset Nina, he begrudgingly said, "I guess I owe you one for coming and waiting for me in this miserable weather. How would you feel about a long drive to Yakima?"

The vents were finally blowing tepidly warm air into the cab. The bird ruffled its feathers, trying to catch as much heat as possible. Its head slowly turned so that one eye looked up at Gunther.

"Yeah," Gunther agreed, as if the bird had spoken loud and clear. "That's what I thought." He pushed the clutch and grabbed the shift lever, then checked himself, looking once more at the raven. "I'll bet you're hungry and thirsty, aren't you?"

Raven didn't understand the words, but he understood the intent. In a weakened voice that was almost inaudible over the grumbling engine and the air rushing from the vents, he croaked, "Guntah."

"Alright little buddy," Gunther said, resolved. "I'm going back inside to get you some food and water. Stay right here. And if those Federal agents show up, don't let them know where I am." He chuckled, and then opened the driver's door, hoping it wasn't a mistake.

Inside the diner he got a Styrofoam cup of water and a hamburger patty for the raven, plus a sandwich and a supersized coffee for himself just in case the pickup broke down in the middle of nowhere. Also, there was no guarantee Walt Bremmer would be at home when he arrived. Or, how Walt might react when he saw the pickup he'd loaned out several months ago pull up in his driveway. Gunther figured there was a fifty-fifty chance he'd be walking away from Walt's house on a bitterly cold winter night, with a sick raven perched on his shoulder.

CHAPTER 97

The morning after the Feds showed up at his office, Frank was scrambling to draft a petition to adopt Nina when his receptionist buzzed on the intercom.

"Cynthia Travers is here to see you, Mr. Miller."

Frank imagined the lawyer standing before Penny's desk, hearing only that side of the conversation.

"Is she with anyone?"

"No sir."

That was a relief. But it did raise a disturbing possibility. Maybe the Feds had no further reason to bother him. Cynthia Travers might be here to deliver the news of Gunther's capture. The German's failure to show last night was an ominous sign that had everyone upset, and Nina in particular. "Tell her I'll be out in a minute," he said, gathering the adoption pleadings into a file folder and stashing it safely out of sight.

He took a moment to calm down and collect his thoughts, briefly replaying the newest confusion in his life.

Clarissa had dropped in earlier to report the contents of a letter she'd received from someone she described as a "friend" in the Order.

"Do you remember me telling you about the Basque woman from Northern Spain?"

"The one you called Livia?

"Yes."

"The same one who kidnapped you?"

"Yes."

"So, what's up?"

"I went looking for Livia because I thought she might be able to give me some pointers for helping to hide Nina. I just received a letter from her, via my friend, and she's offered to take Nina under her protection in Spain."

"And . . ."

"And I think we should take her up on it."

There were red flags for Frank. Livia had kidnapped Clarissa. She hadn't bothered to meet her in person. Being in Spain would place Nina that much closer to the Order's headquarters in Zurich. She would lose contact with people who had fought to protect her: Clarissa, Charlie, Frank and his family, and Gunther. Even Valerie, though Frank didn't think the math guru from San Jose was going to be in much of a position to help. When she had called to report that the third man in the photo was a Vatican official, she had also mentioned that the *wrong kind of person* had shown up at her office. "I might be gone soon," she had warned.

Frank had told Clarissa he didn't like the idea of Nina going to Europe. "And even if we wanted to, Nina is in foster care, and the State of Washington has the ultimate say in where she goes. If she disappears while Anna and I are her foster parents, we'd be responsible for her disappearance. I'd have to lie to the child protection authorities."

"What if she was your legal daughter?"

"She isn't. But even if she were, you can't just pull a kid out of school and expect no one to notice."

"What about home schooling?"

"Even if we could put it all together, I'd still be opposed to what you are suggesting. It's just too risky."

Clarissa practically exploded.

"Frank! Yesterday, two Federal agents came to your house looking for Gunther. The Catholic Church is unwittingly assisting a psychopath who will stop at nothing to take Nina away. The Order has practically limitless resources to pursue her abduction and 'reeducation.' And because Nina arranged to send Gunther's blood to California to try and save a kid's life, medical researchers at Stanford might already know it came from someone in central Washington. Do you really believe that Nina has a better chance here, versus being with a woman who for the past eighteen centuries has been able to successfully elude everyone on the planet, including the Order?"

Frank saw the logic in her argument. But one more entirely personal reason came to mind. If Nina left, Chantha would lose her best friend. Someone to help her survive the vast emotional jungle of the teen years.

When he failed to reply, Clarissa had insisted, "Would you just please consider it?"

"I'll give it some thought," he grumbled. But in the end, it didn't take long to conclude that Clarissa was right. At that point, Frank immediately began to draft adoption forms.

There remained the problem of mandatory school attendance, but Frank suspected the principal would readily accept that his newly adopted daughter was enrolled in a private out-of-state school. The staff and students would certainly be glad to be rid of the troublemaker.

When Frank walked out to the lobby of his law office, he found Cynthia politely paging through a Field & Stream magazine.

"How goes the battle?" he asked.

She returned a rueful look. "If you mean 'did we find Gunther,' the answer is no. Have you heard from him?"

"I promised I'd call if I did, and I haven't."

She appeared to accept this. But there was clearly something else on her mind. "Did your daughter or your friend say anything about Agent Jones's behavior yesterday?"

"I'm not sure what you're getting at." Frank hoped he looked more straight-faced than he felt.

"He left your house suddenly."

"I'm aware of that."

"Did he give a reason?"

"All I know is that he said needed to go somewhere, and could he use the phone to call the local cops for a ride."

"We talked to the sheriff's deputy who picked him up."

Frank continued to play along. "So . . . do you know where he went?"

"I'm not authorized to talk about it," she said, as if he should have known better than to ask.

"I was just wondering."

"It's puzzling," she said, frustrated. "I was hoping you might be able to shed some light."

Frank did his best to sound incredulous, fighting to keep that straight face.

"He really didn't tell you what he was up to?"

"No. We have absolutely no clue why he decided to run off to—" She had almost said it. And they had only known about the Catholic Church because the deputy who'd driven him there had told them. Agent Jones claimed to have no recollection of where he'd gone or what he'd done. It was so unusual they had flown him back to Spokane for medical testing, just in case he'd had a stroke that affected his memory.

Frank offered, "Sorry I can't be of more help."

Cynthia took the hint.

"I'll be in touch. And please call me if Gunther shows up, or if you find out where he disappeared to."

"You have my word." Frank shook her hand, and felt immensely relieved when the office door closed behind her.

Sitting at the front desk, Penny had heard every word. She looked up from her computer screen as he walked by. "Are there any special instructions if she comes back?"

"Treat her with respect, but if anyone asks whether or not you've seen or heard anything, you might want to think about saying no."

Penny's reply was a smile tough as steel.

CHAPTER 98

Another day passed, and Raven failed to return. Gunther's fate remained a mystery.

That evening a meeting was held. Clarissa shared Livia's letter, and a note from Liesel offering to help however she could.

Frank had finished the adoption papers. But even as Nina was saying yes, she saw the conflicting joy and sadness in Chantha's face. Despite becoming full-fledged sisters, they were nevertheless going to lose contact with each other.

Later on, when they were alone in Chantha's bedroom, Nina tried to reassure her.

"I promise I'll find a way to keep in touch."

"But the whole point of disappearing to Spain is so they can't find you. If you try to make any kind of contact with me, they'll find you for sure."

"I'll still find some way," Nina insisted, wishing for the umpteenth time that she could be a "normal" girl.

Something Clarissa had said during their ski lodge session now came back to her.

"We all want what we can't have. It's basic human nature. It will sometimes seem as if you have at your fingertips anything you could possibly desire. But there will continue to be things that will be impossible for you to actually possess."

And here it was. She wanted a sister, and she was getting one. But she wasn't going to be able to enjoy it. Even worse, when she stopped aging in a few years, Chantha would continue to grow older. In what would seem like a few short years to Nina, Chantha would be gone.

More of Clarissa's words echoed in her mind.

"The 'normals' are like snowflakes. We of the Order are like ice cubes. Both melt. But not at the same rate."

"I'll find some way to keep in touch," Nina said stubbornly. But even as she spoke, her breathing hitched.

For a moment it was Chantha who seemed the more mature. She reached out and took Nina's hands and pulled her close, holding her tight while both cried.

CHAPTER 99

Walt Bremmer finished dinner, did the dishes, and threw two extra logs onto a low bed of coals in the stone fireplace. He jacked the logs with a poker, sending a shower of sparks up the chimney.

Settling into a leather rocker, he spread open the *Yakima Herald* newspaper. As he turned to the farm news, he heard the distant whine of the old Ford pickup. It grew in volume as it labored up the gravel drive, finally wheezing to a stop near the front door.

After months of waiting, he'd eventually given up on Gunther and the truck. A wistful smile now creased his weathered face. He folded the newspaper, dropped it onto the floor beside the rocker, and stretched his legs for a moment before standing.

When the knock finally came, he was already leaning with one hand against the doorframe. He grasped the worn brass knob, unsure of what to expect.

Upon seeing Gunther's tired and uncertain face, with a big black raven perched on his shoulder, the laughter began roll out.

"Good Lord, man! Where have you been? And who is your feathered friend?"

Before Gunther could reply, the raven croaked, "Walt!"

"*Holy mother of pearl!*" Walt gaped at the bird, flabbergasted. "*He talks and he knows me!*"

During the long drive, Gunther had rambled on about all the troubles he now faced, as if the bird might somehow understand, possibly even sympathize. His lonely monologue had included where they were headed and the man they were going to see. This had helped to keep Gunther awake and focused on his driving.

"I didn't expect that," Gunther said, quite as surprised as Walt. He stared at the bird, just a few inches from his nose, before extending his arm. Raven hopped down onto it.

"Come on in!" Walt said, backing up, mesmerized by Gunther and the bird. Wood-scented heat mixed with chilly air swirled around them as the door shut. Walt was beaming. "Have you had dinner yet?"

"I had a sandwich in the car."

"Then how about a beer?"

"Beer would be good. Where should I put the bird?"

Walt's gaze settled on a small table alongside the fireplace. "Do you think he's cold?"

"We both are," Gunther confessed. "The heater in the pickup is nearly shot."

"Sorry for that," Walt said. "Those old Ford engines will run forever, but the water pumps and the heater cores are a different story." He pointed to the table. "Set him there. If he wants to go someplace else, I've got no problem with it. Best thing about being a bachelor is not being fussy."

Walt turned for the kitchen, and said over his shoulder, "Does your bird need anything?"

As Gunther carried the bird to the table, he said, "He's probably hungry."

Raven hopped down and turned his head toward the warmth of the fire.

"Think he'd like crackers?" Walt hollered from the kitchen, rummaging in the refrigerator for a can of beer.

"I think he'd prefer meat," Gunther hollered back.

Walt grabbed a plastic bowl filled with fried chicken. He plucked out a thigh before setting the container back on the rack and closing the refrigerator door. He laid the thigh on a plate, returned to the living room, handed Gunther the beer, and walked over to the raven. As soon as he set the plate down the bird began to tear the chicken apart.

"Little fella *was* hungry," Walt observed, watching for a moment as the raven greedily shredded the chicken and gobbled down the bits.

He turned to Gunther, who had pulled the tab on the beer and was taking deep gulps. "Have a seat," Walt said, nodding at the sofa. Walt returned his rocker and settled in. "Now I want to hear the whole shebang of what's happened to you over the past five months."

Gunther collapsed onto the sofa, considering for the umpteenth time two very different story options. The first option involved asking Walt for help in eluding the FBI and Homeland Security. This would require honesty about exactly why he was in trouble. Which would require an explanation about the Order. Because without that piece of information, Walt would easily conclude that the best solution was for Gunther to turn himself into the authorities, who would then deport him to his home country of Germany. The penalty for traveling on a forged passport couldn't be all that serious!

The second option was to tell Walt that he needed to rest up for a while before striking out again on his own. But that wouldn't gain what he needed. It would just be a brief pause in an otherwise desperate flight. It also left no guarantee that Walt wouldn't mention his return to someone. Possibly the woman director at the shelter where he'd stayed in August. If the Feds were being thorough, it could easily lead to his arrest.

Gunther saw there was really only one good choice. And it involved trust. "I'm in trouble with your Federal police," he said.

Walt was surprised. "Did you overstay your visa?" He sounded hopeful.

Gunther shook his head, and launched into an explanation about the Order.

Walt had thought that by the age of 56 he'd already heard everything that was ever going to surprise him. But he now sat staring at a man who claimed to have fought against Napoleon. It opened an entirely new dimension for the word *surprised*.

He sat quietly for a long while, mostly with his eyes closed, thinking of all the reasons why this was impossible. But it was so outrageous that in the end he knew Gunther must be telling the truth.

Something else helped him to believe. As Gunther spoke, Walt studied his body. The skin on his face had no lines. Walt remembered how smooth his hand had been when they first shook back in August. And how quickly Gunther had grown strong after he'd begun working in the vineyards. Now that he thought about it, he'd never seen a scar on Gunther's body, and not so much as a single sun freckle.

There was one final fact that sealed the deal.

Back in early September, Walt had checked with Flo down at the shelter and learned just how injured Gunther was when he'd first come in. "I thought he might die," Flo had confessed. Still, Gunther had been working hard at the vineyard within a few days.

"So . . ." Walt began carefully, "what do you need?"

"A place to stay for a few days. And then a way to get back to Germany. Once I'm there it will be easy enough for me to disappear."

Walt's face slowly morphed from concerned, to thoughtful, and finally mischievous. Still, his first words seem to come out of thin air.

"I never told you, but I had a son who died five years ago. If he'd lived, he'd now be in his early thirties."

Walt's mischievous grin got wider.

"You're about the same height and build, although Jorgen had lighter hair, almost blonde. Yours is medium brown. It would take an active imagination to think you looked like him . . . or at least what he'd look like today."

Gunther still wasn't sure what Walt was getting at.

"Why is this important?"

"Well," Walt said, a conspiratorial edge creeping into his voice. "Just a few months before he died, I was planning to take him on vacation to Germany. He applied for a passport, and I still have it. Of course, we'd have to dye your hair blonde. And I wish your face looked a little more like my son's."

Gunther grew excited. "What if my face was different?"

"You mean like plastic surgery?" Walt was puzzled. "That takes time."

"No," Gunther said. "What if my face were injured? What if I had blisters? Bandages? Do you think I might pass for your son?"

"You mean take advantage of the healing power you just told me about?"

"Exactly. What if I were to scald my face with hot water? Do you think I could pass for your son?"

Walt grimaced at the thought of blisters on Gunther's fine smooth skin. But yes, it might work. And then a new idea came.

"What if I were to come along and tell them you were my son? Who would want to challenge a father taking his injured son on a vacation?"

"You'd do that?"

"Sure," Walt said. "To tell the truth, my life's been a little boring of late. There's not much happening with the vines during the cold." He was enjoying the thought of something very naughty.

Gunther turned serious. "We can't leave immediately."

"Why not?"

"We need to make sure the raven gets back to Nina. We'll have to wait until the weather warms up enough for him to fly home."

"Well, the forecast is for warmer temperatures in a couple weeks from now. We can't use the Yakima airport. A local agent might remember that I lost my son. We'll need to catch a flight out of Seattle. We could swing up north through Wenatchee on the way to Seattle, and drop the bird off fifty miles from Langston."

Both men smiled.

From where he was perched on the end table, near the lively warmth of the fire, Raven sensed that something wonderful had just happened.

CHAPTER 100

Raven reappeared on a gloriously sunny day near the end of February. Nina and Chantha were sitting on a couch in the family room, watching TV. When Nina saw him come sailing across the deck to land on the table, she jumped up and yanked open the French door.

"Raven!" She clapped her hands in joy.

"Nina!" Raven croaked, immediately adding, "Guntah!" He lifted his left leg, to which a strip of paper had been rolled and secured with tape.

Nina walked up and gently lifted him with both hands and carried him back into the house.

Chantha was watching from just inside the French doors. As Nina and the raven entered, she asked, "What's that on his leg?"

"I think it's from Gunther," Nina said, excited.

As if to confirm this, Raven gave an excited squawk.

A few seconds later Anna appeared to investigate the sound. Eyeing the bird, and the bit of paper wrapped around its leg, she said, "Looks like you may finally have an answer." She was happy at seeing Nina so excited. It had been an emotionally challenging winter as the family moved toward adoption and Nina's pending departure. "Let's hope it's good news."

Nina set Raven down on the back of the couch, where he promptly lifted his leg. She sat down beside him and gently worked the tape loose and then unwound the little strip of paper.

"Well?" Chantha demanded.

"It says: *Nina. General Delivery. Wenatchee Post Office.*" She looked up at Anna. "Could we *please* drive down to Wenatchee?"

"Of course," Anna said.

Before they left, Anna called Frank at his office to say that she and the girls had decided to go shopping and they might be a little late coming home for dinner. It would have been nice to share the news, but an FBI wiretap now seemed more of a probability than a possibility. Frank would have to wait to learn what had happened.

The two-hour drive seemed to take forever. When they finally pulled to a stop in the parking lot at the Wenatchee post office, Nina was out and sprinting for the door before Anna could turn off the ignition. By the time they caught up with her, she was already speaking to a gray-haired clerk behind the desk.

"My name is 'Nina.' Do you have a letter for me in your general delivery box?"

The clerk returned a grandfatherly smile. "Let me go and take a look, young lady." He disappeared behind a row of tall shelving, returning a few seconds later holding a thin envelope.

One might have thought it was Christmas morning from the look on Nina's face.

"Let's go out to the car to open it," Anna cautioned, looking around for security cameras. She spotted one, bolted high up on the wall.

Nina followed her gaze, and nodded in agreement.

Back in the Volvo, and with warm air pouring from the vents, Nina ran a finger under the flap to break the seal and then extracted a single sheet. She began to read out loud, in a careful voice.

Dear Nina:

Thank you for sending the raven to warn me. I'm sorry to have kept him for so long, but he was very cold by the time he found me, and I was worried he might not live if I did not take him with me. If you are reading this, he has made it back to you, and I am happy for that. I know how much you treasure him, and I also know that he has helped you to develop one of your abilities.

I have spent the past several weeks with a friend. By the time you read this, I should be safe. I won't provide details, but when my friend returns to the U.S., he has agreed to personally bring Frank Miller a

344

more detailed letter. Also, instructions on how you will be able to contact me if you should want to. My friend and I are planning on spending two months together, so you should not expect Frank to receive that letter until mid-April at the very earliest.

By April, Nina knew she would be long gone to Spain. She paused in her reading, her face a sea of disappointment.

"Don't worry," Anna reassured her. "We'll find some way to get Gunther's message to you."

Nina saw no point in disagreeing, even though she knew any contact might prove to be impossible. She continued to read.

I wish that I could have been of more help to you. I still feel terrible about the kidnapping. If there is anything I can ever do to make up for it, I will.

I hope this letter finds you safe. Please let the Millers know that I appreciate everything they did for me. I hope I have not caused them too much difficulty.

Forever yours, Gunther

Nina slowly refolded the letter and replaced it in the envelope. When she remained quiet, Anna asked, "Would you girls like to stop at a drive-in and pick up some burgers and shakes?"

Nina took a deep breath. "I'm not hungry. But if Chantha wants something—"

"I'm not hungry either," Chantha interrupted. "Let's just go home."

Anna shifted the car into reverse, backed up, and turned for the parking lot exit. "Your father's going to be pleased that Gunther got away. It would have complicated things for all of us if they had caught him."

"Yeah," Nina said. "I just hope he's okay." She couldn't imagine how he had gotten past airport security.

345

CHAPTER 101

Nina's adoption took place in early March before the presiding judge of the Superior Court for Cascade County. Only Frank, Anna, Nina and Chantha were allowed into the courtroom for the sealed proceeding. Clarissa and Charlie were forced to wait in a cafe across the street.

"All rise for the Honorable Royland Bartlett," the woman bailiff said.

The Millers and Nina stood.

A man in a black robe strode into the courtroom. His thinning gray hair was combed over a nearly bare scalp on top. A delighted twinkle filled his eyes as he surveyed the attendees. He nodded approval at the neatly dressed girl standing beside one of his favorite attorneys. There were few cases the judge still enjoyed presiding over, and adoptions were at the top of the list.

Judge Bartlett took his seat behind the high podium, and immediately said, "All of you please sit down and relax. This is a joyous occasion and there's no need to be nervous." A beaming smile confirmed it was a good day. Frank, Anna and Nina took seats behind the counsel table, while Chantha sat in the first pew behind the railing.

The judge now studied Chantha for a moment, gave a brief frown, and said, "Shouldn't I be remembering *you* young lady?"

Chantha felt a moment of panic. Before she could speak, Frank said, "You performed the adoption for our daughter Chantha fourteen years ago, Your Honor."

"Of course!" The pretend frown vanished, replaced by an impish grin, signaling he'd known who she was all along. "Chantha . . . this morning I was reading about you in the caseworker's report, and of course I remember you! Would you please come up and join your family. After all, you're getting a new sister today!"

Chantha rose and cautiously walked to the bat-wing gates in the burnished oak railing. She'd once visited the courtroom with her father to see where he worked and what he did. But she'd never passed beyond the rail. Only those participating in a case were allowed to come inside and "stand before the bar." She timidly pushed and slipped through. Frank stood up so she could sit beside Nina.

"Mr. Miller, you are, as always, a gentleman," the judge said. With a gracious nod he added, "Would you like to proceed?"

It went quickly.

When they left the courtroom, with the order for adoption in hand, Frank said, "After we file this with the Clerk's office, I think it would be a good idea to get Nina a passport."

"Agreed," Anna said.

After the adoption order was filed with the Clerk, a photo for a passport was taken, passport application forms were filled out, and an extra fee was paid for an expedited processing of the request. Within an hour the Miller family was back across the street to celebrate with Clarissa and Charlie.

The next morning, Frank took time off from work to go to the school and change Nina's student designation from "foster child" to "daughter." He met with school secretary Marci Porterhouse, who handled such details.

Marci was one of the few staff at Langston High who felt any degree of sympathy for Nina. It was with open glee that she later shared the news of the adoption with her coworker in the office, Debbi Phelps. A delivery that was perfectly timed so that Boyd Nedrickson overheard it as he arrived for a meeting with the principal.

At the noon break, Boyd informed Josh and John that they'd better "lay off that Nina chic," as she was now legally a Miller, and he "didn't want any blowback from the shyster."

"Sure thing, coach," Josh said. It was no big deal. He'd be graduating in three months, leaving the bush league of high school for big time college football.

John's reaction was the opposite. He still had to deal with Nina for another full year. As the school's quarterback he felt he had a reputation to defend.

At lunchtime on the day after her adoption, Nina suddenly found herself confronted by John at her locker. There were other students nearby, but none seemed interested in taking Nina's side. Most were solidly behind their star player; and those who weren't fans of John Bradley weren't exactly *anti-fans*.

The kids standing around in the hallway quickly melted away from the imminent confrontation, figuring it was safer not to hear what went down. Preferring to avoid the awkwardness of either having to faithfully repeat the dirty deed, or just flat out lie.

"Heard you got adopted yesterday," John said to Nina's back, as she changed out books in her locker.

Nina pretended she hadn't heard.

This only ramped up John's determination.

"Guess you got a slant-eye for a sister now."

Nina spun around. "*What did you just say?*" Her eyes blazed.

John felt the hairs on the back of his neck prickle. Still, he couldn't resist continuing the offensive. "You heard me," he said, chin jutting out, as if inviting her to take a swing.

Had Raven been there, he would have witnessed a blue maelstrom of epic proportion envelope Nina's body. John would later dream that he saw a flash of blue lightning crackle across her face.

She managed to focus her fury this time. So instead of giving some randomly destructive command, like ordering John to go and find a shovel and dig a hole and crawl in, she took a moment to compose herself, and then she laid down a set of rules that would define John Bradley for the remainder of his life.

"You are a mean person, John Bradley. But that is going to end. From now on you will treat everyone you meet with the greatest kindness and respect. You will *never again* say anything racist like what you just said about my sister Chantha. You will give up football.

When you enter college, you will enroll as a sociology major. When you graduate you will find a job working for a government social service agency, where you will do everything in your power to help the poor and those who have suffered. Do you understand?!"

Josh stood mesmerized, absorbing every word, as if his mind were a hard drive with no capacity to deny the commands being loaded. All he could say at the end was, "Yes." Meek as a kitten.

"You may go," Nina said, forcing the energy to spiral down.

Later that afternoon, John appeared in the Vice Principal's office. "Do you have a moment, Coach?" he asked politely.

"Always for you, John. What's on your mind?"

"I'm not going to be able to play football this fall. I'm sorry." And he *was* sorry. But not because he felt any loss over football. He was sorry for the wash of shock that filled his coach's face

"But . . . but . . . you're our *star player!*" Nedrickson sputtered. "You can't just . . . *quit!*"

"I said I'm sorry, Mr. Nedrickson," Josh pleaded, realizing there was nothing he could say that would make it any easier for Coach. There was only one thing he *could* do.

Josh turned and walked out the door, leaving Boyd Nedrickson speechless.

CHAPTER 102

Umberto was on a rant as Pieter drove through the pastoral Swiss countryside, headed for Zurich International Airport.

"That greasy slime-bag priest! I burnt my hand to recruit him! And now that sniveling worm says he's not sure about the girl. He wants more time to think. He's not sure he wants to work with us." His face was flushed a livid red. "How could that meaningless creature possibly refuse a bishop from the Vatican! *How could he possibly refuse me!*"

Perhaps because he senses what a monster you *are,* was Pieter's immediate thought.

He had endured Umberto's ravings, without comment, for the past hour, knowing there was nothing he might say that would change the Spaniard's mind.

Later, as they stood on the tarmac next to the Gulfstream, Umberto finally settled down a bit. His anger perfectly focused.

"You are our last hope. Every day this child grows stronger. It won't be long before she gets to a point where she can't be redeemed, and then there will only be one option left." He didn't elaborate.

Not that Umberto's plans for the girl were any longer Peter's concern. He was about to embark on what he saw as a sacred mission. Nothing else really mattered.

I must be allowed to make things right.

Later, as the jet climbed into the winter overcast, Umberto's words rang in his ears.

"You will need to be swift in taking the girl. And watch out for the American police. I'd go with you, but they know what I look like. It's up to you, Pieter. Get it done!"

What a coward. But that was Umberto.

Pieter fully intended to "get it done." And he'd reached his own conclusion about what was necessary. For what he now intended, he was fully prepared to accept the consequences.

CHAPTER 103

On the day before the drive to Seattle to meet Livia's ship, Clarissa was struggling with something she'd learned that morning. On a phone call to Valerie's office, the colorful spiky-haired receptionist had told her that Valerie was away for a while.

"For how long?"

"I can't say."

"Is there some way I can contact her?"

"I'm sorry, ma'am. Ms. Li asked me to tell anyone who calls that she had something urgent come up and she doesn't know when she'll be back in the office."

"I need to get a message to her."

"I can't guarantee I'll be able to reach her anytime soon." There was a profound sadness in Tina's voice. Clarissa guessed Valerie's office would soon be closed.

Clarissa wouldn't have been surprised to learn that Valerie's notice to Tina had come in the form of a handwritten note. "*Sorry Tina, but we're closing up shop. Don't tell anyone anything. Here's your severance check, plus a bonus for the great work you did. Good luck! My lawyers will handle the details.*"

Clarissa remembered Valerie saying she was fluent in Mandarin and Cantonese. With a pure Chinese ancestry, it was easy to picture her vanishing into the bustle of a city like Hong Kong or Shanghai.

Clarissa thanked Tina and hung up. Then she went to report the conversation to Charlie, who was in his room packing for tomorrow's departure.

Afterwards, she decided to go for a walk. The mid-day temperature had soared into the sixties, and she felt a need to clear her thoughts. A long stroll in the sun seemed like a perfect distraction.

As she left the Bosecker and followed the shoreline trail, there was something even more pressing on her mind than Valerie's unannounced departure. She was worried that Livia might not agree to take her and Charlie aboard the yacht. For Clarissa, that would be a deal breaker. She wasn't going to let Nina go without a guarantee of safety. And the only way to ensure Nina would be fairly treated was if she and Charlie accompanied her to Spain. Afterwards? Who knew what would be best? But until she knew exactly what she was getting Nina into, she fully intended to remain by her side.

After a few minutes she reached the spot where she and Charlie had had their fight in August. Remembering that unfortunate moment broke her concentration. She looked around. Birds were chirruping. A robin was working for worms in the moist soil along the bank. Clumps of pussy willows along the shoreline were bursting with fuzzy white catkins. A light breeze rippled the water, carrying a hint of fish, a trace of wood smoke.

Clarissa began to relax. She found a bench with a view of Langston far out across the lake, and sat down. She closed her eyes to the brightness of the sun reflecting off the water, enjoying the warmth on her forehead and cheeks. Everything seemed right.

As she breathed in the earthiness of the moment, she felt a tingle of resonance.

Charlie saw how upset I was and now he's come to make me feel better.

It was comforting. As the resonance grew strong, she opened her eyes and turned her head to greet him.

And there stood Pieter Silberhof.

Clarissa was off the bench in an instant.

Pieter's cold blue eyes studied her movement, his chiseled face betraying nothing. But in a strange paradox, the rest of his body remained in an open stance that didn't signal an attack. He had stopped at fifteen feet.

Clarissa took a deep breath. "Why are you here?"

"There are two possibilities," he replied flatly, maintaining his distance.

"I don't understand."

"I have a question. And depending upon your answer, I'll know which possibility happens next."

Clarissa glanced up and down the shoreline and saw no one on the trail. There was no chance for help. Against Pieter she was clearly outmatched.

And so it comes down to this.

"What is your question?" she said, leaving no doubt that she was ready to defend herself.

"I had a conversation last April with Liesel. She intimated that you had found something special in this girl. She said this *Nina* was 'the one.' I thought at the time that I understood. But I now wonder if I might have been mistaken."

"About what?"

"I thought she meant that you had finally found a proxy to train for contacting the outside world. And if that is the case, then I'm prepared to do whatever is necessary to prevent that from happening." Pieter paused to let the seriousness of his intentions sink in. "But if she meant *'The One'* instead of 'the one' . . . then I may be interested in discussing another option."

"What would that be?"

Pieter appeared to relax just a little. His voice became less threatening, almost playful.

"I did some research on this girl and found an interesting newspaper account of her parents' deaths in a car accident fourteen years ago. Coincidentally, that was about the time you cut off all contact with the Order. We of course kept tabs on your whereabouts. And it always seemed peculiar to me that you had chosen to remain in a relative backwater like eastern Washington for so many years. But when I read that obituary it became clearer. I learned that the mother was quite an athlete in college. After graduation she became a scientist of some note in the agricultural department of the U.S. government. Everything pointed to the possibility that she was exhibiting the skills and abilities one might expect from one our members."

Clarissa nodded for him to continue.

Any last visage of challenge vanished from Pieter's face. It was replaced by an intensely curious smile.

"Are you admitting that she is *The One?*"

"I suppose it would be pointless to deny it," Clarissa replied.

Pieter nodded. "Would you mind sitting with me for a while? We have much to talk about."

CHAPTER 104

The plan for the morning of March 15 was a deception worthy of a New York Times bestseller.

Clarissa ached to tell the Millers of the deal she'd made with Pieter. He wasn't entirely on their side. But he'd agreed to give her a free hand in relocating Nina. Part of the agreement was that she would forever keep their deal a secret. If the Council learned that he'd allowed Nina to slip away, he would instantly become *persona non grata*, possibly forever.

There still remained the very real chance that the FBI or Homeland Security might be lurking, so stealth had a value.

Frank obtained the loan of a friend's Hummer. The night before their departure, he met his friend along the West Lake Highway at a point where there were no houses. Suitcases were transferred. Later that evening the friend parked the Hummer in a lot near Frank's law office.

An hour before dawn on the Ides of March, Frank drove his Volvo to his office and entered by the front door, carrying a briefcase, appearing as if he had urgent legal work to do. Two hours later, shortly before his staff was scheduled to arrive, he snuck out the back door and walked the short distance to the Hummer.

Anna had left the house with both girls shortly after sunrise and driven to a restaurant in downtown Langston. At breakfast they spoke loudly enough to be overheard by nearby diners about, "going shopping in Spokane."

Frank drove the Hummer to where Clarissa and Charlie were waiting in the Sentra. He then drove behind the restaurant, to the back entrance that was used for deliveries and taking garbage to the dumpster. The girls and Anna climbed in.

By 9am the Hummer was cruising down Highway 97 along the Columbia River, tinted windows ensuring privacy.

Nina had said goodbye to Raven just before they left the house. She had worried that he might not arrive in time, but he swooped out of the sky right on schedule, landing on the deck table.

She laid out a few slivers of beef tenderloin, and then closed her eyes.

An image of *food* swam up out of the blackness. And then the eyes behind the beak saw a troubled blue vortex.

I'm going away and I may not see you again.

?

Because there is danger. Bad people want to come and take me away.

Ravens cannot shed tears. But if he could, he would have. The pain welling up from his heart was nearly unbearable.

Nina was now crying for both of them. Her soft sobs continued for some time before she regained enough control to try and explain where she was going.

It's a country called Spain. I will be traveling there on a large boat. She pictured a mega-yacht she'd seen on the Internet, with three deck levels and a helicopter. A clean white hull, chrome rails, teak decking and trim. *I will miss you so much.* She opened her eyes and saw the bird's head jerking from side to side, as if in denial.

Nina reached into her pocket and pulled out the gold ring he'd given her last summer. She held it up so that he could see it, and then she slid it onto the index finger of her left hand. She closed her eyes once more.

You will always be with me. If I can ever return, I will. Thank you for this present. And for the knowledge you have shared.

The Raven now had one last gift to give. And what came into Nina's mind was powerful and certain.

A blue vortex stood with arms outstretched. One hand grasped a twisting branch of what appeared to be millions of individual strands of red and blue light tangled together in an incredibly complex bundle. The other hand grasped countless threads in every color of the rainbow.

These are all of the animals on Earth. You are the bridge. And the hope.

The image began to fade. Nina stood still, eyes closed, frozen in a moment of revelation. When she finally opened her eyes the Raven was gone.

She went into her bedroom and cried at the enormity of what he had revealed.

Now in the Hummer, she was quiet. Chantha sat beside her, watching with concern. "Are you alright?" she asked.

Not wanting to make the final hours with her sister any more painful, she answered, "Yeah. I'm fine." And then she reached over and grasped Chantha's hand and held it for the rest of the trip over the mountains.

Nina wasn't the only quiet one in the Hummer. Clarissa was remembering the offer Pieter had made, sitting there on the bench, with the sun flashing against wavelets rolling against the pebble beach.

"You never intended to expose the Order using the girl?"

"At first, I did. But eventually I realized it would expose her to more risk than was acceptable. We might have eventually been able to convince reasonable scientists and people at the upper levels of government that our genetics are non-transferrable. But if someone dug deep enough, they might learn what you figured out: that Nina's mother passed on something special to her daughter. And from there it's an easy step to deduce that Nina's children will also carry the trait. If *normals* learned of this, Nina would become the greatest prize imaginable. There would be no easy way to shield her from the consequences. And even more importantly, there would be no way to shield her children."

"Does Liesel know?"

358

"It took her a while to figure it out. But yes, she knows. It's why she offered to help."

"She covered it up well," Pieter said. "Except for that one slip early on, when she told me you had found 'the one.' I'm not sure why she said it in the first place."

Clarissa had wondered the same thing. Perhaps Liesel had been hedging her bets? "Who knows?" she said.

Pieter shifted on the bench, carefully choosing his words.

"For now, I'll run interference so you can escape. Umberto deserves to be taken out into a forest and shot, but we both know that can't happen. I'll tell him the three of you were gone before I arrived. I'll also tell him that I have no idea where you went." Pieter stared at Clarissa for a moment, and then said, "It's better if you don't tell me, even though I'd love to know." He sighed. "Sometimes I wish we could lie. It would make things a lot easier, wouldn't it?"

Both laughed.

She now sat quietly in the Hummer as it crossed the I-90 floating bridge and passed through the Mount Baker Tunnel. Seattle's skyscrapers came into view. A smile brushed her lips. Against all odds, the stern Austrian had proven to be a friend.

Midday traffic was light as Frank merged into the steady northerly flow on the I-5. Three minutes later he took the University District exit and turned west. Glancing at his watch he said, "Two thirty-five. We're right on schedule."

Chantha tightened her grip on Nina's hand and they looked at each other, and then looked away, knowing how easily the tears might come.

In a few blocks, Frank turned right onto a road that ran along the canal. They passed the Chittenden Locks, and continued along the gradual curve that merged onto Seaview Avenue.

The Hummer slowed. "There it is," he said. Up ahead a sign read: *Seaview Boatyard*. A pier extended out into Puget Sound, making a sharp dog-leg to the right.

Clarissa said in a businesslike voice, "Find a spot to park."

The girls again looked at each other and the tears began to form.

Frank pulled into the lot fronting the boatyard. With the engine idling, he turned to Clarissa. "Are you still certain you want to do this?"

"Yes," she said, resolved. "There's no other option now."

"Alright," Frank said, turning the key. The engine fell silent. Before stepping out onto the asphalt he looked at his watch. "They should be here shortly."

Charlie went around to the back and lifted out three bags and sat them side-by-side on the asphalt.

Nina looked out across the moored boats and past the breakwater. A super yacht rode the dull blue chop half a mile out, much like the one she'd found on the Internet. There was even a helicopter perched on the stern.

A tender was speeding in from the direction of the yacht. "They're here," she said, watching as the boat swerved around the end of the breakwater and slowed, then pulled up alongside the pier. There were two men aboard. One jumped up onto the dock and looped a cord onto a dock cleat.

"Okay," Charlie said, picking up two bags.

Clarissa grabbed the third bag, and nodded to Nina. "Time for goodbyes," she said solemnly.

Nina turned, and was confronted by tears streaming down Chantha's face. The words she wanted to speak wouldn't form in her throat, so she walked up and took Chantha in her arms and held her for what seemed like the briefest of eternities. As she let go, she finally found her voice, and whispered, "I promise to keep in touch, somehow."

"Okay," Chantha whispered back.

Nina turned to Frank, and said "Thank you" and gave him a huge hug. And then it was Anna's turn.

Now everyone had tears forming.

"I've got to go," Nina said with a finality that hurt down the core of her being. She turned and quickly joined Clarissa and Charlie, and together they began to walk toward the tender.

"Should I come out with you?" Frank called out.

Clarissa turned her head, but continued to walk. "No," she called back. "Take care of your family." Anna was already holding Chantha. Saying something soft that didn't carry far enough for Nina to hear.

Nina kept her head forward, afraid that if she did turn, she would run back to new family and tell them she didn't want to go. But that couldn't be. She told herself to be brave and gritted her teeth and continued to walk between Charlie and Clarissa.

As they approached the tender the man who stood on the dock raised one hand.

Clarissa had anticipated a challenge, and said, "We're either all coming onboard, or none of us are getting into your boat."

The man looked from Clarissa to Charlie, and then studied Nina for a much longer moment. He finally reached into his pocket and pulled out a walkie-talkie, speaking briefly in a Basque dialect Clarissa hadn't heard in centuries. After listening for instructions, he thumbed the unit off. "Alright," he said. He gestured to Nina, and then held her hand as she stepped into the tender. Charlie and Clarissa climbed down and found seats.

As the tender approached the ship Clarissa felt a strong resonance. She turned to Nina. "Do you feel it?"

"Yes," Nina said, looking between Clarissa and Charlie. "Is that her?"

"Yes," Clarissa said, relieved. Livia had kept her word.

The tender pulled up alongside the ship, to where a ladder had been extended. A crewman first helped Nina, and then Clarissa, up the ladder. Charlie scrambled up on his own.

A woman who appeared to be in her thirties was waiting at the top of the stairs. Not Livia, but most certainly a Basque.

"Welcome to the Esmerelda," she said. "My name is Corrina." She gestured to a woman who stood behind her. "Sandrine will take the young miss and the gentlemen to their cabins where they can get settled in." She nodded politely to Clarissa. "If you would please follow me, the mistress would like to meet with you now."

Nina's face held a moment of panic. Clarissa reached out, took her hands, squeezed them. "We're going to have to trust them. I'm sure you will be safe." She let go and turned back to Corrina. "I've been very much looking forward to meeting her face to face."

Corrina led Clarissa down a passageway, while Sandrine led Nina and Charlie in the opposite direction.

As they walked half the length of the ship Clarissa felt the resonance grow in strength. Nearing the bow, they reached a polished teak door.

Corrina turned, and said, "She is waiting inside." She slid an electronic key into the lock, and with a solid *Click* the door swung wide. Corrina stood aside, and Clarissa stepped through the doorway.

As the door shut, she found herself staring at the back of a woman with black hair that tumbled down, just as it had when they'd met eighteen centuries ago in a field near Zizurkil.

And now the woman turned around and gave Clarissa the greatest shock of her life.

The face looked exactly the same. As if the aging process had completely ceased. No one in the Order was immune to gradual aging. Yet Livia looked a perfect twenty-two.

Now came the distant thrum of engines revving. Clarissa felt the gentle sway of the floor as the ship began to move. As she continued to stare at that perfectly preserved face, she asked, "How is this possible?"

A smile like the smile of the Mona Lisa, barely perceptible, came to the woman's face. "Because," the woman standing before her said carefully, "I am not Livia."

Clarissa was stunned. "Then who are you?"

"My name is Cassandra."

"But how can you look so much like Livia? And . . . you have resonance. How is this possible?"

"And that is the problem we face," Cassandra continued, now quite serious. "It is possible because I am Livia's daughter."

362

www.ingramcontent.com/pod-product-compliance
Lightning Source LLC
Chambersburg PA
CBHW070404260626
47161CB00001B/265

* 9 7 8 0 9 8 9 8 5 1 3 7 4 *